OFFSIDE

RULES OF THE GAME SERIES, BOOK 1

AVERY KEELAN

AVERY KEELAN

Visit my website at www.averykeelan.com

Cover design: Andra M Designs

Developmental editing: Melanie Yu, https://linkin.bio/mademeblushbooks

Line and copy editing: Beth Lawton, https://www.vbproofreads.com/

For anyone who's ever had a Luke.

PLAYLIST

Theme: End Game - Taylor Swift, Ed Sheehan, Future

1. Lose You To Love Me - Selena Gomez
2. Stunnin' - Curtis Waters feat. Harm Franklin
3. Monster - Shawn Mendes, Justin Bieber
4. Rumors - Sabrina Claudio, Zayn
5. This Is What Makes Us Girls - Lana Del Ray
6. There's No way - Lauv feat. Julia Michaels
7. The Bones - Maren Morris, Hozier
8. Do Me - Kim Petras
9. Anyone - Justin Bieber
10. Cherish You - Mikky Ekko
11. Gladiator - Zayde Wolf
12. Unlearn - Benny Blanco feat. Gracie Abrams
13. False God - Taylor Swift
14. Exhale - Sabrina Carpenter
15. If Our Love Is Wrong - Calum Scott
16. Baby - Bishop Briggs
17. I.F.L.Y. - Bazzi
18. Look What You Made Me Do - Taylor Swift
19. Own Me - Bulow
20. Tear Myself Apart - Tate McRae

21. Hold On - Chord Overstreet
22. You Are The Reason - Calum Scott
23. As I Am - Justin Bieber feat. Khalid
24. Eyes For You - Ellery Bonham
25. Get You The Moon - Kina feat. Snøw
26. Lifetime - Justin Bieber

Want more? For the complete Offside playlist, scan the image below with your mobile device's camera while in the Spotify app:

CHAPTER 1
BLINDSIDED
BAILEY

I WAS OFFICIALLY out of my element.

"Do you want something to drink?" Luke asked, his blue eyes twinkling playfully in the candlelight. He was wearing a gray suit with a white dress shirt beneath it—top button undone—and his blond hair slicked back neatly. "Now that you're finally legal, I mean."

"Sure," I said. "Um, you pick something for us."

We were celebrating my twenty-first birthday at one of the swankiest restaurants in the city. I rarely drank, and I couldn't pronounce most of the words on the wine list.

As the only child of two well-to-do lawyers from Chicago, Luke had grown up dining at places like this every weekend. But as the youngest of four children born to a nurse and a teacher from a suburb outside Minneapolis, this was outside my wheelhouse. My family's idea of a big night out was hitting Applebee's, and even that had to be worked into the budget.

He nodded and reached for the wine list. "I'll order a bottle of wine."

Luke flipped through the pages, looking over the selection with the intensity of someone purchasing a new car while I fidgeted in my seat, wishing I hadn't borrowed Amelia's heels. They were half a size too small and pinched my toes like crazy.

Prior to slipping into these torturous shoes, I'd spent the better part of the afternoon putting on makeup and getting ready. My roommates nearly took an eye out helping me apply fake lashes; it was a serious ordeal, and one I vowed never to repeat.

I crossed my legs and surveyed the restaurant to distract myself, taking in the opulent gold accents and framed artwork lining the walls. The other tables were largely occupied by people at least ten years older than us, all well-dressed and well-groomed. I wouldn't have chosen this place myself, given the chance, but Luke had surprised me. It was the thought that counted, right?

After another minute, he shut the menu and set it aside. As if we'd summoned him, our server instantly reappeared. He was astonishingly tall, reed-thin, and looked like he would blow away in a heavy breeze.

"What can I get you started with this evening?" He gave us a bland smile that said he didn't believe we could afford to be here. It was half-true.

"We'll take a bottle of the River Estates Cabernet Sauvignon," Luke said, handing him the wine menu.

"Excellent choice." The server gave us a little bow before turning on his heel and leaving.

I hoped he would return soon so we could order dinner. After living on peanut butter sandwiches for a month to afford the little black dress I was wearing, the thought of seeing a loaf of Wonder bread or a jar of Jif ever again made me want to hurl. Now I was ravenously hungry for real food, though the menu was written entirely in French, which I couldn't speak, let alone read.

Luke reached across the ivory tablecloth and took my hand. He stroked the back of it with his thumb. "I've been thinking a lot about after graduation."

"Do you have news?" Excitement bubbled in my stomach. I leaned closer, studying his face in the candlelight. "Who does Gavin think will bite?"

As captain of Callingwood's Division I hockey team, the Bulldogs, Luke's game had been solid over the last year. A number of NHL teams had showed an interest in signing him, which gave him a degree of bargaining power and almost guaranteed he would go to the league.

The big question now was which team he'd sign with. Specifically, which team his agent, Gavin Harper, could squeeze the best offer out of.

He drew in a breath and flashed me a tense smile. "That's kind of what I wanted to talk to you about, actually."

My stomach fluttered. "Okay."

This was it. We were finally going to make a plan. Long-distance would be tough, but we could do it. It was only for a year while I finished college. I could fly to him, he could fly to me, and in the off-season, we could live in the same city. Plus, we could FaceTime every day. Totally doable.

Our server reappeared, pouring a small amount of ruby wine into each of our glasses and waiting expectantly. It took a moment to realize he was waiting for us to sample it, but I didn't know what wine should taste like in the first place. I watched while Luke swirled the dark red liquid in his glass and tasted it, then nodded in approval. The server filled our glasses partway before leaving again.

"It looks like it'll be Tampa Bay or Dallas," Luke began.

"That's great." I took a sip of my wine, suppressing a grimace. It was astringent, like sour grapes and sadness. How did anyone find this enjoyable? "I know you've been hoping for that."

"I have. But…" He trailed off.

"What is it?" A money issue? Or a disagreement over the terms? Luke wanted a clause in the contract to ensure he'd get playoff time in his first year, should the team make it that far. But not all organizations were willing to agree to that.

"I think we should take a break."

My mouth went dry. "A break?"

Luke nodded. "I'm leaving soon. Let's not make that harder than it needs to be."

I blinked, trying to process his words, but my brain kept freezing like a glitchy computer. *Error: does not compute.*

"You're not leaving until the end of the school year."

"But you knew this was coming…right?" His expression was somewhere between pity and incredulity.

My breath snagged and my eyes pricked with tears. Of course I didn't. If I did, why would I have poured myself into this sexy, low-cut dress I couldn't afford, borrowed Amelia's four-inch heels from hell, and put on this much makeup? Hell, I was even wearing lipstick. *Lipstick.*

Obviously, I thought we'd discuss commitment, not coming to an end.

"Wait." I frowned, working through the subtext behind what he'd said. "Are you asking for a break? Or a breakup?"

He hesitated. "The second one, I guess."

"You *guess*?" My voice climbed an octave, drawing the attention of the people dining around us. Several turned and stared. A few even glared. "We've been down this road before, Luke. This time it'll be permanent."

Luke cringed, making a lowering motion with his hands. "Let's not make a scene, B."

"Oh, I'm sorry." I grabbed my wine and took an unladylike gulp. *Gross*. Slamming the glass down, I shot figurative daggers at him.

"Am I embarrassing you while you break up with me in public *on my birthday*? Is that why you did it here? So I couldn't make a scene?" Hot tears welled again. I gritted my teeth and swallowed. Right now, it was easier to be mad than sad.

"No, it's not—I didn't mean for it to come out like this." He sighed, rubbing the bridge of his nose. "I've been thinking about it for a while, and I wanted to be fair to you. I didn't want to lead you on."

"Right." I laughed coldly. That he'd been thinking about it was a handful of salt in a fresh wound. I was wearing lacy underwear beneath this dress. I'd planned to sleep with him later, while he was working on an exit strategy. How could I have been so oblivious?

"I can't believe you're doing this after you begged me to get back together with you this summer."

"But that's just it," he said. "We've been together for a long time. Pretty soon, the league will rule my life. Where I live, where I play, what I eat, everything. I need some time to myself."

"Uh-huh." I tried to disguise the waver in my voice. "Time to play the field and hook up with puck bunnies, you mean? Just like the last two times."

During our two other "breaks," I waited around for him while he slept with at least one other person. He groveled to get me back after both incidents, and foolishly, I forgave him. I thought he'd actually changed.

"That's not what this is about."

"Okay." I scoffed, crossing my arms and blinking back tears. There was no way I would let him see me cry. "If it's not that, then what is it? There's got to be a reason you're pulling a one-eighty on me. Is it someone else?"

He frowned. "I can't believe you'd even think that."

"Well, I can't believe you'd do this, so I guess we're even." I grabbed the linen napkin off my lap and tossed it on the empty plate. Bracing my palms on the table, I stood, pushing back the red velvet chair. "I have to go."

"Don't leave," Luke pleaded, reaching for my arm. "We can have a meal together, can't we? I still want to be friends."

More like he wanted to be on good terms with my brother, who played for the Callingwood Bulldogs with Luke. Unceremoniously dumping defenseman Derek James's little sister was sure to make for awkward conversation in the locker room before the next game.

Then again, my brother had never stood up for me. Why would that change now? For someone who was a force to be reckoned with on the ice, Derek was a total pushover in real life. He had the spine of an invertebrate.

I yanked my arm out of Luke's flimsy grip. "Not even remotely possible."

"Bailey, don't be like this."

My heart wrenched. Be like what? Upset that he blindsided me? Anyone in my position would be devastated.

"Let me drive you at least."

"Thanks, but no thanks. You've done enough."

Seconds crawled by as I lingered in front of the table, wanting to leave but unable to make my body cooperate. My feet stayed firmly glued to the floor, stuck in some form of malignant denial. This couldn't be happening. This was Luke. My Luke.

I studied his face, tracing the features I knew better than my own. Pale blue eyes framed with thick lashes; strong jawline, cleft in his chin; and a Roman nose that was slightly crooked from a break in minor hockey. I always said it added character to his otherwise perfect face.

It was a face I'd woken up to. A friend who'd seen me at my worst. A lover who'd witnessed my most vulnerable moments.

But this person sitting before me was a stranger.

"You're still coming to the game tomorrow night, right?"

The sadness in my gut morphed into rage. Even now, he wanted me as a groupie.

"You have got to be kidding." I snatched my purse off the chair beside me. "I'll be at the game, but only because of Derek. Not you. I'd cheer against you if I could."

The next morning, I perched at the kitchen island with a cup of coffee and a plate of food that I had zero interest in actually consuming. My stomach turned as I pushed the now-cold scrambled eggs around my plate, trying to muster up the will to eat.

According to the digital clock on the stove, it was a quarter past eight, which meant I'd been staring at my food for nearly an hour. My mother always said a hearty breakfast was the key to starting the day on the right foot, but no amount of food could fix the events of last night. Nothing could, short of a magic wand.

"Good morning!" My roommate Amelia breezed into the kitchen, making a beeline for the coffeepot. Clearly, her day was off to a far better start than mine. She was already dressed in a cropped pink sweater and distressed jeans, and her curly brown hair was woven into a thick braid. I was still unshowered and wearing ratty purple pajamas, my long hair in a tangled rats' nest. My skin was blotchy, my eyes swollen, and my heart empty.

The idea of being single again after a year and a half was akin to being adrift, lost at sea without a compass. I didn't know who I was without Luke. I didn't want to know.

With her back turned, Amelia poured herself a massive cup of french roast, then went to the fridge and pulled out the vanilla creamer. "How was your birthday dinner?" She shut the door with her hip.

"Well—" The words got stuck in my throat. "Not great."

Amelia laughed and stirred her coffee, the spoon clinking against the ceramic mug. "Why, Luke keep you up all night?"

It was like being stabbed in the heart and the gut at the same time.

She spun around to face me, her dark chocolate eyes probing me from over the top of her pink mug. "You do look pretty tired."

Given that I'd been hit by the breakup bus, I was sure I looked more than tired. I probably looked like a troll.

"Uh, not exactly."

She took a sip of her coffee, raising her eyebrows. "Where is Luke, anyway? Is he still asleep?"

Another stab.

"He isn't here." But he should have been.

"Oh." Her forehead crinkled, mild confusion registering. "Did he have to train this morning? I thought Paul said they didn't have dryland today."

"No," I said. "He dumped me."

Amelia froze with the petal-pink mug halfway to her mouth. "*What*?" Her eyes snapped up to mine.

"Yup." I looked down at my plate and took a bite of soggy whole-wheat toast. Since the alternative to eating was discussing the breakup, my appetite had suddenly returned. Amelia stared at me, wide-eyed. I wished I'd printed out a pamphlet I could distribute instead of having to relay every painful detail. A news bulletin of sorts.

I swallowed and added, "He said we should 'take a break.' And then it turned into a breakup."

Part of me still didn't believe it was real, but another part—a bigger part—was resigned to it.

"Sweetie." She set down her cup and walked around the island. Sitting on the stool next to me, she scanned my face with concern and touched my arm gently. "I'm so sorry."

"It's fine."

"What happened? I don't understand."

Neither did I, but that didn't matter. And now I had to relive this horrible breakup conversation over and over again with all my friends and my brother, as well as with my parents. Breaking the news, witnessing their shocked reactions, and enduring their awkward pity. I didn't want sympathy. I didn't want hugs. I didn't want to talk about it—at all.

"We grew apart, I guess."

"Still, you must be devastated. I feel terrible for you, B."

Amelia and I had lived together for over six months and got along fabulously, swapping clothes, sharing makeup, and binge-watching bad shows on Netflix. But we'd met because Paul and Luke played together, which meant that her life, like mine, all but revolved around the team. Now she was looking at me with the level of shock and horror one would expect at the news of a death.

Was she really concerned for me? Or was she worried that she and Paul would be next? *Would* they be next? Like Luke, Paul was a third-year with NHL aspirations. Maybe they all had a pact to dump their girlfriends and live it up for their last year of college.

Or maybe I was the only dead weight.

"Yeah, well…it happens." Avoiding her eyes, I grabbed my plate and stood, pushing the stool away from the counter. "Anyway, I need to shower and hit the library. I have an article to finish before the game tonight."

If it was even possible to focus on writing right now. That part might be a stretch. Or it could be a good escape. I could lock myself away from reality and ignore that my love life had just imploded.

"You're still going to come?"

The question landed like a slap, even though I knew she didn't mean it that way.

"I have to," I said. "Derek would never forgive me if I suddenly boycotted their games."

Besides, I wasn't sure what I would do to fill my time if I didn't.

CHAPTER 2
ALL I DO IS WIN
CHASE

OUR PRE-GAME RITUAL for home games was sacred. Practice skate at Northridge Arena, nap at home, meal at Ironwood Grill, then back to the rink early to warm up and shoot the shit. Lather, rinse, repeat.

It wasn't that we were superstitious, but deviating from this particular sequence of events tended to result in losses.

Okay, maybe we were a little superstitious.

The stakes were especially high tonight because we were playing our rivals, the Callingwood Bulldogs. I couldn't stand the team, especially the captain, and I couldn't wait to crush them.

"Game day, bitches." Our goalie, Tyler, stretched, lacing his arms behind his head. His heavily tattooed biceps flexed, a full sleeve of ink winding down to his left forearm. "You'd better be ready."

I snorted. "Says the guy who kept giving up pucks in practice. I've seen coupons that save more than you."

"None of yours managed to get by, so what does that say?"

While left wing was technically an offensive position, scoring wasn't my primary objective—at least, not on the ice. My areas of expertise were battling for the puck, being strong on the boards, and killing penalties. And, of course, antagonizing the other side to fuck with their heads and cause them to draw penalties, both of which I found immensely rewarding.

I also dabbled in the occasional scrum. Okay, that happened pretty frequently.

"By the way," Dallas said, ignoring our sniping, "we're hitting XS tonight. Including you." He pointed at me with his fork.

"What the hell is XS?" I asked, playing dumb. "A shirt size? I'm gonna need at least a large, dude."

He gave me a withering look. "A new club. Opened last weekend. Supposed to be full of hot chicks."

Of course, I already knew his angle.

Dallas was the pretty boy of the team—the all-American team captain; Tyler was the tattooed bad boy goalie; and, well, I was the asshole agitator. We were roommates, teammates, and made a pretty unstoppable trio when it came to wheeling chicks.

But nightclubs were boring as shit. I could accomplish the same thing at home with a strobe light and watered-down drinks. I'd save paying for cover and a ride too.

And as far as women went, I already had enough numbers to start my own Dickdash service.

I snatched my chicken club from my plate. "I've got a better idea."

"What's that?" Dallas looked up from his plate of fettuccini alfredo, eyebrows raised.

"We could do literally anything other than that."

Why did they bother trying to sell me on this?. We all knew I was the stubborn one. It was impossible to strong-arm me into doing anything I didn't want to do. Coach Miller could vouch for that fact.

Tyler leaned back in his chair. "Since when are you such a buzzkill? I thought you'd be all over this."

Buzzkill was the last word anyone would use to describe me. I never turned down a chance to get fucked up, get laid, or get into trouble. Just not at a damn nightclub. I'd choose literally any other way to unwind after a physically and mentally taxing game.

"All over a party, yes. A bar, fine. But nightclubs are the worst," I said. "Bad dance music, overpriced drinks, too many other dudes in the way. Plus, they're cheesy as fuck."

"Exactly." Ty gestured, as if it were obvious. "Chicks love cheesy. Especially hot chicks."

"Cool," I said. "Have fun with that." I had plenty of options for evening entertainment, hot chicks included. They could go on their merry way, and I'd go mine.

"Come on, man." He glared at me, taking a bite of his burger.

The waitress returned and refilled our glasses with ice water before disappearing again.

"What do you need me for? Can't pull without me?"

"It sure isn't for the pleasure of your company," Dallas deadpanned.

I shrugged. "Let's have people over to our place."

"We do that every weekend." Tyler groaned, tipping his head back and looking up at the ceiling. He raked a hand through his dark hair, and his gaze snapped to mine. "I need a change of scenery."

Personally, I liked it. The party came to us. And when I got bored, I could go to my room to sleep…or do other things.

I laughed. Scenery was a polite way of putting it. "You mean you've finally run out of girls at Boyd to bang."

"That too," said Tyler. "I need to refresh the rotation."

People always gave me a hard time about my reputation, but Tyler made me look like Tom fucking Hanks.

"Either way, I'm down for something different. It's happening. And you're coming, fucker." Dallas leveled his icy-blue gaze in my direction. It might have melted the panties off girls, but it held less persuasive power with me.

"What do you care, Ward?" I tipped my chin in his direction. "You'll end up with Shiv later anyway and you know it."

"Maybe, maybe not." He shrugged. "Depends on how the night plays out."

Bullshit. There was a 98-percent chance he'd ditch out for Siobhan by one a.m. Dallas talked a big game, but he never hooked up with anyone else, even though they weren't technically exclusive. It was a weird dynamic that I didn't understand, though I did like Shiv.

Then again, when things were rocky between them, sometimes he went out in search of a distraction. Not to pick up chicks, but to take his mind off things. Maybe that was the case right now.

"Fine," I said, dipping a fry in ketchup and gesturing with it. "Since you two bar stars are set on going, let's make it interesting."

"Like what?" Dallas asked.

"A wager."

Tyler cocked a dark brow. "Keep talking."

"If we get a shutout against the Bulldogs tonight, we go to XS."

There was a pretty slim chance of that happening. If it did, cool—we'd crush the team I hated most. If we didn't, fine—I wouldn't have to go to a dumb disco.

As long as we still won, of course. That part wasn't negotiable. Win or die trying. We were the only division I schools in our state, which meant the rivalry ran immeasurably deep. It was steeped in decades of hatred and resentment. Boyd had won more championships in total, though in the past decade Callingwood had been stronger overall. As much as it pained me to admit, we'd been pretty evenly matched for the three years I'd been at Boyd.

At any rate, our games were always barnburners. And they really hated that we'd beat them out for a playoff spot last spring. I couldn't wait to crush them tonight, especially their captain, Morrison. He made cheap hits, cherry picked, and was a total bag of dicks.

"And if we don't?" Dallas took a bite of garlic toast, giving me a questioning look.

"We find something better to do with our time." As in, anything else.

He shrugged a broad shoulder. "All right."

"What?" Tyler leaned forward on his elbows and scowled. "No way. That puts it all on my shoulders."

"Not really." I pointed at Dallas. "Your boy over there still has to score for us to win."

That part was a given, though. Dallas's points per game were at the top of the league. His stats were slightly more impressive than mine, which suffered somewhat due to the penalties I drew and took. More time in the sin bin meant less time on the ice. But we each had our roles, and I performed mine well.

"I'd have to stand on my head by myself for three periods to get a shutout," said Ty. "Then as long as one of you idiots on the ice sank a goal, we'd win."

"Fine." I sighed. "We can up the ante. A shutout plus three or more goals for us. At least one goal has to be Ward."

"Easy. Blindfolded and upside down." Dallas took a sip of his ice water. "Let's make it two."

It was like he was doing my job for me.

"Fuck that," Tyler grumbled. "He only has to sneak two shots past Mendez, while I have to block, like, a hundred from their entire team."

He was being dramatic, as usual. The shots on net tonight would likely clock in around half that, if not less. But goalies weren't known for being level-headed; they were their own special brand of crazy. They had to be in order to shake off their frustration and get right back to it after letting a goal in. The mental game goaltending required was intense.

"What's wrong?" Dallas smirked, needling him. "You worried you can't do it?"

Ty scoffed. "Of course I can. And I'm about to."

Tyler's weaknesses also included being proud to a fault, which made him easy to manipulate.

"I hear the Bulldogs tanked their preseason games," Dallas added. "One-four-one. Probably won't be hard."

Had I known the wager would be this easy to win, I would have gotten more creative.

Three minutes into the game, the Bulldogs' goalie failed to block Ward's slapshot straight through the five-hole. Like he was asleep at the stick or something. Then everything went to shit for them. In the first period alone, they took several weak penalties, including tripping, slashing, spearing, and one for too many men on the ice—because apparently, in addition to forgetting how to skate, they'd also forgotten how to count.

As the second period began, we were in great spirits. Meanwhile, the Bulldogs were getting their asses kicked.

I watched as Dallas's backhand narrowly missed the net, hitting the boards and rebounding into the corner. One of the Bulldogs' D-men, Derek James, beat us to it and took possession, but he choked, freezing on the spot. I skated backward in position near the net while our other winger charged. Instead of taking the time to line up like he should have, Derek panicked and tried to pass to his teammate. His shot went wide, and I intercepted the puck in front of the net. With a flick of my wrist, the buzzer sounded again.

Beauty.

With a fist pump, I skated off and hopped onto the home bench.

"Sick goal." Dallas laughed, clapping me on the back. "But you just sealed your fate."

Not even two minutes into the second, the score was 3-0 in our favor—fulfilling the terms of our bet. Maybe I should have set the bar higher. But to be fair, I hadn't expected the Bulldogs to make it this easy for us.

Now the Bulldogs' first offensive line was skating aimlessly like they needed a fucking map for directions to the net. Morrison might have benefitted from a compass too.

The wheels had not only fallen off; the vehicle was on fire.

It was goddamn glorious.

"Tyler still has to bring home the shutout," I said.

Maybe the Bulldogs would pull their heads out of their asses and score one goal so I could skip the nightclub crap. Wait, no. What the fuck? I hated myself for even thinking that. The more humiliating the defeat for Callingwood, the better.

"Please. Have you seen him tonight?" Dallas jutted his chin toward our net. "He's a brick wall."

"We'll see."

"Start planning your hair and outfit," he said. "You're coming."

Fucking hell. A victim of my own success.

"Fine." I leaned over and snagged my water bottle. "Go big or go home. If I'm going to lose this dumb bet, we might as well crush them."

CHAPTER 3

THE HELL YOU ARE

BAILEY

CHEERS ERUPTED from the crowd as the buzzer sounded and the scoreboard changed. Much to my dismay, the bright red letters now read four-nothing, Falcons.

Being the away team always sucked, but it was especially bad when we were getting our asses handed to us like this.

Our goalie, Eddie Mendez, threw his stick and let out a string of colorful curses that echoed throughout the arena. I held my breath, waiting to see if Coach Brown would pull him, but he stayed on. My brother Derek pulled off his blue and white gloves and skated to the away bench, shaking his head. He was upset with himself over the botched defensive play, not with Mendez for letting it in.

And beside the net, Chase Carter—left winger for the Falcons—did a celebratory fist pump and glided over to the home bench to high-five his teammates and gloat like he always did. Irritation rippled through me.

"I hate him," I muttered.

Amelia nodded. "Me too. He's the worst."

I didn't have a strong emotional reaction to many players, good or bad, but Carter was the exception. He was the definition of obnoxious. Cockiness in a crimson jersey.

Smugness on skates.

Sure, he was good—a gritty first- or second-line winger in a

Division I league—but his massive ego was disproportionate to his level of skill. And he was notorious for trash talking and causing fights between our respective teams. Specifically, for initiating altercations that ended with us taking penalties and the Falcons scoring while we were short-handed.

He wasn't just chippy; he was downright devious.

At the end of the regular season last spring, Carter and Derek crossed paths in the second period. Despite Carter's clear instigation, Derek received a game misconduct while Carter got off scot-free. Losing my brother had hurt, given the team was already down several defensemen due to injuries. In the end, we lost by one goal—and missed out on qualifying for the playoffs. Derek was still holding a grudge against Carter. And so was I.

We fell silent again, watching the massacre on the ice continue. Or Amelia did, anyway. I couldn't tear my eyes away from Luke. Even when he was on the bench, it was impossible to focus anywhere but on him for more than a few seconds.

She nudged me with her elbow. "Are you sure you're okay?"

"I'm fine." I wrapped my arms around my body, wishing I'd worn a jacket over my gray hoodie. Boyd University's arena, Northridge Center, was always bitterly cold, but I'd been in such a daze that I hadn't even thought about it before walking out the door.

"Have you guys talked since?"

"Kind of," I said. "Not really."

Luke had sent me a string of increasingly frantic apology texts this afternoon. Not trying to get me back so much as attempting damage control, echoing last night's pleas to remain friends. At first, I ignored him, but after his fifth text, I finally caved and replied, telling him it was fine (it obviously wasn't) and that I just needed some time (as in, forever). Partly because I was a pushover, and partly because I didn't want drama between us to take his head out of the game tonight. Regardless of how I actually felt, I needed to placate him so he didn't blow it for the rest of the team.

Despite that, Luke was almost unrecognizable on the ice tonight—slow, distracted, and all kinds of useless. He had already taken more penalties than he had in any game last season. Stupid penalties too, like obvious hooking and high-sticking. I couldn't even blame Carter for those.

The rest of our team wasn't faring much better. They were clearly upset with their lackluster performance, which was fueling a vicious cycle.

I wanted to tear my hair out over it all.

Amelia tipped forward, squinting at the players' bench. "Ugh. What now?"

Paul and Carter were engaging in some sort of verbal back and forth through the plexiglass dividing the benches. Carter chirped something, and in response, Paul wound up and lobbed his water bottle over the partition, aiming for Carter's head. He dodged it at the last minute and discreetly flipped Paul off while the coaches weren't looking. But of course, the coaches caught the water bottle toss.

Like I said: devious.

Coach Brown shook his head and stormed over to Paul, pointing to the hallway that led to the locker room. Crap. It looked like he was being sent to change early.

Carter leaned his head back and laughed, then fist-bumped Ward beside him. The Falcons' coach shot them a warning look, and their expressions sobered, but I swore I could see the smirk on Carter's face from across the ice the second his coach turned.

"Carter again," Amelia huffed. "That asshole."

"But they're buying right into it," I pointed out. "He's playing them like a fiddle."

"I know. It's a good thing Jillian had to work," she said. "That way she doesn't have to watch this train wreck."

Jillian was our other roommate and had been dating the Bulldogs' goalie, Mendez, for the past eight months. Mendez wasn't faring well tonight, so it was probably better for both of them that she wasn't here to witness the bloodshed.

Four minutes later, the buzzer sounded and the game ended with a final score of five-nothing. It was bad enough to lose to our rival team, but the shutout really added insult to injury. Especially since Luke was usually one of our top scorers.

Amelia and I made our way out of the stands and stood in the concourse, eating concession popcorn and waiting for the team. It took longer than normal for them to change and debrief, probably because Coach Brown was tearing them a new one. Rightly so.

Paul was one of the first to emerge from the locker room, shoulders dropped and face drawn.

Amelia shot me an apologetic look. "Sorry, I've got to talk to him for a sec."

"It's fine." I waved her off. Just because my relationship was toast didn't mean I expected Amelia to abandon hers.

She darted over to greet him, and he leaned down, embracing her in a huge hug that made my heart ache. I clenched my teeth and stuffed the sadness down. But more difficult to ignore was that I was now standing alone in the concourse like some kind of lurker. Other Bulldogs teammates emerged, one after another, but no one came over to me.

No one even waved or said hi.

My stomach twisted. What, exactly, was my endgame here? Did I really think I'd go out with them after Luke dumped me?

I took out my phone and scrolled mindlessly while debating whether I should wait for Derek or call an Uber and bail. My breath caught as Luke trudged out of the locker room, blond hair still damp, expression stony. He glanced over to the throng of people—his friends, who, until today, I'd thought were mine too—then back over to where I was standing alone. Our eyes locked, but he stayed where he was.

After a few awkward seconds where he watched me and I watched him, he walked over to me with a noticeable air of reluctance. Every step was so slow, he was practically dragging his feet.

"Hey."

"Hey." I locked my phone and slid it into my back pocket. "Some tough breaks out there tonight. Good effort, though."

He shrugged, but his tense expression spoke volumes. "We'll get them next time."

"Totally." I nodded. "So..."

We stood, bathed in painful silence, for what seemed like an hour but was probably less than a minute. Humiliation swelled in my gut. Why had I come? Because I thought Luke would change his mind? Or because I thought he'd realize he made a mistake?

I was the one who'd made a mistake.

Starting with him.

"Come on, Morrison," Mendez hollered, waving at him impatiently. The team was clustered around the front doors, surrounded by girlfriends and hangers-on, making their way to the exit. Only two days ago, I would have been there too.

"In a second," Luke called, looking over his shoulder. He glanced back at me. "Uh, I should go."

"Okay."

I hadn't seen Derek yet. He was always one of the last to leave the locker room. But once he came out, he'd be out the door right behind them. I knew where my brother's loyalties fell, and it wasn't with me. It wasn't like he could help, anyway. Tagging along with them was out of the question, which meant I was headed home to cry into a pint of ice cream while watching *Grey's Anatomy* re-runs. I didn't need company for that.

"I'll text you," Luke said.

I wanted to say don't bother, but I nodded and walked away, heading for the women's bathroom. I could hide in there until they left.

As I pushed open the swinging door, my phone vibrated with a new text.

Amelia: Where are you going? Are you coming with us?

Bailey: Too weird with Luke. Heading home.

Amelia: You sure? I can come with you.

Bailey: No, it's okay. I'm fine. Just need some alone time.

I used the bathroom and washed my hands as slowly as possible, trying to ensure they would be gone before I came back out. I'd just tossed my paper towel in the trash when Zara texted, responding to a message I'd sent her earlier about Luke.

Zara: I'm so sorry, hon. Are you okay? Are you at home?

Bailey: No, I'm at Northview.

Zara would have no idea what that meant—she was a fellow journalism major, also on the school paper, and one of only a few friends not enmeshed in the world of hockey—so I elaborated.

Bailey: Boyd U arena. Game just ended so I'm headed home for the night.

Zara: The hell you are. Noelle and I are taking you dancing. Stay put and send me your location. I'll be there in ten.

CHAPTER 4
AIR TRAFFIC CONTROLLER
BAILEY

AN HOUR LATER, I was crammed into a borrowed miniskirt and standing in a nightclub. That I was wearing heels and makeup for the second night in a row illustrated just how drastically my life had gone off the rails.

"Oh my god. That's disgusting." I slammed the empty shot glass on the bar, shuddering. The acrid alcohol lingered on my tongue and burned as it traveled down my throat.

Noelle laughed, handing me my drink. "It's just tequila, B."

"It's awful, is what it is." I frantically sipped my raspberry vodka seltzer, trying to wash away the horrid aftertaste.

"Sorry," Zara said, tucking a lock of auburn hair behind her ear. "I forgot you're not a big drinker. Next round, we'll make it something easier, like blue balls."

"Blue balls?" I recoiled. "That sounds even worse."

"Nah. It's Malibu and a few other things. But it's delicious. Doesn't even taste like alcohol."

"If you say so."

Loud bass reverberated through my body, and I swayed on the spot to the DJ's remix. They had dragged me to a new club called XS on the other side of town. Because it was technically considered Falcons' territory, it was the kind of place I would usually avoid—which made it the perfect place to drown my sorrows. There was no way Luke would be here. None of the team would be. And tonight, the anonymity felt like freedom.

As the alcohol kicked in, warming my veins, thoughts of tonight's game and yesterday's devastation faded into the background. Maybe drinking *did* make my current situation more tolerable.

Zara propped herself up on the bar, resting her elbows on the top and surveying the crowd methodically. "I think you need a rebound, Bails." She raised her brows, watching me as she sipped her rum and coke through a yellow straw. "You know what they say: the best way to get over someone is to get under someone else."

I adjusted my black skirt, which rode up every two seconds. It belonged to Noelle and was about three inches too short for my liking. "Zara, it just happened."

"Exactly." Noelle nodded emphatically, her aquamarine eyes serious. "Beat him to the punch."

My stomach lurched at her unintentional implication that Luke would also be moving on with someone else in the near future. Maybe I did need that blue balls shot after all.

"No way. With the way my luck is going, I'd end up going home with a serial killer."

"Maybe Luke is the cause of your bad luck." Zara shrugged. "When was the last time you two did it, anyway?"

It had been longer than I cared to admit. He'd been busy with training and classes, and I'd been juggling a heavy course load. I'd told myself it was a slump, but the truth was, sex had become more of a chore than anything.

Thinking back, I couldn't remember the last time we'd actually done it. Maybe after the party at Paul's parents' lake house in August? That was over a month ago, but that was normal, wasn't it? Couples had ups and downs. Even if some of the downs lasted a while.

"I don't know," I lied. Heat filled my cheeks. "Awhile."

"Exactly. And it's probably bad juju for Luke to have been the only"—she gestured vaguely to my pelvic area, biting her magenta bottom lip—"passenger."

In spite of myself, and likely because of the tequila, I laughed. "My vagina is not an airport terminal, Zar."

"What's this, now?" a deep voice cut in from behind me.

I turned and jumped, startled to find Chase Carter's imposing figure leaning against the bar behind me, amusement stamped on his gorgeous face.

Agitator for the Falcons, leading the league in penalties drawn last season, and the second-to-last person I wanted to see.

Clearly, he heard the whole thing, right down to my vagina comment. It had been a shit-tastic week, so I wasn't even surprised. Maybe I would get hit by lightning next.

"Speaking of rebounds," Zara muttered under her breath. "*Hello*."

I ignored her and shot Chase a withering glare. "Don't worry about it."

He raised his brows, widening his dark eyes in mock innocence. "But I'm dying to hear more about takeoff and landing."

Noelle giggled and Zara snort-choked on her mouthful of rum and coke, coughing uncontrollably.

"Oh my god." I rolled my eyes, turning back to face my friends.

"Sorry," Zara gasped, pounding her chest with her fist.

"How are the runway conditions tonight?" Chase pressed.

I scanned the bar area for potential weapons, coming up woefully short. "Do you think it would be considered first- or second-degree murder if I kill you with a cocktail stirrer? One could argue it was spur of the moment if I used a weapon of convenience. But I *have* thought about it for a long time."

Chase took a step closer, the corners of his full lips tipping up into a smirk. "And why would that be? We don't even know each other. Or do we?" He tilted his head, studying my face. "You do look kind of familiar. Have we…?"

"No." I made a face. From what I'd heard, it was no surprise he couldn't keep track of his conquests. "God, no. I meant because everyone from Callingwood hates you."

"Is that so?" The facade cracked, and he broke out into a full, smug grin, not even trying to hide his enjoyment.

My level of annoyance was reaching an all-time high. This guy was six feet and three inches—so the sports news community reported—of solid muscle, but the biggest one was his ego.

He was such a shit-stirrer.

Zara, now recovered, watched us but didn't intervene. Noelle's eyes bounced back and forth like she was witnessing a heated tennis match. Neither of them knew who Chase was and, lacking the proper context, had probably fallen under the spell of his good looks.

Rumor had it most women did.

Actually, the word on the street was that women fell under the spell of more than just his looks. Namely, his mythical, magical penis. According to legend, he seduced a beautiful adjunct professor in his freshman year, and she was so distraught when he ended things that she transferred to a college on the West Coast. Then he slept his way through the BU spirit squad and half of the women's hockey team before working his way over to the rest of the campus co-eds and a handful from my school as well.

Because while I may have hated him, not everyone at Callingwood was as loyal to our sports teams.

And despite Chase's personality, which evidently left much to be desired, I'd been told they all came back wanting a repeat performance because—allegedly—he was that good.

Not to mention nice to look at.

The bartender appeared, and Chase rested his forearms on the bar and ordered another drink. I shifted back to face Zara and Noelle, eager to escape. "Why don't we go dance?"

"Sure." Zara bopped along to the music. "I love this song."

Thank god. I grabbed her by the hand, intent on dragging her away, Noelle trailing behind.

"Hold on." Zara came to a sudden halt and set her drink on the bar. She fumbled in her purse, emerging with her phone. Her face scrunched as she studied the lit-up screen. "My mom is FaceTiming me. I've gotta take this. Watch my drink for me, will you? I'll be right back." She gave my arm a squeeze and darted off to the bathroom.

Noelle tilted her head, a scheming look on her face. "You know what? I'm going to check on her." She followed Zara, leaving me standing at the bar with Chase, Mr. Wannabe Air Traffic Controller.

Traitors.

Then again, I could have left. It wasn't like he had a gun to my head. So I guess that made me a traitor too.

Chase turned to me, midnight eyes tracing my face. "You really do look familiar. You go to Callingwood? What's your name again?"

"I give out that information on a need-to-know basis, and you definitely don't need to know."

Taking a sip of my drink, I averted my gaze and focused on the multicolored lights illuminating the dance floor, flashing in a pattern from red to green to blue. He was trying to hit on me, and my poor ego was so bruised that I almost liked the attention. Almost.

Plus, it would really piss off Luke if he knew, which was what he deserved right now. But flirting with Chase would be akin to committing treachery against my brother and our friends. And hooking up with him was definitely out of the question…right?

Despite that, though, I was newly single, not dead, and he was hot. It didn't hurt that his black T-shirt hung perfectly off his broad shoulders, its short sleeves showcasing his buff arms. Arms that could probably pick me up and slam me against a wall with ease.

Not that I was thinking about that.

"Hardly seems fair that you know who I am but you won't even tell me your name."

"Yeah, you'd know a lot about fair," I said. "I've seen you play."

Though unfair wasn't the word I would use to describe his style of play. Chase didn't technically break the rules, at least most of the time. He bent them just enough to make the other team snap and take the penalty instead. Case in point: what happened with Paul earlier tonight.

He was an instigator.

And a heartbreaker.

"Didn't know you were such a fan, Callingwood."

"I'm not." Scanning the room, I searched for someone else—anyone else. But the dance floor was packed with writhing bodies whose identities were obscured by the strobe lights and artificial fog. Besides, I wouldn't know anyone here. We were firmly on Chase's home turf.

Chase took a long pull of his beer, an amused look on his face. I clutched my drink tighter, clamping down on the urge to pour it over his head.

"Is it a highly controlled airspace, or what?"

I glowered at him. "You're such an asshole."

"Tell me, what's the landing strip like?" His broad shoulders shook with laughter.

"Pretty sure your aircraft is too small to find out." I gave myself a mental high-five for thinking on my toes.

He gave me a crooked smile, like he could tell how proud I was of my comeback. "Not bad." He took a step closer, lowering his voice as it took on a husky quality. "But it's definitely an Airbus."

Airbus? I mean, I kind of suspected based on the rumors I'd heard. But he was exaggerating, right? Between the gossip and the way he carried himself, though, maybe he wasn't. Without his hockey gear, he had the most perfect V-shaped torso, but as for what that lead to…

God help me, now I was actually thinking about what he was packing. Had I lost my mind? This was Chase Carter. Impressive body aside, I hated him. It was basically a requirement. The rivalry between our schools ran thicker than blood.

The realization snapped me back to the present where he was still standing next to me, dark eyes watchful. His gaze weighed down on me, waiting for a response.

I released my lower lip from between my teeth. "Oh."

He shifted his weight, stepping closer. I got a hit of his cologne—which smelled way too good considering who was wearing it—and my stomach twirled.

Something tugged between my legs in response, a stirring I hadn't felt in ages. Not even with Luke.

"You seem a little flustered," Chase said.

"More like repulsed."

But if I was being honest, it was a bit of both. It was unsettling how my mind and body were at such odds when it came to him. Clearly, I was rebounding. And a little drunk.

He took a sip of his beer, sizing me up. "I hope you're not a gambler. You have a terrible poker face."

Irritation rippled through me, mingled with sudden self-consciousness. Heat surged to my cheeks. I hoped the lighting was dim enough to hide it.

"I think you're the one who's getting flustered."

He cocked an eyebrow. "Maybe a little."

"Well, either way." I cleared my throat, squaring my shoulders. "The terminal is closed. Indefinitely. Lack of qualified pilots."

"Oh, I think you'd find me highly qualified." His voice dropped even lower, the sound an impossible combination of gravel and silk.

My heart rate skyrocketed as heat from my cheeks flooded the rest of my body. For a moment, I gaped at him, lost for words. Then Noelle and Zara strolled back up to where we were standing. Zara had a puzzled expression on her face, oblivious to the innuendo train wreck she was walking straight into.

"I think my mother just sleep-FaceTimed me." She gestured with her hands, palms up. "Is that a thing? Do you think Ambien can make you do that?"

Noelle shrugged. "I dunno. One time I ate an entire cake after taking an Ambien, and I didn't even remember it the next day."

Chase cleared his throat. "I'd better get back to the team." He nodded in my direction, adding, "Think it over."

Then he sauntered away, like he had innuendo-laden conversations with strange girls at bars all the time. No big deal.

Actually, he probably did.

"Think what over?" Zara's eyes widened.

"Oh, nothing. Just the usual obnoxious Falcon trash talk." I waved her off.

"Is that who he was?" Noelle asked, craning her neck as she watched him disappear into the crowd. She was on the periphery of the hockey world, only mildly aware of its most basic inner workings, and what she did know was solely due to her friendship with me.

"Yup." I drained the last of my drink. "The enemy."

"Hot enemy."

Zara nodded. "I would climb him like a tree, B."

"No," I said. "He's a jerk."

A social media alert popped up on my phone. It was an update for *The Sideline*, a gossip site centered around our local college's varsity athletes. If there was a rumor floating around, *The Sideline* would cover it. Everything from who was doping—allegedly—to who'd just signed a cushy pro contract.

I followed the stupid site solely due to my paranoia that someday, one of the stories would feature me. With the recent breakup, my fears might have finally come true. Hands shaking, I tapped the notification and bit my bottom lip while the page loaded:

The Sideline

Moving on so soon? Which newly single member of the Bulldogs was spotted getting cozy with a new flame at the afterparty tonight? Wonder what his ex thinks about getting 86'd and replaced in the span of a weekend.

My heart roared in my ears as I clutched my phone. Eighty-six was Luke's number. Not that I needed the hint; he was the only Bulldog who was newly single.

He was with someone else already.

Didn't even miss a beat.

But who could he have moved on with so quickly? Then it hit me...Sophie. Sophie Crier. I'd been suspicious about all those late nights since the beginning of the semester when they'd been "working on their marketing group project." When I confronted him, though, Luke made me feel like a crazy, jealous girlfriend. But this explained everything, including his sudden about-face.

"Bailey?" Zara said. "Earth to Bailey?"

I stared at the screen, the display blurring. "Hold on a sec."

Denial creeped in, tempting me like a siren's call. Maybe it wasn't true. Maybe *The Sideline* fabricated the story like they were sometimes known to do. It had to be fake, right? Luke would never do that to me. At least, not again.

I took a screenshot and sent it to Luke.

Bailey: Care to comment?

Three gray dots appeared. Then disappeared. Then appeared. Disappeared…and didn't return. Five minutes later, I was on the dance floor with the girls when my phone vibrated.

Luke: It's not what it sounds like.

Which meant it was *exactly* what it sounded like.

Two could play at that game. But first, I was getting another drink.

CHAPTER 5

SURE, LET'S CALL IT THAT

CHASE

STATUS UPDATE: I still hated clubs. So far, I was seriously underwhelmed by this XS joint. It was cramped and humid, and the DJ sucked. The beers were ridiculously overpriced too. Fifteen bucks for domestic? Fuck off.

Of course, I was here because we'd pulled off a shutout against the Bulldogs. That did take the edge off my current level of irritation. Seeing the look of defeat on Callingwood's faces as they left the ice was damn near priceless. Suckers.

But the only interesting thing that had happened since we arrived was meeting that feisty blond chick from their school. That didn't pan out, but I had other options. It was time to call it. I was too sober for this scene.

"You played amazing tonight," the short brunette next to me said, batting her eyelashes. Her name was Morgan. Or maybe Meghan. I hadn't caught it over the loud music, and I didn't particularly care.

"You a big hockey fan?" I asked.

I was sure she knew next to nothing about hockey. She probably wasn't even at the arena earlier. But my game was on point tonight, so in this case she'd guessed correctly.

She nodded. "Love it."

"Tonight was tough, huh? Thought we were headed into extra innings," I said. "It was close until we got that last touchdown."

"Totally." She made a pouty face. "I'm so glad you won."

See? She didn't know shit about hockey.

And people think I'm the superficial one.

Squaring her shoulders, she stuck out her chest to draw attention to her plunging lace V-neck dress and the plump cleavage it contained."Do you want to go somewhere quieter?"

She was wearing entirely too much makeup, which would probably rub off all over my sheets later. But she was cute enough, and she seemed like she'd be enthusiastic in the sack so why not?

"Uh, yeah. Hang on." I looked over her shoulder for Dallas and Tyler but couldn't find them in the crowd. Whatever, I was leaving with or without them.

Morgan/Meghan stroked my arm with her long, pointy red nails. "Sure." Her hands were fucking freezing. I hoped they'd warm up before they got to my junk.

Before I could open my mouth to say anything further, a soft, warm hand landed on my other forearm.

"There you are." The voice was sugar sweet.

I glanced to my left, discovering my failed pickup attempt from earlier. Long, honey-colored hair, a smattering of freckles along her nose, and eyes that were this crazy hazel-green that I couldn't even begin to describe.

Callingwood.

Our eyes locked and she tilted her head. "I've been looking everywhere for you." She tucked a lock of caramel blond hair behind her ear and gave me a familiar smile, like we knew each other well. Like we hadn't just met.

Morgan stepped aside, withdrawing her hand with a frown. "Is this your girlfriend?"

"Sure. Let's call it that." Callingwood smiled, shooing Morgan away like a pesky animal. She had a good six inches on Morgan, which added insult to injury.

"Seriously?" Morgan glared at me. "You're an asshole. Good

luck with this one, sweetie." She huffed and spun on her red stiletto heel before disappearing into the crowd.

So much for having options.

"Um, hi?" I turned to Callingwood with a frown.

What the fuck? Did she come back just to cockblock me?

I wasn't sure whether she had changed her mind or was simply hell-bent on ensuring I went home alone tonight.

Unfazed by my lukewarm reception, she gestured to her friends. "Zara and Noelle, you remember Carter. I mean, Chase. Chase, this is Zara and Noelle. I'm sure you have some cute friends to introduce them to, right?"

Right. They were like a trifecta of gorgeous girls. My friends would be all over it. Zara was curvy, with long, reddish brown hair nearly down to her waist. And Noelle was more angular. She had a short black bob and golden tanned skin. Both very attractive, objectively speaking, but Callingwood was by far the hottest.

"Sure." I kept my attention fixed on her. "I appreciate the introduction, but I still don't know your name."

I was part-irritated, part-intrigued, and wholly hoping I could still close this. I liked the challenge. I was dysfunctional that way.

Zara laughed, fluffing her long auburn hair. "I don't know why she's being so mysterious. Her name is Bailey."

Bailey. It didn't ring a bell. I couldn't put my finger on why she looked familiar, though, and it was driving me crazy.

"Do you have a last name, Bailey? Or are you a one-name wonder like Rihanna?"

Bailey looked away, taking a sip of her drink. "James."

Like Derek James, D-man for the Bulldogs? Holy shit. That was why she said she hated me. There was no shortage of bad blood there.

"Is Derek your brother?"

"Yup," she said, popping the *P*.

"Ah." I nodded, trying to keep my expression neutral.

Talk about a plot twist. Derek was a fairly average-looking dude; even a little gangly. But his sister was a fucking dime.

Athletic but curvy, with enough to grab on to. Tall too—in her heels, she wasn't much shorter than me.

I was into it. Fully.

Noelle leaned in, lowering her voice conspiratorially. "Bailey is single and ready to mingle. Newly single as of yesterday, in fact."

Bailey shushed her, cheeks reddening. "We don't need to talk about that."

"What?" Zara shrugged. "It's Luke's loss."

Luke…Luke. Then it clicked. Bailey was Morrison's girlfriend. Or ex-girlfriend, it would seem. That was why she looked so familiar. I'd probably seen her in the stands before.

But she was cheering for the wrong side.

"He's an idiot, right?" Noelle chimed in, nudging me.

"Definitely," I agreed. On both parts, actually—it being his loss and his status as a total fucking idiot. Luke Morrison was the worst kind of hockey player; one who took cheap shots and refused to answer for them later.

"Hey, fucker. I thought you might have left." Tyler strolled up, holding a drink in each hand. He had no intention of offering me one. He was just double-fisting.

"This is Bailey, Noelle, and Zara." I gestured to each with my beer. "And this is Tyler, one of our goalies."

"Nice to meet you." Tyler flashed them a grin. He sidled over to Zara and Noelle, ushering them a couple of steps away and striking up a private conversation. He'd probably seen me talking to Bailey and done the math before coming over. He was a damn good wingman, but that wasn't what I needed at the moment. I wasn't sure what I needed, actually.

I returned my attention to Bailey, who was batting her lashes, waiting for me to speak. She was fucking gorgeous—in the way that told me she'd still be gorgeous the morning after.

Not that it mattered; I didn't do sleepovers.

Hooking up with her after decimating their team tonight would add major insult to injury. Unless I was looking to pave the way for a full-on line brawl next time, I should run in the other direction and never look back.

But I'd never been good at doing what I was supposed to.

"Do you want to dance?" I asked.

"Let's get a drink first."

I glanced down at my fresh beer and her half-full drink, but I knew better than to argue. After the chilly reception I'd initially received, she'd warmed to me, and I didn't want to ruin it.

Bailey grabbed me by the hand and turned, threading her way through the crowd as I trailed behind. We squeezed through a group of people clustered in front of the bar. She stood up on her tiptoes and leaned over the counter, looking for the bartender. Her miniskirt rode up, revealing her long legs, defined calves, and did I mention legs for days? I was a leg man, and hers were fucking phenomenal. They'd look incredible over my shoulders.

She was hot as hell.

Unfortunately, after seeing how unsteady she was walking over to the bar, I had a feeling she was drunk as hell too.

"So…" Bailey turned back to face me and stepped closer. Yup, her eyes were glassy. She traced a slender finger down my torso, coming to a halt above my jeans. "Does your offer still stand?"

I wished I could say yes. I really, really did.

"That depends," I said, studying her. "How drunk are you?"

I had a few hard limits—like taking advantage of drunk girls. And I had a feeling she was well past the point of tipsy.

She made a face like I'd insulted her. "What, are you gonna breathalyze me?"

"Should I? You seem pretty wasted."

"Maybe a little." Bailey swayed on the spot, confirming my suspicions that she was significantly more intoxicated than she had been during our earlier encounter. Grabbing the edge of the bar, she braced herself, looking down at the surface. "Okay, maybe more than a little. That last shot is hitting me hard."

"Do you want a glass of water?"

"No, I think I want to leave." Her lips folded into a frown. "I'm getting tired."

Pretty sure "tired" was code for the spins, but I wasn't rude enough to call her out.

"Your friends look a little occupied." I nodded in their direction, where Tyler and Zara were dirty dancing in the corner of the dance floor, accompanied by Noelle and our third-line center, Gabe. "Should I go break it up so they can leave with you?"

Bailey glanced over and paused, brow crinkling. "No…I don't want to ruin their night." She hiccupped. "I'll get an Uber."

In other words, she'd rather ruin my night than Zara and Noelle's, because there was no way I'd let her leave by herself. I'd be surprised if she even made it home.

"You can't leave here alone."

"Sure I can," she said, grabbing her purse off the bar. "Watch me."

I shook my head. "I'll come with you."

"Because you want to get me into bed?" She gave me a coy smile and tripped over her own feet. I caught her elbow, steadying her.

"No, because I want to make sure you don't die."

She shrugged, tossing her long blond hair over her shoulder. "Eh, works for me." She pulled out her phone and typed a quick text. A moment later, from over on the dance floor, Zara checked her phone and glanced up, looking in our direction.

Bailey waved at her friends, pointing to the exit and mouthing, "Bye."

Noelle shot her a questioning look, gesturing as if to say "what gives?"

Bailey waved her off and gave her a thumbs-up, which seemed to pacify her.

"They're okay with you leaving with me?" I asked.

"Oh, I told them who you are," she said. "If anything happens to me, they'll know who did it."

Drunk logic for sure, but whatever worked.

CHAPTER 6

NOT TONIGHT

CHASE

WAS BAILEY ALWAYS THIS CLUMSY, or was this a by-product of how much alcohol she'd consumed? Either way, I had to catch her three times before we managed to exit the club, one of which was a close call after some drunken idiot plowed into her.

We finally made it to the coat check, got our jackets, and burst out onto the street. The din of downtown traffic and cool evening air greeted us, a welcome reprieve from ear-splitting cheesy pop remixes and the scent of sweaty bodies inside. Bailey bit her bottom lip and lingered by the door, hesitating like she was suddenly having second thoughts about leaving with me. But letting her go back into the club in her state was far riskier; she'd be a sitting duck for any creep who came along.

"Let's walk," I said, nodding my chin. "The fresh air will be good for you. I can order a ride on the way."

Ironically, this was the outcome I'd been angling for earlier—going home with her—only minus the fun I'd hoped to have after.

But now that I thought about it, the optics of this situation weren't great. Taking Derek James's sister home when she was drunk off her ass would look pretty incriminating, even if my intentions were good.

"Okay." She trailed beside me until we reached the corner, and I hit the button for the pedestrian crossing signal. A cacophony of horns and sirens echoed in the distance while we waited. The *Walk* signal illuminated, and I took a step out into the street.

Bailey held up a hand. "Wait." She closed her eyes and swallowed audibly. Still frozen to the spot, she took a deep breath and let it out slowly between pursed lips.

Please tell me she wasn't going to puke.

I stepped back up onto the sidewalk. "How much did you drink, anyway?"

She opened her big hazel eyes. Her impossibly long lashes fluttered as she blinked, trying to focus on me. "I dunno." She shrugged, furrowing her brow. "Two vodka sevens and two shots of tequila? No, three shots. One had something else. Malibu, maybe?"

"You don't drink much, huh?" I asked.

"What makes you say that?"

"Just a hunch."

"Not really," she admitted. "I turned twenty-one yesterday."

Which means Morrison dumped her on her birthday. No wonder she was so drunk. Nice touch, dickbag. Not that I was surprised.

We resumed walking at a glacial pace while she made a concerted effort to remain upright. Great. At this rate, we would cover approximately one block per hour. Suddenly, a light mist of rain started to fall. Not enough to soak us, but enough to make us damp in that unpleasant, sticky-clothes kind of way.

"We need to get you home." I pulled out my phone to order a ride. "What's your address?"

"I'm in the brownstones on—" Bailey stopped short, putting a hand over her mouth. Turning, she gagged and proceeded to throw up in the row of tall green hedges beside her. I pocketed my phone, debating whether I should try to help her somehow or just stay out of her way. Before I could intervene, she straightened, wiping her mouth with the back of her hand.

"It's 303 Park Lane," she finished, staggering slightly. "Near south campus."

Based on the way she was teetering from side to side like we were on a boat, this wasn't the last we'd seen of the vomit. I'd bet on it.

"Let's sit down for a second." I guided Bailey over to a low wooden bench beneath a set of trees where we'd be partially sheltered from the rain. The instant she sat, she leaned over the side and retched again. Sympathy hit me; I'd been there before, and it sucked.

"Here." I shifted closer and gathered up her long blond hair, holding it out of the way.

She whimpered something that sounded like "thank you," but it was hard to tell for sure because it was interrupted by her gagging.

A group of loud, drunken people appeared around the corner. I shifted my body to block Bailey from their line of sight as they drew closer, trying to give her some semblance of privacy. Or at least as much privacy as one could have while vomiting on a public street.

"Are you—" I paused while she dry-heaved. "Are you okay?"

Usually, I was the recipient of that question. Things had gotten dire when *I* was the chaperone.

"I think so," Bailey mumbled, pulling herself upright with my help. Once I was convinced she had her bearings, I let her go, and she immediately stumbled.

I wrapped my arm around her waist. "Do you want me to call your brother?"

Her eyes widened. "No. He would freak if he saw me like this. Especially with you."

Good point.

Bailey fumbled around in her tiny black purse, emerging with a package of tissues and gum. She wiped her face and popped a piece into her mouth without offering me one, which was probably for the best; I had a feeling she was going to throw up again and need it for herself.

As we shuffled down the second street, the rain began to fall in earnest, soaking through our clothes. Her place was a good twenty-minute drive away. She wouldn't make it that long in a car without emptying the remaining contents of her stomach on the floor. And if we kept up this pace, we would be drenched by the time we got there.

"Come on," I said, steering her by the arm and changing directions. My place was five minutes away. It was the only option. At least until she stopped throwing up.

But then what? I couldn't put her in a rideshare in this condition. Escorting her to her place on campus at this time of night wasn't viable either, especially after crushing Callingwood in tonight's game. There would be angry, drunken Bulldogs fans prowling campus, and I needed my limbs in working condition.

"Come on where?"

"You asked me to go home with you. So that's what we're doing. We're going to my place."

Bailey frowned. "Oh. Right." She fell quiet for a moment. "Then can we have sex?"

"I prefer my companions sober enough to actually remember our encounter the next day," I said dryly.

"I'm fine, I just..." She stopped and clutched my arm. She threw up again, but this time, she didn't turn away fast enough. She missed the bushes, splattering my shoes a little in the process. One of the shots must have been blue. Lovely.

"Yeah," I said. "It's a no."

"I can rally."

"Look." I spun her around to face me.

She peered back up at me innocently, her lips in a small pout. Somehow, she was still super hot.

"There is no scenario where that is happening tonight."

Another night would be a different story. I wasn't sure what it said about me, but even after seeing her vomit a night's worth of drinks curbside, I would totally hit it. From on top, from behind, you name it.

"But you sleep with anyone with a pair of boobs."

"Well, that's not entirely—"

Her pout deepened. "Am I not pretty enough for you? You seemed to think so earlier."

"You're very pretty," I said, fighting a smile. "And I didn't say never. I said not tonight. Not while you're in this condition. When we hook up—if we hook up—you'll want to remember it."

"Hmm. You are really hot." Bailey sighed dreamily and ran her hands up and down my torso, probing the muscles beneath my shirt.

My cock perked up in response. But sadly, his services wouldn't be needed this evening.

"It's a shame you're such a jerk." She lost her balance and teetered to the side.

I caught her around the waist to stop her from falling off the curb as a car whizzed past. "It's a shame you're so rude."

"More like honest."

"Do you always lack a filter, or is this the booze talking?"

She tilted her head back and laughed. "I have no idea." After a moment, her expression turned serious, inquisitive. With limpid eyes fixed on mine, probing, she asked, "Are you as good as everyone says?"

I shrugged. "You've seen me play."

"That's not what I mean." She dropped her voice to a stage whisper. "I meant *in bed*."

She sure knew how to stroke a guy's ego. Too bad it was the only thing getting stroked tonight.

"Ah. I guess you'll have to find that out for yourself another time."

After an eventful stroll home that took twenty minutes longer than it should have, peppered with small talk and sexual requests that made even me blush, we arrived at the house I shared with Dallas and Tyler.

"Wow, this is fancy," she said, gaping at the modern gray stucco structure. "How do you swing this? Wealthy family?"

Kind of, but I wasn't. Dallas's family, however, was fucking loaded. Hence the sweet digs. I carefully guided Bailey up the three stairs leading to the front door.

"Something like that."

I unlocked the door and pushed it open with my hip while holding Bailey upright with one arm. She stumbled inside, tossing her coat on the floor. Then she flopped down beside the entry mat and unbuckled the straps on her high heels. When she'd wrestled both shoes off, she stood up, barefoot.

Her shoulders heaved with a weary sigh. "I want to go to sleep."

"Right away," I promised. "But you can't sleep in that." I nodded at her outfit. It was damp from the rain, and like my shoes, her white tank top had fallen victim to the blue vomit splash incident.

She was a hot mess. Literally.

"I don't have anything else to wear, though." Bailey frowned.

"Give me a sec." We made our way upstairs, and I led her into my bedroom. I flipped a switch in the attached bathroom so we could see without being blinded by the overhead light. Any of my bottoms would probably fall right off her tiny waist, so a T-shirt was all I had to offer.

Pulling open the top drawer, I grabbed a well-worn red Falcons tee and handed it to her. Sure, I had other shirts. But giving her this felt like a taste of retribution against that dick Morrison.

"Here," I said. "You can change in the bathroom. Washcloths are under the sink if you need one. And mouthwash."

Bailey froze on the spot, staring at the bed. She turned to face me, eyes wide like a deer caught in headlights. "Are you going to sleep in the bed too?"

She looked awfully scandalized for someone who'd asked if she could sit on my face twenty minutes ago.

"Well, yeah. The other bedrooms belong to Dallas—who's probably in there with Shiv—and Tyler. And, for reasons I won't get into, I wouldn't touch that with a ten-foot pole. And I don't fit on our couch." I gestured to myself with one hand, waving an open palm from my head down, as if to illustrate my height. "But you can sleep there if you want. I'll warn you, though, it's not comfortable."

Dallas's stupid modern square-shaped sectional looked cool, but it had these weird immovable armrests and was about as comfortable as a bag of rocks. My ass always ached after playing video games on that thing.

"I don't know..." Bailey chewed her bottom lip. Her gaze darted between the bed and me like she was performing some kind of mental risk calculation.

"I can assure you; I'm not going to try anything."

"Okay." She yawned, rubbing her eyes. "I trust you. I don't know why, but I do."

"I'll go grab you a water."

By the time I returned from the kitchen, glass of water in hand, she had changed into my shirt and was on top of the covers, passed out cold diagonally. Snoring.

BAILEY

Light flooded through the gaps in the curtains, growing progressively brighter. I was thirsty beyond belief. Every muscle in my body was sore, as if I'd just run a marathon. And my head pounded like someone was beating me with a hockey stick.

I groaned and pulled the covers over my head, trying to block out the light—and reality. If I could get back to sleep, maybe I'd wake up later and realize all of this had been a bad dream. What time was it, anyway? I cracked one eye open to discover I was hiding beneath a dark gray duvet, not white like mine…and it smelled like cologne.

Really delicious cologne.

Where the hell was I?

Pieces of last night came back to me slowly. Luke blowing me off at the game, hitting the club with Zara and Noelle, running into Chase Carter…Oh my god—Carter. I threw off the covers and let out a gasp. I was wearing a crimson Falcons T-shirt.

The uniform of the enemy.

I squeezed my eyes shut, slowly counting to five. Maybe I was hallucinating from all the stress. I opened one eye and peeked at my surroundings. Sadly, I was still in the same place: Chase Carter's bedroom. No, not his bedroom. His sex dungeon.

Fine, it didn't look like a sex dungeon, not that I'd know what one looked like. The walls were a crisp, clean white, and the soft cotton sheets and comforter were charcoal gray. There was a small flatscreen TV mounted on the wall, a glass computer desk with a laptop, and an acoustic guitar leaning in the corner. All in all, it was clean and minimalist. It didn't scream fraternity guy like I'd expected. Actually, it was nicer than Luke's bedroom.

But I wasn't the first girl, nor would I be the last, to wake up here. I was probably customer number 238, with a line around the block to take my place. Take a ticket and get in line, ladies.

"Good morning, sleeping beauty." Chase appeared in the doorway and leaned against the frame, clutching a black mug in his hands. He was freshly showered and wearing fitted gray joggers and a white V-neck T-shirt, with his dark hair still damp. And damn, did he look hot—like an athletic wear model or something equally appealing.

I didn't want to know what I looked like. I knew it wasn't good. Or appealing.

He nodded at my shirt. "Red suits you."

I pulled myself upright, yanking the covers up to my chin. I was in a T-shirt and underwear. His T-shirt wasn't that long on me, either. No pants. Not even shorts. Did that mean we had sex? Oh, no. No, no, no.

Nausea roiled through me, and not from the hangover.

"Did we…?" I asked, too embarrassed to finish my sentence. He shook his head. "No."

I eyed him warily, hyperaware of my bare bottom half beneath the blanket. Did he sleep next to me under the covers last night? Did his butt graze my butt? Did I snore? Oh my god.

"I don't take advantage of drunk girls." Chase pushed off from the doorframe and took a few long strides over to stand at the foot of the bed.

My breath stilled, heart accelerating. Somehow, I felt extra-undressed with him so close to me.

"Though in this case," he added, "I think it was you who tried to take advantage of me, James."

"You know my last name?"

"Of course," he said. "You tried to get in my pants."

"I did what?" I frowned, mentally replaying last night's events. The beginning of the evening was fairly clear, but then it got increasingly blurry. Either way, I didn't do *that*. "No, you're the one who was hitting on me with all your lame airport innuendos."

"That was before you got blackout drunk. You came back later and found me. Cockblocked me in the process, I might add." He raised a brow pointedly. "Then you wanted to go home, but it wasn't safe to let you leave alone in the state you were in, so I brought you back here. Nothing happened."

I narrowed my eyes. "Are you sure?"

"We didn't have sex. We didn't even kiss."

"Thanks…I guess." I grumbled. Chase Carter, perfect gentleman? Who knew?

"Oh, don't thank me." His lips quirked. "You made for fascinating conversation on the walk home."

My stomach leapt into my throat. "What did I say?" I didn't drink often, and for good reason. When I was under the influence, I tended to blab to anyone who would listen. My life story, my innermost secrets, it was all up for grabs. It didn't take much to get to that point, either, because I was a total lightweight.

"You've got quite the mouth on you. Made some very explicit requests." Chase smirked and took a sip of his coffee before he continued. "Sounds like Morrison wasn't exactly keeping up his end of the bargain in the bedroom."

I wanted to crawl back under the covers. Or maybe die. Dying sounded pretty good right now.

"But no, I didn't take you up on your many colorful offers. It might have been tempting, if not for the fact that you could barely walk straight. And you threw up on my shoes."

I cringed. "I'm sorry. I'll pay to replace them."

"Don't worry about it. I think I got most of it off." He nodded to the foot of the bed, where my skirt and tank top lay neatly folded. "And your clothes are there. I washed them."

"You didn't have to—"

"Oh, trust me, I did. Otherwise, this place would have reeked of vomit and Malibu."

CHAPTER 7

NO EVIDENCE, NO CRIME

CHASE

COACH MILLER probably scheduled dryland training at the crack of dawn on Mondays specifically to fuck up the start of my week. Out of all the players on the team, I hated early mornings the most, and Miller knew it. We butted heads constantly, and he loved to torture me. Or "build character," as he liked to say.

At least it was over with for today. He'd even gone light on the burpees for once. Now all I had to do was stretch and foam roll, grab a shower, and head home for a good two-hour nap before my first class at ten-thirty. Probably hit the drive-through somewhere in there too. Then back to the rink at four. By the time that was done, I'd be too tired to do much else—which, I suspected, was Miller's intention.

Dallas and I limped into the stretching area and sprawled out on the cushioned red mats, still short of breath from our drills. He leaned over his calf, pulling up on the toes of his black Nike sneakers to stretch out his hamstring.

"Morrison's ex? That's who was at our place Saturday night?" He let out a low whistle, leaning deeper into his stretch. "Are you trying to make life harder for yourself? Now the Bulldogs are really going to have it out for you next weekend."

They had it out for me already anyway. I was public enemy number one, which was perfectly fine with me. It made derailing their game that much easier, just like I had this weekend—like taking shots on an empty net.

"You didn't let me finish. Nothing happened." I stood up and grabbed a black foam roller off the rack, then lay back down with it. "She was too drunk."

"Are you going to call her? Try for a do-over?"

I sucked in a sharp breath as I leaned on my elbow, rolling my glute. The left side of my ass was full of tight, painful knots. I could barely put any weight into it without flinching. It didn't help that Bailey had been sprawled out across the bed, relegating me to a tiny corner because I wanted to give her space. Sleeping that way totally jacked up my back.

"I didn't get her number." *Chump move, Carter.*

Then again, she was too busy vomiting curbside Saturday night. And come Sunday morning, she was skittish after waking up in my bed unexpectedly. When I drove her home, she was silent and stared out the window the whole time. I'd barely had the truck in park when she bolted. We didn't exactly get off to the strongest start.

Plus, there was the whole part where sober Bailey hated me.

Dallas switched sides, grabbing his opposite foot with a groan. "Maybe for the best. Coach probably wouldn't appreciate you stirring that pot. You get into enough trouble as it is."

He wasn't wrong, but she was hot enough that I was still willing to risk it if the opportunity presented itself again.

Hey, I never said I made good choices.

"What about her friends?" I asked. "Did Tyler hit it or what?"

"I think one of their exes showed up and they bailed not long after you guys did. But we met these other chicks and hit up a party at a penthouse downtown. So XS for the win."

"I don't know how your reputation stays so squeaky clean," I muttered. "You're no saint, either."

"I'm just smarter about it. Ever hear the word discretion?" He raised his eyebrows pointedly, wiping his forehead with his red and white Falcons gym towel. Smug shit.

"Whatever," I said. "We can't all be perfect like you."

In contrast to my type-B slacker ass, Dallas was our team's all-star—well-rounded on and off the ice. He played a highly technical game, racked up tons of points, and could stickhandle circles around everyone in our division. In short, it was like he'd been genetically engineered to play; think the Steph Curry of NCAA hockey.

Unfortunately, this also put a huge target on his back. But he wasn't a fighter, and he rarely dropped gloves. That was my job, as was making sure the people who took dirty hits on him answered for it.

"Perfection might be a little unrealistic for you," he said. "I was thinking more along the lines of trying to stay out of jail."

"Yeah, yeah." I waved him off. Wincing, I adjusted the angle of my glute on the foam roller, but that made it hurt even more. Maybe I could get in for a sports massage this week. This cylindrical torture device wasn't helping.

"Oh." Dallas jutted his chin toward the door to the training room, "Coach told me he wants to see you before you leave."

Speaking of torture. Fuck me.

The good thing about Boyd U was that our Division I hockey program was top-notch. The bad part was that Coach Miller was a tyrant. And no one ever got summoned to his office to be congratulated for doing something right.

After a long shower, I took my sweet time getting dressed and finally dragged myself down the hall to his office. Coach Miller sat at his desk with his wire-rimmed reading glasses perched on his ruddy nose, immersed in his phone. His work wardrobe consisted of black track pants with a rotation of Falcons hoodies in black, gray, red, and white. Today's choice was black, which I hoped wasn't a bad omen.

"Hey, Coach." I rapped on the gray metal doorframe and stood at the threshold, praying he wouldn't order me to come in. "Ward said you wanted to see me?"

"Sit." He pointed at the chair in front of him without glancing up from his phone.

Dammit.

Not only did I not want to get chewed out, but this was eating into my nap window. Maybe I could make up an excuse about having a class soon. Nah. After my bumpy sophomore year, Miller was up my ass constantly. I was pretty sure he had my schedule memorized inside and out. He probably even did spot checks to make sure I was in my classes.

But I didn't have a choice, so I obeyed, plopping into the worn black leather seat across from his solid-oak desk. He continued to scroll on his phone, face contorted into a sour frown. I scanned the walls of his office, lined with trophies and photos from tournaments and championships dating up to twenty years back. Man, Miller used to have a nice head of thick, wavy brown hair. Maybe that's why he was so pissed off all the time. I would be mad at the world too if I went bald.

After another minute, he locked his phone and set it facedown. He placed his elbows on the desk, studying me warily from beneath his red Falcons cap. "I finished my semester check-in with your professors."

"Okay…" This wasn't leading anywhere good, given that he'd done all of this by eight o'clock on a Monday.

"Long story short, you're on probation."

"Probation?" I echoed. We'd gone down this road last spring, and it was an utter waste of everyone's time and paperwork. After a month or so, I pulled my grades up enough to pacify them, and we all moved on. The theatrics and procedural crap were unnecessary. Why were we doing this again?

"Not officially, thank god." He glanced up at the ceiling. "Because then I would have no choice but to pull you from the line."

"Phew," I said, leaning back and crossing an ankle over my knee.

"No, Carter," he snapped, pinning me with an icy gaze. "Not *phew*. You're still on probation with me. With the program. I spoke to the athletic director about it. We're trying to keep it under the radar this time because repeated probations look bad for you *and* for the program."

"What's the reason you're putting me on probation?"

"You really don't know? Your grades are in the goddamn toilet. Just like last year."

Well, that wasn't a surprise. Since school started three weeks ago, I'd dedicated approximately twenty minutes to studying and completing assignments. It was my last year at Boyd. I wouldn't be staying to graduate, so I gave no fucks whatsoever about my grades.

College was merely an annoying detour along the way to the league. At least I didn't have to worry about losing a scholarship on top of everything else. I was paying my own way through this circus.

"I'll address my grades," I told him.

"You'd better." He gestured to his phone. "You've failed two quizzes in history already. And you have a term paper due next month that's worth a third of your grade. I expect you'll expend extra energy on that paper to ensure you don't fail the class."

"Yes, I will." Extra energy having someone else write it for me, maybe. That history class was drier than cardboard.

"While we're on the topic of problematic behavior, I heard about your antics at that little end-of-school party you threw this spring."

What, specifically, had he heard? He would take issue with several things, I was sure, some of which weren't exactly legal. Asking for details didn't seem like a good idea, though. Then he might start digging.

"I'm sure whatever you heard was greatly exaggerated."

He shot me a look so searing my skin prickled. "I'm told there are pictures. You better hope that is not the case."

Shit. Maybe we needed to confiscate phones at the door. No evidence, no crime, right?

"I have eyes everywhere, Carter. If it happened, assume I've already heard about it."

Cute how he was trying to scare me. But if that last part were true, I would have been kicked off the team freshman year.

He added, "Stop gallivanting around with girls, getting into fights, and acting like a teenage idiot."

I almost pointed out that at twenty-one, I was not, in fact, a teenager. Then I realized that was his point. Instead, I nodded. Silence was usually the safest bet in these situations.

"Look," he said, his tone marginally less hostile. "You add a lot of value to the team. And I appreciate your knack for getting into your opponents' heads. But you have to reel it in a little off the ice, or you're going to ruin all your hard work. Understand?"

"Yes," I muttered. "I understand."

"You can't impress the scouts from the sidelines, Carter. Get it together or get benched. You're dismissed."

"Yes, sir." I stood up and threw my gym bag over my shoulder before heading for the door. There was still enough time to catch some sleep before class.

"And Carter?"

"Yes, Coach?" I turned back to face him.

He snatched a pen from its holder with a worrying amount of violence. "Consider this your first, last, and only warning."

CHAPTER 8
YOU THOUGHT ABOUT IT
BAILEY

I DIDN'T DARE TELL Jillian and Amelia where I spent Saturday night. When I got home Sunday morning, they assumed I had been at Zara and Noelle's, and I didn't correct them. Zara and Noelle had agreed to cover for me too, angels that they were.

Plus, nothing even happened with Chase. So why open that can of worms?

Even without telling Jillian and Amelia about Chase, things were strained at our place. Like neither of them knew how to act around me now that I wasn't Luke's girlfriend. I hadn't realized that as far as most of my "friends" were concerned, that was my identity.

Now it was like I was a stranger instead of their roommate and friend. Or like I had a communicable disease and they were scared of catching breakup-itis.

Maybe I could move into the *Callingwood Daily* office and live there.

I successfully avoided Luke for the first part of the week, which required considerable effort given the overlap of our lives. On my way to English Lit on Tuesday, I nearly ran smack into him on the quad. Fortunately, I had reflexes like a ninja, and I ducked behind a tree so he didn't see me. At least he was alone.

You could say I was taking the whole post-breakup no-contact strategy to the extreme. If I wasn't in class, I was holed up in the *Callingwood Daily* office. I didn't even settle in to study on campus for fear of Luke strolling by. But now it was Wednesday, and contact with him was inevitable, because taking a class with my boyfriend had seemed like a great idea until he was suddenly no longer my boyfriend.

Heart racing and hands clammy, I pulled open the lecture hall door for ASTR201 - Introductory Astronomy: Stars and Galaxies. Luke and I had registered for it together last spring because we both needed to fulfill an intro-level science requirement. Astronomy seemed better than biology with its gross dissections or chemistry with all its math. Foolishly, I'd even thought it might be romantic to go stargazing for an assignment.

Now I was sorely regretting that decision. I would rather have cut up a thousand frogs (sorry, frogs) or done a million equations than be shut in a room with Luke for an eighty-minute lecture.

If only he'd get sucked into a black hole.

Heart thundering in my ears, I paused in the doorway, scanning the tiers of laminate countertops and attached seats for his familiar blond hair and his standard gray and navy Bulldogs zip-up. When I didn't see him, I released a sigh of relief. He wasn't here yet. Maybe he wouldn't come. I grabbed a seat off to the side in the back for an optimal sight line while maintaining minimal visibility myself. Then I waited, like a tightly coiled spring, but the lecture began, and he never showed. Thank god. He'd probably withdrawn and taken a W. I was considering it if he didn't. But I couldn't afford to eat the tuition like he could.

While I was packing up my stuff after the lecture wrapped up, my phone buzzed with a half-hearted *sorry about the breakup* text from my brother. It was approximately five days too late and lacked the comfort—and sincerity—one would expect from a sibling in this scenario. But maybe he felt conflicted, given that Luke was not only his teammate but one of his close friends. That was, after all, how we'd met.

Following astronomy, I headed back to the *Callingwood Daily* office, my makeshift home these days, to complete some work on the newspaper and catch up on homework.

Zara, Noelle, and I sat at the round table, revising articles for tomorrow's issue while snacking and drinking coffee. A few other students who also worked on the paper milled about the office, copying documents and doing various administrative tasks.

Zara glanced up from her silver MacBook. "By the way, can you cover the Hawks game on Friday? Liam called in sick."

"It's Wednesday," I said, biting into my chocolate chip granola bar. "He already knows he's going to be sick this Friday? How convenient."

"I know, right?" Noelle took a sip of her iced french vanilla coffee, rolling her eyes.

"I wish he understood that having the sports beat means he has to cover *all* the sports," I said. "Not just the ones he likes."

I sank my teeth into the chewy oat bar in my hand, taking out my irritation on the snack. For some reason—probably misogyny—Liam had a grudge against women's sports. He also disliked volleyball. When the two collided, as was the case with the Callingwood women's volleyball game this Friday, he was often unable to perform his duties for a variety of reasons. Stomach bug, sinus infection, sprained and/or broken limb, stuck in traffic, too hungover, mental health day, dental emergency, flat tire, family commitment, family funeral, and a suspicious number of sick and/or dead pets.

Funny how that worked.

Needless to say, Liam didn't pull his weight at the paper. He should have been pulled off the sports section long ago. But our faculty advisor, Professor Johnson, was fairly hands-off—which in most cases was a good thing—and tended to avoid intervening. As a student-run group, unless we really wanted to raise hell with administration, there wasn't a whole lot we could do other than tolerate him and count down until he left.

"On the bright side," she said, "he'll be gone next year. Then all the sports coverage can be your baby."

I sighed wistfully. "Can't wait."

Hockey had been a religion in our household when I was growing up. Derek and I learned to skate shortly after learning to walk. Dad poured a backyard rink every winter, and we spent every waking hour on it. We both played hockey when we got older. Unfortunately, hockey was an expensive activity, and our family could only afford for one of us to play. Since Derek was better, he won, and I had to stop in middle school.

But I still loved it, which meant I was a total hockey nerd to this day. Stats, awards, records, rookies, and scores. I followed all of it. Points, goals, assists, you name it. I was a sports nerd in general. I could, and often did, school Liam on stats any day of the week.

I thoroughly resented that Liam had the sports beat simply because he happened on the scene a year before me. If it had been merit-based, it would have been mine by now.

Zara stretched out, propping her feet up on a spare chair beside me. "Are you done with that scholarship application?"

"Not yet. They want my entire life story. I'm surprised they didn't ask for a DNA sample too."

"I'm rooting for you. I think you have a good shot." She gathered up her long curtain of auburn hair, twisting it and securing it with two yellow pencils. On her, it was messy chic. When I attempted it, I looked like the nutty professor.

I gave her a half smile. "I hope so."

It was hard to gauge what my chances were, really, when the entire process was so complicated. I met the minimum GPA requirement, but that was one of a zillion factors. The application package included a lengthy form, personal essay, academic and personal references, resume, biography, and full transcript submission.

And that was only the initial round, where they narrowed it down to five finalists. If I made it to the next round, I'd be interviewed by a panel of journalism faculty members, several of whom had received prestigious awards at various points in their careers.

Intimidating would be putting that mildly.

To be fair, the amount of work was warranted given the scholarship amount. It was hefty, the kind of scholarship that would keep me from having to worry about money next year at all—I might even have some breathing room financially, as hard as that was to imagine. And it would definitely help ease my student loan burden once I graduated.

I desperately wanted the scholarship. Desperately needed it. Hoped I would be the lucky one of countless applicants who landed it. But I knew it was a long shot, so I was trying to temper my expectations.

As it drew nearer to dinnertime, the other students began to file out of the office. Eventually, the three of us were the only ones left. Noelle was working on an English paper, Zara was doing research for a psychology project, and I was *trying* to focus on my *Video and Audio Production* textbook. But my mind kept circling back to the weekend—and not because of Luke.

"So?" Zara checked to make sure the coast was clear, then leaned over the table. She waggled her perfectly sculpted eyebrows. "How was he?"

"Who?" I played dumb, fighting the telltale rush of warmth crawling up my neck.

"The super hot guy you went home with, silly. Chase?"

"I wouldn't know. We didn't sleep together," I said. "Thank god."

"Why not?" She gestured dramatically. "He was the perfect rebound. Tall, dark, and horny."

"I was too drunk, for one. I threw up on the way home. Several times, according to him. I can't say, as I don't recall much from that window of time." Specifically, I had no idea what I'd said, and I had a strong hunch I'd aired some dirty laundry. The only question was what.

Zara cringed and sucked in a breath. "Oh no."

"Sorry, B." Noelle winced.

"The last two drinks were my idea, so I have no one to blame but myself."

"Do you think you'll see him again?" Zara asked.

With my luck, I probably would. But I planned to avoid hockey games as much as possible going forward. I was already thinking up excuses to bail on Saturday's rematch against the Falcons on home ice. I was debating between fabricating a twenty-four-hour stomach bug or group project emergency. Because the idea of seeing Luke *and* Chase in one place was, frankly, horrifying.

"No way." I shook my head. "He's an asshole."

"Are you sure about that?" Zara asked, tipping her chin thoughtfully. "It sounds like he helped you get home and he didn't take advantage of you."

"Low bar there, don't you think?" I asked.

She shrugged. "Maybe, but it's still more than I could say for half the guys I know."

"Fine," I said. "So, he's not a creep, but he's still an asshole. And a player."

Emphasis on that last part.

"That's a shame," Noelle mused, tapping her glossy lips with her purple pen. "He had total BDE."

"BDE?" I repeated, confused.

"Big dick energy."

"Ugh, gross." I hid my face in my hands. "Sorry I asked."

Zara poked me with her pencil. "You know you thought about it too."

Snippets of our airport terminal conversation came flooding back to me. Specifically, the Airbus part. My face heated against my fingers.

"Definitely not."

CHAPTER 9
THAT TOOK A TURN
BAILEY

SATURDAY AFTERNOON ROLLED AROUND before I knew it, hitting me smack in the face. I tried to back out of attending the three o'clock rematch on home ice against the Falcons. I really, really tried. I did *not* want to see Luke, and I wasn't sure I could face Chase after last weekend, either. Unfortunately, despite my best efforts, Derek guilt-tripped me into attending. Just like always.

"I don't think it's a good idea," I had told him.

"You have to come," he'd said. "You're good luck, Bails."

No pressure there.

Why, if I was such good luck, had the Bulldogs lost the last three games I attended? I kept that question to myself, not wanting to mess with Derek's head before the game.

Pathetically, I didn't have any other plans anyway. If I didn't go, I'd be doing laundry or sitting in my room surfing Netflix. Watching my brother play for a few hours wasn't asking much. I would pretend it was freshman year all over again—before Luke and I ever met.

I wished it was.

This time, at least, I would cut loose immediately after to avoid the awkwardness. I'd start with that, then maybe I could leave earlier and earlier as the season went on, eventually not coming at all. If I eased into it gradually, maybe Derek wouldn't notice or care as much.

Or maybe things would magically get less awkward with Luke. But probably not.

To say our season was off to a rough start would be an understatement. By the start of the third period, the Falcons were leading again with a score of four to two. Not great, but at least we were on the board.

Dallas Ward stole the puck from Paul, flying into our end zone like a streak of lightning. He dodged Derek's defensive efforts, leaving him in the dust, and passed to Carter, who was perfectly positioned, as usual. The guy had the hockey IQ of a genius. It was infuriating.

Carter dug into the ice like a machine and came at the net before anyone could get near him. He wound up and sank it into the bottom left corner with a clean wrist shot, raising his stick up in victory as the puck sailed in.

It was a beautiful play, executed so quickly that Mendez didn't stand a chance of stopping it. And as Carter's third goal of the evening, it was a hat trick too. The Falcons fans in the crowd went wild, whistling and yelling his name. Chants of "nineteen" echoed around the arena as the Falcons on the bench gave him congratulatory fist bumps and helmet taps.

Ugh.

Both Carter and Ward were on fire tonight. Our team, not so much. But a score of five to two with fifteen minutes left meant we still had a fighting chance—in theory. Games could change on a dime. If everything was dialed in, it was more than possible to score two consecutive goals in the span of a minute or two. Then all it would take would be one more to tie it up.

It all boiled down to whether the Bulldogs stayed focused or let that fifth goal rattle them. Unfortunately, I had a feeling it would be the latter.

"Dammit," Amelia groaned, covering her face. Her cheery-red nails hid her anguished expression. "The score is going the wrong way."

"Still better than last week," I said.

Chase hopped back onto the ice for another shift. Our gazes collided, and an electric jolt ran through my body. Goose bumps popped up on my arms beneath my black puffy down parka. He flashed me a drop-dead gorgeous cocky smile and winked before skating off to the other end.

Jillian poked me in the ribs. "Um, did Carter just wink at you?"

My stomach did a flip-flop, heart bounding against my ribcage. He did. He definitely did. What the hell was he thinking?

"Huh?" I squeaked, my voice was unnaturally high. "No. Must be a puck bunny nearby." I turned around, pretending to survey the rows of seats behind us. The only other people seated nearby were a family of five with a baby and an elderly couple. Jillian and Amelia turned to look too, confirming as much.

"Hmm," Jillian murmured, biting her coral-painted bottom lip. "Doesn't look like it. And it definitely wouldn't be me or Amelia. We don't even know him."

"Neither do I," I lied.

And I definitely didn't sleep in his bed last weekend, either.

"I really think he was winking at you, B," Amelia agreed, leaning closer. "That's so weird. Do you think he's trying to piss off Luke?"

"Why would Luke care?" I asked flatly. "He's the one who broke up with me."

"Oh, come on." She snorted. "You and Carter? You know that would piss him off."

As the stands emptied after the game, I said goodbye to Jillian and Amelia and headed for the side doors so I could make a hasty exit. It was gorgeous outside for late September, which meant the twenty-minute walk home would be pleasant due to the sunshine and, more importantly, the lack of Luke's presence.

"Bailey!" Jillian called. Her long, dark curls swayed as she frantically waved me over. "Come here for a second."

Dammit, Jill. I couldn't imagine what she needed that we hadn't discussed during the two-and-a-half-hour game. Maybe I could pretend I hadn't heard her? Nope, too late. She caught my eye. Reluctantly, I made a detour and headed in her direction.

"What's up?" I stuffed my hands in my coat pockets and bounced on my heels, stealing a nervous glance at the fluorescent-lit hallway that led to the dressing rooms. I felt like a ticking time bomb being here. She'd better make it quick.

Jillian drew in a breath, speaking quickly. "I forgot to ask you about tomorrow. What time do you want to go to the mall to get those—"

Before she could finish, Luke walked around the corner—with Sophie by his side. Jillian stopped short, mouth open in surprise, and I froze on the spot. My stomach clenched as my gaze landed on where their hands were tangled together. Our breakup was so fresh it was almost like there was some other girl standing with my boyfriend. Only he wasn't my boyfriend anymore. They looked lovey-dovey in a way that, prior to Friday, Luke and I hadn't been in ages…if ever.

Suddenly, it was hard to breathe. This was not happening. Could not be happening.

They ignored us and strolled over to join the group a couple of feet away. Jillian's eyes darted over to them, then back to me. "Uh, I'm sorry, Bails. I didn't know she was here. I swear."

But she knew they were together, didn't she?

Everyone did. How long had this been going on? It was hard to believe there hadn't been any overlap. Was there some big cover-up?

And if there was…did my brother know?

As if I'd accidentally summoned him, Derek emerged from the locker rooms and made a beeline for Jill and me. He glanced in

Luke's direction but didn't react to seeing him with Sophie. Almost like he was used to the image already.

Derek sighed, running a hand through his sandy brown hair. "Hey, B. Jill."

"Hey." I was tempted to raise the Luke issue but knew it wasn't the time. "Uh, good game." Normally I would have something more constructive to offer, but my brain was short-circuiting. I glanced over Derek's shoulder at Luke and Sophie. I couldn't help it; it was like a train wreck I couldn't tear my eyes away from. Sophie was everything I wasn't: petite, girly, feminine. She wore skirts everywhere, had the longest eyelashes I'd ever seen, and didn't know the difference between spearing and slashing.

"Not really." Derek shook his head, jaw tight. "I don't know what's going on lately. We can't seem to get our shit together."

"All teams go through a slump once in a while," I said, hiking my purse strap up on my shoulder. "I'm sure it'll pass soon. Anyway, I was just leaving. I've got a deadline." Not true, but it was easier to pretend I had a reason to be somewhere else.

"I'll text you about tomorrow," Jillian said, expression apologetic.

I nodded. "Sounds good."

My eyes landed on Luke and Sophie again, lingering in some form of twisted self-torture. With her small frame and long platinum blond hair, she looked like a real-life Barbie, and he was her Ken. They were probably a better couple than we could have ever been. Which meant the past year and a half I'd spent with him was a complete and utter waste.

A lump formed in my throat. I needed to get out of here, stat. The good news was, I could see the exit. The bad news was, reaching it would require walking past the entire team, including Luke and Sophie. A necessary but unpleasant task.

Just as I started to make another break for it, Paul muttered, "Here comes Carter." He jerked his chin toward the locker rooms. "What does that asshole want?"

Suddenly, Luke was the least of my problems. I came to a screeching halt, swiveling in the direction Paul had indicated. There he was, in all of his gorgeous, arrogant glory. Broad shoulders in a well-tailored navy suit with a determined expression on his face. Chase Carter.

And he was heading right for me.

Chase weaved through the crowded concourse purposefully, side-stepping the spectators milling about. Several girls stopped and stared, not even trying to hide that they were ogling him. One or two tried to talk to him but appeared to be too tongue-tied to speak. Even a few of the guys he passed were visibly dazzled by his presence.

It was like a scene from a goddamn movie. All he needed was a spotlight and his own soundtrack.

He was magnetic. Hypnotic. Utterly addictive to look at.

As he drew closer, all the conversations around me faded out, and an eerie silence fell over the group. He came to a halt beside me, throwing an arm around my shoulders.

"Ready, James?" He snapped his gum, giving me a wink.

It was the equivalent of an atomic bomb going off in my personal life. Everyone stared at us, wide-eyed, but no one said a word. We could have heard a puck drop fifty feet away.

Jillian and Amelia looked like they'd seen a ghost. Derek eyed Chase warily, which wasn't totally unwarranted given his reputation. And Luke clenched his jaw, his face turning redder than the Falcons' home jersey. Sophie looked up at him questioningly, but his eyes were laser focused on us.

Not even on us. On Chase.

Chase flashed Luke an easy grin and gave him a nod. On its face, it looked cordial, but in reality, the smile was more smug than friendly, and it was peak passive aggressive. It was a "what are you gonna do about it?" smile. This, of course, had the intended effect. Luke glowered at him, his expression murderous, but he didn't speak. Really, what could he say?

Chase inclined his head to the doors. "Let's go."

"Uh, sure." I glanced back over at Amelia and Jillian, already dreading the interrogation I would surely receive later. "I'll see you at home."

"Okay," they echoed in unison, heads cocked and voices lilting in confusion.

They weren't the only ones who were confused.

I awkwardly waved goodbye to the stunned group of witnesses as Chase steered me away, his arm still draped around my shoulders. My brain was having a hard time getting up to speed. It didn't help that I was close enough to get a contact high from his delicious cologne.

He was still touching me…and I didn't completely hate it.

Even though I still hated *him*. Obviously.

Chase wordlessly maneuvered me back through the crowded concourse and over to the side exit that led to the players' parking area.

"What are you doing?" I hissed, stealing a glance at him once we were out of sight of my friends.

"Rescuing you, apparently."

"I don't need to be rescued."

He chuckled, low and deep. "You sure about that?"

CHAPTER 10
AS A FRIEND
CHASE

"WHAT THE HELL, CARTER?" Bailey pulled away from me and came to a stop on the sidewalk outside the arena. Her eyes flashed with anger. "Where are you taking me?"

Late afternoon sun glinted off her dark blond hair, bringing out the green and gold in her hazel eyes. Unlike most girls I met at nightclubs, she was even more attractive in a normal, everyday setting, free of all the makeup and tight clothing. And like when we first met at XS last weekend, she had reverted back to hostile mode.

Just my luck: one of the hottest chicks I'd ever met hated my guts. Or was she hot because she hated me? Maybe it was a bit of both.

I didn't want to examine that too closely.

But it was probably both.

"To my truck." I pointed with my keys to the corner of the parking lot, where my black F-150 was parked several rows down.

"And then what?" She unzipped her black puffy jacket and slid it off to reveal a white short-sleeved V-neck underneath. It dipped down in the front, showing the slightest hint of her round, perky cleavage. But I managed to keep my eyes above shoulder level. Mostly.

"Whatever you want."

"I don't even like you," she said.

"You don't even know me."

"I know enough." Bailey drew in a breath and paused, watching me.

I said nothing. Just watched her back and waited her out.

Pinching the bridge of her nose, she let out a defeated sigh. "Fine."

I'd received warmer receptions from women, to say the least.

We weaved through the parking lot at a pace that was, fortunately, much faster than last weekend's drunken excursion. I always ran hot after games from the physical exertion and metabolic boost that followed. Combined with the unseasonably warm fall weather and my dark suit pants, I was running at a thousand degrees. I loosened my tie as we walked and slipped it off, followed by my suit jacket. I hated the fucking dress code for games. What was the point?

"Are you stripping now?" Bailey asked dryly.

"I can if you'd like." I unbuttoned my collar and rolled my sleeves up to my forearms. I was roasting. Was I nervous or something? What was going on? "But then you'd have to pay me, and I don't come cheap."

"That's not what I hear."

Bailey came to a sudden stop in front of my truck instead of getting in. She looked at me, to the vehicle, then back at me. Her expression hardened.

"I changed my mind," she said, planting her hands on her hips. "I don't want to go anywhere with you."

I arched an eyebrow. "You're telling me you want to go back inside?"

"Well, I can't now. You blew up my life."

Really? Seemed to me like her life blew up, oh, approximately last Friday. It had just been raining shrapnel ever since. But it was easier to blame me, I supposed.

"I think you're overstating things here."

"Not even a little. Everyone is going to be pissed at me."

I snorted. "For what? Moving on? Morrison sure did. Though it was a downgrade, if you ask me."

Almost imperceptibly, she flinched. I immediately regretted what I said, even though it was true—that girl Morrison was with had nothing on Bailey. Not even in the same league. But tact wasn't my strong suit, and she seemed vulnerable in a way I wasn't used to dealing with.

She straightened her spine, glaring at me. "No, for sleeping with the enemy."

"I don't think literal sleeping counts." I strolled past her and opened the passenger-side door, holding it for her. "Unless this is your way of hinting at something."

"Definitely not."

All I wanted was to get inside my truck and blast the air conditioning directly at my face. Stop by home and change into a T-shirt and jeans instead of this ridiculous suit. Then inhale at least three plates of food. I would figure out the rest later.

If her company factored into any of the above, all the better.

Unfortunately, she was hell-bent on arguing with me.

We stood, locked in a standoff, while I cooked under the sun, waiting for her to get in the damn vehicle. My truck chimed, reminding us that the door was still ajar. James might be the only person I'd ever met who was *less* argumentative while drunk.

Time to de-escalate the situation a bit.

Taking a few steps, I drew closer until she was within arm's reach. I didn't actually touch her, but that was the point. "James." I dropped my voice, keeping it low and smooth.

"What?" she huffed, crossing her arms over her chest.

"Do you have other plans tonight?"

Her mouth scrunched up. "No."

"So what's the problem?"

"Everything?" She gestured between us. "You, me, this?"

I ducked my head, catching her eye. "Are you hungry?" It was just a guess, but it was dinnertime and would explain some of her irritability. And I was definitely starving. A massive burger was in order, stat. Maybe two.

As if on cue, her stomach gurgled loudly. Her cheeks flushed pink, which was pretty adorable. She jutted her chin defiantly. "No."

"Great," I said, ignoring her reply. "What are you in the mood for?"

She looked down at her black Converse. "I don't know. Pizza? Burgers? I'm not picky."

"Let's swing by my place so I can change, and then we can grab some food. My treat."

"Okay," she grumbled, finally climbing into the truck.

After stopping by my place, we ended up at Burger Bar in the trendy brewery district nearby. We ordered their signature boozy milkshakes, burgers, and fries, and somehow, I even talked her into sharing an order of onion rings with me, but I was borderline worried she'd poison them if I wasn't careful.

"I hope you know I'm not going to sleep with you." Bailey took a sip of her chocolate-Kahlua milkshake, eyeing me warily from the other side of the booth.

I grabbed an onion ring from the middle of the table and set it on my appetizer plate. "Technically, you already did."

"If you use that loophole to tell everyone and give them the wrong idea, I will strangle you with hockey tape."

"Relax, James. I was kidding. I didn't think you'd sleep with me tonight."

Sober Bailey had made it abundantly clear on Sunday morning that she was not, in fact, a one-night stand type of person. I had no delusions about that changing soon. Though obviously, I wouldn't turn her down if it did.

"Oh really?" She raised her blond eyebrows. "Then what about all that crap you said to me at the bar?"

"I was teasing you." I shrugged, biting into the gigantic onion ring. Oh my god. It was almost orgasmic. Food always tasted exponentially better after games.

"Yeah, right."

Our server returned, quickly setting down our plates. She slid Bailey's chicken burger with sweet potato fries over to her, followed by my loaded double cheeseburger with regular fries, before disappearing again.

"Well, it's half-true," I said, picking up my burger. "I was teasing you in a playful way. Obviously, I was hitting on you too."

There was no point in denying that part. Hostility aside, she was freaking gorgeous. My attraction to her grew every time we hung out. What muddied the waters was whether she was attracted to me now, in the absence of tequila.

I was pretty sure she was. But the death stare made it hard to tell.

Bailey leaned over the table, brow crinkling. She lowered her voice, like she didn't want anyone to overhear. "Does that actually work with other girls?"

Did she want honesty here or what? I guess that's what I would give her.

"Most of the time," I said, taking a bite of my french fry.

"Seriously?"

"You came back, didn't you?"

"That was the tequila talking," she snapped.

Damn. She was cute when she was annoyed.

"Huh." I stroked my chin. "Isn't that a country song?"

She placed her palms flat on the table, resting her forehead on them. "You are exasperating," she muttered, still facedown.

"Back atcha." I just wished I didn't enjoy it so much. Liking the dynamic we had going on was problematic. But I put the fun in dysfunctional, so I guess that wasn't a huge surprise.

Bailey lifted her head, curtain of golden hair falling in her face as she looked up at me. "Why aren't you out celebrating your win and hat trick against us with all your Falcon buddies?"

"I don't know," I said honestly. In fact, I was missing at my own house party at this very minute. My phone, switched to silent, had been blowing up. "I guess that scene gets old after a while."

"What, you don't like having a crowd of doting fans throw themselves at you? That seems like it would be right up your alley."

Honestly, being here with her, getting the gears, was far more appealing than being surrounded by a bunch of people who didn't actually know me but claimed to think I was great because I could hit things with a stick.

I swallowed a bite of my burger. "Don't you ever find it…superficial? That whole scene?" I asked. "We're joined together by this single common thread, but otherwise, I'm not sure most of us would even be friends."

She should know, as it looked like she was about to be excommunicated by Captain Dickhead. I'd seen it happen before. But she hadn't grasped what was coming yet, which made me feel bad for her. She didn't deserve that.

"Deep thoughts from Carter over here," she said. "I thought you were supposed to be Mr. Life of the Party. Don't all the Falcons love you?"

"Ha, no. Ward and I are solid. And Tyler's cool, odd duck that he is. But I'm pretty sure half the team would throw me under a Zamboni if they thought it would help them make the league."

Bailey blinked slowly at that. "Okay." She shook her head as if to clear it. "Did you seek me out at the bar because you knew who I was?"

"No, I didn't know. Not until you came back, anyway."

"But you came up to me tonight to piss off the team," she said.

"Honestly?" I pinned her with my gaze. "Partly. But also, it looked like you could use a friend." When I'd walked out of the locker room, that stricken look on her face was all I could see. It pissed me off, especially because that douche Morrison had put it there. I couldn't not do something.

She bristled. "I have friends."

"And what were they doing while your ex was parading that chick around right in front of your face?"

Another flinch. Maybe I should filter my thoughts around her. I never really had, but surely I could learn.

"Amelia and Jillian are caught in the middle," she said, looking down at her plate of food. "I'm sure this whole situation isn't easy for them."

An odd pang tugged at my gut. Sympathy? Pity? It was unfamiliar, and I didn't like it. At any rate, these friends of hers sounded shitty.

"It's nice that you're thinking about their feelings," I said. "But who's thinking about yours?"

She raised her eyebrows. "You were thinking of my feelings tonight when you abducted me in front of everyone?"

"Of all the ways you could have left the arena tonight, do you honestly think that wasn't the best-case scenario?"

"I guess..." She shifted in the booth, avoiding my eyes. "But you were trying to rattle Luke. Don't act like you were doing me a favor."

Rattled didn't even begin to describe it. I would have paid good money to capture a photo of Morrison's face when I threw my arm around her shoulders. It was the perfect mixture of rage, disbelief, and jealousy. As much as she was protesting right now, there was no way she didn't enjoy that as much as I had.

"I'd say it's a win-win, wouldn't you agree?" While technically, Bailey wasn't his business anymore, I was well versed in the inner workings of the male mind, and to Morrison, she absolutely was. That meant there was a 100 percent chance that he was losing his shit right now. The smug as fuck smile I flashed him pretty much guaranteed that.

Morrison wasn't a direct threat on the ice—he didn't even engage in fights when he was challenged, let alone start them. But he would send his minions to do his bidding, which meant I would probably need to look out for Bailey's brother and a few of the forwards for a while.

There was a decent chance of a full-on line brawl with Callingwood in the future because of what I'd done.

Dammit. I had enough fires erupting in my own life, most of them self-ignited. Now I'd thrown kindling onto the perpetually smoldering feud between the Falcons and the Bulldogs.

Coach Miller was going to have my head.

"As much as I may hate him right now," she said, "I am still firmly Team Bulldog."

I shrugged. "Whatever you need to tell yourself."

Part of me did admire her sense of loyalty, however misguided it was.

When Bailey left the table to use the bathroom, I checked my texts. Ignoring most of them, I wrote Dallas back.

Dallas: Where the fuck are you?

Dallas: You ditched us.

Chase: Something came up.

Dallas: You mean someone.

Chase: Exactly.

The server came by with our bill, leaving the black leather folio on the end of the table. Bailey lifted her hand like she was going to make a grab for it.

I leaned over and yanked it out of her reach before she could. "Don't even try."

"You can't pay for me," she said, blond brows knitted. "This isn't a date."

"I'm well aware. And I'm still not letting you pay."

"I don't know whether I should thank you or throttle you." Bailey sighed, slipping on her jacket. "Does that mean I owe you now?"

I pulled out my Mastercard and handed it to the server. "Well, you did grace me with your sunny personality over a meal, so I guess we're even."

"Har-har." She rolled her eyes.

"Though you do seem marginally more pleasant now that you've eaten. Emphasis, marginally."

"I guess I was kind of hangry. I spent all my money on—" She stopped and cringed. "Never mind."

She almost let her guard down. Interesting.

"Do tell." I pressed forward, lowering my voice. "Hookers and blow? Me too."

Bailey laughed. "Nothing nearly that interesting, sadly."

"Well, the night is young."

The drive back to Bailey's place was filled with conversation. She was easy to talk to, as long as we avoided any mention of hockey, the Bulldogs, or the Falcons. Signaling, I took a left, pulling into the parking area for her brownstone complex. I eased into the visitor spot and put my truck into park, leaving the ignition running. At least she was sober enough to get upstairs without falling down them this time.

"Here." I held out my hand. "Give me your phone."

"Why?" Bailey pulled away and hugged her phone against her body, eyeing me suspiciously.

"So I can look at porn, James. What do you think? So I can put my number in it."

"Who said I wanted your number?"

"Who else are you going to text next time shit gets weird?"

She unbuckled her seat belt, still clutching the phone. "Why would you want me to text you?"

"Maybe I need a friend too."

"You need a friend?"

"Why not?" I shrugged. "Like I said, half the team would throw me into a skate sharpener if they had the chance. Maybe three-quarters. Coach Miller might even get in on that action."

Bailey chewed her bottom lip as she scanned my face. I raised my eyebrows, waiting.

"Fine." She unlocked her phone before passing it to me. "But I'm not giving you mine."

I quickly entered myself as a contact and handed it back to her. "Text me sometime."

"As a friend."

"Right," I said. "As a friend."

CHAPTER 11

DON'T MAKE ME CHOOSE

BAILEY

CHASE'S TRUCK engine roared as he pulled out of the visitor parking lot and turned back onto the street. In a daze, I made my way down the sidewalk and up the three concrete stairs to my front door. My head was spinning, my hands were shaking, and I was questioning everything I thought I knew.

I had dinner with Chase Carter. And I kind of liked it.

Clearly, there was a snag in the space-time continuum, and I had been transported to an alternate universe. Or the apocalypse was nigh. One of the two, anyway.

I unlocked the deadbolt and held my breath, praying no one else was home. It was shortly after nine, so the odds were in my favor. The navy blue door swung open with a creak, revealing a dark, quiet, and blessedly roommate-free house. I hung up my parka and heaved a sigh, the tension in my body easing. Maybe it was a little pitiful to be home alone on a Saturday night, but the solitude was a welcome reprieve from the interrogation I was sure to face in the near future.

I flipped on the porch light and headed to the kitchen for a glass of water before going straight to my bedroom. Amelia and Jillian were probably staying over at the house Paul and Mendez shared with Luke, but there was still a chance they would come home tonight. And if they did, I would definitely pretend to be asleep.

Then I walked upstairs, pulling out my phone to survey the extent of the damage to my personal life. Not surprisingly, I had three missed calls and fifteen new texts. I already had a pretty good idea what they said, and I had no interest in engaging in discussion about Chase, my personal life, or any combination thereof. Instead, I opened each message without looking at its contents, then left them all on read to let everyone know I was still alive.

Not that it was my safety they were worried about.

It was loyalty.

The following morning, I was sitting at the island eating a bowl of strawberry granola with milk and minding my own business when I was ambushed. Jillian and Amelia descended the staircase in tandem, like they'd been plotting military strategy upstairs. They came into the kitchen, pinning me with gimlet eyes and circling like sharks.

My stomach sank, appetite vanishing. Jillian came to a stop and leaned against the counter, facing me. Amelia continued to pace nervous circles on the tile flooring. Their outfits even coordinated. Both wore black sweaters and dark jeans. Whether the clothing choice was intentional or not, this was clearly a straight-up intervention.

Jillian was only five-three and a hundred pounds soaking wet, and Amelia wasn't much bigger, but the effect of the two of them combined was oddly intimidating.

"Carter, B?" Amelia gestured wildly, her perfectly arched brows knit together. "What in the world is going on?"

I glanced up from my half-empty bowl and set my spoon in the pink milk. "We're friends," I said. "That's all."

Jillian crinkled her nose. "Why?"

Annoyance simmered in the pit of my stomach, bitter and burning. It wasn't like I was president of the Chase Carter Fan Club all of a sudden, but her condescending tone rubbed me the wrong way.

Especially when they all kissed Luke's ass constantly.

And especially when she'd barely spoken to me all week.

"Why not?" I slurped my coffee, intentionally being obnoxious.

Amelia blinked rapid-fire, like a machine gun of disbelief. "But you hate him. We hate him."

"And I used to like Luke. Funny how things change, huh?"

"I—" She faltered.

Jill's white Apple Watch vibrated, and she looked down, frowning. "I have to take this." She rushed back upstairs, ponytail bouncing as she took the carpeted steps two at a time. *Something was off.*

"Is she fighting with Mendez?" I asked Amelia.

Jill and Mendez had been dating for over a year, but their relationship had been volatile from the start. They were both crazy jealous and prone to toxic behavior like flirting with other people and ghosting each other. In the spring, they'd gone through an especially tumultuous patch where they fought every weekend, complete with dramatic blowouts, door-slamming, and phone hang-ups. There were a lot of alcohol-soaked tears on her part. And sometimes his. But things had been more stable with them lately. Slightly.

Something flashed across Amelia's face that I didn't quite catch. "Er, no. They're fine. I think it was about work."

At nine o'clock on a Sunday? Jillian worked at a swimwear boutique, and they didn't even open until noon. Plus, she was a sales associate, not management. It didn't add up.

"Stop changing the subject." Amelia retrieved a black mug from the cupboard and filled it from the pot of coffee I'd brewed earlier. "Seriously, B. Chase Carter? Do I need to be worried about you?"

"No, I'm fine," I said brightly. "Peachy." I did feel pretty good, all things considered. Earlier this week, Zara told me about a trick her old therapist taught her. Picturing the person who'd wronged you in diapers—because only babies or small children act that way, or something like that. I'll admit, I was skeptical; it sounded silly, not to mention a little weird. But I tried it with Luke, and actually, it kind of worked.

He was a man-child.

Despite the horrible way it had come about, I was starting to think I was better off. A huge weight had been lifted from my shoulders. No more walking on eggshells, no more trying to please him, and maybe, most of all, no more worrying about what he was doing behind my back.

Being attached to someone wasn't the same as being in love with them, but I hadn't quite realized that before. That's not to say the fallout from the breakup was easy to deal with. My social circle was crumbling around me, and I had a hunch Luke was putting on the pressure with his friends to speed the destruction along.

At any rate, Amelia's concern lacked authenticity, given that this was the first time we'd even spoken at length since last Sunday. I had tried to connect with her, but she'd made excuses about being busy. When it came down to it, I doubted anyone was truly concerned for my well-being; their own agendas trumped their loyalty to me.

Amelia narrowed her eyes. "If you say so."

"Moving on," I said. "Do you want to catch a movie this week? That new rom-com, *Kiss Me,* just came out. It looks super cute." With the way things were going, I could definitely use the escapism of a happily ever after with a side of movie theater popcorn and giant bag of candy.

"Um…I don't know." She looked away, setting her mug down. "I'm pretty busy with this group project I have for Developmental Psych, plus there's a game on Tuesday night. And I think I might go for dinner with Paul on Thursday. I'm pretty booked. Sorry, B."

"Okay. How about we do something tomorrow or Wednesday then?" I took a bite of my cereal, finishing the last of it and debating whether she would judge me for drinking the strawberry milk from the bowl. Then I did it anyway, because I no longer cared.

She fidgeted with the sleeve of her yellow sweater, picking off a piece of lint with her gold-painted nails. "I have to work on that project then too."

Uh-huh.

Fine. I would ask Zara and Noelle.

"Is this about me and Luke?" I asked, setting down the bowl.

"Breakups aren't contagious, Amelia. You can still hang out with me."

"No..." She trailed off, wincing. There was a long pause before she continued. "It's just that Paul is really pissed about the whole Carter thing."

What on earth? Who the hell was Paul to be angry with me for anything? We were barely even friends.

"Who I hang out with is none of Paul's business. Like, literally zero percent."

"He sees it as being disloyal to the team." Amelia took a sip of coffee, hiding behind the gigantic mug so she didn't have to meet my eyes.

I gritted my teeth. "I didn't realize I was a part of the team. Which position do I play?"

"You know what I mean," she said. "Luke is one of his best friends."

And I was supposed to be one of hers.

"But it's fine for Luke to be disloyal to me as a person?" I snorted. "To dump me on my birthday, after having probably cheated on me *again*? I don't see anyone giving him grief."

Of course they wouldn't. He was team captain; practically their god. It was a high school clique dynamic to a T, and he was the ringleader. Then it hit me: Luke was the mean girl of the Bulldogs. He was Regina George. On skates.

"Please don't put me in a position where I have to choose, B."

I stood up and put my bowl and spoon in the dishwasher. Slamming it shut a little harder than necessary, I turned back to her. "I'm not the one who's doing that," I said. "Your boyfriend is."

CHAPTER 12
I REMEMBER
CHASE

THE WEEK WAS WELL UNDERWAY, and I hadn't heard from Bailey yet. Maybe I never would.

"You saw her again, didn't you?" Tyler asked, pulling on his black undershirt. We'd hardly seen each other since the game on Saturday. He had been practically living on campus, working overtime on a group project for one of his accounting classes. Unlike me, his dedication to high performance on the ice also extended to his grades.

"Who?" I fought a yawn. Breakfast skates were brutal. Six a.m. was too early to be awake, let alone on the ice.

"The girl from XS. James's sister."

"How do you know that?"

"I saw you go up to her after the game, dumbass. Is that why you bailed on our place? And on meeting us at O'Connor's?"

Avoiding his probing gaze, I grabbed my stick from the rack. It was trashed from the game on Saturday. I scraped it across the black rubber flooring near the doorway, removing any leftover tape residue from the bottom edge of the blade.

"Kind of." I secured the black cloth tape to the heel of the blade and methodically wound it around, working over to the toe end. "It's a long story."

It really wasn't. By the time I dropped Bailey off at home, it wasn't even ten, and my friends were expecting me to meet them. But I wasn't in the mood to get shit-faced at a pub while yelling to be heard over loud music. Maybe I was too sober to see the appeal. I got halfway there and made a detour for home instead, which marked the first time I'd stayed in on a Saturday in my entire college career. It wasn't that bad, actually. And for once, I was in great shape for Sunday's dryland training.

He smirked. "I bet."

"Nah, not like that." I ripped the tape off from the roll and rubbed the end down with my thumb so it laid flat against the blade.

"Why not? Couldn't close?"

I shook my head, carefully smoothing the tape. "That wasn't the point. We were hanging out as friends."

"You. Friends with a chick." He laughed, sliding a foot into one of his skates. "Right."

"Why not?"

"Do you want the reasons in alphabetical or chronological order?"

"Hilarious." I placed my stick back on the rack by the door. Sitting down on the bench, I grabbed my skates from my equipment bag and loosened the laces. "How was O'Connor's, anyway?"

"Fine. Same old." He reached over, attaching his skates to his red and white leg pads. "But speaking of female 'friends,' Kristen was pissed you didn't come."

I tightened my skates, glancing back up at him. "Why? I didn't have plans with her."

"She seemed to think otherwise."

"I haven't even talked to her since spring." It had been well over four months, almost five. We weren't a thing. Never had been. This was why repeat hookups were a bad idea.

And after what Kristen had done, she'd guaranteed there would be no encore.

Ty shrugged. "I never said chicks made sense. Just letting you know."

I made a mental note to avoid her. Or to continue to, anyway.

"By the way..." He angled closer, lowering his voice. "Word has it there will be a couple scouts at the game on Saturday."

I glanced around to see if anyone else was listening. They were too engrossed in some story that Justin, a sophomore defenseman, was telling. It involved a raw steak and male nudity. I didn't want to know any more than that.

"How'd you hear about that?" I asked.

"I have eyes and ears everywhere."

It was true. Ty was freakishly in tune with the goings-on of NCAA hockey; injuries, scouts, who was signing with whom. "I'm giving you a heads-up in case the intel is correct. I'm not telling everyone, though, so keep it between us and Ward."

"Roger that." We were playing New England U this weekend. They were having a hot start to the season so far, but maybe that was a positive; I generally played better against strong competition.

"Make sure you don't choke."

"Thanks for the vote of confidence," I said, standing up. "You're a peach."

"Anytime."

After class, I headed to Starbucks downtown to meet my mom for coffee. She'd been called into the city last minute on a work emergency. Funny how she managed to come in for that but rarely ever to see me. I should have been used to it by now, but the sting never fully went away.

I walked up to the corner where she'd taken a table and two chairs next to a fireplace. She'd already ordered us both coffees. "Hey, Mom."

She stood and wrapped me in a big embrace infused with her familiar floral perfume. "How are you, honey?" She held me out at arm's length, inspecting me for a moment before releasing me.

"Good. How about you?" I pulled out the small metal chair and sat. My knees pressed up against the underside of the tabletop. The whole set, made for average-sized people at most, was about two sizes too small for me.

"Oh, keeping busy," she said. "Work has been hectic, and Rick got a big promotion last month."

"That's great." I tried, and failed, to sound like I meant it. My stepfather, Rick, and I weren't exactly poker buddies. We had never gotten along. I was sure he would have greatly preferred if I didn't exist. But he made my mom happy—mostly, at least—which was what ultimately mattered to me.

"How's school?"

I avoided her eyes, pretending to be suddenly fascinated by the label of my drink. "It's going."

"How's hockey?"

"Good." She would know more if she ever came to my games. They lived roughly an hour away and hadn't made it to one of my games since my freshman year. I wasn't asking for every weekend, but once or twice a season would be nice. Sometimes our away games were even closer—but still, nothing.

Maybe it reminded her too much of my father.

"You know, it'll be ten years in April," she said, like she was reading my mind.

My throat tightened. "I know." *Well aware that my dad has been dead for a decade, Mom*. Did she think I'd forget?

There was a weighty pause.

"Would you like to do something to commemorate the date? I could fly Sera down for the weekend..." She trailed off.

Would I? Honestly, not really. Did that make me a bad person? I wasn't sure.

I always remembered April twenty-first—I just did it in my own way, which started with getting obliterated the night before. The timing worked out well because exams were usually wrapping up and everyone else was looking for an excuse to party. It was a win-win: numb the pain for the evening and feel too sick the following day to function, let alone have feelings.

My coping skills were top-notch.

"We could do a small memorial service for him," she added. "Plant a tree in his memory."

This tree suggestion was so left field for her. Although she *was* making an effort, which was a nice change of pace. But we weren't a touchy-feely family by any stretch; we barely celebrated birthdays. Maybe she was back in counseling—the idea had *therapist* written all over it.

"I'm good with whatever you two decide. It would be nice to see Sera if she can get away." Though I strongly doubted my sister would want to fly in from Arizona to stick a twig in the dirt.

She patted my hand on top of the too-small table. "It's important to talk about him and remember him, you know."

I stiffened and clenched the to-go cup, the cardboard collapsing slightly beneath my grip. Drawing in a breath, I tried to quell the irritation brewing in my gut.

"I know. I do." I remembered him fine.

How he taught me how to skate; That he taught me how to shoot, how to deke, how to lift the puck; I remembered putting on his jersey and sprawling out on my parents' bed to watch him play on TV.

And I remembered that the reason he was on that fucking helicopter was because he was trying to make it home for my hockey tournament.

When I arrived home a few minutes past five, Siobhan was in the kitchen, stirring something in a gigantic stainless pot on the stove. I wasn't sure we even owned a pot that big, but maybe she'd brought it over. At this point, she was essentially our fourth roommate.

Siobhan glanced over as I came in the door. "Hey, stranger." She took a spoonful of sauce and blew on it before she took a taste. Then she frowned and shook her head, snatching up a spice shaker from the granite counter. Whatever she was making smelled delicious, like garlic and Italian spices mixed with heaven.

"I miss one Saturday night, and you're all acting like I defected to the other side in a war." I opened the fridge and pulled an apple out of the produce drawer. "Where's Ward?"

"He's washing my car."

Weird chore for him to take on, but sure. They'd been dating—or doing whatever they did—since May, and I stopped trying to make sense of their dynamic not long after. Shiv fed us a lot and was cool in general, so I couldn't really complain.

"I'm making spaghetti," she said. "It'll be done in half an hour or so."

"Nice." I tossed the apple and caught it, lingering in the doorway to the kitchen. "Maybe you could give me some advice."

"You're right." She stirred the sauce, then gave me a once-over. "That shirt and those pants don't work."

"Not that." I glanced down at my jeans and black T-shirt. "But ouch. And good to know."

"I was kidding. You live in jeans and tees, Carter. You're safe from the fashion police. What was it?"

I hesitated. Maybe I shouldn't have brought it up.

"Wait." She set down the wooden spoon and narrowed her dark blue eyes. "Is this about that girl you've been talking to?"

Oh my god. How did everyone know?

"You know what?" I shook my head, backing out of the kitchen. "Never mind. I don't even know what I'm asking, anyway." I honestly didn't. How to make someone text me? That was literally impossible. All I could do was wait, like I had been, while slowly going crazy…like I had been.

Not that I was into her as more than a friend.

A really hot friend.

Dammit.

"I didn't mean to embarrass you."

"You didn't," I grumbled.

She tilted her head, studying me. "You know, this is a good look on you. It's pretty adorable."

"What?"

"You're smitten," she said. "Don't worry, I won't tell the guys."

"No, I'm not." I tore away from her gaze, sinking my teeth into the apple.

"Uh-huh. Whatever you say."

After eating dinner with Dallas and Shiv, taking another shower, and wasting more time than I should have looking up sports stats, I reluctantly cracked open my laptop so I could work on my history paper. It wasn't due for a month, which would normally mean I wouldn't even look at it for roughly twenty-nine more days. But maybe scrambling at the last minute wasn't an optimal strategy as far as my grades were concerned.

As soon as I opened Word, my phone lit up beside me. Lightning quick, I grabbed it. I should have ignored it and focused on the assignment, but maybe it was important.

Bailey: Hey, it's Bailey.

Bailey: I never thanked you for taking care of me that night. You didn't have to do that.

Chase: Well, I kind of did. But I didn't mind.

Bailey: I'm sure you were happy to see that we lost again tonight.

Chase: Didn't know, but ouch. The streak continues.

Bailey: You're crushing us in the standings. Gonna need you to throw a couple games at this rate.

Chase: Sure, I have a price. It's probably not even that high.

Bailey: I'm afraid to ask.

Chase: How are things? Any more weirdness?

Bailey: Eh, they're so-so.

Chase: Well, you know who to call.

Bailey: Ghostbusters?

Chase: Or me. But maybe an exorcism would help break your losing streak.

Bailey: You'd better hope the tables don't turn, chippy.

Chase: Don't worry, they won't.

I stared at my phone with a stupid grin plastered across my face. Maybe Shiv was right. Maybe I was smitten. But I had no idea what to do about it.

CHAPTER 13
BETTER THAN YOU
BAILEY

WEDNESDAYS WERE THE NEW MONDAY—THE worst day of the week. Because Wednesdays meant that ASTR201 with Luke returned with a vengeance. There was no way I'd be lucky enough to avoid him again.

From the moment I woke up, a thick, black storm cloud of dread loomed over me. Even Zara and Noelle remarked that I seemed edgy in our Research Methods class. After parting ways with them, I headed over to The Dish for a late lunch I didn't want to eat but knew I needed. I lingered over my chicken and brown rice bowl while time moved at warp speed, rocketing me closer and closer to astronomy.

Fueled by adrenaline, I speed-walked to class early and grabbed the same spot—off to the side at the back. Then I unpacked my things and prayed. With every minute that ticked by, my nerves climbed a little higher. I waited, jiggling my foot and tapping my pen against the desktop until someone sitting in front of me turned around and shot me a dirty look.

The clock hit two p.m. and Professor Walsh began his lecture on the properties of stars. Still no Luke. I heaved a sigh, muscles relaxing. I lucked out again—or so I thought. Two minutes after class started, he rushed in and found an empty seat near the front. As he did, he turned around, making eye contact before I could look away.

The hairs on the back of my neck stood on end for the entire lecture. I steadfastly focused on my notes and the slides at the front while I ignored Luke's attempts to catch my eye. Class ended, and I quickly gathered up my pens and books, sliding them back into my bag with one big sweep of the arm. If I could get out fast, I could avoid him.

"Bailey," Luke called. "Wait." He scaled the steps two at a time, dodging other students in the aisle to reach me.

Worst-case scenario confirmed. The desperate need to escape seized me, and the dark cloud that had been with me all day morphed into a category-four hurricane of anger and panic. I speed-walked down the aisle, making a beeline for the doors at the back. Unfortunately, he beat me to the end of the row and was standing in wait when I got there.

"If I throw a stick, will you leave?" I asked, tone flat.

He glared at me. "I came over to say hi. What's your problem?"

Other than the fact that you exist? Nothing. Nothing at all.

"Don't talk to me," I said, brushing past with my book bag wedged between us. His woodsy cologne wafted around me, both familiar and unpleasant. "In fact, don't even look at me. Pretend I don't exist, and I'll do the same in return."

Luke followed close behind like a toxic shadow I couldn't shake. "What the hell has gotten into you?"

"Gee, I don't know. Maybe it's how you got a new girlfriend the day after you dumped me." I came to a stop at the exit while people filtered past us, then turned to face him. If he didn't care about making a scene, then neither did I. "Or it could be the part where you're trying to turn my friends against me."

As I finished, the last handful of people left and the doors shut behind them with an ominous click. Suddenly, we were the only two left standing in the empty lecture hall. Alone in the beige-walled prison under fluorescent lighting. The literal last place I wanted to be.

"Why are you being so hostile?" He threw his arms out, palms up. "Sophie doesn't have a problem with you."

What had I ever seen in him? He was delusional, self-centered, entitled.

"Are you kidding me? Why would she? I never did anything to her." I shook my head, pushing my hair out of my face. "You didn't even miss a beat."

Luke's square jaw clenched, and he took a step closer, fists balled. It might have been intimidating, if not for the fact that we were nearly the same size. And even though he was an asshole, I wasn't scared of him in the physical sense.

The only damage he had ever inflicted on me was emotional.

"Like you're one to talk." His voice took on a bitter edge. "Carter? What the hell is that about?"

"What do you care?" I jutted my chin.

"He's…he's not a good guy," Luke spluttered, a red flush flooding his face. He was easy to rile up, which made him the perfect target for Chase.

"And yet, still better than you."

"He's going to—"

"Hurt me?" I smirked. "After putting up with you, I think I can take care of myself." I turned on my heel and pushed open the heavy swinging doors, letting them close behind me with a bang.

Unfortunately, Luke wasn't good at letting things go. I'd experienced that firsthand many times. Wednesdays were going to be the equivalent of *Groundhog Day* combined with *Friday the 13th*. An endless loop of unpleasantry with him.

Maybe the W on my transcript would be worth burning those tuition credits on after all.

I headed through the glass-roofed atrium toward the library. My phone chimed, and I was greeted by an equally irritating text from my brother, who'd apparently lost his mind.

Derek: You can't do this, B.

Bailey: What?

Derek: Date Carter. It's crazy.

Bailey: I didn't ask for your permission.

Derek: We have to talk. Can you do coffee?

Bailey: To talk about Carter? No.

Derek: Not just that.

Bailey: I'm pretty booked this month.

Students passed by me, chattering as I stood outside the library entrance, glaring at my phone. I wasn't even dating the guy, and I was being forced to defend myself. Was this 1950? Did I need a chaperone or something? And was Luke getting grief about Sophie? Of course not. My life was the only one under the microscope.

It was infuriating. I was simultaneously being scrutinized and ostracized.

Later that evening, I was in the kitchen pulling a mug out of the cupboard to make tea with when the doorbell rang. Footsteps sounded, so I didn't bother answering the door. I wasn't expecting any deliveries, but because of Jillian's online shopping addiction, we received packages several times a week. Sometimes it seemed like she was single-handedly keeping Amazon afloat.

I opened a new box of tea bags, selecting a chamomile-orange blend. Amelia rushed past while I grabbed the kettle from the stove and filled my lucky green mug.

The door squeaked as she swung it open. "Hey," she said, voice a little too bright to be natural. Clearly, it was not the UPS truck like I'd thought.

There was a chorus of replies as several voices greeted her in response, including one all-too-familiar male voice. Mid-pour, I glanced up and missed the mug, nearly scalding myself in the process. There stood Paul and Mendez—with Luke and Sophie in tow.

Apparently, Amelia and Jillian had invited people over without letting me know. Or including me. Not that I would have joined in.

Then I realized: it was a freaking triple date. Couples' night at our house.

And Luke's attendance was payback for earlier.

To add insult to injury, I was in scrubby loungewear; old gray sweats and a baggy concert tee, the kind of thing you only wear at home without company. My hair was in loose, messy waves around my shoulders. I was the picture of unkempt and decidedly not prepared to see my ex with his brand-new girlfriend.

I froze for a moment, wanting to die and cry at the same time. Self-preservation kicked in. I grabbed my mug and bolted straight upstairs. After I'd shut my bedroom door, I leaned against it, breathing heavily, my heart rate exceeding any normal, healthy upper limit. Laughter echoed upstairs through the heating vent beside my desk. They proceeded to talk boisterously in the living room like everything was completely normal. But none of this was normal, at least not to me.

Was it too late to transfer schools? Even Boyd had to be better than dealing with this. Okay, maybe not. The Falcons were still a pretty tough sell.

Sophie had Luke, and while that stung, it hurt more that she was taking over my old life. My place. My role. She stepped right in and replaced me, like we were interchangeable puzzle pieces.

I didn't really miss Luke, but I missed the sense of belonging, like I was part of the group. And I definitely did not enjoy my new social-outcast status.

Over on my desk, my cell lit up. I set my tea next to it, my heart doing an unhappy ka-thunk when I saw the message.

Amelia: Sorry, B. Was supposed to be the four of us. Didn't know Luke would tag along.

Bailey: Right.

Amelia: Plus, I mean…it is my place too.

Bailey: Good point. In that case, I'll invite Lauren over to watch The Bachelor next week.

So what if it was petty? Lauren was a fellow journalism major I'd met my freshman year during my Introduction to Online Media class. But more importantly, Lauren and Paul dated shortly before he met Amelia, and according to my brother, Paul had been completely and madly enamored with her. Legend has it he cried and refused to leave his room for a week, even to shower, when Lauren dumped him.

Needless to say, Lauren was a major sore spot for Amelia, who had never invoked such a strong emotional reaction in Paul herself. Amelia once threatened to break up with him in the midst of a fight, and he'd simply shrugged and said, "If you feel you need to, go ahead."

I flopped onto my bed and scrolled social media in search of distraction, but all the highlight reels only made me feel worse. Smiling group shots, girls' nights out, and happy couples were fresh reminders of everything I didn't have. It didn't help that Noelle was hostessing until close tonight and Zara had a date with some new guy from Tinder, effectively exhausting all my other friend options.

Normally, I would have enjoyed something like wandering around a bookstore solo for a while, but in light of the party downstairs that I hadn't been invited to, even that seemed a little depressing.

Setting down my phone, I hopped off the bed and raided my closet. I changed into a nicer pair of black jeans and a cute gray sweater. I felt less shlubby, but I was still trapped in my room. I desperately wanted to get out of the house and take my mind off things for a while—and I didn't want to do it alone.

There was only one other person I could think of.

It was crazy. One hundred percent certifiable. But it was still better than being here.

And maybe, just maybe, I wanted the excuse.

Bailey: SOS

Chase: SOS? Silk Or Satin?

Chase: Personally, I'm a fan of both

Bailey: Carter.

Chase: James.

Bailey: I'm being serious. I'm trapped in my room and I need help.

Chase: You know the lock is on the inside, right?

Bailey: Yes, smartass. But Amelia invited people over to our place and Luke showed up with them.

Chase: awkward.gif

Bailey: At this point, I might climb the fire escape to get away.

Chase: Just left an evening lecture. Wanna hang?

Bailey: Sure.

Chase: I can be there in 20.

Chase: But use the front door, James. We don't need your clumsy ass falling off the fire escape.

Bailey: Har-har.

A rush of exhilaration ran through me, like when a rollercoaster suddenly plunges down a steep drop. It was excitement, effervescent and bright, mingled with hints of fear.

Two minutes later…

Bailey: Speaking of the front door, can you do me a favor?

Chase: What kind of favor?

Bailey: Not that kind.

Chase: Dammit.

Bailey: When you get here, can you come to the front door?

Chase: And say hi to my BFF Morrison? It would be my pleasure.

CHAPTER 14

AS A FRIEND

BAILEY

NINETEEN MINUTES LATER, after I'd done a significant amount of frantic pacing, hair fluffing, and generalized freaking out, the doorbell rang. I bolted out of my bedroom and ran down the stairs, tripping on my own feet halfway down and nearly wiping out.

Not that I was nervous or anything.

Unlocking the front door, I swung it open to find Chase wearing a white tee that hung off his frame perfectly and a pair of broken-in jeans. He looked like a walking cologne advertisement. It wasn't fair for one person to be so attractive all the time. Everyone should have bad days. I definitely did.

"Hey." He flashed me a smile that did something decidedly non-platonic to my body.

I grinned back at him like an idiot, because I was a little panicked. And oddly short of breath. This entire scenario was surreal; a little like playing with fire while sprinkling kerosene on top to keep it interesting.

Then I remembered to actually speak. "Hi." My eyes fell to the large brown paper delivery bag in his hand. "What's…?"

Chase glanced down, like he'd forgotten what he was holding. "Oh, a delivery guy gave me this as I was coming up the stairs. Then he bolted," he said, expression apologetic. "Said they paid online already."

Oh, so it was a triple dinner date too. How cute. Vomit.

"There is zero chance I'm delivering that by hand," I said. "I'll yell for one of them. Come in and give me one sec." I waved him inside and slipped into my leather boots, quickly tying the laces.

Before I could call for anyone, footsteps echoed, and Amelia came around the corner. "I heard the doorbell. Is that our—" She stopped short when her eyes landed on Chase.

Not a second later, Satan himself appeared, clad in dark-wash jeans and a pale blue polo with his hair slicked back. He stood next to Amelia with a gleam of malice in his eyes that made the usual shade of blue go ten times colder.

"I thought I heard someone." Luke took in the brown paper bag Chase was still holding and smirked. "You pick up a part-time job, Carter? Always good to have options for when you don't make the league."

"Yeah," Chase deadpanned. "I applied to be a giant dickbag first, but they told me you already filled the position."

I choked back a laugh, trying to disguise it as a cough. The smirk faded from Luke's face as his cheeks flushed with anger. He opened his mouth to say something, then closed it. He'd never been all that quick on his feet verbally—only when he threw the first punch or had time to plan what he was going to say—which meant that, right now, he was drawing a blank.

"Fuck you, Carter," Luke snapped, turning and walking away. "Jackass," he muttered.

Chase shook his head as Luke rounded the corner. His jaw was tight, like he wanted to say something but was holding back.

"So." I ran my hand through my hair, likely undoing all the primping I had done in anticipation of his arrival. "We should get going."

Amelia snapped out of her daze and took the bag of food out of Chase's hand. "Uh, thanks," she muttered, not looking at either of us. Without another word, she turned and disappeared into the living room.

Had my roommates always been this awful? Or was this a recent development? Either way, they'd done an about-face on me, going from my supposed good friends to wanting nothing to do with me. We were like strangers now.

Maybe I'd underestimated how much social influence I'd been granted solely due to being the team captain's girlfriend. Which was actually pretty gross.

"Anyway." Chase's tone lightened, and he propped himself against the doorframe, flashing me a heart-stopping smile. "Ready?"

"Absolutely." I grabbed my olive utility jacket off the hook and pulled it on as we walked out the door. Chase waited while I fumbled with my keys briefly and locked the deadbolt.

"I'm sure they're watching us," I said, glancing up at him. "The windows in the living room look out onto the street."

He cocked one brow. "Well, in that case." He threw his arm around my shoulders again, enveloping me in masculine warmth and his intoxicating scent. It was a sort of leather-vanilla cologne, maybe, mixed with something clean, like soap or laundry detergent. Whatever it was, it made me want to bury my face in his neck for a bigger hit.

Then I remembered how, up until recently, I thought I hated Chase. Was I losing my mind?

We descended the three concrete stairs that lead to the sidewalk. With the size difference, his arm fit around my frame perfectly, unlike with Luke, who was nearly the same height as me. Not that it had mattered, since we had rarely engaged in public displays of affection. Or private displays of affection, for that matter…Unless bad sex counted.

"That was pretty awesome." I laughed. "Did you see his face when he saw you standing there?"

"I've never seen someone turn that shade of red," he said. "If I'd kissed you, his head probably would have exploded and splattered all over the wall."

Well, there's a thought.

I glanced over his shoulder, back at the oversized bay window. The outlines of a few figures seated on the couch were visible. My sense of spite went into overdrive, overruling my common sense.

"Okay," I said. "Do it."

Chase looked at me with a gleam in his deep brown eyes. "What? Really?"

"Sure." I shrugged. "It's just a kiss."

I think.

Not like I was going to kiss him back.

Right?

His lips curved into a half smile. "If you insist."

Nervousness tore through me like a bullet. I tensed, expecting him to get it over with right away. But he kept his arm around my shoulders and guided me several more steps until we came to a stop in front of the passenger side of his truck.

Instead of opening the door, he grabbed my hip and turned me to face him in a slow, deliberate motion. My breath stilled as he stepped forward, fencing me in with his arms. His broad frame surrounded me, engulfing me from the front and sides, while my back was pressed against the metal and glass of the door. Trapped. In the best possible way.

Now that I was within his gravitational field, the pull was impossible to resist. His dark eyes held mine for a moment before falling to my lips. He paused, pulse ticking in the base of his throat. My heart stuttered as I watched him, waiting.

"What are you doing?" I whispered.

"Kissing you." His gaze snapped back up to meet mine. "Properly."

He cupped my face in his hands. My eyelids fluttered shut as he dipped closer and his lips found mine. Without thinking, I parted my lips, and he slanted his mouth against mine, deepening the kiss. He tasted like icy mint and heartbreak. Everything else ceased to exist.

I splayed my fingers against his chest, then grabbed at the fabric of his white T-shirt. A small sound of appreciation rumbled from the back of his throat in response. He slid a hand to my nape and tugged at the roots of my hair, angling my face up a fraction and pressing me against the truck.

I'd never been kissed like this before.

It was like falling.

He pulled back slightly, his lips tipping into a smile, before he covered my mouth with his again. It was playful, questioning. I could have gone on doing this all night—nibbling, tasting, teasing. I'd forgotten why we even started in the first place; didn't care, didn't want it to stop.

After another moment, he eased back. My breath was ragged, my heart racing. I was so lightheaded that the truck behind me was the only thing keeping me upright.

"Well," he said. "I think that was pretty convincing."

It sure convinced me.

I tried to keep my voice level. "Yeah. I think so too."

CHASE

The look on Morrison's face tonight? Awesome.

Getting to spend time with James? Even better.

Kissing her? Fuck me, I'm in over my head.

BAILEY

Moments later, we were in Chase's truck, pulling out from where he'd illegally parked on the street. My brain was still scrambled from the kiss, but I was trying to keep it together for appearance's sake. He probably kissed girls like that all the time. I doubted it meant anything to him.

I wished I could say the same.

"For the record," I said, "I'm not clumsy."

He stole a glance at me, a smile playing on his lips. "Is that why you nearly fell off the curb outside XS?"

"I did a lot of things that were out of character that night." Apparently, I was still doing them. But I couldn't blame the alcohol anymore.

"Okay, where to?" Chase signaled left and shoulder-checked, pulling out onto the main thoroughfare.

Momentarily distracted by his large hands gripping the steering wheel and the memory of how they'd felt on my body, I scrambled for an idea, coming up woefully empty-handed.

"I think it's your turn to decide."

"Pretty sure I decided last time," he said. "I was trying to be nice, but now I'm dragging you around wherever I want. Prepare for a wild night of adventure and crime."

"You're joking, right?"

He shrugged. "I guess you'll have to see."

After another fifteen minutes, we pulled into the entrance for a natural park area tucked away not far from downtown.

Trees lined the parking lot, stretching out for miles in each direction, their leaves in their full autumn splendor, painting the landscape with burnt orange, umber, and gold. It was breathtaking.

Chase parked and killed the ignition, then grabbed a gray Carhartt from the back seat before getting out and locking the truck. I climbed out and took in the scenery, enjoying the soothing effect the fresh air was having on my frazzled brain. Small talk and physical distance between us on the drive had helped somewhat, but I still hadn't fully processed that kiss.

I wasn't sure I ever would. It was the sort of kiss that I'd likely always remember.

Even if it wasn't real.

"This way." Chase nodded to the right. We started down a paved pathway into a dense patch of trees painted in rich fall shades, walking close but not touching.

"What is this place, anyway?" I asked, zipping my coat as we walked. It had cooled off significantly since the week before. There was a nip in the air that promised of winter coming.

"The real name is Hammond Park, but people call it End of the World," he said. "Sometimes I come here to think."

"Ah, so not often then."

He grinned, bumping me with his elbow. "Hey, now."

Moments later, a glass-walled shack appeared in front of us in a clearing, surrounded by metal bistro tables and chairs. The sign out front read *Uncommon Coffee Co*.

"Oh no." I shook my head. "If I drink coffee this late, I won't sleep tonight."

"Cool your jets, Grandma. We ain't here for coffee." Chase pulled the door open and gestured with an open palm for me to enter first. The heavenly scents of coffee and chocolate filled the cafe, which was decorated in reclaimed wood, giving it a rustic, hipster charm. A chalkboard menu displayed its offerings in pastel shades of the rainbow behind the counter.

"We're here for that." He pointed to the left-hand side, where a pink handwritten header read, *World's Best Hot Chocolate*. Listed beneath it were original, dark chocolate, white chocolate, peppermint bark, salted caramel, raspberry truffle, peanut butter cup, roasted coconut, hazelnut twist, and spiced gingerbread.

"This is incredible." I happened to love hot chocolate. It reminded me of skating rinks and bonfires in the winter. Of gliding along the ice, watching my breath plume in front of me, beneath a sky blanketed with stars. Of that blissful, fleeting feeling of being free.

"The salted caramel is almost as good as a blowjob," Chase said.

I shot him a look. "TMI, Carter."

"What?" He shrugged. "Just saying."

"We need to get you a mute button."

"Anyway, it's good. You could get tea or something gross instead if you want." He waved to the menu board vaguely. "But I don't know how anyone could turn down hot chocolate."

"Hmm." I hummed, still waffling between original and the salted caramel. The heavily pierced and tattooed barista at the counter waited patiently while I hemmed and hawed. The flavors did sound good, but it was hard to beat a really amazing cup of classic hot chocolate.

"Know what you want?" Chase asked, stepping up to the register.

I grabbed the zipper of my tan leather crossbody bag. "I can pay—"

"Yeah, no," he said. "What should I order for you?"

Was this how it was going to be? Maybe I'd actually met the only person on earth more stubborn than I was.

"Salted caramel."

He winked at me. "Good choice."

We collected our drinks before heading back outside. The cocoa was every bit as good as he promised; the sweet milk chocolate was perfectly balanced by the slight savory undertone of the caramel.

As we wandered along the path, the sun began its descent below the horizon, casting the sky in shades of dusky violet and warm pink. Leaves crunched beneath our feet, and a slight breeze picked up, rustling through the trees and ruffling my hair.

"This is the second date-like non-date we've ended up on," I said, clutching the red paper cup in my hand. Probably more date-like than anything I had done with Luke in ages, come to think of it.

"It is?"

Oh, sweet summer child. Of course he wouldn't know. Girls came along and threw themselves at his feet. Or his other body parts. No wining and dining required.

I stole a glance at him. "Let me guess, you don't go on dates."

"Not really." He took a sip of his hot chocolate, dark brow furrowed. "But isn't this something you'd do with your friends? Get drinks, sit around, and gossip and shit? You know, chick stuff."

"I guess so," I said. "You want to do chick stuff with me?"

"Why not? My life is testosterone overload most of the time. It gets old. Plus, guys are smelly. Dallas after a game could be a biological weapon."

We came to a fork in the path, and he pointed to the left. Ahead was a rickety staircase built into the hillside, its wood gray and weathered with age. It didn't look like it could support Chase, let alone both of us, but he knew what he was doing. I hoped.

I laughed. "This is your ulterior motive? Not to mess with Luke, but so we can get mani-pedis and have pillow fights?"

He cocked a brow, gesturing for me to go up the stairs first. "For the record, you texted me tonight."

"You kidnapped me from the arena before that." I took a tentative step, testing the surface below my foot before climbing the steep staircase. Chase followed, his line of sight likely somewhere near my ass. My mind ricocheted back to the kiss earlier, my knees going weak at the memory.

"And before that, you cockblocked me at XS."

I glanced back at him. "You came up to me first, Mr. Wannabe Airline Pilot."

"Fair enough." He grinned. "I'll pass on the mani-pedis, but I'm down for a pillow fight any day of the week. Preferably in our underwear."

Oh.

Picturing Chase in underwear wasn't helping me keep my mind straight after that kiss.

He came to stand beside me on the landing, halfway up the stairs, and I poked him in the side. "Don't be dirty."

"What?" Chase said with mock innocence. "I wasn't."

I raised my eyebrows.

"Fine, I was. But the offer stands."

CHAPTER 15
DESPERATE TIMES
CHASE

BAILEY and I finished scaling the wooden staircase built into the earth and rounded a corner at the top, coming out at an opening in the trees. I was a little winded, not because I'd just climbed two stories' worth of stairs—I could do that in my sleep—but from my proximity to her.

I was losing my chill.

"Wow," Bailey breathed. "You can see all of downtown."

She followed me to the wrought-iron bench that sat at the very edge of the hillside. In front of us lay the city skyline, its lights twinkling in the dusky purple twilight. Skyscrapers lined the jagged horizon, some of the windows still lit from within. And a steady stream of cars moved over the connecting roads in a blur of red and white.

I still wasn't sure what had possessed me to bring her here, somewhere I had never brought anyone else—or even mentioned it to.

"The view from here is amazing." Shifting her weight, she crossed her legs.

I couldn't help but stare. They were long and shapely, and I hadn't been able to get them out of my mind since XS.

"The view right here's pretty nice too."

Her lips curled, and her cheeks darkened almost imperceptibly in the dim light. She shot me a look that said she couldn't tell if I was messing around or not. Which meant my game had gone to shit lately. Probably due to lack of practice and aforementioned absence of chill.

"How do you know about this place?" Bailey's round eyes searched my face, her expression turning serious.

"Sometimes I come here for runs in the off-season. You know, to mix it up and get off the dreadmill." I stretched my legs out in front of me, draping an arm along the back of the bench. "Then I stop and undo all my hard work with a sugar-laden drink at the end. It's all about balance."

"Must be paying off if you guys are schooling us in the standings this badly already."

"Guess so." I shrugged. "You should probably jump ship while you can. It's not too late to join our bandwagon."

She laughed, shaking her head. "Keep dreaming."

We fell quiet, looking out at the view, but it wasn't an awkward silence. It was kind of nice being with someone who, like me, didn't feel the need to fill every second with idle chatter. After a while, we slipped back into small talk about school, hockey, and other friend-appropriate topics.

Until my internal stream of thoughts butted in before I could stop myself.

"No offense to you, but I don't get the Morrison thing," I said. "You're cool. And that dude's got about as much personality as a carton of white milk."

"Oh my god." She stopped mid-sip and huffed out a little breath of air. "Somehow that fits perfectly."

I drained the last of my hot chocolate. "Seriously, what did you see in him? Asking for a friend." I paused. "Okay, that friend is me. I'm a nosy fuck."

I'd thought about this more than I cared to admit, and I'd still come up empty-handed. Bailey was smart, hot, and funny; she could have had her pick of almost anyone. I couldn't reconcile why she'd give that douchebag the time of day, let alone date him for an extended length of time.

Was this what jealousy felt like? I didn't like it. At all.

Bailey frowned, looking out over the cityscape. "Honestly, I don't know. We started dating freshman year. I guess sometimes you get attached to people and let things go on longer than they should. I was young and naive, I guess."

"Yeah, you're really getting up there now. Twenty-one, yikes." I sucked in a breath. "Talk about ancient."

"Wait." She furrowed her brow. "When's your birthday?"

"January third." As a kid, it sucked. Parties and presents were perpetually overshadowed by Christmas and New Year's. But it was an awesome birthday as far as hockey was concerned, because I was always the oldest in our birth year division. Combined with being larger than average, I was often a giant among the other players.

"So, you're older than me," Bailey pointed out.

"Semantics," I said, waving her off.

"You're giving me gray hairs as we speak, so maybe you're right." She paused, crinkling her nose. "Besides, didn't I tell you everything about Luke when I was wasted and sharing my life story?"

"Not really."

She only touched on a few things that night. Namely, that Morrison was a cheating piece of shit who lacked game in the bedroom, and that he didn't eat pussy, which was a fucking travesty. But I didn't want to make her feel self-conscious, so I didn't intend to get into that right now—or ever, unless it became directly relevant because we were hooking up.

I mean, I hoped it would become relevant down the line, but I couldn't gauge whether that was a possibility just yet. Maybe I'd signed my own death warrant by friend-zoning myself.

"There is no story," she said, zipping her olive green coat up to the very top and burrowing her face into the collar. "We were dating; now we're not. The end."

I let out a low whistle. "Okay, moving on."

"Why do you get to interrogate me about my love life?" She turned to face me and tilted her head, hazel eyes pinning me with a probing look. "How come I can't ask why you're such a fuckboy?"

I raised my eyebrows, meeting her gaze with a level look. "I think you just did."

Well, *that* didn't bode well for down the line. Plus, fuckboy struck me as a little extreme. I did have some standards. They were just…broad. Let's be real. I was young and single, and girls threw themselves at me, so why would I say no?

Though I was in the midst of a serious drought at the moment —not necessarily by design, but because every text that popped up on my phone offering a hookup was from someone other than Bailey. I had thought about trying anyway, just to see if I could get myself out of the mindfuck I was in, but I didn't really *want* to.

Objectively speaking, it made zero sense because I had no real reason to think we would hook up ever, let alone any time soon. But certain body parts of mine didn't care for reason or logic, so here I was. Practically a born-again virgin.

And obviously not telling a single soul about any of this.

"Then answer the question."

I shrugged. I didn't have a good answer and felt a little dumb for it. "Because I can?"

"Guys are wired so differently," Bailey murmured, looking down at her red paper cup.

"What makes you say that?"

"Because I could never…do that. With someone I didn't know."

Knowing what I knew now, I was thankful we hadn't slept together that night. She would have regretted it, regretted me.

"Not to poke holes in your theory here, or make judgments about good or bad, but lots of girls do."

"I guess so." She hummed, tucking a lock of hair behind her ear. "Maybe it's just me."

"It's not a bad thing," I said.

"I don't know. It's not like it's worked out for me so far, either."

I knew exactly what she was referring to, but again, I didn't want to make her feel self-conscious by bringing it up. Knowing some of the personal shit I did while she didn't *know* that I knew made for a massive fucking moral dilemma. It was one-sided and unfair, but I also didn't want her to think I was teasing her or being a dick.

Bailey shivered, rubbing her arms. "I should have worn a warmer coat."

"It's getting pretty chilly," I said. "We should probably head back. Maybe your roommates went out or their company's gone by now."

"Dare to dream."

We stood and headed for the staircase. It was even darker now, most of the light coming from the streetlamps lining the park. A gust of wind kicked up, blowing a pile of dead leaves on the ground in a miniature funnel.

"You know, this is a little spooky." She started to descend the stairs, with me following behind.

Speaking of nice views, I would follow her anywhere, any day.

"What, walking around a secluded forest with a guy you don't know that well?" I said with a shrug. "Maybe a little."

"Good place to dump a body," she mused, gripping the handrail as she scaled the stairs. "But wouldn't it have been easier to off me after the bar?"

"I prefer a long con, myself."

"Ah, I see."

On the path back to the parking lot, she caught her foot on a tree root that was hidden in the ground, tripping and losing her balance. I grabbed her elbow to steady her. "I got you."

"Thanks," she said, a little breathless.

Rather than continuing our trek, we froze, looking at each other for a beat. Adrenaline hit me like a rush after a goal. She gazed up at me, lips slightly parted, and then I realized I was still holding on to her arm. It was like a moment in a cheesy movie where the characters would lean in and kiss, but I wasn't going to push my luck twice in one day.

Even if I really wanted to.

Even if she did kiss me back earlier.

"So much for not being clumsy." I gently let her go.

"I'm not," she insisted.

I stole a glance at her, fighting a smile. "Maybe just clumsy around me."

"Maybe so."

The lights were out at Bailey's place when we reached her street. I pulled in illegally again and shifted into park. Leaning over to her side, I ducked my head to see out the passenger-side window.

"Doesn't look like anyone's home."

Bailey glanced over to confirm. "Praise God." Exhaling a sigh of relief, she turned to look at me. "Thank you for tonight. It helped a lot."

"Anytime."

Silence fell between us again, but this time, it was awkward. Super awkward. Like maybe I should hug her, but the physical space between us made it too difficult to gauge her reaction to me getting closer. So, like a chump, I did nothing.

"I guess I owe you now," she said, unbuckling her seat belt.

"I'll definitely be collecting on that."

Bailey grabbed her purse and dropped her chin, giving me a stern look. "Are you being dirty again?" Her voice was low, a little husky, and it definitely made me want to be dirty.

"No," I said. "Unless you want me to be."

Her lips tipped up at the corners. "Text me, okay?"

"I will."

By Friday evening, Bailey and I had texted back and forth almost constantly, but I still hadn't come up with an opening to see her again. And it was taking my head out of the game, which was fairly fucking dire given the scouts in the stands.

We were getting our asses handed to us, down zero to two, so I wasn't the only one having an off day. Coach Miller finished reaming us out and stormed off, slamming the dressing room door behind him. The rest of us glanced at one another, every expression a mix of guilt and irritation with the rest of the team. There were still six minutes left in the first intermission to stew.

From beside me on the bench, Dallas studied me. "What's up with you?"

"Other than my game being shit, you mean?"

"Your default setting is vaguely pissed off at the world." He gestured at me. "And right now, you're oddly mellow. Even with this game in the toilet."

"Preoccupied, I guess." I didn't dare tell him with what.

"Well, un-occupy yourself, fuckface," he said. "I can't carry this game alone."

Fair point. A lot of the guys were coasting tonight, which wasn't helping me get my head straight. But it wasn't an excuse, either. Usually, I would be the one reaming everyone out.

"Plus," he lowered his voice, "scouts, man. Get it together. What happened to the fire you had the last few games?"

"Two of those were against Callingwood, and I fucking hate them, so..."

It helped when I genuinely wanted to cause bodily harm to a good portion of the other team, especially their captain. I didn't have nearly the same size ax to grind with New England U tonight.

"So pretend we're playing them. Get mad, bro. I need your head in this."

I nodded. That could work. I would pretend everyone was Morrison out there and crush them accordingly.

A few minutes later, we headed back out, and Dallas and I hopped onto the ice for the first shift. Palmer, one of our D-men, immediately took a stupid-ass penalty for tripping. Idiot.

We headed into five on four play. I was at the high slot to disrupt cross ice passes and block shots from the point. The Wolves' right winger wound up and passed to their center. Not today, bitches. I skated forward to intercept it, blocking the shot—with my fucking ankle. Searing pain shot through my foot, radiating up my leg.

Somehow, I managed to skate forward and beat the defender to the rebound, sending it over to Ward. He lined up and sank it in the top right-hand corner. With a fist pump, he skated off to our bench.

"Nice one," I said, sitting beside him.

"When I told you to try, I didn't mean sacrifice your sorry ass."

"It's fine," I lied. It was throbbing like a motherfucker. But we needed that goal.

Dallas shook his head. He knew it was bullshit. "Are you going to invite that chick to Ty's birthday next weekend?"

I hadn't thought that far ahead. Would Bailey want to go? Did she even like big parties? Plus, that was so far away. If I waited that long, it would be a week and a half before I saw her again.

Then the perfect opening hit me. It might involve actually doing my schoolwork, but hey, desperate times and all.

CHAPTER 16

A TAD DRAMATIC

BAILEY

Chase: You're a journalism major, right?

Bailey: I am. Why?

Chase: Does that mean you're good at editing?

Bailey: What's your angle, Carter?

Chase: My history paper is a fucking tire fire.

Bailey: Wish I could help, but I don't know anything about history.

Chase: Turns out, neither do I.

Chase: Help me, James. I'm just a pretty face.

Bailey: I guess I could read it over and make sure it flows smoothly. Email it to me - b.james@Callingwood.edu

Chase: I owe ya.

Chase: In fact, I'll give Morrison an extra hit next time we play the Bulldogs. I'll crush him for you. Like a bug.

Bailey: Oh my god, don't do that. Still Team Bulldog here, remember?

Chase: For now.

Bailey: Forever.

Chase: We'll see.

Bailey: We really won't.

TURNED out that texting with Chase before bed was recipe for insomnia. I was way too keyed up to sleep. Given that I had an early class on Tuesday mornings, this was a highly problematic development. I pulled out all the stops—reading a boring textbook, rewatching comfort shows, even chamomile tea, but nothing could calm the buzz in my body.

Finally, I took some melatonin and fell asleep sometime around midnight, only to be startled awake by a loud crash, like something falling over and hitting the ground. Probably the neighbor's cat, who loved to prowl around on our fire escape. I sighed, rolling over in bed to find the glowing red letters of my alarm clock staring back at me—3:12 a.m. Might as well go pee while I was up.

After sliding out from under the covers, I shuffled to my door and down the hall with my eyes half-closed. As I reached for the bathroom door, it swung open, and I ran smack into a large male body.

I jumped back. It was probably Paul or Eddie.

But in the dim moonlight streaming in, I caught sight of a familiar face. It was my brother.

"Geez!" I put a hand to my chest, my heart racing like I was watching a game in overtime. "Derek, what are you doing here?"

"Shh," he said, grabbing my arm. "Keep it down."

"You're in my hallway in the middle of the night, and you're shushing me?" I whisper-yelled. "I want an explanation."

Derek bent closer, his voice low. “Can we go downstairs at least?”

“Fine,” I hissed.

He turned and headed down the steps. I followed behind and flipped on the light over the stove. I poured a glass of water while he sank onto a stool at the island, slumping over the laminate counter. I could pee later; right now, I needed to know what the hell was going on.

“Explain.” I rested both elbows on the counter, pinning him with my stare.

He lifted his head, regarding me with his brows knit together. His dark blond hair stood up everywhere, he had dark circles beneath his brown eyes, and his sweatshirt was rumpled. He looked like he’d just woken up after a night of terrible sleep.

His throat bobbed. “I was with Jill.”

“*What*?” The glass I was holding nearly slid out of my hand. I knew something suspicious was afoot, but hearing him say it out loud was a different story entirely.

“Would you keep your voice down?” He glanced at the stairs nervously. “No one is supposed to know.”

But I bet Amelia did.

I stared at him, my breath growing faster. A whirlwind of hurt, betrayal, disappointment, and anger swirled in my gut. Our parents hadn’t raised us to be the kinds of people who did things like this; Derek knew better.

“How could you—how could she—” I shook my head. “I don’t understand. Eddie is your friend.”

“I know.” Derek ducked his head, his jaw clenched. “It’s complicated.”

“I’m sure it is. How long has this been going on?”

He looked back up at me and shrugged, guilt all over his face. “Since August?”

“You mean this has been happening for months? What the hell, Derek?”

Then it hit me. Oh my god. I bet it happened at Paul’s parents’ cottage. After a huge blowout fight with Jill on Friday afternoon,

Eddie stormed off and went back to the city instead of staying at the lake house for the weekend with the rest of us.

Jill had been really upset, crying and taking it hard, but then she'd gone to bed early. Then my brother had done the same not long after.

And they had always, always flirted.

"I know."

"She's using you," I said, anger overtaking my other emotions. "I don't know what for, but something. It's not like her motivations can possibly be innocent here. You're a side piece."

Now I had to look at her every day and pretend I didn't know this? How twisted was that? How many people were covering it up? Had Luke known too and not told me?

He blew out a heavy sigh. "I have feelings for her, okay? It's not that simple."

"You're an accomplice to a crime," I snapped, placing my glass in the dishwasher.

I had always suspected he had a crush on Jill. But this ran deep. So deep that he was compromising his morals and ethics, and potentially hurting one of his friends—and teammates—for her.

As for Jill, she'd always been self-centered. But this was low, even for her.

"What about you?" Derek's expression turned harsh. "Carter?"

"I didn't know he had a girlfriend." I cocked my head. "What's her name?"

"That's not what I mean, and you know it."

My skin prickled at his tone. Of course I knew. I just didn't care.

He added, "Carter is one of our worst enemies, B. Me, the whole team."

"Oh, grow up," I said. "It's just hockey."

"Hockey is one of the most important things in my life. You don't even respect that anymore."

"You're literally screwing your friend's girlfriend, and you're giving me grief about a consensual relationship between two single people?" I asserted, throwing a hand in the air. "And for what it's worth, Chase has been ten times nicer to me than your best buddy Luke ever was. Or you lately, for that matter."

"I know I've been a shit." He sighed again, shaking his head. "I've been so preoccupied with this Jill stuff that my head has been up my ass."

I crossed my arms over my pink pajama top, leveling him with an icy glare. "I'm glad we can agree on something."

"I've been avoiding everyone because I'm scared it'll come out." His tone was forlorn, like he wanted me to feel sorry for him, but he was the creator of his own problems. It wasn't like him to play the victim like this.

"As you should be," I said. "Why doesn't Jill break up with Eddie? Are you scared it'll mess up his game?"

As ridiculous as it was, hockey came before everything else for the team, even personal relationships. It was totally within the realm of possibility that they'd cover this up to preserve their goalie.

"It's more complicated than that."

I arched an eyebrow.

Derek glanced over at the stairs again, leaning in closer and lowering his voice. "Last time she tried to end things with him, he threatened to kill himself."

My stomach lurched. I blinked, trying to process the details. "That's messed up."

"I know," he muttered.

Though as terrible as it was of me to think, part of me wondered if it was true. If this intel came from Jill, it likely couldn't be trusted. She was playing puppeteer with my brother like a pro.

"If that's true, he needs help." I wiped at the countertop in front of me. "Her staying with him is only fueling the problem."

"I know," he said again, defeated.

I studied his face in the shadowy light. Our mother's eyes, our father's nose, hair the same color as mine. Never once did I think he would be capable of this.

"I don't even know what to say to you right now," I told him. "I'm beyond disappointed. This is wrong and you know it."

"You aren't going to tell anyone, are you?"

"No." I shook my head. "But I hope you wise up and do the right thing. I'm going to bed. Lock the door behind you, please."

After we texted Monday evening, Chase sent me a copy of his essay and scammed me into coming over to help him with it the following day. And by scammed, I mean he was both incredibly charming and insufferably persistent until I relented. In other words, impeccably on-brand for him.

That's not to say I minded. But that was a whole other ball of hockey stick wax.

Plus, it was a nice distraction from my rapidly disintegrating social life and the new Derek-Jill revelation.

That's how I found myself in Chase's bedroom for the second time, albeit under dramatically different circumstances. A bedroom that smelled of the delicious lingering leather-vanilla scent of his cologne. Had he applied said cologne before leaving to pick me up?

Combined with my three outfit changes while waiting for him and the sparkly pink lip gloss I swiped over my lips on my way out the door, there were some major questions as to what, exactly, we were doing.

But I wasn't ready to unpack that yet.

I perched on the end of the bed across from the computer desk, rifling through my backpack for the printout I'd marked up with my suggestions. Chase faced me, straddling the computer chair, and turned his red Falcons baseball cap backward, then rested his arms on the seatback.

"I made a few edits." I handed him a copy of his paper with my corrections and suggestions marked in red ink. Using track changes within Word would have been less work for both of us, but this way he had to do more heavy lifting by inputting the changes manually, rather than accepting them all with one click of a mouse button. While I didn't mind helping him, I wouldn't enable him, either.

Chase scanned the front page, then glanced back up at me with his dark eyes wide, like a deer in headlights. "Holy shit. I didn't think it was that bad."

"It's not. You've got some good insights, and the conclusions are well-supported. It's just a little…jumbled."

"That sounds like a candy-coated way of saying it sucks."

I shrugged. "My rough drafts are messy too. You have to revise and rewrite to polish a piece."

"Ugh." He folded his arms over the back of his chair again and hung his head, sighing dramatically. His forearms flexed, veins tracing their length. I watched, mesmerized, for a split second. Since when had I developed a thing for forearms? And had his hands always been that big?

"That sounds like so much work."

"That's sort of the point of schoolwork, Carter."

Chase was a top-notch grinder—one of the grittiest players on the Falcons, known for his physical gameplay. He made life hell for our defense, cleared bodies out of the way for snipers to score, and won puck battles more often than not. For someone who was a powerhouse on the ice, he was awfully lazy when it came to school. He was intelligent, that was obvious; he just needed to apply himself.

"Not gonna lie; it's incredibly hard to give a fuck about any of this knowing it won't matter down the road."

"It matters now," I said. "I thought you were on probation."

"I am. Dicks." Chase rolled his eyes.

"What if you need to finish your degree later? You never know. You could get injured or something."

"If that happens, I'll have bigger problems than the lack of a degree. I'm basically unemployable in any other capacity." Chase raised his dark eyebrows. "Can you picture me wearing khakis and working in a cubicle, James?"

"No," I admitted. It was so ill-suited to him that it was almost comical.

"And let's face it," he said. "I'm way too corruptible to be a cop. So, for the greater good of society, help me polish this turd of a paper and keep my grades up enough to stay on the team. I have to get signed. It's that or homelessness for me. There is no in-between."

I shifted, criss-crossing my legs. "Anyone ever tell you that you're a tad dramatic?"

"I prefer to think of it as having a zest for life." His mouth tugged at the corners.

"You have something, that's for sure."

Chase got a gleam in his eyes that said he was definitely up to no good.

"You're going to stay while I work on this, right?" He lowered his voice, a tactic he used, I realized, to get into my head…or maybe my pants. Yet, even knowing that, the voice totally worked. At least on the first part. Possibly a little of the second.

Maybe being in his bedroom wasn't a good idea after all.

I raised an eyebrow, hiding all my inappropriate thoughts behind sarcasm. "You picked me up, so I'm not sure I have a choice."

"That's true." He nodded. "Do any of us really have a choice? Or is free will merely an illusion?"

"I actually do have an exam to study for, so if you want company, there's no need to get all philosophical on me. All you have to do is ask."

I grabbed my textbook and binder and scooted back on the bed until I was sitting against the headboard. I wasn't all that eager to spend time at my place, anyway. Lately, I felt like a stranger in my own home. Things were tense with Amelia and Jillian, and they were downright hostile when Paul was there, which was more often than not.

"You're the best." He spun around to face the computer, cracking his knuckles and stretching his neck. "I'm going to bang this out in no time."

I suppressed a laugh as I bit back a dirty joke. Maybe I'd been spending too much time with Chase after all.

CHAPTER 17
NEAR MISS
BAILEY

"TIME FOR A BREAK," Chase announced, shoving the keyboard tray back into place. He arched back in his chair, stretching out his long legs.

I glanced up from the bed, where I was sprawled out on my stomach reading my *Data Journalism and Methods* textbook. "But it's only been an hour."

"It's five o'clock, which means it's time to eat. We need brain food, James. It's science."

I groaned. "Let me guess, and then we're going to need second dinner. And a snack. And a pencil sharpening break. Better yet, maybe we can go chop down a tree and handcraft some pencils so you don't have to finish your essay."

He grinned. "Probably, but let's start with pizza."

We abandoned our study materials and relocated downstairs. Chase hopped over the back of the couch, parkour-style, and plopped down beside me. It was a surprisingly nimble move for such a large human, even an athlete.

"Pizza will be here in twenty-five. Time for…video games?" He turned to me, head cocked.

"Sure." I couldn't focus on my dry as dirt textbook knowing food was on the way.

"Really?" His eyes lit up. "I was shit testing you. I didn't think you'd say yes."

"I know," I said. "But I have three brothers. Didn't exactly have anyone to play tea party with growing up. We played *NHL '07* all the time."

Much to my mother's dismay, I had never been a girly girl. When she found out about her "surprise" pregnancy after she'd had three boys, she was excited for frilly dresses, Barbies, and tea parties. Then I was born, hating all things pink and preferring Derek's dump trucks to my dolls. I even cried when I was five because Santa brought me a purple and pink Lego set; I wanted the "real" multicolored Legos my brothers had.

He smirked. "So you're saying you're good at video games?"

"Oh, I'm better than good."

Which Luke hated. To him, having a pair of boobs was a disqualifying condition when it came to playing. He was less than thrilled when I wanted to join and even more annoyed when I beat them, which was often. He had always wanted me to go hang in the kitchen with the other girls like a good hockey girlfriend should.

"Sweet." He stood up and turned on the game console. "None of the chicks I know ever want to play. I think Shiv would like to strangle Dallas with the controller cord at this point."

"Who's Shiv?"

"Siobhan. Dallas's, ah…well, I don't know what they are. But she's cool. You'd get along with her." He scrolled into the team selection menu, and we built our lineups.

"You might not be quite as thrilled after I school you."

He scoffed. "Never gonna happen."

By the time the pizza arrived, I'd beaten him twice.

"What do you know?" Chase turned to me, giving me a sly once-over. A thrill ran through my body. "Hot and nerdy. You're full of surprises." He set the controller aside and got up to answer the doorbell.

Wait. Did he just call me hot?

…And nerdy?

"Hey, let me pay," I called out, standing up.

"Too late." He shut the door, a truckload of food in his arms. Two large pizzas, wings, breadsticks, Caesar salad, and freshly baked chocolate chip cookies. It was nice, in contrast to Luke's restrictive chicken breast and broccoli diet he paid a nutritionist thousands of dollars to create. "I paid online when I ordered. Don't even think of trying to sneak me cash, either."

"But you paid for dinner that other night and hot chocolate..." Luke literally kept track to ensure we took turns. Everything was always even.

"You're helping me with my paper, remember?" He shrugged.

I followed him into the kitchen and propped a hip against the black granite counter while he set out the boxes of food.

"Speaking of your paper," I said, "how far did you get on it?"

"Page four." He handed me a square white plate from the cupboard.

I suppressed a groan. His essay was twenty pages long, and I had a feeling I wasn't getting a ride home until it was finished.

Three hours later, I was hopped up on carbs and cookies, re-writing my notes for my exam. Chase worked so slowly that I had time to focus on my own schoolwork. I couldn't get off-track and fool around on my phone, because he would immediately use it as license to do the same.

"This fucking history class is going to be the end of me." Chase snapped his green pencil in half and tossed it into the stainless-steel garbage can beside him with a clang. "It was the only social science elective that fit my training schedule."

I set down my blue ballpoint pen and shook out the cramp in my hand. If writing things out on paper made for better retention, I'd ace the exam. Having my laptop would have been nice, but I hadn't planned to stay this long. I should have known to plan for contingencies when Chase was involved.

Not that I was complaining about spending time with him.

"What's your major again?"

"Econ." He turned the chair around to face me, and a small smile played on his lips.

My stomach flip-flopped, and not from all the sugar.

"You must be more than a pretty face if you're studying that." I had taken microeconomics last spring as part of my breadth requirement for journalism, and it was like a full-on foreign language to me. Production and pricing decisions, market outcomes, consumer theory. I had barely maintained my 4.0 that semester.

He shrugged his broad shoulders. "I barely knew what economics was when I chose it. I did an internet search for the top five majors with the fewest papers, and here we are."

"Shut up. You did not." He probably did.

"Sure did," he said. "Math isn't hard. It's all the reading and writing crap that gets me."

"Crap?" I gasped, placing a hand on my chest. "Blasphemy. You're talking to a writer, you know. That's my bread and butter."

"It just doesn't come easily for me, and I have a low tolerance for frustration."

"You don't say."

He grabbed a new pencil from cup on his desk and tossed it in the air before catching it easily. "Lucky for me, I have you to help me with that stuff now."

"Oh, this isn't a permanent tutoring arrangement."

"Of course it is." He shot me a lopsided smile. The room got ten degrees warmer, and my heart picked up speed.

"Finish the essay, Carter." Fighting a smile, I shook my head and returned my attention to my notes. Or tried to, anyway, because the tension in the room had suddenly grown heavy. Palpable. Suggestive.

Instead, he stood and came to sit beside me, the bed sinking under his weight. I could smell the fresh mint on his breath, feel the warmth of his body. His cologne, mingled with soap and laundry detergent, formed some kind of heavenly mixture that should have also fallen into the controlled weapon category.

"So when are you going to come see me play?" His arm brushed against mine, skin against skin, sending a shiver down my spine.

I glanced up at him, finding his dark eyes serious and watchful. "What are you talking about? I've seen you play plenty of times."

"Yeah, but when are you going to come and cheer for me?" His mouth tugged into a boyish grin.

Who could say no to that? Not a single straight woman alive.

It was the flirting equivalent of a trick shot.

"You could sit with Shiv," he added softly, nudging me with his elbow. "You know, on a night we're playing someone else."

It would have to be. Watching Chase play against Callingwood would be way too uncomfortable; imagining it brought up all sorts of mixed feelings. I was loyal to a fault, but after everything that had happened lately, maybe my loyalty had been misguided.

Everything I thought I'd known was slowly unraveling. Or not so slowly, when it came to him.

Heat rushed up my neck, and I dropped my gaze. "Technically, I should still cheer against you since both teams are in the same division and vying for points."

"I won't tell if you don't." Chase's voice dropped, innuendo-laden and impossible to resist.

The air in the room took on an electric charge. I lifted my eyes, meeting his. His pupils dilated and he paused, studying my face reading me better than I think anyone ever had. My body hummed in response to his perusal, and my breath grew shallow at his proximity.

When he turned his body to face me, his expression shifted from contemplative to determined and—.

"Carter!" a deep voice yelled, followed by a door slamming. "Yo, I need a hand bringing something in."

The high I was riding vanished.

Chase furrowed his brow, like he felt the same way. "Guess the roommates are home. Want to meet Ward?"

"Sure." I drew in a breath, trying to regain my mental footing, but I was in quicksand. Knowing what kissing him felt like was a special kind of torture because now I knew what I was missing.

I followed Chase down the wooden staircase into the living room. There stood Dallas Ward, offensive sniper for the Falcons.

While Chase was a total instigator, Dallas could shoot and stick-handle circles around anyone on our team.

He was almost as tall as Chase, with a sharp jaw, dark chestnut hair, and arresting blue eyes. With him was a beautiful raven-haired girl who had dark blue-green eyes and rosy Cupid's-bow lips. They were the most beautiful couple I had ever seen.

I used to think Luke was good-looking, but he was a potato compared to the three of them. Were all the people on his team gorgeous up close? And their girlfriends? So far, everyone looked like they were straight from the cast of a network television drama. I certainly didn't fit in.

"This is Bailey." Chase gestured to me. "Bailey, Dallas and Siobhan. Or Shiv."

Dallas's eyes widened. "This is the famous James?"

Oh god. Was I famous because Chase liked me or because I threw up on his shoes?

"It's so nice to meet you," Shiv said, giving me a warm smile. Most of the hockey girlfriends I knew didn't appreciate the presence of new girls, but her greeting was sincere, like she actually meant it.

"Likewise," I said.

Dallas jerked his thumb at the front door. "Can you give me a hand, man? I need help with a bookshelf."

"Bookshelf?" Chase cocked a brow. "Shiv, are you domesticating him or what?"

Siobhan grinned. "What can I say? He's finally housebroken. It's a proud day for us all."

"Yeah, yeah." Dallas rolled his eyes, smacking her on the butt as he walked past her to the entry. The door slammed shut behind them, and Siobhan stepped closer to me, eyes twinkling.

"So, you and Chase, huh?" She lowered her voice.

"Oh, we're just friends."

I wondered how many "friends" he'd kissed. Then I wondered how many "friends" Siobhan had met...Especially lately.

Not that it was technically any of my business.

"Of course." Siobhan winked at me. "Dallas and I are 'friends' too. How long have you and Chase been, um, hanging out?"

Were we hanging out? I guess we were. What did that even mean? My relationship experience consisted of one short-lived high school boyfriend and Luke. I was not well versed in the workings of the dating world.

But this wasn't *that* kind of hanging out…Was it?

How did I not know what I was doing?

"About a month?"

"Huh." She nodded thoughtfully. "Well, I could really use some more estrogen around here to balance things out. He's a good guy. I hope you can put up with him long-term."

I wasn't sure that would be the problem.

CHAPTER 18
OWN IT
CHASE

COULD I have completed that essay a little faster? Probably. Was I motivated to speed up the process when James was in my bedroom, looking adorable as fuck on my bed? Not really.

When I got home from dropping off Bailey, Dallas was sprawled out on the living room couch, a bottle of beer in hand with his other arm draped around Shiv. In the dark, a horror film flashed on the oversized flatscreen, complete with revving chainsaws and splattering blood. Those two were a match made in weirdo horror-loving heaven. I wasn't squeamish about guts and gore, but I never really got the appeal of scary movies. If I was going to sit through a movie, it either had to be funny or have lots of car chases and explosions. Or, well, be a naked movie.

I paused in the doorway to the living room. "Hey."

In the background, there was a bloodcurdling scream from the TV.

Dallas picked up the remote and paused the movie. "How's your ankle?"

"Hurts like a bitch, but it's slowly getting better," I said. "What are you two psychos watching this time?"

"*Chainsaw Slaughter 6*." Shiv grabbed a handful of popcorn from the bowl beside her. "It's the best one of the whole series. Wanna join?"

It sounded better than economic theory, but I had a quiz tomorrow, and Coach Miller had been watching me like a hawk since our little chat. He'd been cornering me on a weekly basis for updates, which was really code for trying to catch me in a lie since he'd already talked to my professors. If I wanted to keep playing, there wasn't much room for error.

"I still have to finish some schoolwork, but thanks for the offer."

Dallas tilted his head, studying me. "Schoolwork? Is this Bailey's influence or what?"

"Coach is up my ass about my grades again." I shrugged. "It's buck up or get benched, and we all know you're fucked without me."

"Back to the Bailey thing," he said emphatically, ignoring my jab and blatant attempt to change the subject. "You've seen her a lot lately. Taking this toying with Morrison thing pretty far, huh?"

"Nah, I like spending time with her."

He pointed at me with the neck of his beer bottle. "Because you like her."

Beside him, Shiv widened her eyes and gave a little shake of her head as if to say, "I didn't tell." I believed her. Unfortunately, Dallas was good at reading me. Plus, hanging around a girl this long without banging was basically a dead giveaway. The only other girl I was friends with was Shiv.

Besides, let's be real—not even I believed my intentions with Bailey were platonic. But was that what Bailey wanted?

"Maybe."

"Don't even try to act cool. We already know, dumbass," Dallas said. "But I wanted to make sure *you* did. You're not always the most self-aware."

Dammit.

Okay, whatever. I could own it.

"Fine," I said. "I like her."

"I like her too. Can we keep her?" Shiv gave me a puppy dog face.

"I have no idea," I said honestly. With how often we had been talking lately, it was hard to imagine my life without Bailey in it.

But I'd known her all of a month, and I wasn't entirely sure where we were headed. For all I knew, she could get back with Morrison tomorrow and never speak to me again.

"She does seem cool," Dallas agreed.

"She is."

He smirked. "Which means you have no business with her."

"Thanks for the vote of confidence, man." I flipped him off before continuing upstairs to my room.

"Love you too," he called.

When I got into bed later, it still smelled faintly like Bailey—something sweet, like her perfume, mixed with something else that I was pretty sure was just her. And hockey help me, I liked it.

I was so screwed.

Tuesday evening's practice rolled around, and Coach Miller bag skated us for the first half as punishment for playing so poorly against New England U. He was sneaky that way. He hadn't done it the day after the game or the day after that, so we thought we were in the clear. But midweek?

Surprise, motherfuckers.

Now everything hurt and I was dying. To make matters worse, I was dumb enough to carpool with Dallas and Ty, which meant I got dragged to O'Connor's after practice. I mean, the pub part was fine. It was the crowd that frequented the pub that I was ambivalent about. O'Connor's was puck bunny and former-hookup central.

"Solid practice," Dallas said. He drained the last of his rum and coke and set it on the black laminate tabletop. "Aside from the part where half the team puked in the garbage can at center ice."

"At least none of us did." I shrugged, pushing my chair away from the table to stretch out my legs in front of me. My ankle still wasn't 100 percent going into practice, and it was agonizing coming out. "Plus, by Miller's standards, only half the team is practically a pass."

Ty smirked, tipping back his beer. "And you even got a few shots past me during drills for once. Good for you, little buddy."

"I guess your strategy of flopping has to work sometime," I said. "Maybe you should learn to lift the puck."

"Maybe you should—"

From out of nowhere, a soft hand touched the back of my neck and startled the crap out of me. I jumped in my seat and jerked around to find a pair of blue eyes with heavy eye makeup staring back at me.

"Hi, handsome." Lindsay slid into my lap, looping an arm around my shoulders. She crossed her legs, causing her very short, very tight black skirt to hike up a little more.

I shifted my weight uncomfortably. Would it be rude to tell her to get off my lap? Diplomacy wasn't exactly my strong suit. Even if I did mental gymnastics to justify this—like reminding myself that I was still technically single—it felt disloyal as hell.

"Hey." My voice fell flat. In the background, Ty rolled his eyes and stood up to grab another beer.

"Long time no see," she said breathily.

Objectively speaking, Lindsay was hot, albeit in a very overt, heavily made-up way. Earlier this year, I made it a mission to hit it and flirted with her like crazy. We did a whole back and forth thing and got pretty close, but it never quite came to fruition.

Despite that, there was zero response in my body to the events that were unfolding now. It was like watching the entire thing happen to someone else.

"Yeah. Been a while."

"Are we going to pick up where we left off last time?" She bit her lip, tracing a pink fingernail along my chest. "Remember?"

I craned my neck and reached around her for my beer. "Er…no, not really."

I hadn't seen Lindsay since sometime this summer. Between hockey, school, and James, it felt like a decade had passed since then. I had no recollection of where we'd left things. I may or may not have been wasted at the time. Odds were, I was.

"About christening the bathroom next time we were here?"

Oh. That.

I'd been half-lit at the time, trying to close after we'd been making out off in the corner next to the pool tables. Lindsay was on the hook, too, until her friend passed out at the table and she had to take her home. I'd all but forgotten about that.

She nodded to the hallway behind us, lowering her voice. "You said you were going to tear off my panties and—"

I winced and held up my hand, cutting her off. "I don't think that's a good idea."

"Or…" Lindsay angled closer, undeterred. Her breath was warm against my ear and smelled like some kind of fruity alcohol. "We could go back to my place with my friend Melanie over there. She loves hockey players." She pointed to a busty brunette standing by the pool table, talking to a few other guys from the team. Her friend noticed us, and waved at flirtatiously.

August me would have considered this winning the hookup lottery, would have been all over it, would have been booking a ride home with both of them already.

October me would rather go home and watch *SportsCenter*. Or text James.

Was this seriously happening?

I shot Dallas a *what the fuck* look.

Dallas cleared his throat, leaning over the table. "Carter's got a girlfriend, Linds." He nodded at me.

She turned and gaped at me, expression a mixture of disbelief and irritation. "*You* have a girlfriend?"

I nodded because it did seem like the simplest way to let her down easy. "Yeah. It's new."

"Oh." Her glossy lips formed an *O* for a moment as she paused. She tossed her dark hair and shrugged. "Well, she doesn't have to know."

Lord help me. She didn't know how to take a hint. Or a flat-out rejection, apparently.

"I'm flattered, Lindsay. Really, I am." I tried to push her off me while she resisted my efforts. "But I'm going to pass."

Lindsay narrowed her eyes. "You're serious right now? After the big game you talked last time?"

Funny how I pursued her for a while, doing the whole sexy cat and mouse thing, but the minute I lost interest, she wanted me immediately.

"Can't do it."

"Whatever, Carter." She stood up, tossed her hair over her shoulder, and stormed away in a huff.

Once she was safely out of earshot, Dallas let out a low whistle. "Never thought I'd see the day."

"Neither did I."

His eyes jumped to the pool table behind me. "Guess your loss is Tyler's gain." I followed his line of sight to find Lindsay and her friend hanging off Ty at the bar. Cool. More power to him.

Lindsay shot me a defiant glare, like she expected me to be jealous. I smiled back because I seriously did not give a shit.

"But dude." Dallas lowered his voice, giving me a look so probing I felt borderline violated. "What the hell is going on? Have you even made a move on Bailey?"

"Not really," I said, peeling the label off my bottle. "You and your fucking bookshelf made sure of that."

His mouth dropped open. "Oh my god." He guffawed, shoulders shaking. "No wonder you seemed off when we got home. Sorry, man. I didn't expect you to have company that early in the evening."

"It's fine," I muttered.

"But you're going to find your balls again and make a move, right?"

I nodded, taking a sip of my beer. "Yup."

In theory.

"Soon." He lowered his head and gave me a pointed look.

"Soon."

But she'd just broken up with Morrison. And what if this feeling was one-sided? Or I scared her off by pushing too soon? Or I went for it and she rejected me?

Was it fear of seeming opportunistic about her breakup with

Luke holding me back? Or fear that I'd scare her off if I was flat-out wrong about things? Or was it the fear of rejection? That was something I'd never dealt with before, and it was scarier than I wanted to admit.

Maybe it was all of the above.

BAILEY

I was having a fantastic day. First, I convinced my astronomy instructor to let me unofficially switch class times, citing unforeseen (and nonexistent) school newspaper conflicts. I would still have to write the final exam with my actual class—including Luke—but Professor Walsh agreed to let me sit in on the Thursday morning lectures instead. I practically danced out of his office. It was like a gigantic meteor had been lifted from my shoulders.

Then Noelle drove Zara and me to our favorite lunch place off campus to enjoy overpriced but delicious chopped salads the size of our heads.

"You didn't have to buy me lunch," I said to Zara, and I meant it. Fifteen-dollar salads were hard to justify, but my gigantic chicken Caesar was heaven in a bowl. Somehow, salads always tasted better when someone else made them.

She shrugged, taking a bite of her spicy Thai noodle salad. "It's the least I could do after you agreed to cover the volleyball game tomorrow night on short notice. Again."

"I don't mind."

Technically, I had plans with Chase. He invited me over for Tyler's birthday, but he understood when I told him I'd be late. It was an early game at least, so it wouldn't eat into the night too much.

"You know I would have taken one for the team if I could," she said. "But no one wants to read a sports article written by me. My knowledge starts and ends with the fact that the ball goes over the net."

I laughed. "It's okay. You have a date tomorrow night anyway, don't you? How are things with Caleb?"

Caleb was her Tinder date from last week, a slightly older veterinarian with a three-year-old daughter. Different from her usual type, but maybe that was a good thing. Usually Zara gravitated toward bad boys, with bad outcomes as a result.

"Amazing." Zara's eyes sparkled. I'd never seen her so excited about someone.

"It's their third date," Noelle said in a sing-song voice. "Someone's going to get lucky."

Zara blushed, which was the first time I had ever seen her look bashful. "Well, maybe. We're kind of taking it slow."

I wasn't sure it could be much slower than Chase and me, who'd yet to even establish our intentions. I was pretty sure he almost kissed me the other day, but now I was second-guessing myself. Maybe he really did see me as just a friend, and the flirting was for fun. It was hard to tell with him sometimes.

Ugh.

This limbo we were in was both exhilarating and exhausting.

"I'll wear ear plugs tonight in case," Noelle said.

Zara's cheeks turned a deeper shade of red. "It's not my fault the walls are thin."

"Speaking of that," I said. "This might seem a little out of left field, but have you guys given any thought to living arrangements for next year?"

A gust of wind from the open door blew in, chilling us all. I pulled on my plaid scarf, wishing we had grabbed a table closer to the back.

"Not really." Noelle shook her head. "That's still so far away. Depends on what happens with our rent, I guess. Last year our landlord raised it 10 percent, so if she does that again, we might look for something else. How come?"

I swallowed a bite of food. "I was wondering if you might want to get a three bedroom."

"That would be awesome," Noelle said. "We would have so much fun."

Zara took a sip of iced tea, nodding. She set down the glass as a confused frown crossed her face. "But wait. Why don't you want to stay with Amelia and Jillian?"

"Uh…We aren't really getting along lately."

"Really?" Noelle frowned. "What's going on?"

"What's not?" I snorted. "Everyone hates me because of Luke. And they're using Chase as an excuse, since he's supposedly enemy number one."

"That doesn't make any sense. Luke broke up with you. And you're a free person." Zara stabbed at her noodle salad aggressively.

"Tell me about it," I said. "But it's so uncomfortable I don't even want to be there anymore. If I could afford a place on my own, I would be out tomorrow."

Noelle winced. "That sucks, B. I'm sorry. I don't know why they would be so shitty."

"Luke is the ringleader, I guess. What he says goes."

"But what about your brother?" Zara asked. "Doesn't he stick up for you?"

I sighed. "No…That's its own story entirely."

Definitely didn't want to get into that right now. Or ever. I was still hoping Derek would come to his senses and end things with Jillian. As it was, I couldn't look either of them in the eye.

"Anyway," I said, "if you know anyone who needs a roommate, let me know. I would legitimately consider it. It's pretty brutal at home."

Noelle grinned. "Good thing you've got Chase to distract you."

Now it was my turn to blush. "We're just friends."

I think.

CHAPTER 19

ANYTHING YOU WANT

BAILEY

THE VOLLEYBALL GAME ended with Callingwood winning three-two. In theory, a close score like that should have made for an exciting match. In reality, I had no idea what happened. I took notes, but I'd done it in some kind of bizarre autopilot mode. The conscious, thinking part of my brain was stuck on the fact that Chase was picking me up. I was trapped in an emotional loop that cycled through excitement, fear, uncertainty, and lust, changing as often as the colors on a string of blinking Christmas lights. Torn between wanting to throw myself at Chase and wanting to run the other way. Half-tempted to kiss him to see what happened, but also fairly convinced that was a terrible idea. Worse still, not sure whether I cared if it was.

In other words, I was a mess.

Chase was already waiting in the loading zone as I navigated the crowd of spectators exiting through the glass arena doors. I climbed into his truck and buckled my seat belt. The kiss idea jumped up a few notches in my mind the second I got a good look at him. But if he wanted to kiss me again, wouldn't he have done it already? He'd had ample opportunity.

My attention fell to his phone. It was lying in the center console, notifications going wild. The ringer was on silent, but the screen lit up with messages every few seconds.

Right.

I shouldn't have been surprised.

Chase glanced down as he put his hand on the gearshift but paused and pulled it away before putting the truck in drive. "For fuck's sake." He rolled his eyes, shaking his head. "Do you mind if I respond to Ward so he leaves me the fuck alone about this fantasy hockey trade? He sent me an offer that expires in an hour, and now he's texting me with a countdown every three minutes. Dick."

A tiny stab of guilt pricked at me for assuming the worst about him.

"Sure," I said. "Go ahead."

"Pretty sure he's already a little drunk," Chase added. "He's not normally this high maintenance."

I crossed my legs, shifting to face him. "What's the offer?"

"I don't know." He raked a hand through his dark hair. "Didn't even review it. I was on my way out the door and didn't want to be late picking you up. I'm sorry. I'll be two seconds."

To Chase's credit, he completely ignored his phone most of the time. When we were together, he was mentally present, and his attention was fixed solely on me. It was more than I could say about most people I knew, friends or otherwise.

"I don't mind, but now you've got to show me. I'm curious about what his offer is."

Chase unlocked his cell and read the message. "Ha." He snorted. "As if." He held the device out so I could see the screen.

I studied it for a moment. "What's the rest of your team look like?"

He took his phone back and navigated the screen briefly before handing it to me again. Chase obviously knew more about hockey than I did, but I didn't agree with his conclusion.

"I don't know," I said. "I think I would take it."

He shot me a dubious look. "Smith for Taylor? Ward is trying to screw me."

"Taylor is overvalued, and he's off to a weak start. Have you seen his stats lately? He hasn't found his groove since they traded

Petrov last season. He's coasting. I don't think he's going to turn it around."

Good job, Bailey. Geek out on sports. Guys loved that. I had already opened Pandora's penalty box, though, so it was too late.

Chase looked at the screen, then back up to me. "Keep talking…" He furrowed his brow, dark eyes thoughtful.

"Smith is a sleeper. He's been a little slow to develop, but he's shown serious promise over the last six months. I think he's going to have a breakthrough season. Plus, Dallas threw in a first-round draft pick with his offer. With Richardson coming up soon, I would be all over that." I stopped my rambling and drew in a deep breath.

And cue backlash in three…two…

I waited for him to argue with me like Luke—and most guys—did. To tell me all the reasons my opinion was wrong or stupid. Derek was the only one who could engage in remotely civil debate with me about sports. Even then, he tried to pull the hockey player card when he was losing.

Chase tilted his head, looking at me like I was an alien. Then a grin broke out on his face. "You know what?" He shrugged. "I'll bite."

My heart exploded.

"Wait, really?" Surely, I'd misheard.

"James, you just dropped more knowledge than half the guys on the team could. It makes total sense."

This may have been the moment I fell for him, but I'd never admit that out loud.

"Plus," I added, "if you take the trade and I'm right, Dallas will be extra mad that he did it to himself."

Chase grinned. "I like when you talk dirty to me." He nodded at the phone. "There's a lot of money riding on this pool, so if I win big because of this, I'll buy you something nice."

"I'd settle for a hot chocolate."

"I'll take you for that any time you want."

Dark hair tumbled over his brow as he typed out a text to Dallas, frowning in concentration. He looked so heartbreakingly perfect, but what lay beneath the surface was a tangled mess of contradictions I didn't understand. He was all sharp edges and swagger from a distance. But closer up, there was softness and vulnerability too.

The man, the myth, and the legend, yet—human.

I didn't know what to make of it.

I didn't know what we were doing.

"You can skate, right?" He stashed his phone in the console again. It stopped lighting up every two seconds, which confirmed that my initial assumption—that it was a roster full of girls—may have been hasty.

"Why?"

"Just curious. Maybe I like to plan ahead. But if you can't, I mean…you can admit it." A smirk played on his lips. He shifted the truck into drive, signaling to pull out of the loading zone. We waited while throngs of people milled about, blocking the way.

"Who do you think you're dealing with here?" I asked. "I've been skating since I was three."

"Figure skating?" Finally, a clearing opened, and he eased the truck onto the road, heading for the freeway exit.

"Psh, no. Hockey."

He stole a sidelong glance at me, lips tugging up. "You played hockey? That's awesome."

"Until middle school. I mean, not very well. My skating was fine. Good, even. It was the other things that were the issue, like stickhandling."

"I could teach you how to stickhandle."

I suppressed a laugh. "*Carter*."

"What?" He widened his eyes in mock innocence. "You know, I think you're the one with the dirty mind, James."

Maybe I was.

Twenty minutes later, we made our way up the sidewalk to Chase's house. The street was packed with cars, and low bass throbbed out onto the street.

He glanced over to the front window, which looked into a living room crammed full of people. "Wow. It's filled in since I left."

"Ah," I said, because nerves had hijacked my brain and I couldn't formulate a more articulate response. What was I doing at this Boyd blowout anyway? I wouldn't know anyone besides Chase and—sort of—Shiv and Dallas. And I couldn't expect Chase to babysit me all night.

He opened the glass front door and held it for me. "You ready to fraternize with the enemy?"

"I don't know," I said, shooting him a tentative glance. "Is the enemy nice?"

Maybe they were nicer than my supposed allies. It wouldn't take much these days.

"Nah, we're all terrible people," he said, nudging me toward the kitchen. "Let's go grab a drink."

We walked through the hallway and past the living room full of people I didn't recognize. My panic continued to escalate.

"Is Shiv here?" I asked, scanning the house. "I feel like I need another girl if I'm going to survive this."

"Sure is," he said. "Not sure where, but we can look for her."

As we walked into the kitchen, Dallas strolled in the back door. "Carter," he said, giving him an air pistol. "Just the person I wanted to see. We're out of beer."

"How the hell?" Chase gestured. "It hasn't even been two hours, Ward."

"Didn't go as far as I thought it would." Dallas shrugged, leaning against the kitchen counter. He was definitely tipsy. Which explained the bad trade he'd offered Chase.

Chase sighed. "You blew up my phone for the past hour and didn't think to mention this?"

"Thought we had more in the beer fridge out in the garage. But we don't, and you're the only one sober enough to drive." Dallas gave him another air pistol. Yep, drunk. "Thanks, man."

"You fuckers can't plan for shit." Chase glanced down at me, expression apologetic. "Sorry. Want to run back out with me?"

Shiv came inside from the patio door and shut it behind her. "Or you can stay here with me. Dal can go with Chase. We were about to play a drinking game. I think there's still one beer in the fridge."

"I can stay," I said, "but I have to go easy on the drinking. I don't think Chase wants a repeat of the night we met." I peeked up at him and grinned.

He laughed and gave my shoulders a squeeze. "Well, at least it got us here."

Half an hour later, we wrapped up one round of a drinking game during which I drank water instead of beer because I was still genuinely afraid of repeating the incident at XS. People began to filter out of the basement, leaving me with Shiv and Aaron, a second-year player from the Falcons.

Shiv said, "I was undeclared to start. But I changed to psychology when I transferred to Boyd this year."

Suddenly, there was a crash of breaking glass from upstairs.

"Oh my god," she muttered. "I swear, sometimes…"

"Want help?" I asked, pushing to stand.

"It's okay. I'll be right back."

Aaron turned to me. "You're a journalism major too? I hear the Callingwood news lab is amazing."

"It is," I said. "But the Boyd alumni connections are supposed to be great for securing a job after graduation."

"Yeah," he said. "My friend got hired—"

A long shadow appeared, blocking the overhead light in the stairwell like a solar eclipse. We both turned to find a gigantic hockey player lurking in the doorway. Chase raised his eyebrows but said nothing. He didn't need to.

Aaron paled. "Uh, I think I forgot something in the living room." He darted around Chase, taking the stairs two at a time.

Chase sauntered over, swinging the beers he was holding. "Sup."

"You're so mean."

"So they tell me." He cracked one of the beers and handed it to me. "But I saw Shiv upstairs and I couldn't find you. I was worried."

"Oh, Shiv had to go clean up a broken glass. Aaron and I were talking about school."

"Sure you were." Chase smirked.

"He's a journalism major too," I said, holding his gaze evenly. "But if I didn't know better, I might say you were jealous."

He shrugged but didn't deny it. "Just pointing out how single-minded and filthy most guys are."

"Including you?"

He stood closer, giving me a look that did something decidedly unfriend-like to me inside. "Baby, I'm the filthiest."

I laughed. "I know."

"Anyway." Chase took a sip of his drink, his throat bobbing.

My eyes lingered for a beat on his lips as a flicker of desire ignited within me.

He cleared his throat and continued. "I came to see if you were staying here or if you wanted to go home later."

My heart went ka-thunk like a rusted old car. "Staying here?" I *may* have thrown some extra personal items into my bag in case this scenario arose, but I genuinely didn't think it would.

"As a friend, James. But if you want to go home, I'll stop drinking after this so I can drive you. This is my first beer."

I chewed my lip, considering. I was fairly certain that if I stayed, it wouldn't be as a friend, despite his assurance.

Did I want that? I sure did. But I was also a little scared. Okay, a lot scared.

"I don't need a chaperone to get home."

He leaned against the wall, biceps bulging as he folded his arms. "There's a blue stain on my favorite pair of white sneakers that says otherwise."

I groaned, embarrassment flooding my gut. "I don't know."

His eyes caught mine, questioning. Tempting. I wanted to say yes.

"Come on." He nudged my foot with his. "I'll let you wear my Falcons shirt again."

"Never," I said. "I'd rather sleep naked."

It was meant to be sassy but was *way* off the mark. I blamed being in such close proximity to him; my brain was going all sorts of haywire.

His voice dropped, turning husky. "That can definitely be arranged."

"Carter." I narrowed my eyes at him.

"James." He copied me, but he couldn't keep a straight face. A smile broke through that was hopelessly endearing and intentionally designed to be that way. "Plus, if you stay, I can kick your ass at video games later."

"Okay," I said. "But you know I'll be the one kicking your ass. Again."

"Oh yeah?" He raised his brows, coffee-brown eyes dancing. "Let's make it interesting. If I beat you, then you have to wear my Falcons shirt again tonight."

"What do I get if I beat you?"

Our gazes locked and a smile played on his lips.

"Anything you want."

CHAPTER 20
NOT IN A RUSH
BAILEY

SIOBHAN DESCENDED THE STAIRS, a fresh drink in her hand.

"Sorry about that," she said. "I keep telling everyone solo cups only, but do they listen? *No*. I swear, someday I'm going to replace everything in this house with plastic." Her eyes landed on Chase and me. She came to a halt halfway down the staircase, a knowing smile on her face. "You know, I just remembered that I was supposed to go…"

Chase grinned. "It's okay. We were coming up."

"Right," I said.

Before I could move, he grabbed my hand, curling his warm, strong fingers around mine.

"Come on," he said. "I'll introduce you to everyone."

Several hours and two more broken glasses later, Shiv and I were curled up on the living room sectional, chatting while the guys played beer pong in the basement. A few other people were scattered around the living room, chatting and drinking, half watching an NBA game on TV.

"You transferred schools this year?" I asked.

"Yeah." Her blue-green eyes darted around the room to check for eavesdroppers. She leaned closer, dropping her voice to a hush. "After I broke up with my ex, he went totally off the rails. He kept showing up at my dorm, and the school wouldn't do anything about it. Eventually, transferring was the only option."

I could kind of relate, though at least Luke wasn't quite on that level. If he showed up for another couples' night at my house, though, I was going to whack him with a frying pan.

"That's awful." I gave her a sympathetic look.

"But it's also embarrassing," Shiv added quietly, taking a sip of her gin and tonic. She pursed her dark magenta lips. "Like, how bad was my judgment that I dated someone so crazy? That's why, when people ask, I tell them I transferred so I could switch programs."

"His behavior isn't your fault," I said. "My ex isn't exactly a prize, either. Sometimes people hide who they really are, and it takes time to see through the façade."

Was that the case with Luke? Or had I ignored the red flags from the start? As a freshman, I'd been inexperienced and naïve; starstruck at the idea of being pursued by a hot, popular hockey player. Looking back, I recognized a lot of little warning signs. Some not-so-little ones too.

She shrugged, dropping her gaze. Starting over like that would have to be difficult, especially in a brand-new city. If I didn't have Zara and Noelle, I would be adrift socially right now too. Heck, I still kind of was.

"How has it been at Boyd so far? I hear good things about it."

"A little tough. Most orientation stuff is geared toward freshman. They pretty much expect sophomores to be settled in already."

"It's still early in the semester," I said. "I'm sure it'll get better once you start doing more group projects and that kind of thing."

"I hope so." She sighed, tucking a lock of raven hair behind her ear. "I met Dallas at the gym over the summer. But it's been hard to meet other girls. Most of the guys on the team don't have girlfriends, either."

A pang of sympathy hit me, because I knew all too well what it felt like to be on the periphery. "We should go for lunch sometime."

"Yeah?" Siobhan's face brightened. "I'd love that."

"*James*," Chase's voice rang out. It was low, commanding, gruff.

Siobhan froze. Her questioning look probably mirrored mine. I'd never heard him use that tone before, especially not toward me. Heavy steps echoed from the hallway.

He barreled into the room, eyes zeroing in on me as he closed the distance between us.

"Sorry, Shiv, I need to borrow her for a sec."

"No worries," she said, standing up. "I'm going to go beat Dal at beer pong."

Chase took me by the elbow, ushering me through an archway into the dark, empty dining room. He shoved his phone into my hands and leaned against the table, watching me expectantly.

I looked up at him, scanning his face. "What is it?"

"Are you aware of what fuckface is saying about you?" He nodded at the lit-up screen, his jaw tight.

Brow furrowed, I studied the display. Then I blinked slowly, processing what I'd just read. It was a screenshot of a text from Luke, claiming that he was still hooking up with me on the side. Specifically, calling me his "side piece."

That lying asshole.

My teeth set on edge. "Where did you get this?"

"We aren't all enemies," he said. "And not everyone on your team likes their captain."

"Like who?"

He shrugged. "Palmer, Reed. I played minor hockey with them. And they can't stand Morrison."

"Oh," I said. "I had no idea."

"It's not exactly something they can broadcast if they want ice time. But that dumb shit put this in a group text with almost the entire team, minus your brother, so in this case, he won't know who ratted on him."

The entire team? Resentment smoldered in the pit of my stomach, threatening to ignite.

Then I caught myself. No. Nope. Nuh-uh.

I wouldn't let Luke rile me up and ruin my night—especially not when I was with Chase. Pressing my lips together, I exhaled through my nose, expelling thoughts of Luke from my brain. Begone, demon.

I handed Chase his phone. "For a minute there, I thought you were mad at me."

"No." His brow creased, his tone softening. "I'm mad at *that*."

Chase glowered at the display again. The cords in his neck were tight, his breath uneven. Thinly restrained power and strength radiated off him, like he was a predatory animal ready to attack.

He looked ten times bigger when he was angry.

"Why do you think he would write that?" He gripped the phone so tightly it looked like he would crush it in his bare hand.

"Would I be standing here if it were true?"

"I know it's not true, James. That's why I'm so pissed." He was still holding my elbow loosely with his other hand, like he'd forgotten about it. "Morrison is spreading bullshit because he's got a problem with me."

Trashing my reputation did fit Luke's usual MO—never mind that I was his friend's sister; he was all about revenge over reason, spite over smarts. Though it was an odd move, given that he was with Sophie. Did he want her to think he was cheating? Did she not mind if he was? I had so many questions, but honestly, I wasn't all that interested in the answers.

"He is," I agreed. "But who cares what he says?"

Chase's jaw ticked, his grip on my arm tightening a notch. "I care."

"Why? He's a loser anyway." I should have been mad, probably. Or sad. But I didn't want to wage war against Luke; I wanted him to go away. Permanently.

My lips parted in surprise as Chase slid his hand from my elbow and rested it on my lower back. He pulled me closer, turning me to face him. Behind the anger in his eyes was something softer—tenderness mingled with desire.

"Because he's messing with you."

"It's only messing with me if I let it bother me," I said. "Besides, anyone who actually matters would know it's a lie."

Maybe I should have been upset, but it was more ridiculous than anything. Especially when I had pages worth of late-night texts from Luke asking if he could come over to "talk," followed by my responses repeatedly shooting him down. I had no shortage of receipts proving that post was bullshit, but I didn't feel the need to prove it in the first place.

Plus, I was more than a little distracted at the moment. Chase's hand was still on my back, his scent enveloping me. The closeness of our bodies was exponentially more exciting, both physically and emotionally, than any text messages ever could be.

"Still." He shook his head, gaze dropping back to his phone. His face clouded over like he was going to rain down his wrath on the next person unfortunate enough to cross him. "I'm going to flatten him on the ice."

I touched his chest. "Carter."

He lifted his head. Our eyes locked, and something clicked into place inside me. His expression relaxed, shifting from murderous into a sullen pout.

"You can if you want to. But I'm fine," I said, flattening my palms against his black T-shirt. His heart pounded against my hands, strong and steady. "Really."

Besides, if happiness was the best revenge, then I was 100 percent winning right now.

"I still don't like it," Chase grumbled. He locked his phone and slid it into his back pocket. Then he pivoted both of our bodies, coming to stand in front of me with the dining table at my back.

My breath snagged as he rested his hands on my sides, his large fingers spanning my hips. He drew in a breath and ducked his head to catch my gaze.

"I'm sorry," he said, voice gentle. "Didn't mean to lose my shit. Believe it or not, I hardly ever do."

"It's okay." I braced my hands on his biceps, stroking lightly with my thumbs. His muscles were taut beneath the warmth of his smooth skin.

He regarded me for a long moment. "Do you want to get back to the party?"

Did I? Not really. A dark, quiet room with him was infinitely more appealing. Especially with the way things were heading right now.

I shrugged, biting back a smile. "I'm not in a big rush."

Chase's expression shifted, turning hungry, predatory. "Me neither."

He slipped his hand beneath the hem of my shirt, fingers digging into my bare skin, and pulled me against him. Anticipation flooded my body. Angling low, he inched closer until our mouths were almost touching. Almost. Then he lingered, teasing. Waiting for me to close the space between us. I inhaled, taking in his scent, the heat of his body so close, then I tilted my head, and our lips came together, instantly melting into a deep kiss.

A whimper escaped from the back of my throat as his tongue brushed against mine, pushing deeper into my mouth. He caressed my jaw, then moved his hand to my nape. Gripping the roots of my hair, he secured my head in place and moved his mouth against mine, deepening the kiss until I was completely lost in him.

A wave of desire unlike anything I'd ever experienced crashed over me. It was heady and intoxicating, relentless and persistent, growing stronger with every sweep of his tongue.

I slid my hands to his lower back, palms resting on the stacks of lean muscle. Drawing in a jagged breath, Chase grabbed the backs of my thighs and set me on the tabletop. Then he nudged my knees apart and positioned himself between my legs until our bodies were flush, creating a delicious hint of friction where we touched.

Heat pooled between my legs, wanting and needing, as he pressed against me. I took his bottom lip between my teeth, and a low rumble emanated from his chest. He skimmed my bare stomach with his fingertips, tracing the waistband of my jeans, and a pulse settled between my thighs.

In the background, laughter spilled out from in the living room, snapping me back into the present. I'd all but forgotten where we were.

We broke apart, breathless. My heart roared in my ears.

He shook his head, voice husky. "You're killing me, James."

"Why's that?" I whispered.

Chase lowered his head, planting a row of kisses down my neck. "Because I don't want to stop. But if I keep kissing you," he murmured against my skin, "I won't be fit to be around other people for a good, long while."

He pulled back and smoothed my hair with a playful grin. "Later, it'll be a different story."

After some distraction in the form of our impromptu make-out session, food, and video games, Chase's mood improved significantly. But I did kick his ass at NHL again—and Dallas's.

Chase and Tyler thought it was hilarious. Siobhan was stifling giggles, or at least attempting to. And Dallas was furious, which only added to our collective amusement.

"Ooh, want some cream for that burn?" Tyler laughed, taking a swig of his beer. "She schooled you both."

"How?" Dallas threw the white game controller onto the empty leather armchair beside him, slapping his leg. He turned to Chase and me, throwing a hand in the air. "Like, what just happened?"

Chase shrugged, giving me a lazy grin. "I'm pretty sure she's a wizard."

"That's what happens when you grow up with three older brothers."

"Rematch," Dallas declared, picking up the controller again. He navigated back into the main menu and opened the settings. "The game is rigged," he muttered, squinting at the screen. "Something's wrong with it."

From the armchair, Siobhan rolled her eyes, twirling a strand of hair around her finger. "It's a good thing you're pretty, Dal."

"It's okay to lose sometimes, Ward." Tyler propped his legs on the ottoman, not even attempting to hide his grin.

Dallas shook his head. "I never lose."

"Actually, I'm getting tired." I stifled a yawn, wondering if Chase would come to bed when I did, or if he would stay up with his friends like Luke always had.

Chase shot me a glance. "Want to call it a night?"

"I think so."

He set the game controller on the glass coffee table and stood, stretching his arms. His black T-shirt hiked up, revealing a sliver of washboard stomach that I did my best to ignore. Though after being pressed up against him earlier, I already knew his abs were spec-tac-u-lar.

"Yeah," he said. "I'm good too. Let's go."

At that, tiny fireworks erupted low in my belly. We were going to bed—together.

I pushed off the couch and stood up, then made my way out of the room with Chase following close behind.

"Later, losers," he said to the guys as we headed up the staircase. "See ya, Shiv."

"This isn't over, James," Dallas called. "I want a rematch tomorrow."

Chase laughed, the rumble low and deep in his chest. We started up the stairs, and he put a warm hand on my lower back, leaning in to murmur in my ear. "You do know Ward is going to stay up all night playing now, right?"

A tingle ran down my spine and goose bumps popped up along my arms when his breath hit my neck, but I tried to act normal. Keyword: tried.

"You're saying he's a sore loser?" I asked under my breath. "Gee, couldn't tell."

"It's not personal," he said. "And it's not because you're a girl, either. It's that no one ever beats him. Which is what makes it so great."

Chase let his hand linger on my back as we continued down the hall. I was dying inside in the best possible way. He followed me into his room and closed the door behind us.

As soon as it clicked shut, I was hit with a whack ton of nerves. Suddenly I was jittery—skittish in a way I wasn't usually with him. Sure, there was always a hefty dose of sexual tension between us, but most of the time, it manifested in teasing and banter, play-fighting and flirting.

Right now, it was manifesting in me being coiled tighter than a spring.

After tonight's kiss, everything felt different.

We'd moved out of the friendship gray zone tonight. Our mutual attraction was out in the open, and the chemistry between us had proved to be explosive.

He switched on the lamp on the nightstand, bathing the room in dim yellow light. Then he turned away from me and pulled clothing from the wide dresser beneath the flatscreen TV. I threw my bag on the bed and rifled through its contents. I had a clean tank top, underwear, shorts, and best of all, a toothbrush. After spending the night with Chase under disastrous circumstances before, having the ability to brush my teeth this time was a huge relief.

Hygiene was important, after all. Not because I would be kissing him again or anything. But, you know…just in case.

Okay, even I knew we were about to kiss again. That was why the tension was through the roof and I was practically vibrating.

"I know I lost our bet, but you can still grab a shirt." Chase nodded to the tall dresser beside him. "If you want."

Want. Not need.

Was it wrong to want to sleep in one of his shirts even though I had my own?

Probably.

And yet, I was totally going to do it.

"Speaking of that," he said. "Since you won, are you going to collect?"

"I haven't decided what I want yet."

He grinned. "I could give you some ideas."

Heat spread through my body. My cheeks were likely the reddest they had ever been. He winked at me and went into the bathroom, shutting the door behind him. I perched on the edge of the bed in hopes of catching my breath.

The good news was, I definitely wasn't tired anymore. The bad news was, I was so keyed up that I might never sleep again.

And I had no idea what, if anything, was about to happen.

CHAPTER 21
THINK SO
CHASE

BAILEY WAS in my room for a third time, and I wanted to pinch myself. I'd have said third time's the charm, but I had no delusions about getting lucky tonight, and I was more than okay with that. Just getting to spend time with her, especially alone, had me flying higher than I'd ever been.

As I returned to my room with two glasses of water in hand, Bailey came out of the bathroom wearing a faded blue T-shirt from one of my minor hockey teams. It hugged the curves of her torso in a way that made me borderline jealous of the fabric. And the icing on the cake was the pair of black shorts she'd paired it with that showed off her mile-long legs.

I must have done something right in my life to end up here.

I walked over to the nightstand and set both glasses down before turning to face her. When our eyes met, I couldn't keep the stupid grin off my face.

"You look so much better in my shirts than I do."

Her lips curled into a wry smile. "You just want me out of the shirt."

Well, that was also true. But James in my shirt was still pretty awesome.

"It may have crossed my mind."

We stood, considering each other in the dim light for a couple of heartbeats. Faint chatter and video game sounds floated in from downstairs. My gaze fell to her mouth, and she caught her bottom lip between her teeth, her expression clouding over. She was nervous, but it was hard to tell whether it was in a good, excited way or a bad, anxious way.

"James." I took a step forward, cupping her chin with my hand. Her skin was soft and smooth beneath my fingers, which were callused from my gloves and time in the gym.

She looked up at me through impossibly dark lashes, eyes wide. Her breath was quiet and shallow, like she was nervous or aroused, maybe both. "Yeah?"

"We don't have to do anything tonight if you're not ready."

I wanted her so bad it hurt—literally—but more importantly, I wanted it to be right. Until then, I was going to compile a very long, very detailed list of all the things I would do to her in the future.

Plus, I had a hunch I could corrupt her a little if I was patient, and that would be well worth the wait.

"I know," she said softly, looping her arms around my neck. "But what if I want to?"

All the blood left my brain. That was it. I was done.

I sucked my bottom lip, trying to get my head straight. I'd gone into this thinking we would just sleep tonight, that maybe it was for the best, because I didn't want her to freak out after if we did fool around.

But no guy in his right mind could look at her and say no. And I wasn't in my right mind at the best of times, let alone when I was around her.

My voice turned hoarse. "You might have to spell things out for me. I don't want to push you."

"Okay," she said breathily. Her eyes were smoky, eyelids heavy. "Can we just kiss? Make out a little?"

"Of course," I murmured, wrapping my other arm around her back.

Her expression turned serious, and she looked up at me, hesitating. "No sex."

"You're in charge here. I would never pressure you."

Her eyelids fluttered shut as I slid my hand down to her neck and covered her mouth with mine. She let out a little sigh, parting her lips and granting me access. My tongue pushed inside her mouth, claiming, and she opened wider in response. She tasted better than I remembered, every single time.

Mouth still locked on hers, I took a few steps back, walking her over to the bed. Grabbing the backs of her thighs, I pulled her down with me so she was sitting in my lap, straddling me. Her legs spanned my hips, hair tumbling all over the place in a curtain.

Having her on top meant she would hopefully feel more in control. But the view was phenomenal too.

Bailey pulled back, gold-flecked eyes meeting mine. They were endless, captivating.

She let out a little gasp as I lifted my hips slightly, moving against her. Dipping closer, she found my lips again, her confidence growing. In response, I gripped her calves, squeezing, my hands sliding up to her thighs. The mental to-do list I'd created was multiplying by the minute, like kissing every inch of her body. At this point, I could fill an encyclopedia with ideas.

She tangled her hands in my hair, tugging, and I drew in a shuddering breath, grasping her tighter. Sliding under her shirt, I clasped her smooth, bare skin and moved my hands up her ribcage, stopping just below her breasts.

She kissed me again, deeper this time, and arched her back, grinding against me. It was delicious torture. Neither of us was wearing much, just two thin pairs of shorts, which meant she could feel exactly how much I wanted her in the moment. I wanted to touch her, to slip my hand beneath her waistband and find out if she was as wet as I suspected, but I wouldn't push it.

Usually, making out was a means to an end for me. But doing nothing but kissing her was fan-fucking-tastic. Maybe I was going soft. Except I was hard as hell and about to end up with a major case of blue balls.

Still worth it.

Bailey broke our kiss, inhaling sharply. "Wait." Her cheeks were flushed pink, breath heavy.

"You okay?"

"More than okay." She gave me a shy smile. "But I don't want us to get carried away."

I nodded. I couldn't disagree with that. If she wanted me right now, it would be almost impossible to say no.

"It's pretty late, anyway."

"Yeah." Bailey sighed and rested her head on my shoulder. Her breath was warm against my neck, which only made me harder. "I was up early."

"Me too," I said, rubbing her back. "Breakfast skate." On a *weekend*. Like I said, Coach Miller loved to fuck with me.

She crawled off me and onto the bed, getting under the covers on the far side. I slid in beside her and rearranged the pillows.

"Come here." I wrapped my arm around her, pulling her closer.

She yawned and snuggled in against me. She radiated warmth, along with the scents of her perfume and shampoo, which together created something so delicious that I wanted to bury my face in her neck and inhale her all night long.

Pretty sure I would have felt trapped with anyone else draped around me like this. I couldn't say for sure, though, since I'd never been a cuddler. I wasn't a touchy-feely person, aside from the usual "touch-me, feel-you" one-night stand scenario.

But with Bailey, it was perfect.

She lay on my chest while I stroked her long, silky hair, having a mini-panic attack. Because I was getting exactly what I wanted, even though I definitely didn't deserve it.

I woke up to find Bailey sitting in my desk chair, clutching a mug and absorbed in what she was looking at on her phone. Her caramel hair was piled in a messy bun, and she'd cinched the drawstrings on a pair of my gray sweats tight and rolled the waistband down. She looked fucking adorable.

"What time is it?" I asked, propping myself up on one elbow. My desk lamp was on, and it was still dark outside.

She peeked up at me. "Around five thirty." She took a sip from the white mug she was holding. "I helped myself to the Keurig downstairs."

"Oh my god, James. It's the middle of the night. What are you doing up?"

"Reading." She shrugged. "I couldn't sleep."

My chest clenched, growing tighter until it was hard to breathe. I rolled out of bed and shuffled to the bathroom to brush my teeth. Our eyes met as I swung the bathroom door back open and paused in the doorway.

"Do you have anywhere to be this morning?"

Bailey shook her head. "Not until after lunch."

I moved close and touched her shoulder, stroking with my thumb. "Why don't you try to get back to sleep? If I get a few more hours, I'll be much more functional."

Her expression was guarded, her eyes wary in a way I couldn't interpret. I got back under the covers as she bit her bottom lip, assessing me. My breath stilled, the tension in my body growing with every second that passed. Somewhere along the line, something had gone wrong.

"Okay." Setting her coffee on the desk, she stood. Then she padded over to the other side of the bed and slid in beside me. The blankets rustled as she adjusted the pillows and pulled the covers up over her chest until only her head poked out. "I was kind of cold anyway."

"You could take a hoodie. They're hanging in the walk-in closet." James in my hoodie would probably be the only thing cuter than her in one of my shirts.

"Noted," she said. "Next time."

Next time. I guess that was a positive sign. But something was clearly wrong.

I shifted to face her. She turned her head my way, full lips parted slightly and breath soft. Her face was so fucking perfect that it almost killed me.

"What's going on?" I asked. "Why can't you sleep?"

"Just couldn't stop thinking. Sometimes I wake up early when my brain is working overtime." She rolled to her side, big hazel eyes locking on mine. "Why were you so upset about that text Luke sent to everyone?"

Couldn't even attempt to dodge that question or deflect with humor, because I hadn't just been upset. I had been livid. Still was. I wanted to shove that phone down his throat.

"Was it because you thought it might be true?" Her forehead crinkled. "Did you think I would do something like that?"

"No, not at all." I fumbled inwardly, trying to find a non-pathetic way to phrase it. "I know you can handle yourself, but it triggered something protective in me. You're one of my favorite people."

Her lips curved into a small smile, her gaze softening. "Who are your other favorite people?"

"It's mostly you, I guess. Not a big fan of humankind in general." Maybe this was a little crazy, given the length of time we had been hanging out, but it was the truth.

"Ah," she said. "Well, now you're stuck with me."

"Thank Gretzky for that."

We fell silent for a moment, considering one another. Lying with her like this felt more intimate than anything I'd ever experienced. It made my heart ache a little, and I didn't even know why.

"One more question." Bailey looked away. She sucked in a breath and paused, the moment heavy, and then the words came out in a rush of air as she glanced back up at me. "Have you been with anyone since we started hanging out?"

There was another tug in my chest, because suddenly I knew this was what had kept her awake.

"I mean…" She winced. "I know it's not my bus—"

"No," I said. "It's okay. But the answer is no, I haven't."

She eyed me warily, which kind of hurt. But I understood. I knew my reputation preceded me.

"Look," I said, touching her cheek. "In the interest of total transparency, I haven't been with anyone whatsoever since you and I started talking."

Her brow creased. "Would you tell me if you had?"

The puzzle pieces continued to snap into place. She'd told me about Morrison and all of his shady-ass behavior the night we met. Disappearing for days, calls and texts from other girls late at night, flirting right in front of her face. Hockey knows I was no saint, but he was next-level trash for treating Bailey the way he had.

It stung a little to know she thought I would do those things to her. But I guess getting past that would take time.

"Have you ever known me to be anything other than uncomfortably honest?"

She gave me a half-hearted smirk. "Good point."

"I'll always give you the truth, even if you might not want to hear it." I covered her hand with mine, squeezing, and laced my fingers in hers.

Her eyes dropped to my hand, then back up to my face. She bit back a smile, letting out a little huff of breath. "Okay."

We fell quiet for a moment, and she scooted closer, nestling against my chest. I rested my cheek against her hair, inhaling the clean scent of her shampoo. She sighed as I ran my fingers up and down her arm, back and forth.

"I don't want anyone else, James."

"You don't?"

"Not even a little," I said, kissing the top of her head.

"Think you'll be able to sleep now?"

"Yeah," she said. "Think so."

CHAPTER 22

PEOPLE YOU KNOW

CHASE

AFTER DROPPING Bailey off and giving her a not-so-brief goodbye kiss on the front step, I was flying way too high to return home and face the guys. I was so hopped up on hormones that I wasn't sure I could carry on a coherent conversation. Hell, even driving was a little dicey.

Instead, I took a detour and grabbed a gigantic drive-through coffee before running a bunch of errands I had been putting off. With the good mood I was in, everything seemed a lot more tolerable, even the boring-ass drugstore. While out and about, I fought the constant urge to text James. I didn't want to come off as clingy.

I was probably overthinking that one, but this was uncharted territory for me. I had no idea what I was doing. At all.

Then I hit my room for some earnest study time before our afternoon practice. So far, my increased effort had paid off—and admittedly, it was a lot less stressful living without an ax hanging over my head.

An hour into *Economics of Sport*, a loud bang at my door broke my focus.

"You ready?" Dallas bellowed. "Your turn to drive."

We piled into my truck, and I turned on the ignition. I drew in a deep breath, bracing myself. The inevitable gears were coming any minute now, and I had already made peace with it. Bring on the teasing.

Dallas leaned forward, trying to catch my eye. "So, Bailey spent the night."

I nodded. "Sure did."

"You're grinning like a lunatic," Ty said from the back seat. "Just FYI."

I stole a glance in the rear-view mirror. He was right.

"Can't a man be happy?" I said, turning away to shoulder-check and easing out of the passing spot. "Damn, guys."

He snorted. "Did you even get laid?"

"Not that it's your business, but nope." If I was this loopy now, I was going to be straight-up cracked out after that happened.

It was going to be great.

Fuck, now I was thinking about sex with James at the most inopportune time.

Dallas leveled his icy-blue stare my way, snapping me back to reality. "I can't believe you have a girlfriend. That's wild."

"I don't know if she's my girlfriend."

But somehow, I felt like a gigantic asshole saying that. It wasn't like that would be a bad thing.

Oh, shit.

I really was in deep.

"Dude," he said, laughing. "She definitely is."

"Like you're one to talk." I waved a hand in his direction. "You and Shiv have been dancing around that issue for way longer."

"I don't know." Dallas shrugged, leaning back in the black leather passenger seat. He quieted, looking stung by my remark. "That's on Shiv, man."

"Really?" Ty and I said in unison.

"Yeah." He frowned and glanced down at his phone, his jaw tight. "We've talked about it, but she didn't want to slap a label on it. Ball's in her court on that one."

Weird. The number of chicks who would love to tie Dallas Ward down—both figuratively and literally—could line a city block. What was the holdup?

Then I wondered whether Bailey felt the same way as Shiv. Did she want to put a label on it? *Should* we put a label on it?

BAILEY

With everything that had happened with Chase, I'd barely thought about my roommate situation. Blessedly, between part-time jobs, group projects, and other commitments between the three of us, I hadn't seen them in days.

I was reminded, rather rudely, when I came downstairs Monday morning and instantly encountered Amelia, who was seated at the round kitchen table, eating a bowl of oatmeal. My stomach sank, my appetite for breakfast vanishing. But my need for caffeine was urgent, so I'd have to deal with it. And at least it wasn't Jill.

Strolling into the kitchen, I gave her a limp wave.

"Hey." Amelia's lips curved into a bland smile. "I feel like I've barely seen you lately." Her honey-brown eyes scanned me methodically, probing. She assessed me like an enemy spy, results to be reported back to Commander Luke.

"Yeah," I said. "Just been really busy with class and such."

"Where were you the other night?" she asked casually. "You didn't come home." She was trying to sound friendly, but beneath the pleasant veneer, there was an undertone of nosiness.

"Where do you think?" I grinned, turning to the cupboard to retrieve a mug. Thinking about the goodbye kiss yesterday made me feel warm and tingly…Not to mention all the kissing that came before.

Who knew kissing could be like that? I had been seriously ripped off until now.

Amelia's mask slipped, and she gaped at me, wide-eyed. "Seriously?"

"Sure was," I said. "It was great. He's great."

"So you guys are actually…"

I poured the coffee and blew on it. "Yup."

"Carter," she said, dumbstruck. "Chase Carter."

"What about him?" I clutched the mug, replicating her bland smile from earlier. She shook her head a little but didn't reply.

"Anyway, what did you get up to all weekend?" I asked.

Amelia hesitated, spoonful of oatmeal halfway to her mouth. She looked down at the white ceramic bowl, avoiding my gaze.

"Not much on Friday. We went over to…uh, Sophie's with everyone on Saturday."

"Cool." I meant it. I literally did not care. "Now, if you'll excuse me, I have to get ready for class."

When I got out of the shower, I found a text from Chase waiting for me, and my mood instantly lifted.

Chase: You know what you need?

Bailey: I'm afraid to ask.

Chase: A makeup birthday. Like a do-over.

Bailey: If only.

Chase: Oh, it's happening. Let's do something this week. Dinner. Anything you want.

Bailey: But it's not your fault Luke is an ass.

Chase: It's not yours, either.

Chase: Maybe I want an excuse to take you out before I'm away for hockey all weekend.

Bailey: Sure, I'd love to.

Chase: Great. I'll even throw in an autographed picture of me as a belated birthday gift.

Bailey: I'm a lucky girl.

Chase: I know, right?

After Amelia's weird half-interrogation Monday morning, I knew my living situation needed to change, and I couldn't wait until next year to live with Noelle and Zara.

After all, how could I live somewhere Chase wasn't even welcome? Heck, I didn't feel welcome myself.

Random roommates were out of the question, so I combed the rental ads. A one-bedroom was out of my budget, but maybe I could swing a studio—or maybe I was being delusional, based on the prices I was seeing. Still, there had to be a way. Even if it wasn't the nicest place, at least it would be mine.

Late Monday evening, I dropped the bomb on Jillian and Amelia while they were watching TV. They were curled up together on the big couch, sharing snacks and utterly engrossed in a show they were bingeing on Netflix.

I couldn't tiptoe around it any longer. The elephant in the room was taking up more space by the day.

Heart pounding, I lingered in the living room doorway. There was a tiny pang in my gut. A month or two ago, I would have been in there hanging out with them. Now I could barely bring myself to enter the room.

When they didn't immediately notice my presence, I rapped on the doorframe to get their attention and drew in a deep breath.

I hated confrontation. Especially when it was two on one.

"Hey," Amelia said. "What's up?"

I cleared my throat. "Um, so…I'm thinking of breaking the lease," I said. "Actually, no. I'm planning to. In the near future."

They both turned and stared at me like I'd suggested we burn the place down.

Amelia grabbed the remote and turned the TV volume down. "Where are you going?"

"I don't know yet." Anywhere but here.

Jillian set down her bowl of chips, curling her lip into a snarl. "Then why are you moving out?"

Gee, I can't imagine why.

"Let's be honest," I said, folding my arms. "This isn't working out for any of us anymore. I don't even feel comfortable having Chase over here, and that's not fair to either one of us."

"Well, you can," Amelia snapped. "No one is stopping you."

"So he can get into it with Paul and Luke? Hard pass. And speaking of Luke, he's here too often for my liking."

Jillian scoffed. "He was here once."

"Exactly. One time too many, as far as I'm concerned."

"But he's still our friend, B." Amelia raised her eyebrows, like she'd dropped some kind of truth bomb.

"Clearly," I said. "That's why I'm giving you notice now so you can find another roommate."

"And what if we can't?" Jillian asked.

"That sounds a lot like a you problem."

"You signed the lease too," Amelia said. "That means you're still on the hook legally, even if you move out."

"Then I guess you'll have to sue me." I shrugged. "Literally."

And good luck with that because I had no money to my name. I lived on scholarships and student aid. But they could try. I would rather eat money I didn't have than deal with them any longer.

Jill furrowed her brow, blinking at me like I was some kind of hallucination.

"This is so irresponsible. I guess I shouldn't be surprised, based on who you're dating."

"Excuse me?" I shot her a scorching glare. "Don't you *even*."

Talk about glass houses. It would take a tiny pebble to shatter hers to pieces.

She recoiled, probably because I'd never spoken to either of them like that. I wasn't sure I'd ever used a tone that sharp before, maybe not even with Luke. But I was out of patience—especially with her.

"Anyway, just a heads-up," I said, turning to leave.

"We can't find someone in the middle of the semester like this," Amelia called.

I looked back over my shoulder, giving them a knowing look.

"Oh, I don't know, guys. Maybe you could ask my brother. He's here a lot, isn't he?"

They both stared at me, dumbfounded, but didn't respond. I started for the stairs with a heavy heart. Beneath my anger toward them was no small amount of sadness. As crappy as they'd been lately, losing two friends—or two people I'd thought were my friends—still hurt.

CHAPTER 23
NOT BROKEN
CHASE

BAILEY CURLED up against my chest as we lay in my bed, watching an NHL game. We chatted idly, only half following the game as neither of us was particularly invested in the teams playing. As far as a weekday evening went, it was pretty perfect. Except for one thing: the conversation we needed to have.

The sure to be difficult, guaranteed to be uncomfortable, hopefully not disastrous conversation.

Maybe it was too soon to talk about this, but it would weigh on my conscience until we did. And I refused to do it the night we went out for dinner, potentially fucking up her birthday twice in one year.

The whole situation made me furious. I literally treated one-night stands and casual hookups better than Morrison had treated his own girlfriend. It was wrong on every level.

Here goes nothing.

BAILEY

Chase picked up the remote, turning down the volume on the TV. "Hey, James?" He shifted to look at me and studied my face, voice low. "How much do you remember from our walk from XS to my place?"

"Not a lot," I said, shaking my head. "I remember getting sick. Vaguely. That's about it. Why?"

His brows knit together. "Because you told me something that night, and I don't think you remember."

Alarms went off in my head, complete with blaring sirens and flashing red lights. I was certain the gist of this conversation was: he didn't like me anymore because of it, and now he was ready to end things between us. Already.

Cue maximum panic mode.

I scrambled to sit upright. "You're bringing this up *now*? That was ages ago."

"I held off because it was something personal," he said. "I didn't want you to think I was teasing you or being a dick. But with the way things have changed between us, it feels wrong for me to know this when you don't know that I know."

My breath snagged, heart pole-vaulting into my throat.

No.

I didn't. I couldn't have. I wouldn't have.

"What did I say to you?" I whispered, panic winding up my neck like a vise. "Tell me, please."

"You told me that Morrison sucked in bed." Chase paused, uncharacteristically hesitant. Time slowed as I held my breath, waiting for him to continue. "Specifically, that he didn't go down, and that you faked it with him on the regular."

Just like that, my dignity evaporated into thin air. Not even my closest friends knew that second one, and I'd told Chase the night I met him? Good lord. And it was infinitely more humiliating given how much more experienced he was than me.

"Okay." I wriggled out of his embrace, slid out of bed, and stood up. "If you need me, I'll be at home dying of embarrassment. Tell my parents to get a nice headstone. Gray marble, something like that."

"Wait. Can we talk about this, please?" He reached over and gently grabbed my hand.

Humiliation simmered in my gut, caustic and searing, threatening to boil over. I spun around to face him, cheeks scorching. "Why do you even like me if you know this?"

"What?" Hurt flashed across his face, and his lips tugged into a frown. "I like you for a million reasons, and none of them have to do with sex."

"That's a relief," I said, "because I seem to be defective in that department."

Chase tugged my hand, pulling me to sit beside him. He rubbed my skin with his thumb, making slow, smooth strokes. "You're not defective."

"Sure feels like it." My voice cracked, and I drew in a jagged breath, trying to quell the sob lurking in my throat. The only thing more embarrassing than this would be ugly crying in front of him.

"Oh man." He sighed, dropping his head to his hands. Seconds ticked by as his back moved up and down with long, smooth inhalations and exhalations. His hands fell to his sides as he lifted his chin. "I'm an asshole. I didn't mean to upset you. I've been thinking about how to talk to you about this for a while now because I didn't want to fuck it up."

"You didn't," I said, fighting back a wave of tears. "It's fine."

Somehow, I felt bad that he felt bad. Which only compounded my overall distress. A complicated mix of shame, sadness, regret, and fear swirled within me.

And maybe, just maybe, a tiny bit of relief.

"James." Chase angled himself to face me. He took my hands in his, which were warm, slightly callused, and comforting. "I'm not judging you. I promise."

I looked at our hands, avoiding his eyes. "You should be."

"Trust me, you're not the one I'm judging in this situation."

"I honestly want to die right now," I said, shaking my head as I stared at the textured gray comforter. "I can't overstate that enough. No one knows that. I can't believe I told you."

"No, I'm glad you did. I don't want you to feel like you need to fake anything with me." He leaned closer, brushing a stray piece of hair out of my face. "If something I'm doing isn't working, I'd rather know. That's why I wanted to talk about this."

"To talk about how I'm broken, you mean?"

"You're not broken," he said softly. "Lots of girls can't come from penetration alone. It's pretty common. Normal."

In theory, I knew this. The internet and women's magazines said as much. But it didn't make me feel less inadequate, like I was faulty—or like certain parts of me were, at least.

Chase scanned my face, dark eyes patient as he waited for a response.

I didn't know what to say, so I shrugged. "Okay."

"It could be what the other person was doing." He raised his eyebrows, speaking carefully. "Or not doing…Or not doing properly."

"I don't know." As much as I liked the idea of throwing Luke under the bus, I was pretty sure there was something wrong with me. I drew in a breath and held it until my lungs felt like they were going to explode. "It's just really hard to get me off."

"I'm up for the challenge." He grinned. "Literally."

A sad half laugh escaped from the back of my throat. He was too smooth for my own good. Even when I felt like hiding under a rock permanently.

"I mean, I can…" I fumbled, searching my brain for a way to explain without delving into uncomfortable details. "I'm sorry. This is hard to talk about without bringing Luke into it." Luke would sulk afterward if I didn't have an orgasm—as if that was going to somehow help it along. Though the fact that I faked it so often had some disturbing implications. Either Luke never noticed or, worse still, he knew and didn't care.

"It's okay," Chase said. "You can talk about him."

"He would complain because only certain positions would do it for me, or I took too long. Sometimes it was easier to let him think I had." And now I'd shared the most intimate details of my former relationship with Chase, things even Zara and Noelle weren't privy to. Great.

"He did *what*?" His brows snapped together. "What kind of

sorry excuse for an athlete is he? Fucking dick." His jaw ticked, and he exhaled heavily, shaking his head. "Sorry. It just pisses me off to know you were treated like that."

"I don't know," I said. "I think it's a me problem." It had to be when it was that elusive and difficult to reach. There were maybe two things that worked—some of the time—and that was it. Even then, it was about as reliable as a rain dance.

"Not even a little." He smoothed my hair away from my face.

I sucked in a shaky breath. "Agree to disagree."

"Not on this one. Morrison is a fucking idiot. Full stop. It's the eleventh commandment."

This time, I laughed for real. He leaned in, brushing his lips against mine. The tension in my body loosened as I returned the kiss, lips opening against his. He pushed inside my mouth, but it was tender, gentle. As we pulled apart, he wrapped his hands around my waist, pulling me closer to him.

"You're not a means to an end, James."

The urge to cry returned, and I swallowed hard, nodding wordlessly.

Chase tipped forward, his lips grazing along the curve of my neck, which was a welcome distraction.

"Plus, the idea of getting you off is so fucking hot," he murmured.

"Really?" It was hard to wrap my mind around that. Sex had always seemed like it was more about pleasing the guy.

"Hell yeah." His gaze met mine, and he bit his bottom lip, nodding. "Do you know how many times I've thought about that?"

"No idea."

"A lot." Chase's eyes danced.

"Ah, so you do have a dirty mind."

"Dirty for you."

I laughed and shook my head.

He picked me up and moved both of us back until we were propped against the headboard . "Can we talk about this a little more? Or are you too uncomfortable?"

"Yes and yes." I grimaced. "I'll try."

"Just to clarify," he said, "you have had an orgasm before. So you can."

"Right. It's really hit or miss. Heavy on the miss." My cheeks flared with heat, and I worked overtime to maintain eye contact with him.

"Then it's a matter of finding what works. Some of that is trial and error. But if you fake it, I won't know what works."

Fair point. But there had been so much pressure to live up to some imaginary standard where orgasms came freely and easily during sex no matter what the position, speed, or angle. In reality, it was like trying to spot a freaking unicorn that only appeared in the woods twice a year between 8:00 and 8:05 p.m. when the moon was full. Theoretically possible, but incredibly rare.

"I guess that makes sense."

"Do you know what works? Like, is it hit or miss even when you're alone?" he asked carefully.

Oh my god. Speaking of wanting to die. Another swell of humiliation crashed over me, and I looked away, gaze dropping to the comforter again. "We are not talking about that."

"Okay," he said. "We don't have to." He fell quiet, stroking my hair. But we'd gone this far, so I guess nothing was too personal anymore. What did I have to lose?

I sighed. "Yes, even alone."

"Hmm," he hummed, rumbling low in his chest. "Have you tried a vibrator?"

"What?" I squeaked, eyes snapping back up to his.

"Like a sex toy," he said. "It might help."

"During sex or alone?" I cringed. Surely, I had used up all nine of my lives by now. It would be a great time for a sinkhole to open and swallow me up.

He shrugged. "Either."

Luke's ego—and male parts—would have deflated faster than a slapshot if I had suggested using a vibrator. Hell, he would have freaked out if I'd even *owned* a sex toy, which was one reason I didn't. The other being that I was kind of intimidated by the idea.

"Don't most guys have a problem with that?"

"No," he said, perfectly straight-faced. "Why would they?"

Sometimes Chase forgot that not everyone had the titanium self-assuredness he had been blessed with. Particularly when it came to their manhood. But he had BDE for a reason. Nothing fazed him. Case in point, this entire discussion.

"I don't know." I chewed my bottom lip. "I guess I thought it might make them feel threatened."

"Baby, I can do all kinds of things to you that a little toy can't." He gave me a mischievous smile that, despite the situation, had its intended effect. Something inside me really, really wanted to find out what those things were.

"I bet," I said, suddenly a little breathless.

"But in this case, it might help you get over the hump, so to speak. Especially alone."

"Hump? That was the worst pun ever." I groaned, flopping back onto the bed and staring up at the ceiling.

"I know, right?" Chase leaned on his elbow beside me. He traced a finger along my ribcage, down to my hip. "Look, it's just a theory. But being more comfortable with your body alone might help you be more comfortable with your body with me. Does that track? You can tell me if you think I'm wrong."

"No." I sighed. "It does."

"You still haven't answered my other question." He ducked his head, catching my eye. "Have you?"

I covered my face with my hands. "What do you think?"

"Oh, I think we should go shopping." He grinned.

"Shopping?"

"Yeah," he said. "You know, pick up a little something for you."

"I don't know." I crinkled my nose. "The idea of a sex toy seems so freaky."

"It's okay to be a little freaky. You can be freaky with me."

I pressed my lips into a line for a minute, considering. "Fine. I'll be open-minded."

"Good," he said, holding eye contact. "And as far as you and I go, I'm in this for you. I want to make you feel good. Remember that, okay? You can trust me."

"I know." Somehow, I did.

CHAPTER 24
CANDY STORE
CHASE

THE WEEK DRAGGED on in a monotonous cycle of school, practice, and dryland until it was time for Bailey's birthday dinner. Ever since our talk, we were closer than ever, but sometimes I could still sense her holding back. Even so, I'd win her trust or die trying.

After suffering through a morning of classes, doing my best to focus and failing, I bolted off campus and headed over to Ice Life to have James's skates sharpened. Could have done it at the rink during practice, but I wanted the excuse to window shop for shit while I waited.

Unfortunately, they were having some epic one-day sale I hadn't been aware of, and the place was packed. Normally, I would have bailed, but I had a few hours to kill, and I wanted to check out a bunch of newly released equipment, so I decided to stay and deal with the crowds. Plus, I was more than a little distracted thinking about seeing Bailey later. Completing schoolwork or doing anything else remotely productive wasn't an option.

I navigated through the throngs of shoppers over to the skate-sharpening counter in the rear corner. There was usually no wait, but today the line was at least a dozen people deep.

When I joined the lineup, Morrison suddenly appeared from out of nowhere like a preppy little demon summoned from the depths of hell. Pale blue polo, slicked-back blond hair, and an overwhelming aura of entitlement. That he'd been handed everything his entire life was written all over his cocky face.

What were the fucking odds?

I balled my hands into fists, squeezing until my knuckles turned white; I wished they were around his neck. I'd always hated the guy, but it was next-level at this point.

Pulling out my phone, I sent Dallas a quick text about the practice plan for later. Then I popped a piece of extreme mint gum, taking my hostility out on it. And I checked our fantasy hockey results to find that James was right about taking the trade. After last night's games, I was in second place overall, while Dallas had fallen to fourth. Nice.

Despite my blatant attempt to ignore him, Morrison slithered my way, coming to hover close enough that I was engulfed in a cloud of his too-strong, obnoxious cologne. His presence was irritating on every level.

He nodded at the skates in my hand. "Are those Bailey's?"

The fuck?

"Anyone ever tell you that you're a creep?" I asked.

Morrison squinted his watery blue eyes, glaring at me. Or attempting to, anyway. He didn't have enough spine to lend the weak glare any credibility.

"Anyone ever tell you that you're a dick?" he countered.

I grinned. "All the time, man."

A compliment, really, considering the source.

The winding line moved forward, turning right, which created a buffer of people between us. No longer able to needle me, Morrison lost interest and wandered off.

Once I dropped Bailey's skates off at the counter, I browsed the store, making a conscious effort to avoid him—not because I was scared of him, but because I was scared of what I might *do* to him.

He talked a lot of shit for someone who couldn't back it up. I should pummel him for the text message thing alone. But I couldn't afford to lay him out off the ice. Good thing we were playing them again soon.

As I rounded a corner near the sticks and tape, I ran into

Morrison again, standing near the CCM display. Like the gods wanted me to beat his ass. The fates were practically begging me to do it.

Of course, leaving the area because of him wasn't an option, so I carried on browsing the shelves like he wasn't there.

He glanced over at me, setting down the stick he was holding. "Enjoy it while it lasts, Carter." His voice oozed with syrupy smugness. "We both know you're a rebound."

Ah, fuck it. We were tucked away in an aisle at the back. No one around to see. Probably no cameras, either.

I pivoted to face him, and his expression instantly shifted from cocky to apprehensive. His eyes darted around, confirming that we were very much alone. I prowled in his direction, taking my sweet-ass time closing the distance between us. Daring him to run away and relishing how his discomfort visibly climbed with every step I took.

There were so many things I knew, so many things I wanted to say. But I wouldn't sell out James. He wasn't worth it.

Intentionally invading his space, I came to a stop a little too close. He stiffened and shuffled back, flinching slightly as he hit the metal shelving behind him. We stood nearly nose to nose, although nose to forehead was a more accurate description.

"You're real mad that she moved on, huh?"

His jaw clenched, but he didn't respond. Of course not, now that we were alone and within swinging range.

"Got anything else to say?" I asked.

A beat passed. I raised my eyebrows. He glared at me, still silent.

"Yeah," I said evenly. "That's what I thought."

My phone beeped with a text message. Her skates were probably done.

I nodded at him. "Later, fuckface."

After narrowly refraining from committing a felony, I channeled all my leftover aggression into our afternoon practice and crushed it. It was a great way to forget about that asshat and head into an evening with James. My mood was sky high. Until I had to deal with her roommate.

Amelia answered the front door, giving me a death stare. She paused, uttering a massive sigh like my very existence was an imposition. Right back atcha, Amelia.

"I guess I'll go get her." She flipped her hair and flounced away, leaving the door hanging wide open without inviting me in. I could see why Amelia got along with Paul so well, considering how friendly and charming they both were.

I stepped inside the entryway, taking her absence as an open invitation to do so. A minute later, Bailey came down the stairs, eyes brightening when they landed on me. Her dark blond hair was loose around her shoulders, and she looked hot as fuck in a pair of black jeans that showed off her legs, paired with a pink sweater that was just tight enough to keep drawing my eyes to her chest.

I was trying to behave, but damn, it was hard—literally—when I was around her.

Following a lengthy hello kiss and another in front of my truck for good measure, we finally made our way into the vehicle. I waited, letting the truck idle as Bailey buckled her seat belt. Turning to me, she tucked her hair behind her ear and batted her eyelashes.

"Where's my autographed picture, Carter?"

"My bad." I grinned. "I guess we'll have to hold a private photoshoot later."

Bailey reached over to my side of the truck, poking me in the bicep. "You're going to offer up things and not deliver them?"

I dropped my voice, giving her a look. "Oh, I can deliver."

Her eyes widened slightly, pink lips curving into what could only be described as a flustered smile.

It was cute as hell.

She shifted her weight, biting her bottom lip. "I guess we'll see."

"Guess so."

Hopefully tonight. I mean, I could be patient. Would be patient. But I could still hope, right?

———

Bailey had told me about her birthday debacle in great detail, including the stupid stuffy French restaurant. I hadn't known her long, but even I knew it was the opposite of the type of restaurant she would enjoy. So I intentionally kept it low-key when it came to choosing a place and picked a little Italian restaurant near campus. It had brick walls, fireplaces burning in the corners, and candles on the tables, but it wasn't fancy or uptight by any measure.

"This is so cute," Bailey said as the hostess ushered us to our table.

"Yeah," I said. "Kind of has that whole homey thing going on. Great pasta too."

After we'd ordered appetizers and entrees, she left the table to use the bathroom, and I quickly checked my messages. Dallas had texted me several times to let me know Shiv was now homeless and would be staying with us for a while. I wrote him back, then set down my phone as Bailey returned to the table.

"Hey, I have some good news."

She sank into her seat, placing her napkin on her lap and looking at me questioningly. "What's that?"

"Shiv's place burned down," I said.

"Um." Bailey did a double-take, blinking several times. "*What*?"

"Wait." I held up my hand and shook my head. My brain wasn't firing on all cylinders around her. Although I wasn't entirely sure why. I didn't even get nervous before games—pumped, yes, but not nervous. I could count the number of times in recent history that I'd been nervous on one hand, and they were all around Bailey.

That's not to say it was a bad type of nervous. It was more like a massively heightened state of awareness with a dash of idiotic happiness thrown in. And maybe a pinch of plain stupidity, as evidenced by what I'd just said.

Sometimes, every shred of my game vanished around her.

"I mean, that isn't the good part." I grimaced. "Obviously. And it didn't actually burn down. There was a kitchen fire in another unit, and the smoke damage to her side of the building is so extensive that she has to move out. No one was hurt or anything."

"Phew," Bailey said, taking a sip of ice water.

"It happened this morning, I guess, so she's crashing with us for a few days. Ward said she's been searching for rentals all day and having an impossible time finding a studio or one-bedroom."

"Yeah, I couldn't find much, either. They were either really gross or incredibly expensive." She made a face. "You wouldn't believe the going rates."

"Ward also mentioned that she was thinking about trying to get a roommate because it's cheaper to split a two-bedroom. That was the good news part. I mean, you do need a place to live…" I trailed off. "Maybe it's meant to be."

While it would be convenient for me if Bailey was closer to my friends, the truth was that I mostly wanted her out of her current living situation. Between Morrison showing up and the messed up secret affair between Derek and her roommate, it was toxic as hell. It left me low-key worried about her whenever she was at home.

And if Morrison showed up in her living room one more time, I might not avoid that felony again.

Bailey hummed thoughtfully. "But she probably wants to live near Boyd, right? And I need to be close to Callingwood because I don't have a car."

"Maybe you could find something halfway. Near the train line." I shrugged. "A short commute might be worth it if you're happier."

"True."

"It's just a thought. Would you consider it?"

"I totally would," she said, pressing her lips together. "But I don't know if she would. Can you, like…float it by Dallas to have him float it by her?"

"You're adorable."

"What?" Bailey shrugged, her cheeks turning pink. "I don't

want to make it awkward. We've only met twice. Maybe she thinks I'm a weirdo."

"I doubt that very much, James." I squeezed her hand over the table. "But I'll talk to him."

Dinner went longer than I had anticipated, probably because we hadn't run out of things to say. Two hours later, we lingered over dessert, slowly finishing a slice of raspberry cheesecake and a piece of tiramisu we'd shared.

I watched Bailey take the last bite of tiramisu, trying to keep my mind from thinking about all the dirty things I wanted to do with her mouth.

"I like that you eat," I said. It sort of slipped out, like my internal narrative tended to. She was super tolerant of it, all things considered. Because sometimes it was random as fuck. Like right now.

"Huh?" She paused, fork hovering in midair.

"So many girls I know never seem to eat." I shrugged, scooping up the second-to-last bite of cheesecake. "Then it makes me feel bad for eating in front of them. Like, I'm a large human being. I train every day. I need a ton of calories. It's awkward to be the only one eating all the time, you know?"

Bailey grinned. "If you think that's impressive, you should see me breathe. I'm world class."

I laughed, then I caught myself staring at her for a beat longer than was probably normal. Couldn't help it.

"What?" She leaned closer, round eyes scanning my face in the candlelight.

"Nothing," I said. "All good."

Was this what falling for someone felt like? It was a trip.

Once I took care of the bill, it was time for the grand finale: skating at Northview Arena. The prospect of skating and James together had me legit feeling like a kid in a candy store.

I pulled into the deserted parking lot, illuminated by pale yellow streetlamps. Grabbing a spot at the front near the doors, I eased in and killed the ignition.

"Wait." Bailey tilted her head, studying me. "We're skating at your rink?"

"Yup."

Her hazel eyes narrowed suspiciously, then widened suddenly, and she let out a little gasp. "Are we breaking in?"

I unbuckled my seat belt and reached for the bag with our skates. "Is it breaking in if you have the code?"

"Well, are we allowed to be here?"

"Define allowed," I said, hoisting the black duffel onto the middle console. "I mean, it's a free country. We have the constitutional right to freedom of movement."

"Carter…" She made a little *eek* face.

"We're not *not* allowed." I shrugged. "No one's booked the ice. Plus, I'm on Coach Miller's good side these days, so we should be okay."

Bailey groaned. "So we're definitely breaking in."

She was such a rule-follower. Adorable.

"Public skate just ended. We have plausible deniability if we get caught, like maybe we were confused and didn't know it was over." I smiled innocently.

"You get out of a lot of trouble with that smile, don't you?"

"Sure do," I said, leaning over to kiss her on the cheek. Her skin was so soft, and she smelled so good…Bad idea. Now I wanted to kiss her on the mouth, and if I did that, we'd probably never make it out of the truck.

I really needed to get it together.

"Come on," I said. "They don't flood the rink for another two hours."

"You're sure?"

"Don't worry. I've done it dozens of times before."

She shot me a wary look, like I'd brought millions of girls here. The truth was, I'd never liked anyone else enough to want to take them skating, but I wasn't sure she would find that reassuring, either.

"Alone, James. When I need to work off energy because I'm pissed off or whatever."

"So you commit crimes habitually," she said, fighting a smile. "Good to know."

I winked at her. "You knew who you were getting."

CHAPTER 25
YOU WIN
CHASE

OUR STEPS ECHOED as we navigated the deserted hallways of Northview Arena. I entered the security code next to the dressing room entrance without looking, and the red metal door unlocked with an obedient click. Leaning against it with my hip, I pushed it open and gestured for Bailey to go first.

"Wow," she breathed, scanning the giant 3D logo in the middle of the floor, the rows of glossy crimson lockers, and the custom LED lighting.

"Pretty sweet, huh?" The Boyd dressing rooms had been completely renovated the year before I started, courtesy of a massive donation by an anonymous alumnus. I was awed the first time I saw them too. They were sleek, modern, and would put most of the dressing rooms in the NHL to shame.

Taking her hand in mine, I led her over to my locker at the end of the room, nearest the entrance to the ice. It would be difficult, but I was going to try to keep this G-rated while we were in here. I wanted to actually get in some skating with her.

For a little while.

After that, all bets were off.

I may have had some plans for later.

"Yeah, your dressing room is way nicer than ours." She caught herself, plump lips folding into a frown. "Wait. Don't tell anyone I said that."

I set our skates on the bench beside us, glancing back over at her. "When were you in the Bulldogs locker room?" As usual, the question slipped out before I could stop myself. And it didn't sound nearly as casual as I would have hoped.

Bailey stepped closer, wrapping her arms around my neck. Instantly, my willpower disintegrated. Fuck G-rated; if I kept it PG-13, I would consider it an accomplishment.

"To do a piece for *Callingwood Daily*, you big caveman." Her hazel eyes glinted playfully.

"Ah." I ran my fingers down the sides of her ribcage, spanning the curve of her waist over her soft pink sweater. Even with her height, she was still a good measure shorter than me, not to mention way smaller. I loved how she felt beneath my hands—pliant and feminine.

I tilted my head and leaned closer, my mouth meeting hers. Bailey let out a little sigh and parted her lips, letting me taste her. I took her bottom lip, sucking on it before pushing into her sweet mouth with my tongue.

Gripping her waist, I pulled her closer, warm curves pressing up against my body. She stood on her tiptoes as I deepened the kiss, taking, tasting, claiming. Desire surged through me, my cock growing harder by the second. Then I remembered where we were. If we didn't stop now, we would never make it onto the ice.

I slowly pulled back, breaking the kiss, even though every fiber of my body was begging me not to. Bailey looked back up at me, eyes more golden than green in the light of the room.

"For the record," she said, booping me on the nose with her finger, "you're cute when you're jealous."

"I was just curious." I shrugged, reluctantly releasing her.

Her lips tugged. "Sure, Carter."

Opening the digital lock, I hung up her bag and my gray canvas jacket, then quickly threw on a black lightweight training hoodie over my T-shirt. Bailey opted to keep her coat on over her sweater, claiming she was cold. Why were chicks always freezing? The high today was sixty-four degrees, which was shorts weather as far as I was concerned. But I ran at a million degrees year-round, especially when I was moving.

We slipped off our shoes and laced up our skates. Then I tossed in the rest of our stuff before securing the locker again. Probably wasn't necessary at his time of day, but it was a force of habit.

From the home bench, I opened the gate for Bailey. She skated backward, blond hair flying loose in the breeze. "Come on, slowpoke." She made a come-at-me gesture, arms spread wide.

"You're not half bad." I stepped onto the ice with a huge grin. She was so fucking cute.

"Oh, I've got moves you've never seen."

"I bet." I took a few easy strides in her direction, coasting. "Gonna show me?"

Bailey turned away from me, calling over her shoulder. "You'll have to catch me first."

I picked up speed, drawing closer to her but holding back a few feet. Then I let her get away from me a few times, intentionally missing by a narrow margin when I reached for her. Finally, I couldn't wait any longer. She made it to the corner, and I picked up speed, carefully grabbing hold of her. I came to a stop, spinning us both and pushing her into the boards.

She looked back at me, lips softly parted. "I guess you win."

I had her in my arms, so I definitely did.

"Looks like it."

I pinned her up against the plexiglass, wedging a thigh between her legs. She let out a little gasp, her eyes glazing over.

"This is so much better than the other kind of boarding," I murmured, my attention falling to her full, kissable lips. "But now I'm going to get turned on every time I'm in this corner during a game."

Hand sliding up her neck, I held her in place as I crashed my lips to hers again. Kissing her was unreal, like everything else in the world instantly vanished the moment our lips came together.

And each time, she relaxed a little more. Softened somehow.

Maybe it was a trust thing. Either way, it drove me crazy in the best possible way.

After a minute, we broke apart.

"Carter?" She held on to my forearms, breathless and wide-eyed. I was too, and definitely not from the skating.

"Yeah?"

"I'm going to lose my balance if you keep kissing me like that."

"I got you," I said, voice husky. "I won't let you fall."

Skating didn't last long.

We burst into the locker room in a frenzy of kissing and groping. I sat on the bench and got out of my skates in ten seconds flat. Beside me, Bailey struggled with hers, not as accustomed to getting in and out of them quickly.

"Here." I picked up her legs, turning her ninety degrees and taking her feet into my lap. I quickly loosened the laces, tugged off her skates, and placed them out of the way on the bench.

Then I pulled off my hoodie and tossed it aside. I picked her up, pinning her against the wall beside the lockers. Our lips collided, and everything exploded. It was different from any kiss we'd shared before: hurried and needy, hungry and wanting. Gripping the backs of her thighs, I lifted her off the floor and thrust against her, pressing between her legs. A whimper escaped the back of her throat. She wrapped her long legs around me as I pushed into her again, and she tilted her hips in rhythm with me.

Her mouth moved against mine, fingers digging into my shoulders. I was in the zone. So into her that it put me into some kind of trance. And so lost in her that at first, I barely heard the faint rumble of wheels rolling down the hallway. Then they got louder—and closer.

I tore my lips from hers, freezing as I listened to the approaching sound.

"What?" she asked.

"Shit," I muttered. "It's Roy."

"Who's Roy?" Bailey whispered, scanning my face nervously.

"Our custodian." I glanced over my shoulder, calculating.

Her eyes widened. "We are so busted."

"No, don't worry. It'll be fine." I had no real reason to think that, but I didn't want her to freak out. At least it was probably just Roy. I was 95 percent sure. If it was Coach Miller, we might have a problem.

"I'll deal with him," I said. "The bathrooms have stalls. You can hide in there."

Bailey nodded. "Okay." She darted around the corner, and a split second later, the door swung open. Roy walked in, pulling the janitorial cart behind him.

Thank Gretzky.

Scrambling to sit, I leaned an elbow on my bent knee and attempted to seem casual. The fact that I had a massive fucking hard-on made it a difficult task.

I waved at him. "Oh hey, Roy."

"Chase?" His brow furrowed, then he glanced around the locker room in confusion. "What are you doing here so late?"

"Needed some extra ice time," I said. "Coach said I had to work on my crossovers. You know how it is. The grind never stops."

I'd done this numerous times before for practice purposes, but the one time I ran into someone, my presence here wasn't even a little legitimate.

His eyes fell to the bench, landing on the second pair of skates. God dammit, why didn't I hide Bailey's stuff? With no blood supply above my waist, I could barely carry on a conversation, let alone strategize.

Roy cleared his throat. "I see." He gave me a knowing look, fighting back a smile. "Well, I'll start in the offices and let you get out of here before I circle back. Have a good night, son."

"Thanks," I said. "You too."

He pulled the door open, and it swung shut behind him.

"All clear," I called softly. Bailey tiptoed back into the changing area. Her face was six shades of red.

"Oh my god," she said, covering her mouth. "Is he gone?"

"Yup. We're good. Just a close call."

She didn't need to know that we were totally busted. But I was pretty sure Roy wouldn't tell anyone. He was a nice guy. I always gave him a hundred bucks at Christmas as a thank you for cleaning up after our gross asses. If he kept this under wraps, I would double it.

Our eyes locked, and Bailey stifled a laugh, shaking her head.

"See?" she said. "I knew you were trouble."

BAILEY

The sexual tension between us was high after I spent the night with Chase last weekend, but it was nothing compared to the atmosphere in the truck after the arena.

The ache between my legs made it impossible to focus on anything else.

I kept stealing glances at him in the darkness of the vehicle, his face illuminated by flashes of streetlights. Strong jawline, sinewy forearms, large hands that I desperately wanted all over my body again. It was torture. And by the tension he was holding in his body and the way he gripped the steering wheel, he felt the same way.

It was only a ten-minute drive, but by the time we made it through the front door to his house, I thought we both might spontaneously combust.

Wordlessly, he led me upstairs to his room and let me enter first. I slid my bag off my shoulder and set it next to the nightstand with shaky hands. I couldn't turn around. Couldn't look at him just yet. Desire thrummed in my veins, dizzying me like a drug. He'd been hesitant with me so far, afraid to take things any further…but I wanted him to.

Chase shut the door behind him and closed the distance between us in a few long strides. Suddenly, he was pressing up against me from behind, a wall of muscle and warmth. His intoxicating scent surrounded me, relaxing me while simultaneously arousing me.

He gathered up my hair, tucking it over one shoulder to expose the opposite side of my neck. I leaned back against his body and let my eyelids flutter shut as I tilted my head, surrendering. His lips landed on the skin below my ear, planting a trail of open-mouthed kisses down to my collarbone. The ache in my legs grew, begging for his touch.

"Those little moans you were making in the locker room almost did me in, James." His voice rumbled in his chest, flush against my back. Warm, slightly rough palms smoothed down the sides of my arms, leaving behind a trail of goose bumps.

"Too bad we were interrupted," I said.

He grabbed my hips and turned me to face him, grinning wolfishly. "But now we've got all night."

My breath caught as I regarded him, working through the implications. As great as the prospect sounded, it created a lot of pressure.

My expression must have given me away, because his softened.

"Remember our talk?" His tone was gentle.

I was standing on a precipice now, deciding whether to jump. But the truth was, I already had.

"I trust you." I nodded, sucking on my bottom lip before releasing it. "I want…you."

Chase's lips tipped up. "Yeah?"

"Yeah."

Midnight eyes traced my face, dropping to my mouth. Then they sank lower, skimming the rest of my body in a way that made me feel naked while fully clothed.

Chase lifted his gaze back up to meet mine. My stomach fluttered as he placed a hand between my shoulder blades, easing me onto the bed. He leaned on his elbows, hovering over me. The hard length of him pressed up against my pelvis, sending desire coiling between my legs.

He nuzzled my neck, inhaling deeply against my skin and exhaling with a low groan.

Luke had wanted sex.

But Chase? He wanted *me*.

His broad hands landed on the strip of bare skin beneath the hem of my sweater, lifting it slightly.

"Can I?" he murmured.

I nodded. "Yes."

Carefully, he tugged it off over my head and tossed it aside. He sat back on his knees and bit back a grin, shaking his head.

"Baby, you're so hot, and you don't even know it."

With one hand, he pulled off his black T-shirt and dropped it to the floor. He loomed over me again, bracketing my arms with his while his smooth skin radiated heat against my bare stomach and chest. His lips met mine as I ran my fingertips down the hard planes of muscle that covered his stomach, probing, exploring.

He rolled so we were on our sides, facing each other. Then he smoothed a hand down my ribs, landing on my hipbone. Skimming across to the center of my stomach, he toyed with my waistband, his eyes on my face, waiting—a question. With an arm around his neck, I pulled him closer and kissed him again.

With nimble fingers, he undid the button on my jeans and unzipped them. Then he broke apart from the kiss to slowly tug them off before cupping between my legs over the fabric of my black lace underwear. He groaned as I grabbed him—rock hard and huge—over the top of his pants.

Tugging, he moved my underwear aside and slid his fingers against my center. My hips jerked in response, and I drew in a shuddering breath as pleasure rippled through my core. Warmth spread across my skin, and the ache between my legs grew, the sense of want growing into a desperate need.

Ducking low, he placed a row of kisses down my chest while reaching behind my back to undo my bra with one hand. He slid it off and cupped my breasts, kissing his way back up my neck.

"Let me take care of you," he said against my skin.

"What do you mean?"

Chase pulled back, his dark eyes hungry, his lips curved.

"I want to eat your pussy, James."

Heat shot through my body. My heart thudded against my ribcage, and I held my breath for a beat.

"Okay." I nodded.

He flashed me a wicked grin before kissing his way down my body, alternating licking and sucking. Strong hands skimmed my ribcage, past my hips, landing on my inner thighs. Planting a kiss over the center of my underwear, he slid his hands under and slowly pulled them off.

Chase spread my legs apart, exposing me to him. He ran his hands over my hips and down to my knees and back, his eyes gleaming with desire.

"Fuck, baby. Your body is so beautiful. Every single inch of it."

I waited breathlessly, and he turned, planting soft kisses on my inner thighs, working higher until he was almost where I needed him. He circled his arms around my outer thighs, wrapping my legs around his shoulders.

Shifting his body, he settled between my legs and flattened his tongue against my center. My breath hitched and I jumped slightly.

He grabbed my left hand, lacing his fingers with mine, all the while teasing and caressing, coaxing me with his tongue until it felt too good to focus on anything else. I shifted into a state of hyper-awareness. Of his hands, his lips, his tongue. It was like seeing color for the first time.

My muscles eased as the warm sensation within my belly grew, drowning out all my other senses. His mouth moved against me faster, growing more purposeful. I squirmed as the intensity of the sensations grew, verging on unbearable.

I gasped, legs jolting. "Ohmigod."

Chase rumbled a low, throaty laugh against me. He released my hand, snaking his free arm under my leg so both were wrapped around my thighs. Keeping the same pace and pressure, he worked me with his tongue in long, devastating stokes. A breathy whimper escaped me, my back arching in response. It felt so good, almost too good to continue. I desperately needed release, but I never wanted it to stop.

My breath quickened, shortening into shallow pants. I grasped his dark silky hair with one hand, tugging at the roots, and fisted the covers with the other.

He used his arms to pin my thighs down, keeping me open for him while my hips bucked, my pelvis tilting. Pulling me down the bed, yanking me closer to him, he devoured me as I came apart with a moan.

Chase kept going, working my body with his tongue until I was almost too sensitive to continue. Then he pulled away and planted a gentle kiss between my legs, followed by a trail of them up and down my inner thighs. My knees were weak, legs unsteady, even though I wasn't standing.

He shifted back up to the head of the bed and leaned on one elbow. "Hey, baby."

"Hey." As I came down from the high, I was acutely aware of how naked I was, especially since Chase was still partially clothed. He'd seen every single inch of my body. Every. Single. One.

I turned, scrambling to grab my tank top and underwear off the floor, and slid them on quickly. He picked up my shorts and handed them to me.

"How are you doing?"

"Um…Dazed?" No further discussion necessary—I couldn't have faked that if I tried. I wasn't even sure what had just happened. It was like an out-of-body experience that I hadn't fully returned from.

"Good." He grinned. "That was so fucking hot."

Chase waited until I slid into my shorts and then grabbed hold of me with big, strong hands. "Come here." He lifted my hips up slightly, pulling me toward him on the bed and wrapping his arm around me.

Brows knit together, I studied him. I was more than a little confused.

"I feel like I'm leaving you hanging."

He shook his head. "Not at all."

"But you didn't—"

Chase caught my eye, stroking my hair. "It's not a hockey game, James. I'm not keeping score." He kissed my lips softly. "But if I was, I'd definitely want you to win."

CHAPTER 26
CHICK FLICKS
BAILEY

I'D NEVER BEEN PROVEN wrong about so many things in such a short period of time. Or been so happy to be wrong in the first place.

After kissing outside the truck at his place, inside the truck, and outside it again, Chase walked me to my front door and wrapped me in a big hug. I inhaled his scent, relaxing against the warmth of his embrace. Everything was easy with him in a way I'd never thought possible.

He pulled back, broad hands sliding down to my waist, holding my gaze for a beat, and he gave me a smile that made my knees go weak. "I'll call you tonight, okay?"

"Okay," I said. "And good luck this weekend."

We lingered, looking at each other on the front step. Mostly because I didn't want him to leave, but also partly because I didn't want to go inside.

He frowned, expression clouding over. "You can stay at my place while I'm gone if you want."

"Without you?"

"Yeah," he said. "To get a break from your roommates, I mean. Shiv will be there alone, so…" He shrugged. "She would probably like the company."

"Actually, we did make plans to get together for dinner."

He raised his eyebrows. "For apartment hunting? That's awesome."

"To talk about it more, at least. Maybe make a list of places to check out."

The idea of moving out was such a relief that I fantasized about it all the time lately. Right now, I was all but relegated to my bedroom when Jillian and Amelia were home. I had eaten more meals at my tiny desk than I could count. Though after our confrontation the other day, they had given me a wide berth. If I was in a room, they wouldn't even enter. But I practically needed a coat and gloves to weather the chilly atmosphere.

In Jillian's case, she was probably treading carefully because she didn't want me to tell everyone what I knew. Maybe that was the case with Amelia too. Seemed like everyone was complicit in their little web of lies.

"See?" His face brightened, a smile peeking through. "You could stick around on Sunday until I get back. It shouldn't be too late. Probably shortly after lunch."

"That was your angle all along, wasn't it?"

"Sure was." He glanced at his watch, smile fading. "Oh shit. I really do have to go, or I'll be late for practice." Tipping forward, he gave me a quick peck on the lips and released my waist. "We can talk tonight. I'll text you the door code too."

As he jogged down the steps, I unlocked the door and pushed it open. Please don't let anyone else be home.

No such luck.

Jillian was standing in the entryway, putting on her coat as I walked in. I slid off my shoes and brushed by her, ignoring her presence completely.

"Bailey," she said, voice tight. "Can we talk for a minute?"

My entire body tensed. I was a pretty level-headed person overall, more prone to sweeping things under the rug and forgiving too easily than fighting. I rarely lost my temper, rarely even raised my voice, but this moment was incredibly close to becoming an exception.

Turning to face her, I made every effort to keep my voice level.

"Why?"

She straightened her shoulders, throat bobbing. "About what you said the other day. You're not—you're not going to tell anyone, are you?" She scanned my face nervously.

I shrugged. "You mean, besides Chase? Because he knows all about it."

Keys in her hand, she froze on the spot, and the color drained from her skin. The look on her face was so horrified it was almost comedic. Someone she hated knew one of her darkest secrets. Poetic justice.

"But your brother…the team." Jill gestured vaguely.

As if I would care about the team at this point.

"Yes, Derek is my brother, which is why I'm so upset. Otherwise, I wouldn't really care about what sorts of shady things you got up to, Jill."

She chewed on her bottom lip, expression turning guilty, but said nothing.

"Imagine how you would feel in my shoes," I said. "This isn't fair to him. To either of them."

"It's complicated."

"So I'm told." I hung my bag on the hook and turned, heading for the staircase. "As for telling anyone, I haven't decided yet. Maybe you should make things easier on both of us. If you put an end to this messed-up situation, then I won't have to make that call."

It was an empty threat. I could never do that to Derek. But she didn't need to know that.

By the time I got to the *Callingwood Daily* office after lunch, my annoyance with Jill had faded, and I was back to cloud nine over Chase. It really was a wild experience. I'd never felt this way before. Ever.

With Luke, I thought I should like him because everyone did. He was good on paper—or so I thought—and had tons of girls eager to date him. Naively, I had been wowed that he was even interested in me.

But I'd never been giddy about him or filled with that intense, inescapable infatuation. It had almost been one of those *you don't know what you don't know* situations.

But I knew now, and it was amazing.

I pushed open the door, making my way over to join Zara and Noelle at the oversized round table. I could feel their eyes on me as I set my bag down and pulled out my laptop and notebook.

Zara tilted her head, examining me. "Well, isn't someone in a good mood?"

"You practically skipped in here," Noelle added in a sing-song voice.

"I would say danced," Zara volleyed. "Or maybe pranced?"

I shrugged, but I couldn't keep the dopey look off my face. Words eluded me. My brain was hormone and happiness soup.

"Wait." Her jaw dropped. "You saw Chase again last night, didn't you? Did you guys finally…?"

I bit my lip. "Maybe."

They both squealed.

"Well, no." I held up a hand. "No sex. We just fooled around a little."

Or, you know, a lot.

Zara raised her eyebrows. "Must have been some fooling around if you're this giddy."

A rush ran through me at the memory. "Oh, it was."

"That's awesome." Noelle swatted me playfully. "Especially after what you said about Luke."

Oh my god, how many people had I told? I'm never doing shots again.

"Aw, B. I'm so happy for you." Zara bounced in her seat.

Noelle nodded. "Me too."

We fell quiet for a while, working on homework and newspaper tasks.

"Speaking of good news," Zara said, squinting at her computer screen. "I have some more for you. Well, some partial good news."

"What's that?" *Could it be?*

She nodded at her laptop. "I got an email from Liam. He wants to give up part of the sports beat. Says he'll split it with you. If you're willing, that is."

Okay, so I was partially right. I thought maybe he was throwing in the towel altogether, but I guess I could only get so lucky. I should have been excited about this, but now I would probably have to actually work *with* him.

Ugh. And there would be strings.

I sighed. "What's the catch?"

Did he want me to pay him for the honor? Take credit under his name for the stories I wrote? Nothing would surprise me.

"He wants to keep covering hockey exclusively."

Oh, even better. Jerk. Why was Liam so attached to covering hockey specifically when he was a casual fan at best?

"Of course he does." I huffed. "You should ask him what our record is right now. I bet he couldn't even tell you without pulling out his phone."

Conversely, I could list the stats for the top ten teams off the top of my head. Who was leading in each metric, who was living up to expectations, and who was disappointing this season.

Zara shrugged, giving me a sympathetic look. She knew I was right. "Is that a yes or a no?"

"You know it's a yes," I said grudgingly. "Maybe he'll lose interest in hockey eventually too."

"Did you see that list of spring internships?" Noelle asked, poking me with the end of her pen. "They're all remote. There's, like, ten of them. I saw something sports-related on the list and thought of you."

My ears perked up. "No, where was this posted?"

"On the career portal." She nodded at my laptop. "Went up this morning. You should check."

Hope thrumming, I reopened my browser, navigated to the Callingwood career website, and logged in with my credentials. Scrolling through the listings, I scanned the descriptions. There was one for a fashion website I'd never heard of, a food website I was vaguely familiar with, a local news station, a national fitness brand…and *Penalty Box Online.*

You know, only the foremost source for hockey news.

Oh my god.

Lightning fast, I double-clicked the listing.

Penalty Box Online
Hockey Content Writer - Paid Internship

- *Commitment: approximately 5-10 hours per week*
- *Duties: creating website content, social media posts, and copywriting, as well as researching industry topics*
- *Requirements: journalism or communications major with a strong GPA; passion for hockey; in-depth understanding of game, player, team, and league issues; ability to consistently deliver high-quality work on short deadlines*
- *Potential to transition into a part-time permanent position with good performance*

Unblinking, I stared at the screen. This was it. Exactly what I needed. The perfect resume boost.

Then I snapped back to reality and caught sight of the clock behind Zara. I bolted out of my chair, gathering up my things.

"Sorry, I have to run. Shiv is picking me up soon."

Noelle raised her eyebrows. "Shiv?"

"Uh, Chase's roommate's girlfriend," I said. "We're apartment hunting. Long story."

———

An hour later, we were camped out in the living room with takeout Mexican food and homemade margaritas. Plus a plan to watch every rom-com on Netflix we could find. It was nice to have a girls' night in again; I hadn't done it since things went sideways with Amelia and Jill.

"Chase told me about the fire," I said, taking a sip of my strawberry margarita. "That's terrible. I'm glad no one was hurt."

"Yeah." Siobhan pulled her legs under her on the sofa and turned to face me. "Except most of my stuff was ruined because the smoke damage was so extensive. Rental insurance is covering it, but it's still a pain to replace it all. Especially when I'm trying to live out of a suitcase in Dallas's room."

"I bet he doesn't mind that part." I picked up my chicken taco and bit into it. Heavenly. Between dinner out with Chase and takeout tonight, I was getting totally spoiled. It was a nice change from my usual broke college student fare.

She laughed, tucking a lock of dark hair behind her ear. "All three of them have been good about it, actually. I think Ty is probably the least thrilled to have a girl around all the time, but he's managing. Either way, I don't want to overstay my welcome."

"Have you had the chance to look at any two-bedroom places yet?"

"I've got a list of potentials I thought we could look at." She hesitated. "I hope I'm not getting ahead of myself. If you have anything in mind, we can totally go look at those too."

I cringed. "Honestly, I haven't even had the chance to look. I was pretty swamped this past week."

Shiv gave me a look, the corners of her mouth quirking. "So I heard."

"What did you hear?"

"Oh, Chase said you guys hung out twice. And he told me about your little skating date. I have to say, that's pretty adorable."

"It was fun," I said, cheeks warming. "Until we got busted by the custodian in the middle of making out." Sharing this tidbit was probably the margarita talking.

Her eyes widened, and she covered her mouth, giggling. "Shut up. You did not."

"Well, almost. More like a close call, I guess." I shrugged. "Has Dallas ever taken you skating?"

"No." She shook her head. "I'm a Florida girl through and through. I don't think I could even stand up in skates, let alone use them. Ice is a spectator-only surface for me."

"Florida? Wow, you're pretty far from home, huh?"

"By design," she said. "The ex and all that. I wanted a buffer several states wide."

Jeez. "Does he still try to contact you?" I pried, but she'd brought it up, so it seemed safe to broach the subject.

"Sometimes." She took a bite of her enchilada. After she swallowed, she expanded. "My social media is on total lockdown, which helps to some degree. But a while ago, he got my phone number from a mutual friend. He called over and over again in the middle of the night. You should have heard Dallas when he answered. I changed my number the next day."

Siobhan pulled in a deep breath and let it out slowly. "I guess that's why I've kept Dallas at arm's length." Then she gestured to the living room. "Obviously that hasn't worked very well. I mean, I'm crazy about him. But I'm still a little gun-shy."

"I get that," I said. "Your ex almost makes Luke look good."

Luke was an asshole, to be sure. And inexplicably hell-bent on messing with my life now that I had moved on. But her ex sounded next-level, like the kind that could be dangerous. The damage Luke could inflict was likely limited to spreading ridiculous lies and trying to annoy Chase to death. If anything, Chase was the bigger threat to him.

"I dunno. Luke sounds terrible." Siobhan dipped a tortilla chip in guacamole. "I heard about that text message thing."

"Right? Who does that?" I hummed. "Actually, it's pretty on-brand for Luke. I think he was trying to cause trouble between Chase and me."

She grinned. "Oh, I don't think Chase is going anywhere. Not to sell him out or anything but…" She paused. "Okay, I'm selling him out a little, but he's cute about you."

I couldn't fight back my goofy smile. "I can't believe I used to hate him."

"You did?" Shiv tilted her head questioningly.

"I thought I did, anyway." I frowned. So much had changed recently that it felt like up was down.

"In your defense, he can be a total pain in the ass on the ice." She laughed. "Dallas says he's one of those players you love if they're on your team and hate if they're on anyone else's."

"Sounds about right," I said, standing to put my empty plate in the kitchen. "Should we watch *Love in Summer* first or *Accidentally Engaged*?"

Siobhan shrugged. "Let's work through the list alphabetically."

"Binge-watching all of these under Dallas's profile is going to mess with his Netflix suggestions," I pointed out. Right now, his home screen was full of *John Wick*, stand-up comedy, and horror movies.

She giggled, taking another sip of her margarita. "That's the best part. They'll be notifying him about upcoming chick flicks till the end of time."

CHAPTER 27
PART OF THE GAME
BAILEY

I SET my phone on Chase's nightstand and slid beneath his covers, leaning against the wooden headboard. It was strange being in his bedroom without him; his presence permeated the room like a ghost. And the bed smelled just like him, infused with that intoxicating blend of his cologne and his natural scent.

Not that I'd been inhaling the pillowcase or anything.

Oh my god, I really liked him. It was terrifying.

A moment later, my phone vibrated. My stomach did a little twirl as I grabbed it, hitting the green Accept icon. "Hi."

"Hey, baby," Chase said, his voice deep and hypnotically suggestive. It did something to my brain—and other parts of my body. "What are you wearing?"

I laughed. "Are you drunk?" Somehow, I could tell by the lilt in his voice.

"I mean…" He trailed off. "Maybe a little."

In the background, one of the guys yelled, "More than a little, you fucking lightweight."

"Ignore Ward," he said. "Lightly buzzed at the most."

"Don't you have another game tomorrow?" I shifted, pulling the soft gray comforter higher around my torso to combat the chill in the air. Chase was like a portable furnace; I was never cold when he was in the bed with me.

"It's all good. I'm a machine."

"I'm sure." My gaze drifted across the room, landing on the white door to Chase's walk-in closet. Then I remembered what he said about his hoodies. "Are you at the hotel?"

Sliding out of bed, I held the phone between my ear and my shoulder. I opened the closet, studying its contents for a second. Like everything else of Chase's, it was neatly organized and broken into categorical sections. I pressed my lips together at the sight of it. He was so tidy all the time.

Reaching past the suits, I grabbed a white Falcons sweatshirt off one of the hangers and slipped it on. It was too big in the way that made it fit just right and broken-in enough to be soft and cozy.

"Yeah," Chase said. "Some of the guys snuck out, but we stayed behind to have a couple beers here instead. Then I got to thinking about you in my bed, so here we are."

I couldn't lie; it put my mind at ease knowing he hadn't gone out. Not that I thought Chase would do anything, but lots of guys with girlfriends hooked up on the road. Learned that one the hard way.

"The bed does seem awfully empty without you hogging all the space."

Pulling back the covers, I crawled back under them and settled in. His bed was a dream. The mattress wasn't too soft or too firm, the comforter was fluffy, and the pillows were clouds of perfection. It was so much better than my cheap IKEA setup.

"Me?" His laugh was deep, beckoning. "James, you're adorable, but you sleep diagonally."

He had me there; I was a chaotic sleeper. At home, I took up my entire double bed. I also tossed and turned so much that sometimes the edges of the fitted sheet came off the mattress. Though my sleep wasn't as restless when I was with Chase; maybe because I had less space to sprawl out.

"I never told you what I was wearing." I shivered, pulling the soft cotton cuffs of his sweatshirt so they half-covered my icy hands. I swear the guys kept the thermostat set to refrigerator.

Maybe Shiv and I could turn up the heat a degree or two while they were gone.

"If you're trying to distract me from your bed-stealing ways, it is absolutely working," he said. "Go on."

"One of your hoodies, of course."

He may or may not get it back, but I wasn't going to tell him that part. Maybe he wouldn't notice if it disappeared.

"Ah." Chase sighed. "And I'm not even there to see it."

"Tomorrow," I said. "How was the game?"

"Awesome." He chuckled. "I got into a fight. I won, obviously."

My shoulders shook with laughter. It was so on-brand. "Of course you did."

He'd been involved in at least a minor tussle in every game I had seen. Then again, the Boyd-Callingwood rivalry ran deep, so that may not have been solely his fault. Likely not all of his games were so heated.

Except he practically had a PhD in antagonizing.

"The other team took a five-minute major for it," he said, feigning innocence. "I didn't start it."

"Sure you didn't." I shook my head, smiling. "There's no way you'd instigate something like that. What about the rest of the game?"

"We won four-three," he said. "I got two assists."

"Nice. That'll be good for your stats." Though they were strong enough to begin with this season.

"How'd the apartment search go with Shiv?"

"Good," I said, fighting back a yawn. It wasn't even that late. I had no excuse for being so tired other than heavy Mexican food and one super-strong margarita. Shiv mixed drinks like she was trying to tranquilize an elephant. "We made appointments to look at a few places on Wednesday. They're all pretty central; right around the river district. About ten minutes from your place."

Siobhan and I had combed the rental ads scrupulously, narrowing it down to the three top contenders for now. If those didn't pan out, then we had two backups to consider. But there was a cute little two-bedroom with a balcony on Green Street that I had my hopes set on. It was recently updated, on a good street, and two minutes from the train. Big windows, sunny living room, and—best part of all—two bathrooms. Exactly what I pictured for the perfect starting-over apartment, so I was praying no one would snatch it up before we could go look.

"Perfect," he teased. "Then you can swing by our home game when you're done."

My throat tightened. "You know you're playing us, right?"

"Yeah. Still too weird?" Chase asked, tone softening. "It's okay. I get it."

"I'm not sure." I drew in a breath and held it for a beat. It was weird, but maybe it always would be. "Can I think about it? It's just about Derek at this point. It's a little…awkward for me."

Who would I even cheer for? Both sides? Neither?

"No worries," he said. "If not, maybe the next one."

He was trying to hide it, but there was a hint of disappointment in his voice that hit me right in the gut. All of a sudden, I felt wildly guilty. I'd attended Luke's games religiously. All of them.

I hadn't been to a single one of Chase's.

"You know what? I'll come," I said. Shiv and I would sit far, far away from Jillian and Amelia. Like, on the other side of the arena. Before and after might take some extra vigilance, but I would figure it out.

Plus, I wanted to see Chase play.

His voice brightened. "Yeah?"

"Yeah." Another yawn creeped in as I was speaking.

"Sweet," he said. "You sound tired, baby. I'll let you get to sleep. But I'll see you tomorrow, okay?"

"Sounds good," I said. "Night, Carter."

"Night, James."

CHASE

James in my bed without me. Self-inflicted torture.

I ended the call, staring down at the screen. Picturing James under the covers. Her pouty lips. Those soft sighs. Long legs tangled in mine…

Then I glanced up to find Ward standing in front of where I was sitting on the edge of the hotel bed.

He observed me, lips quirking. "How's your girlfriend?"

Not even going to argue that point again, although, strictly speaking, we hadn't defined it like that.

I kind of wanted to. But how would I approach it? I wanted her to be mine in a very basic, very primal way—caveman-like, as she'd said in the locker room.

"Good," I said. "Making apartment plans with Shiv."

"Yeah." His posture stiffened, expression shifting from amusement into something unreadable. "Shiv mentioned that."

I narrowed my eyes, studying him. "You don't want her to leave, do you?"

And Ward gave me grief about Bailey. This dude.

"What?" Dallas made a face, but he was a terrible actor. "No, it's fine. I'll be glad to have my space back and all that…" He gestured vaguely around the room, which did precisely nothing to help sell his lie.

"You do realize the places they're looking at are only, like, ten minutes away, right?"

At this point, I was stoked about spending time at Bailey's place someday. Not being public enemy number one in her home would be great.

"Yeah, I know."

Ty strolled over, amber beer bottle in hand. "Enough gossip, bitches. Are we playing poker or what? Davis and Fitz are in too."

"You want to get taken to the cleaners again?" I asked. "It's like you two never learn."

Not that I should complain. A little extra pocket money never hurt. And they made it so damn easy.

"You got lucky," Dallas grumbled.

I cocked a brow. "The last five times?" Standing up, I reached into my back pocket and pulled out my wallet.

Ty held out his free hand, beckoning for the buy-in money. "Put up or shut up."

Many hands later, it was down to Fitz, one of our senior defensemen, and me. He wasn't a bad poker player, though not quite as good as he believed. He played in tournaments recreationally, which gave him an inflated sense of confidence.

And made him the perfect mark.

Ty dealt the final card. The river gave me the nine of spades I'd desperately needed.

Beauty.

"Call." Fitz raked a hand through his copper hair—his tell. He had something, just not something big enough to beat me.

"Flip 'em," I said, nodding at his hand.

Fitz turned over his cards to reveal a full house: three eights and two kings. Not bad.

Then I flipped my cards over, displaying a straight flush in all its glory: a nine, ten, jack, queen, and king of spades.

Fitz's eyes bulged, and he slapped the round tabletop. His face reddened beneath his freckles, and he made a fist, pounding his thigh beneath the table.

"Dammit, Carter!"

"Bullshit," Dallas muttered. "Did you have those up your sleeve or what?"

Ty cleared his throat. "Ahem, the dealer is right here, jackass, and that shit wouldn't fly at my table. I have fucking eyes."

"What?" I shrugged, pushing the cards over to Tyler to put away. "You thought I was bluffing?"

Fitz gestured with the neck of his beer, still baffled. "You went in big on a pair of twos a few hands ago."

"All a part of the game, my friend."

That pot had been small, the payoff huge. Because it made Fitz think I was a reckless idiot, which was why he went all-in against me just now.

I ended the night two hundred dollars richer. Can't say I didn't warn them.

CHAPTER 28
DOUBLE DATE
CHASE

THE BUS RIDE home felt like days.

When I walked in, Bailey was curled up on the living room sectional with her silver laptop propped up beside her. She looked adorable wearing black leggings paired with my white Falcons hoodie. Definitely an added perk to coming home.

Her hazel eyes lit up when they landed on me. “Hi, stranger.”

She closed her computer and stood to greet me as I rounded the couch. Wrapping my arms around her waist, I ducked my head to kiss her. Her warm vanilla scent surrounded me, always smelling vaguely like a cookie or something equally delicious that I wanted to devour—literally.

Her lips parted, and our mouths slanted, deepening the kiss. She drew in a soft breath, arms sliding to rest on my shoulders. My hands smoothed down her ribcage, past her hips, cupping her perfect ass. And instantly, I got hard. Maybe I should have done this somewhere else, because I was getting way too turned on in the middle of the living room.

The front door swung open, and Dallas barged in like a goddamn rhinoceros. “Don’t mind me,” he called, clomping by. For someone so graceful on the ice, he had lead feet at home. “Just going to find Shiv.”

Mood-killer.

"Sorry we ran late," I said, tracing her jawline with my finger. "Some of the guys took forever to get their act together and check out from the hotel after the game."

She blinked slowly, lips forming a little smile. "It's okay."

"C'mere." I threw an arm around her, tugging her onto the couch with me. Bailey flopped down beside me, exhaling with a sigh and shifting ninety degrees so her long legs draped across my lap.

I scanned her face and let my gaze drift down to her torso, clad in my white sweatshirt. It was a little oversized on her, but in the most perfect way. And I knew the curves beneath it were phenomenal.

I wanted to throw her down on the couch and ravage her. But I didn't want her to think that was the only thing I was interested in, especially after a few days apart, so I held off.

Our gazes met again, and it felt like coming home; being with her felt like home.

"What were you working on?" I asked.

"Well…" She sank her teeth into her bottom lip. "I was reading an internship posting Zara sent me."

"With what company?"

She was playing coy for reasons I couldn't quite discern.

"*Penalty Box Online*." She grabbed her laptop, turning it to face me.

I skimmed the description and the requirements.

"James." I glanced up at her. "This sounds perfect. You're going to apply, right?"

She made a little noncommittal sound and did a half shrug, dropping her gaze. "We'll see. I'm not sure I'm qualified."

I studied the description of the internship again. "Babe, it sounds like they created this for you."

. . .

She rolled in her lips like she wanted to argue but didn't. I hated that she thought so little of herself and her abilities sometimes. I hated the reason why even more. Fucking Morrison.

"Don't self reject," I told her. "You've got nothing to lose by applying."

"Yeah." Her gaze turned distant for a beat, and she nodded. "You're right. I'll do what you would do. Assume I'm awesome and that everything will work out."

"Exactly. You're going to stay over Wednesday, right?" I flashed her a crooked grin, one that almost always got me to yes.

"Yeah, I can." She smiled, suddenly shy. "I'll get some of that stuff done early. And I don't have class until ten on Thursday. Unless you need to be up early."

"I have dryland that morning, but I can come back after. I should be home around eight." Crawling back into my bed to find James in it was my literal idea of heaven.

"That works," Bailey said. "I still have a group project to deal with tonight anyway. We're having issues between group members, and I have to play mediator." She rolled her eyes, letting out a huff of annoyance that was more cute than angry.

I wasn't sure I'd ever seen her really angry. Irritated, yes. But never losing her temper. It was probably inevitable with my dumb ass, though.

"Unfortunately, I have a lot of schoolwork to finish before tomorrow too," I said. "And now that I can kiss you freely, I'm not sure I would be as productive with you here as I was last time."

"Let's be honest." Her green-gold eyes traced my face, pink lips tipping upward. "You weren't trying to be productive then, either."

Was I that obvious? Damn.

"I may have been buying some time," I admitted. "But Ward has consistently bad timing."

Her jaw dropped, her mouth forming a little *O*. "So you *were* going to kiss me." She swatted my arm playfully.

I smiled. I was busted and I knew it. "I was sure going to try."

"You can kiss me now if you want," she said, her voice turning breathy.

Coming closer, I twined a hand in her hair, pulling her to me. Our lips came together softly. She placed a cool hand along my jaw as she kissed me back.

I could only describe it as a shut-off switch for my brain, because everything else faded away. The moment stretched out forever. All that existed were her sweet lips moving against my lips in the most achingly perfect way and her body pressed up against mine.

Slowly, we broke apart. Her lips curved into a shy smile again. Then her expression turned serious, and she studied my face.

"Speaking of schoolwork, how's that probation going?"

"Thanks to you and to the good grade I got on my essay," I said, "I am officially out of the woods on that one." And I was trying to keep it that way. Unless I lost my cool and beat the shit out of Morrison in the near future, which was a strong possibility and would absolutely be worth it.

Ideally, though, I'd clobber him on the ice, thereby helping the team while avoiding jail.

"Really?" Bailey's face brightened and she squeezed my hand. "That's great."

"Yeah, but I still have to watch myself. Like at the game against you guys this week."

Maybe I shouldn't have mentioned that part. Coach Miller had been giving me regular "stay the fuck in line" pep talks—which we both knew were warnings.

Her brow creased, and she shifted her body weight. "Are you sure it won't be worse if I'm there?"

"No, it'll be fine." I shook my head. That didn't come out the way I wanted it to. Having her there would be so much more than fine. "It'll be great," I assured her. "I'm looking forward to you coming. I can keep my cool."

I think.

Dallas strolled into the living room. "Dinner? Yes?" He raised his dark eyebrows, pointing at Bailey, then me. "I can cook."

"Wait. You guys go away all weekend, work your butts off, then you come back and cook for us?" Bailey asked.

I mean, Dallas would be doing all the work in this scenario, but if I got credit by association, I wouldn't complain. Grilling wasn't really a two-man job, but I guess I could stand beside the barbecue and pretend to help.

Two hours later, we had perfectly grilled steaks, loaded baked potatoes, and a masterpiece of a Caesar salad, compete with fresh bacon crumbled over top.

The company wasn't too shabby, either.

Bailey set her fork down on her plate and took a sip of water. Her lush lips landed on the glass, drawing my attention. All I could think of was her mouth on my mouth. Or, well, other places.

"You know," she said, "I haven't heard any embarrassing stories about you from your friends yet."

I swallowed a bite of medium-rare steak with trepidation. There were embarrassing stories, and then there were *embarrassing stories*. But I could trust Ward not to throw me under the bus. Didn't need some of those tales getting out, least of all to James.

Some of the guys on the team might need a small reminder.

"Hmm." Dallas furrowed his dark brow. "That's a tough one. I feel like most of them implicate me too."

"All the better." Shiv leaned over in her seat, nudging him with her elbow. She pushed her curtain of dark hair over her shoulder and looked at Ward expectantly. "Start talking, Dal."

He glanced over at me. We shared a brief, silent understanding that he wouldn't completely ruin my life, and I would do the same for him. *Thanks, man.*

"I don't know," he said, drumming his fingers on the wooden table. "There are some good ones from that juniors tournament in Finland. Like the restaurant thing."

Ah, that was a fun trip. It was the summer before freshman year, the first time we'd been afforded any real freedom while we were away for a tournament—with the trouble to show for it.

"Yeah," I agreed. "That was kind of funny."

And low on the embarrassment scale, comparatively speaking. At least my clothes stayed on in that one. *Nice save, Ward.*

Bailey tilted her head, pausing with a fork full of Caesar salad. "Why, what happened?"

"On our first night there, they let us go out on our own," I said. "Ward and I headed downtown, far away from the touristy stuff near our hotel. You know, to get an authentic local experience."

"Obviously we didn't speak a lick of Finnish," Dallas added, taking a bite of his loaded baked potato.

Shiv and Bailey watched us, rapt, as we continued.

"We rolled up to this restaurant, and it was packed, so we figured it had to be good." I tossed back.

"But with the language barrier, communicating with the hostess was an issue," he said. "She pointed at a table, then to a group of people who were already seated. We nodded and were like, yeah, we want a table too. Then she seated us at the end of this long table, right along with these other people. We thought it was strange, but we were like, okay, maybe communal dining is the Finnish way."

I huffed a laugh at the memory. "The other people were giving us funny looks, but we thought it was because we were American. The server kept bringing us courses of food, one after the other. We didn't get the chance to order off the menu. Again, it was odd, but we rolled with it."

"They even poured us wine without asking," Dallas added. "When we were finished, we went to pay, and they wouldn't take our money." He paused, taking a sip of his beer, his lips curving against the mouth of the bottle. "Because we crashed a wedding reception by mistake."

"We left a huge tip and booked it out of there," I said, snickering.

Shiv tipped her head back, letting out a throaty laugh. "How is this the first I'm hearing of this?" She recovered partially, shaking her head. "Oh, it's a good thing you two are pretty."

"Sure is." Bailey bit her lip. Her shoulders shook beneath my white hoodie as she attempted to fight back a fit of giggles and failed.

I waved them off, fighting a sheepish smile. "Yeah, yeah."

Dallas looked down at his plate, cutting off a piece of steak before glancing up again. "There was also the Amsterdam thing on the way home."

Bailey turned to face me. "Amsterdam…?" Her brow knit together, expression turning wary.

I laughed, squeezing her thigh beneath the table. "We did edibles, James. Magic brownies. We didn't hit the red-light district."

The father of one of our teammates handled the travel arrangements for the entire team. We got stuck with a random thirty-six-hour stopover in the middle of the Netherlands. Obviously, we had to seize the opportunity to check out a "coffee shop."

"But edibles are tricky, and we had no idea what we were doing. So, of course, we overshot and ended up super high," Dallas explained. "Like, *super* fucking high."

Bailey and Shiv exchanged a look over the table that was somewhere between amusement and *these idiots*.

"Then we got the munchies," I said, "so we found a McDonalds. We ordered everything on the menu, and with the exchange rate, it worked out to like two hundred dollars by the time we were done," I recalled. "You know, I bet we could have dined at the fanciest joint in Amsterdam for that."

"To be fair, those were the best chicken nuggets I've ever eaten." Dallas's expression turned wistful. "Worth the twenty-five bucks."

I guffawed. "Because you were higher than a fucking kite. You were dipping them in your strawberry milkshake, dude."

"Once we got back to the hotel, Carter lost his phone. We ransacked our room looking for it—using his phone as a flashlight. Finally, I wised up and decided to use my phone to call his. And he screamed when it rang in his hand."

Shiv laugh-snorted, slapping her palm on the table, and Bailey broke into a fit of giggles. It wasn't my sharpest moment, but it was funny in retrospect. I'd been pretty fucked up before, but that took the cake. Or brownie.

"Then we turned on *Anchorman*," I told them. "We were a solid half hour into the movie before either of us realized the TV had been on mute the entire time."

"Oh my god," Bailey shouted, hazel eyes crinkling. "You two are such a gong show."

Dallas chortled. "I blame Carter. It was all his idea."

"I believe you," Bailey said.

"What?" I shrugged, picking up my bottle of beer. Beneath the table, Bailey shifted her weight, accidentally brushing her leg against mine and momentarily diverting my attention. "It's legal there. When in Rome. Er," I stumbled, "Amsterdam." See? She had a crazy amount of power over my brain.

"I think the lesson here is that you should never be released into the wild together without proper supervision," Shiv said, still fighting back a chuckle.

"In our defense, we were only eighteen," I said. "I like to think we're a little bit smarter now."

"I should hope so." Bailey wiped away a tear of laughter. "You a closet pothead, Carter?"

"Ha, not really."

"That's not a no." Her brow crinkled, expression sobering. "But what about drug tests?"

"I'm talking a couple times a year, max. In the off-season." Usually. Ty was another story, with an encyclopedic knowledge about how to outwit drug testing and several successes doing so.

"Ah," she murmured. "You really are corrupt."

"Trying to reform," I said. "Kinda. Why? Are you telling me you've never done that?"

She scrunched up her nose. "Once or twice. I just didn't like it."

Huh. I couldn't picture Bailey doing anything illegal. Or breaking the rules in general, for that matter. Wasn't sure how she ended up with me, but definitely wasn't complaining.

"Ah, my rule-follower." I patted her thigh beneath the table, letting my hand linger on her leg. She shot me a sidelong glance that was more than a little suggestive, which instantly turned me on again. Dammit.

Not long after, Shiv drove Bailey home so they could swing by and check out the exteriors of the apartments on their list. To, quote, "assess the sketchiness factor of the area and check out walkability to nearby Starbucks." Chick priorities, I guess.

Wednesday couldn't come soon enough.

CHAPTER 29
FACE OFF
CHASE

THE ARENA WAS PACKED. But that was always the case when we played Callingwood. The stakes were especially high tonight because Bailey was in the stands with Shiv. Hell, I didn't merely want to win; I wanted to annihilate the Bulldogs. You know, male pride and all that. Not to mention the ever-present desire to crush Morrison in every possible way.

Unfortunately, our teammates were on a different page. I wasn't sure what the fuck was going on, but they were sloppy, disorganized, and undisciplined. Ward and I were pulling most of the weight—and putting in ridiculous amounts of ice time as a result.

Even worse, Ty was having an off game, and the two goals he let in so far were weak as hell. One or two more, and Coach Miller would have to pull him. Though with our defense failing to show up, I had little confidence our backup goalie would fare much better.

With less than five minutes left in the first period, I hopped back on for another shift. I mean, why not? At this rate, I might as well stay out here the whole time.

As the blades of my skates connected with the ice, the Bulldogs lost possession of the puck and it slid across the blue line into their zone. Paul and I raced for it, but I made it there first. Before I could bring it out, he pulled up in a blur of navy and gave me a forceful shove, trying to separate me from the puck. We got stuck in the corner, locked in a heated puck battle. He attempted to stick-check, and when that failed, he accidentally-on-purpose slashed me in the hand with his blade. Hard. I sucked in a sharp breath as searing pain shot through my left hand and wrist.

Cheap motherfucker.

I hated him almost as much as I hated Morrison.

The whistle sounded as the ref called a justified minor penalty. And one that was more than needed for us. We could use the one-man advantage right now. I was nothing if not consistent in my ability to draw penalties from other teams.

Hand throbbing, I headed to our bench to make a line change, skating past the visitor bench on my way. As I passed, Morrison tipped forward, nodding at the scoreboard. "How's it feel being down by two points after the first, Carter?"

This was his idea of trash talking. Pointing out the score.

"A hell of a lot better than being a free agent with shitty stats," I said. "Must be stressful, man."

Coming out of high school, Morrison was good enough to get into Callingwood, a respectable Division I school, but not good enough to get drafted to the NHL. He had a massive inferiority complex to show for it. Given his recent poor performance, he was set to flounder as a free agent when he left college next spring, praying a team would pick him up as scraps. Couldn't happen to someone more deserving.

"I've got lots of interest from the league." He glowered at me, squaring his shoulders from where he sat on their bench.

"Sure," I said. "Even farm teams need a fourth line."

Morrison was legitimately one of the most overrated players I knew. Had two mediocre years in the NCAA, followed by a short-lived hot streak in his third, which somehow landed him a captainship he didn't deserve. He promptly shit the bed for his final season.

Unfortunately for him, one good year in college did not a professional career make. It took consistency and steady growth as a player. But that meant hard work, which was probably where the wheels fell off for his spoiled ass. All the money and training camps in the world couldn't compensate for a total lack of grit. That was why I had a future in the bag and he didn't, unless leeching off his wealthy parents counted.

His upper lip curled in a sneer. "Has Los Angeles wised up and dropped you yet?"

"At least I got drafted," I told him. "Guess there are some things your mommy and daddy can't buy."

Much to my frustration, our game didn't improve during the second period. Plays were falling apart left and right, and we could barely get a shot on net. Halfway through, Ward finally managed to get a goal on the board, and then we immediately gave up one more.

Fifteen minutes in, the score was three-one Callingwood. And the Bulldogs weren't even playing well. We were just playing that poorly. To make matters worse, the officiating in the second was trash, with blatant infractions against us flying under the radar. Several hooks on Ward, including one on a scoring opportunity. Bailey's brother boarded me, plain as day, and it didn't even get a whistle. *What the hell, refs*?

The only thing we were doing right was playing a physical game with lots of hits. It wasn't doing squat for our scoring chances, though.

I watched from the bench, praying to the hockey gods while we scrambled around the ice, trying to run out the clock. If we could escape the second period without letting in any more goals, there was still a chance we could salvage this tire fire in the third. Some patented Coach Miller verbal ass-kicking in the dressing rooms might do the trick.

Reed sent the puck offside, and the linesman blew his whistle, stopping the play. The linesman headed to the benches to talk with the other officials while Ward and I hopped back on for yet another shift—sweaty, still winded from the shift before, and hitting the wall.

I was so fucking tired.

I was positioned a couple of feet away from Morrison for the faceoff. Unlike me, he was brimming with energy. He was as perky as a cheerleader. I wasn't sure why—he'd contributed exactly zilch to their three goals. If anything, the Bulldogs were winning despite him.

I'd suspect performance-enhancing drugs, but then he'd probably, well, perform better.

Morrison skated by me and came to a sudden stop, trying to spray me with ice and failing. If he could get near the puck for more than half a second, I would check his sorry ass into the next state. But I couldn't afford an interference penalty for hitting him when he didn't have possession, especially when we were losing.

"Cart*er*," he said, dragging out the last *R* in the most aggravating way possible. "I forgot to ask, how are things going with my ex?"

Clearly, he'd been working on that zinger since we spoke during the first period.

"Fucking fantastic." I flashed him a cocky grin. "Thanks for asking."

Morrison was intentionally trying to rile me up. I was the king of riling up my opponents, which was why I wasn't going to take the bait. He needed to know that he was insignificant. Completely insignificant. And I had to keep my head in the game.

"You know," he said, "I popped that cherry."

My molars clenched so hard they nearly disintegrated.

Forget what I said. Consider me riled.

I glared at him, nearly paralyzed with rage. "Shut the fuck up, man."

How badly the team needed me in the game rivaled with how badly Morrison needed a fist in his face. But if I got a game misconduct, there was zero chance we'd turn the score around. And that was *exactly* what he wanted.

"Ooh," he said, laughing. "That bother you?"

The sex part? Not really. What James did before me was none of my business. Besides, there wasn't much to be jealous about when I knew all about Morrison's pathetic bedroom performance.

Him talking about her like that, though? Yeah, it bothered me. A lot.

"No." I shook my head, pivoting back to the faceoff. "But show some goddamn respect."

Morrison laughed again, but it was hollow, forced. He didn't have any other cards to play. Idiot.

Where was the linesman with the puck? My patience was waning by the second.

After being released from unofficial probation, the last thing I needed was to get right back on—or to receive a multiple-game suspension. Especially when Coach Miller had given me yet another stern lecture this morning about "staying on the right path." I was living under a goddamn microscope.

And yet, the temptation to cause Morrison bodily harm was almost too great to ignore.

I wanted to rag doll him.

"Huh," he said, studying me intently like the creep he was. "Interesting…"

I glanced over at him again. "Did you not hear me the first time I said to shut the fuck up?"

"Just surprised you don't care more about her." He shrugged. "Or maybe it's not that surprising, given your reputation."

The edges of my sight grayed out, my vision tunneling and my aggravation levels topping out. My frustration was at a record level. Even worse, I was frustrated about being frustrated.

No one got to me like this. Ever.

Because I *did* care, and he was lucky for it. I cared about James too much to throw everything I knew in his face. I never would, but damn if I didn't want to. Hell, I'd love to send out a Callingwood-wide email with a CC to his parents to show them what garbage he'd turned out to be.

At this point, I was dangerously close to choking him with my Vapor FlyLite. But even my hockey stick deserved better than Morrison.

"Do you want me to smash your fucking face in?"

"Oh, I don't think Bailey would approve…" he retorted.

The minute he said her name, my blood pressure spiked so high I nearly stroked out. Everything went red.

Taking a penalty was inevitable.

My gaze snapped over to the bench, where Coach Miller was busy talking to the guys. Taking a few quick strides, I came to a stop in front of Morrison, staring him down with my jaw clenched like a bear trap.

It took every shred of self-restraint I had to keep my gloves on.

"Listen fuckface. I'll put you on notice once and only once." My voice was laced with menace and poison. "Feel free to shit talk me all day long, but leave Bailey out of it. Don't talk about her, don't talk to her. Stay the hell away from her, and you and I will be fine."

Morrison glanced over my shoulder, probably to check if Paul was standing by in case he needed rescuing. But Paul would never be fast enough to save his sorry ass from me.

"Or what?" he said, trying and failing to sound tough.

"Do I need to spell it out for you?" I lowered my voice so the other players wouldn't hear. "I'll break your fucking legs, move on to your arms, and go from there. Your pathetic career will be over before it starts."

Morrison's expression went blank, and he blinked at me slowly. Too many big words to comprehend, I guess.

I skated closer. "Are we clear? Or should I start now?"

"Carter!" Coach Miller yelled. He threw both arms up in a WTF gesture.

"Watch your ass," I bit out before turning away.

I skated back into position, and the linesman finally appeared and dropped the puck. Dallas won the playoff, sending the puck back to me. I caught it and skated up the side before passing it to Davis.

Or trying to pass it, anyway, because my aim was off, and the puck traveled way over to the left—inadvertently turning over to a forward on the Bulldogs instead. He flew straight down to our end on a breakaway, hammering out a slapshot that Ty barely managed to block.

A botched play that was fully my fault, all because I couldn't complete a basic backhand pass.

Fuck me.

Morrison got in my head.

And now he knew I had a weakness.

BAILEY

I perched on the edge of my seat, my entire body tensed like a bowstring. Because attending a match between the Bulldogs and the Falcons wasn't emotionally draining enough on its own, the game tonight had been incredibly tight—and physical. Like both sides were out for blood.

With less than two minutes left in the second period, both teams were practically dead on their feet, exhausted from beating the crap out of each other on the ice for the previous thirty-eight minutes of play. There had been more hits and infractions tonight than I'd seen in ages. Chase was obviously hitting anything that moved, but the other players were unusually aggressive too. Derek was on some kind of rampage, which was completely out of character for him. Even some of the tamer players were piling on. The Bulldogs were targeting Ward in particular, probably because he was their most skilled opponent. And they were going after Chase because, well, Chase.

The officials had started letting some of the less serious penalties slide, probably so they weren't playing four-on-four for the entire twenty minutes each period.

After a turnover, Chase got a hold of the puck on their end and brought it up. Paul headed in his direction, accelerating with the obvious intent to initiate a massive hit. My breath caught and I braced myself, but Chase glanced over in the nick of time. He pivoted out of the way, and Paul slammed into the boards at top speed, making a loud crunch.

I burst out laughing. Good thing we weren't near Amelia.

"Oof." Siobhan cringed, biting her raspberry pink lip. "Tough break for that guy."

"A well-deserved one," I said.

"Falcons aren't playing very well." She shivered, zipping up her teal puffy coat. The frosty arena was even colder than usual, which only added to my mental and physical discomfort. "Not like normal, anyway." She sighed, raking a hand through her long, inky waves.

"Yeah, neither team is." The Bulldogs' three goals had largely been luck. I shifted my weight, crossing and uncrossing my legs because I couldn't sit still. "Too busy trying to kill penalties while killing each other."

We watched as Chase zoomed around one of our defensemen and right up to Mendez. He wound up and took a screamer of a shot on the net. It was heartbreakingly close but bounced off the crossbar with a defeating clang. Luke took possession off the rebound and skated up the far side, heading for the Falcons zone.

Chase turned and barreled straight for Luke like a shark that had detected blood in the water. Technically, someone else should have been covering Luke, and technically, Chase was taking himself out of position. But this was about more than hockey, especially after they'd been sniping back and forth all game. This was a way for Chase to clobber Luke with some degree of plausible deniability.

And Chase *really* wanted to make that hit. I'd never seen him skate so fast.

A split second before Chase caught up, Luke glanced over and realized he was about to get demolished. Instead of reacting, he froze, and Chase plowed into him with his shoulder, leveling him with a devastating open-ice check.

It was one of those brutal hits you'd see on TV, replayed in a "top ten hits of all-time" clip compilation.

Almost in slow motion, Luke went flying and landed in a heap on his side.

Chase skated off without looking back.

The crowd erupted into a roar while the players on the Bulldogs' bench, including Derek, protested loudly, calling for a penalty.

Siobhan turned to me, her blue-green eyes wide. "Is the guy Chase flattened your asshole ex?"

"Yup. Sure is." I adjusted my gray scarf, tucking it beneath the collar of my coat. It was soft and warm, but I could have used at least two more layers of clothing. Or maybe long underwear, not that it would be the sexiest thing for Chase to find later.

"That didn't look good." Shiv sucked in a breath through her dazzlingly white teeth, grimacing.

"Nope," I said. "Sure didn't."

The referee blew the whistle, halting the play. I watched as Luke lay sprawled out on the ice, dazed. As much as I hated him, I didn't like to see players get injured. Needless to say, I had mixed feelings. Luke definitely deserved a solid check—just not to be, like, severely maimed.

Moderately maimed, maybe.

But I didn't want Chase to get in trouble, either.

Cheers erupted from the Bulldogs fans as Luke slowly pulled himself up and skated over to the bench, his balance unsteady and with a pronounced limp. As he stepped off the ice, the Bulldogs' trainers ran to his side and helped him into the dressing room. He would be out for the rest of the game due to the league's concussion protocols. Maybe longer, depending on the injury his leg had sustained.

But would Chase take a penalty? Or worse? The hit itself was clean, technically speaking; he'd kept his elbow tucked, and there was no contact with Luke's head. But there was no doubt he'd intended to run Luke down. It wasn't even a little gray.

Shiv and I watched, waiting on pins and needles and frozen rear ends, as the officials conferred off to the side.

"Please don't let it be a game misconduct," I muttered, rubbing my frigid hands together, which was about as effective as rubbing two ice cubes together.

"I hope not," said Shiv. "The Falcons need him in the game."

The referee signaled, calling a two-minute minor against Chase for charging.

"Phew," I said, the tension in my body easing. It was more than fair, considering he'd traveled a significant distance out of his way to make the hit.

Siobhan nodded. "Thank goodness."

The Bulldogs bench broke into a second round of loud complaints, calling for a stiffer punishment. Chase shrugged and skated over to the penalty box, smirking the entire way. I had a feeling he would have gladly taken a lengthier penalty.

Unfortunately, there were fewer than twenty seconds left on the clock, which meant that the Bulldogs would start the third period on another power play while the Falcons were left shorthanded again.

I hoped that wouldn't come back to haunt them.

CHAPTER 30
NOT FIRST
BAILEY

AS THE SECOND INTERMISSION STARTED, Siobhan and I made our way up the stairs, heading into the concourse to stretch our legs. And, hopefully, to regain feeling in our lower halves. Not only was the arena cold, but the seats were rock hard, and my butt had gone numb. We might as well have been sitting on the ice surface below.

She sighed. “Maybe the third will be better.”

“I hope so.” It was difficult to believe it would, but Chase decimating Luke could be good for the Falcons’ morale. Or Chase’s morale, at least. I pointed to the pink sign at the far end of the hallway. “I need to run to the bathroom.”

“Okay,” she said. “I’m going to hit the concession for a hot chocolate. I’ll turn into Elsa soon if I don’t get something to warm me up. Do you want one too?”

“That would be great, thanks.” It would pale in comparison to the hot chocolate from End of the World with Chase, but Shiv was right—the arena’s chill had seeped into my bones. Next time I was at Northview, I would have to remember to bring a blanket.

When I turned the corner to exit the women’s bathroom, I caught sight of Amelia and Jillian standing outside. Icy dread flooded my body faster than I could blink. Couldn’t escape them at home, couldn’t escape them at the arena.

They were wearing short skirts with bare legs, which struck me as highly impractical, given the venue. Heck, even my outfit wasn't cutting it, and I was in jeans with a flannel button-up beneath my puffy coat.

Jillian's eyes flickered over to me, and she nudged Amelia, leaning in to say something under her breath, burgundy-painted lips moving silently. I was in the process of walking around them when Amelia turned, glowering at me with heavily made-up eyes.

"You'll be happy to know that your boyfriend injured Luke."

She wasn't entirely wrong. I was *not* broken up about Luke leaving the game.

Pivoting a quarter turn, I came to a stop and straightened my shoulders. While it may have been two on one, at least I had height on my side. Now that we were face to face, I was more perplexed than ever by their nightclub-esque makeup and outfits.

"And?" I gave a one-shoulder shrug. "Refs saw the whole thing. He'll do his time in the sin bin for it."

Nothing more could be done, anyway; it was too late to review the call. I supposed the Bulldogs could try to make Chase answer for it during the third period. Operative word being *try*. So far, they hadn't been successful in actually hitting him—aside from a single cheap shot from behind. I was going to take *that* up with Derek later.

Amelia jutted her delicate chin, her dark eyes flashing with anger. "He might be out for more than just this game, thanks to Carter."

"Oh." I kept my tone flat, face impassive. Was I supposed to care? Luke could retire for all it mattered to me. In fact, I'd welcome it. Then I wouldn't have to see his face at games.

My attention traveled behind them, searching for Shiv in the crowd. Maybe I could text her.

"He was gunning for Luke. It was a super dirty hit," Jillian added, voice dripping with contempt.

Cue record screech. I'd seen a million dirty things on the ice tonight, and the majority of them had come from the Bulldogs.

I leveled them with a steely glare. "You're joking, right? Did you see Paul take a run at Chase? The only difference between Chase's hit and the one Paul attempted was that Paul missed."

Amelia's face darkened. I'd struck a nerve by bringing Perfect Paul into the argument. In her eyes, he could do no wrong. Probably because he was second in line for the throne after King Luke. Plus, Paul taking himself out by mistake was more than a little embarrassing.

"Totally different," she snapped. "Everyone knows Carter's cheap."

As Amelia finished her sentence, Siobhan approached, holding a cardboard tray containing our drinks.

She bristled, glaring at Amelia. "What's *your* problem?"

"What's yours?" Jillian butted in, putting a hand on her hip.

Shiv raised a sculpted eyebrow, wielding a disdainful *you're beneath me* look that would rattle even the most confident person. Being knockout gorgeous like she was helped with the intimidation factor too.

"Chase is my friend. And hockey is a contact sport," she said, like they were the dumbest people on earth. "Put on your big girl panties and get over it."

A bark of laughter erupted from me before I could stop it. Jillian opened her mouth to respond, but quickly closed it again. Amelia squinted, her eyes darting back and forth like she was trying to formulate a retort. A beat passed, and background chatter from people milling around filled the silence between us.

"Well, this has been unpleasant," I said cheerily. "See you later." I wasn't interested in the digs aimed at Chase they would eventually come back with.

Shiv and I turned and weaved through the crowded concourse. She handed me a hot chocolate from the tray and removed the other one before tossing the tray into the blue recycling bin we passed.

"Sorry for butting in," she said with a slight frown. "Who was that, anyway?"

"Um, no one important. Just my roommates." They'd be no one soon enough. Practically counting down the days until they were.

"No wonder you want to move out," Shiv muttered beneath her

breath. Then she spun to face me, her turquoise eyes wide. "Oh my god. Wait, did I make life miserable for you? Holy shit, I have such a big mouth."

"Nah. You didn't make it any worse than it already was." If anything, putting them in their place lately had helped keep them in check. A few months ago, I would have let them run me over, and I would have cried over it every night. "Let's hope we find a place soon, or we'll both be living with the guys."

Halfway through the third period, it looked like things might improve. Chase got a shorthanded goal, assisted by Dallas. The energy in the arena shifted…until the line changed. Then the defense completely fell apart and they immediately let in another goal for the Bulldogs.

From over on the bench, Chase shook his head, clearly frustrated.

For the remaining ten minutes, the Falcons made an admirable effort to make a comeback. Chase was practically killing himself trying. But it wasn't enough, and the clock ran out with a score of five-three Bulldogs.

My heart dropped. Damn.

To be fair, they had been on a long winning streak until now—losing eventually was unavoidable. But the timing wasn't great. I hoped this wasn't going to ruin Chase's mood, since we planned to hang out later.

Or do other things later.

I wasn't sure what those things might be yet.

As people filtered out of their seats, I told Shiv I was going to see my brother and shot Chase a text saying the same. Then I waited by the visitor dressing room, not particularly caring who I might run into. But Derek was one of the first out for a change.

"B?" Derek shot me a confused smile as he emerged from the hallway. "What are you doing here?"

My irritation ramped up a notch. Of course he wouldn't know; we had barely spoken in weeks.

"I was here with a friend, watching Chase."

He frowned. "Carter?"

"Yes, Carter. And what the hell was that with him, anyway?" I gave him a little shove. He stumbled back, clearly not expecting it.

Regaining his footing, he shot me a look. "What are you talking about?"

"Hitting Chase from behind." I threw my arms up. "That was dirty."

"Refs didn't seem to think so." Derek shrugged, but he couldn't hide his guilty expression. He knew he'd been wrong.

"You and I both know they miss stuff all the time," I said.

"Why are you so upset about the other team?"

Other team? I didn't play for the freaking Bulldogs, but okay.

"Why are you starting shit with Chase to impress Luke?"

"I'm not," he said. "Hitting is part of the game."

I stamped my foot. "Bullshit, Derek. You never make hits like that." I could count the number of times Derek had made an overly aggressive check on one hand. This was definitely personal.

"I still don't understand why you're hanging out with Carter." Derek shook his head. "Are you cheering against us now too?"

"Maybe I am." I drew in a breath and exhaled heavily. "Just don't, okay? If you're not going to support me in this, the least you could do is stay the hell out of it."

Spinning on my heel, I turned and walked away. I navigated around the throngs of people crowding the arena lobby, impatiently side-stepping anyone in my way. The confrontation with Derek had soured my mood; now the noise and bustle of the crowd was wearing on my last nerve, and I was eager to get out of here.

In the distance, Chase stood with a group of people. I couldn't make out who he was with, but he was grinning, appearing largely unfazed by their loss.

My stomach fluttered, emotions softening at the sight of him. Other, more primal parts of me came to life as I drank in his broad shoulders and tall frame, clad in a perfectly tailored charcoal suit. Six feet and three inches of beautiful, muscular male, and he was all mine. I was more than a little happy to be going home with him. Though I wasn't entirely sure what would happen when we got there. I had been mulling that one over for a few days now, torn between brain and body and heart.

But my mood tanked again as I emerged into a small clearing to discover a pretty brunette to Chase's right, hanging off him. Or trying to, anyway. She laughed, tilting her head back to showcase dazzlingly white teeth framed by bright red lips. Don't get me wrong, Chase was funny, but she was clearly playing it up. Then she tilted in, placing her hand on his forearm. I stiffened. Whoever this girl was, she was way too comfortable with touching him. Chase withdrew his arm and took a step back, looking about as uncomfortable as I felt.

She wasn't taking the hint. At all.

My chest tightened, my heart picking up speed. I tamped down on a movie reel of flashbacks from my former life that cued up inside my head. This was not the same. He was not the same. I trusted him.

Despite that, I had the nearly overwhelming urge to turn and walk the other way.

With no small amount of trepidation, I straightened my shoulders and continued forward. Finally, I came to stand beside Chase, gently touching his firm shoulder.

"Hi," I said.

He swiveled to face me, and his eyes lit up. "Hey, baby." Ducking down, he gave me a quick peck on the lips and put his arm around my waist, pulling me against him. His familiar scent enveloped me, firm body warming mine, and the turmoil within me receded.

Chase nodded to the girl. "This is Kristen. Kristen, this is James. My Bailey. I mean, Bailey, my"—he faltered, brow creasing—"girlfriend?"

His sheepish stumbling was so adorable, I couldn't hide my ridiculous, goofy grin. I probably looked like I belonged in a toothpaste commercial. Chase was rarely anything other than confident and completely self-assured, which made his slip especially endearing.

Not to mention, girlfriend did have a nice ring to it.

As I turned my attention to Kristen, my smile went from real to fake. But I could pretend to be polite, at least. "Nice to meet you."

"You too." She smiled back at me, but it didn't reach her eyes either. I had a feeling I was going to have to get used to that.

As we walked up to Chase's truck, he reached past me and opened the passenger-side door. Then his hands landed on my waist, and my entire body thrummed in response to the contact, warmth flooding my veins. He moved in closer, his mouth finding mine, and I closed my eyes as my lips parted against his. The kiss was soft and brief but loaded with promises about later.

We pulled apart, and I looked up at him, raising my eyebrows teasingly.

"Did you give yourself a promotion back there?"

He froze on the spot and opened his mouth, but shut it again quickly, his brow furrowed. It may have been a first for Chase. Immediately, I felt bad. I had thought he would banter back.

"I didn't—"

"I'm messing with you, Carter," I said softly. "I like it. I mean… if you like it."

He grinned, squeezing my waist. "I definitely like it."

A rush ran through me, excitement mingled with desire. We stood in silence for a moment, both smiling.

"Movie night?" I asked.

"Sounds perfect."

We both knew we wouldn't be watching a movie. At least, not first.

CHAPTER 31
ALL YOURS
CHASE

THE BAD NEWS was we'd lost to Callingwood.

The good news was James hadn't run for the hills after my not-so-smooth slip of the tongue in front of everyone. And the best news of all was we'd slapped a label on things, and I could actually, officially, call her my girlfriend.

Oh, she was stuck with me now.

I eased my truck out of the space and navigated through Northview's parking lot, then turned onto the main road. Home was only a ten-minute drive away, but right now, that seemed like a lifetime. My mind was firmly locked in one-track mode.

All I wanted to do was get James into my bed, get her naked, and have a little repeat of the other night. Or a big repeat, as the case may be. Maybe multiple repeats? Hmm…

"What did Luke say to you earlier?" Bailey asked, snapping me out of my happy, horny daze.

"Nothing important." My grip on the steering wheel tightened a notch. "Just shooting off his mouth when he shouldn't be."

Brutal honesty was my default setting, intentionally or not. But in this case, she already knew Morrison was an asshole. I had nothing to gain by upsetting her with those details.

"You sure laid him out," she said.

Satisfaction washed over me like a warm, fuzzy hug. I really did. According to my insider sources, I fucked up Morrison's knee nicely. Pity it wasn't his smug face, but a knee injury would keep him out longer, so I would call it a win.

I shrugged, stealing a glance at Bailey. "It was a clean hit."

"Kinda gray when you factor in the charging." A smile played on her lips, and she made a so-so gesture with her hand. "Not that I'm complaining."

"Maybe he'll learn to keep his head up." Despite my best efforts otherwise, the words came out clipped.

Bailey caught it immediately. "Are you sure he didn't say something?" Her brows pulled together, hazel eyes scanning my face.

"Nah, I just prefer not to lose to Callingwood." Even if I did take him out of the game in the process, losing to Morrison's team annoyed me. Especially in front of James.

"You still played well tonight," she said, as if reading my mind. "No one can carry a game alone. Even with Dallas's help, it was virtually impossible."

Yes and no. I should have done more to move the needle. Another assist or goal would have gone a long way in generating momentum for our side. But I'd let someone take my head out of the game for a good portion of it, and that was on me.

"You're a little biased, James, but I'll take the compliment." I winked at her, patting her thigh. "Besides, the only thing that matters to me right now is that I get to take you home."

"Smooth talker." Bailey let out a soft, husky sigh. In my periphery, she raked a hand through her long waves, breaking into a bashful grin. It was so easy to get her flustered and so damn cute when she was.

Signaling, I made a left onto the main thoroughfare of my neighborhood. My mind circled back to all the things I wanted to do when I got her upstairs, starting with having her soft, perfect lips against mine and moving south from there. She made this little sound the other day—a cross between a whimper and a moan—that I desperately wanted to hear again.

What color were her panties tonight? Whatever they were, I wanted to take them off with my teeth. Then I could kiss my way back up her gorgeous legs and take a nice, long detour between them.

"I think…" Bailey trailed off. She drew in a deep breath. "I mean, speaking of that. I've given it a lot of thought, and I think I'm ready," she said. "To have sex, I mean—with you."

At her admission, I nearly drove right off the road.

It took me a good couple of seconds to reboot my brain. Even in the midst of entertaining all sorts of dirty thoughts inside my head, I wasn't expecting her to say that. But I was sure fucking glad she did.

"Great," I said. "Do you want me to pull over now, or?"

She giggled, swatting my arm. "No, you perv. I wanted to tell you when it wasn't in the heat of the moment so you knew I meant it."

"Well, I'm all yours."

I really was. In every sense.

Factoring in tonight's loss, I was still coming out way ahead. Fuck the game. What was hockey, again?

After committing several traffic violations and executing the worst parking job ever, we made it back to my place and went straight to my room. I followed Bailey inside, shutting the door behind me and locking it.

The first thing I wanted to do was ditch all these goddamn layers. I'd taken my suit jacket off in the car, but I was still in my white dress shirt, sleeves rolled up to my forearms, plus gray suit pants. And she was in jeans with a red button-up plaid shirt.

Very cute, and yet very much in my way.

The clothes needed to go—now. At least some of them.

As I took a step toward her, the doorbell rang downstairs. Irritation bordering on rage gripped me. Fucking hell, why was this happening? I swear to god, if this was Ward somehow interrupting for the third time, I might kill him—best friend or not.

"Should you…?" Bailey looked up at me, forehead crinkled in question.

Definitely not. Unless the house was literally on fire, I was more than happy to ignore all distractions.

I shook my head, pulling her closer. "I'm not expecting anyone."

I slid a hand up her neck and grasped her jaw. She looked up at me, gaze soft. I knew in that moment that I was done, a goner. Not just in over my head; I was well past the point of no return.

Falling, fallen, fucked. In the best possible way.

I tilted my head, leaning in to kiss her, and her eyelids fluttered shut as our mouths came together. She parted her lips, letting my tongue slip inside. A soft groan escaped the back of my throat; she tasted better than ever, each and every time.

Her fingertips dug into my shoulders, and I slid my free hand around the curve of her waist, down to squeeze her ass. Somehow, kissing her both satisfied my desire and fueled it.

Then the doorbell rang twice in a row, followed by an insistent banging on the door downstairs. Bailey jumped, startling, and we pulled apart.

"Maybe it's important," she said.

At this point, it fucking better be.

"Okay." I sighed, reluctantly releasing my hold on her. "I'll go check."

Sprinting down the stairs, I quickly adjusted myself so I didn't commit some kind of act of indecent exposure in the process of answering the door.

It wasn't Ward or anyone we knew, nor was it important. It was a pizza delivery guy with enough food to feed a small village who'd gotten the wrong house.

Despite my attempts to explain otherwise, he remained stubbornly convinced that he did not, in fact, have the incorrect address. What's more, he argued with me about what my address *was*. Negotiating nicely to get him the hell off my front step took far longer than it should have and used every ounce of patience I possessed.

After he finally left, I jogged back upstairs and pushed the door to my room open. I stopped on the spot, and my heart bounced off my ribcage like a puck hitting a goalpost. Bailey was perched on the edge of my bed, looking at her phone—wearing my red Falcons T-shirt.

It was everything.

"Sorry." She set her phone on the nightstand, lifting her eyes to meet mine. "I was writing Shiv back. She said they're going to O'Connor's for a couple of drinks."

Good.

I hoped they stayed there. All night.

I shut the door behind me and locked it again. Spinning around, I couldn't help but slowly scan up and down her body, drinking in the sight of her and growing more intoxicated by the second.

Dark blond hair loose around her shoulders, lush lips parted. My shirt. And tiny gray pajama shorts showing off her slender, endless legs. Legs that might be over my shoulders later, in a different way than last time. Or in both ways, maybe.

Both would be great.

I gave her a crooked grin and finally regained my ability to speak. "Nice shirt."

"Isn't it?" Bailey's mouth tugged into a flirty smile. "I'm a big fan of number nineteen. He's pretty cute."

"What did I do to deserve this?" I asked, stepping closer. Whatever it was, I'd repeat it on the daily.

As I reached the bed, she pushed herself to stand and nibbled her bottom lip. "Just being you."

Her hands landed on my shirt, slowly unbuttoning it from the top down and helping me shrug it off. She slid her fingers down my bare torso, probing. Then she took hold of my belt and unfastened it, followed by my pants. I quickly stepped out of them, pulling my socks off at the same time. Suddenly, I was left standing in front of her in nothing but black boxer briefs.

Her turn. But first…

"Are you nervous?" I brushed the hair out of her face and slid my hands down to her waist, gripping over top of the worn cotton.

Bailey's eyes drifted shut for a beat before opening again and focusing on mine. "A little."

"You don't need to be nervous with me, James."

"I know." Her expression softened. "Are you?"

I gave her a small smile. "Maybe a little."

Brutal honesty strikes again. But she'd told me the truth, so it was only fair. Feeling like this was a first for me, at any rate.

"Really?" she asked quietly, blond brows pulling together. "Why?"

A million reasons came to mind. Because I cared about her, which was uncharted territory for me, sexually or otherwise. Because I wanted it to be good for her. I was usually confident I had that under control, but I suddenly found myself sweating. And because she was so fucking beautiful that it made me ache a little inside.

I tried to capture all the reasons in one sentence. "Because I'm so into you that it's insane."

It was. It was like a drug. It might be my undoing.

She hummed a little sigh, smiling. "Same here."

Not to mention I'd been waiting for this for a long time and had no shortage of built-up sexual frustration. Part of me wanted to bend her over, pull her hair, and fuck her into next Friday, which was definitely not on the table tonight. I was more than okay with that; I just needed to slow my roll a little. Somehow.

I stroked the hem of her T-shirt—my T-shirt—between my finger and thumb. "You know, this is very, *very* sexy on you," I said. "Maybe you can put it back on later."

Bailey nodded silently, reaching down to help me pull it over her head and tossing it onto the floor. Her lacy white bra showcased her plump breasts perfectly. I sucked in a breath, hardening even more. Damn.

I traced a finger along her bra strap, down the valley between her breasts, and back up to the other side. She drew in a small breath, goose bumps popping up along her skin.

I dipped under the waistband of her shorts, toying with the elastic. "Same with these."

She tugged them down and stepped out of them. All that was left was the lacy white bra and matching panties, combined with miles of smooth, touchable skin. Not quite naked but hot as fuck.

My hands spanned her hips, and I picked her up, then I placed her on the bed so that I was on top of her, between her legs. God, she looked fucking good beneath me, and she felt even better.

I slid my hands under her thighs and gripped her plump ass. She let out a breathy moan as I peppered kisses along her neck, lifting her against my hard cock. This was perfect. Now we needed to replicate it *without* clothing.

Not yet.

Get it together, Carter.

Instead, I grabbed her hands and pinned them to the bed. Then I ducked my head, capturing her mouth with mine. Bailey giggled against my lips, half-heartedly squirming in my hold.

Still holding her hands, I pushed myself up so I was hovering over her while she lay back on my pillow.

I raised an eyebrow. "Looks like you're stuck, James."

"You like being in charge, huh, tough guy?" Her lips curved.

Sure did. In truth, I wasn't applying much pressure. If she wanted to, she could easily pull away. And if she told me to, I'd let go instantly. It was more about the perception of being restrained.

"I like playing around with you." I grinned, drifting closer to barely brush my lips against hers, then pulling back again. I paused until she met my gaze. "But if you say stop, it's a hard stop."

"I know," she said softly. "I don't want you to stop."

I lowered my voice, watching her face. "But do you like me being in charge?"

So far, I had pretty good instincts when it came to her. And I had a strong hunch that I was right about this, but I wanted verbal confirmation.

Her pupils dilated. "Kind of."

"Kind of?" I said. "Or yes?"

"Is it weird if I say yes?" Her breath grew shallow.

"No," I rasped. "I like it. But I don't want to overstep and upset you. That's why I asked."

Color flooded her cheeks. "Yes."

Knowing this took my fantasies to a whole new level. Oh, the possibilities. So many possibilities.

We would have to ease into that, but maybe I could take my foot off the brake a little.

"Mmm," I murmured, studying her—flushed cheeks, parted lips. "That's fucking hot."

Bailey's eyes gleamed, the shyness fading away. "Why?" She tugged against my hands playfully. "What would you do if you were in charge?"

I shook my head, biting back a smile. "Oh, James. So many things."

"Tell me one." Her voice was breathy.

Damn, where would I even begin?

Spank her, blindfold her, tie her up, have her talk dirty to me, talk even dirtier to her, edge her, have her touch herself in front of me…

I could go on all night. God knows I'd had time to think about it.

But we had to walk before we could run, skate before we could shoot, and all that.

"In time."

Ducking behind her ear, I brushed my nose against her skin, inhaling her sweet scent and holding it in my lungs for a beat. She sighed as I trailed a line of soft, open-mouthed kisses along the curve of her neck. Moving down to her shoulder, I gently sank my teeth into her flesh.

"Right now, I do have one thing in mind."

"What's that?" The words were a whisper across her lips.

"Making you come all over my fingers."

Now that I'd gotten her there with my tongue, I was confident I could do it with my hands too.

And hopefully after that, with my favorite body part.

She nodded, watching me. "Okay."

I kissed her again, reaching behind her back and undoing the clasp of her bra before slipping the straps off her shoulders. Taking her nipple in my mouth, I sucked, swirling my tongue around her perfect pink tip. She tilted her head back and let out a sigh, raking her hands through my hair. I palmed her other breast, squeezing before releasing her nipple from my mouth and moving to the other side.

Smoothing a hand down my abs, Bailey grabbed me through my boxers, pressing her palm against me, sending pleasure surging through my body. Holy fuck. This didn't bode well for my stamina later.

Breathe. I needed to focus.

Her back arched as I skimmed the sides of her torso. I nipped and sucked my way back up her neck and across her jawline, kissing her on the mouth before pulling back again.

I wanted to see her face for this.

I slipped my hand beneath the waistband of her underwear, caressing the soft skin of her lower abdomen. At the contact, she drew in a jagged breath, lids fluttering closed as I moved lower and rubbed between her legs with the pad of my finger.

She was so warm and wet, soft like silk. All I wanted was to be buried inside her, balls deep. But not yet. I'd keep things slow, savor her a bit, and make sure she was ready.

My fingers glided against her again, and she pushed against my hand, needy and wanting. Blond hair against my pillow, squirming with pleasure. Seeing her like this was the hottest thing ever.

"Baby, you're so fucking wet."

She let out a little gasp, hips undulating against me. I slid one finger along her clit, sinking lower to slip inside. Another finger followed, and I stroked. My thumb moved to press her nub, working in rhythm with my fingers.

Her breath quickened, cheeks growing flushed as I kept stroking her. She whimpered, biting her bottom lip as she rocked her pelvis in rhythm with my movements.

"Do you like how that feels?"

Her eyes flew open like I'd surprised her. She looked at me, lids heavy and eyes glassy, but she didn't respond.

"Do you, James?" I repeated, dropping my voice. When she didn't reply again, I pressed her gently with my thumb.

She drew in a shaky breath. "Y-yes."

"Are you going to come for me, baby?"

"Mm-hmm," she moaned, nodding slightly.

I moved a little faster as her breath quickened. Her pussy clamped down on my fingers, pulsing as she writhed beneath me. She cried out, growing even hotter and wetter, right at the edge.

Fisting her hair at the nape, I tugged gently, angling her face and devouring her mouth. I rubbed her, unrelenting, as her legs started to tremble. She clutched at my arms, her nails digging into my skin, crying out against my lips as she came apart.

Still kissing her, I eased off with my fingers, gradually letting her down. Giving her a breather so I didn't completely overstimulate her, I broke apart from her lips.

She drew in a shaky breath, watching me, her grip on my arms relaxing.

"Hi, baby." I ran my free hand through her hair, tracing down her neck, down her arm.

"Hi," she said, still breathless.

"Need a minute?" I asked.

She drew in a breath, cheeks still flushed pink.

"Maybe one."

CHAPTER 32
ALL MINE
BAILEY

AS MY HEART rate slowed to normal, my brain resumed functioning, and a tidal wave of thoughts hit me.

This was happening.

Suddenly, I was nervous again. Mostly nervous I wouldn't live up to what Chase expected. His sexual experiences could probably fill an encyclopedia, but mine would fit on a Post-it note.

Plus, he was big. A lot bigger than Luke. Yeah, things could stretch, but…how much? And would it hurt?

Chase held himself up on his elbows, hovering over me.

"Where'd you go just now?" His dark hair, now messy, tumbled over his forehead as he studied my face.

"I'm here," I said softly, placing my palms on his upper arms. His skin was warm and smooth beneath them.

I wanted this. Wanted him. For more reasons than I could count—desire, intimacy, curiosity, affection. Because I cared about him and I wanted to be close to him. I wasn't having doubts; it was more like an awareness of the gravity of the decision. One I couldn't go back from.

He ran the pad of his thumb along my lower lip. "Do you have any idea what you do to me?"

There was such fondness in his eyes that my nerves abated instantly.

"No idea."

His lips turned up in a small smile. "There are no words."

I ran my hands along his muscular shoulders and pulled him closer. I could feel how hard he was as he pressed against me and kissed me deeper, claiming, demanding.

With his mouth still moving against mine, he slid his hands along my torso, tugging my lacy underwear down and picking up my legs to take them off. I found his boxer briefs and pulled them down. He lifted himself and slid out of them, all without breaking contact with my lips.

Breaking our kiss, he sat back on his knees and leaned over. He pulled open his nightstand drawer and fished around for a second, emerging with a condom wrapper. In a flash, he tore it open, unrolled it, and was hovering over me again.

Then his brow knit together. "Hang on." He grabbed a pillow from beside me on the bed and, lifting my hips, slid it under me. "Better angle," he said, probably noting my confusion.

More evidence that he knew a lot more than I did about what was about to happen.

Chase leaned over me again, bracketing me with his arms. He was so big, so broad, his body an imposing presence surrounding me from every angle. Barely contained desire thrummed off him, like he was straining to hold back. But I'd never felt safer or more cared for.

I looked back up at him as his dark brown eyes caught mine, serious and questioning.

"You sure, James?"

I nodded, touching his jaw. "So sure."

He gripped his shaft and slid inside me slowly, an inch at a time. His mouth dipped to meet mine again, tongue pushing inside. I drew in a breath against his lips as he pushed all the way inside and the stretching sensation grew into a vulnerable sense of fullness. It was intense, but it didn't hurt.

When he was seated inside me, he stilled, pulling away from our kiss to look at me. He wrapped one strong hand behind my neck, gripping, holding me firmly in place beneath him. And with the other, he stroked my hair.

"Tell me if I'm being too rough, baby."

"I will."

Chase thrust slowly, intentionally, moving his body against mine. My breath hitched as pleasure instantly flickered between my legs. I closed my eyes, circling my hips to meet his movements, losing myself in the all-consuming feeling of him inside me. It was even better than I had imagined. And he was definitely right about the angle.

"You feel fucking amazing." His voice was low and husky, strained.

His words only added to the frenzy building within me. I dug my fingers into his back, needy and desperate for more.

He sank into me with the same undulating strokes, relentless and demanding. The pleasure between my legs continued to grow, expanding through my core and turning into a need, an urgency for release. Bringing his head down, Chase planted his lips against my neck, sucking and kissing, driving me to the brink.

It was too much and not enough all at once, and I was teetering on the edge of explosion. I moaned as heat flooded my body, the nearness of an orgasm seizing hold of me like a drug.

"There," I whimpered.

Chase smiled against my skin and thrust deeper, sending an overwhelming swell of pleasure through my core.

"Here?" He slid his hand down to my left hip, pinning me in place as he pushed into me again, creating a sense of agonizing ecstasy.

"*Yes*." All my control disappeared, and instinct overtook me. I wrapped my other leg around his torso and dug in my heel. "Please don't stop."

"I won't, baby."

With that, I let go. My legs trembled as my skin turned feverish against his. Chase moved closer, covering my mouth with his and tugging the roots of my hair. With another drive of his hips, everything exploded. I cried out against his lips, clutching his back with my fingers desperately as I fell, losing myself completely in the rapture.

He tore his lips from mine, thrusting into me again.

"Oh my god," I moaned. The peak went on and on, seemingly endless, as I pulled him tighter against me until it finally receded.

"Fuck," he groaned, increasing his pace. "You're so fucking hot."

He dragged his other hand from my hip to grab my ass, pulling me against him roughly and pumping into me harder. Then he slammed into me one last time with a growl, muscles straining.

Chase stilled, dropping his head to my shoulder, his heart pounding in his chest against mine.

Drawing in a shaky breath, he lifted his head to look at me with a tired grin.

"You're amazing. And so sexy when you're moaning beneath me."

Still recovering, I gave him a tiny smile. I was so high I might not ever come down.

He leaned in, kissing me softly before he pulled out of me. Then he stood and turned away, throwing the condom in the trash. I waited as he pulled back the covers and climbed in beside me, hauling me closer in his arms.

We snuggled as he ran a hand through my hair over and over again until my body was so relaxed that my muscles felt like Jell-O. I nestled against his chest, lost in a warm, fuzzy trance. Like I'd expected, taking this step had shifted things between us. A new kind of intimacy had formed, like being truly seen for the first time.

And my heart was full in a way it had never been.

He traced a fingertip along the logo of the T-shirt I was wearing. "See? Told you my shirts look better on you."

"I'm partial to this one myself."

"That's my favorite on you too." He sighed, falling quiet for a beat. "It's weird."

"What's weird?" I asked, glancing up at him.

He rested his cheek against the top of my head. "I didn't know what I was missing until I found it."

My breath caught. I almost wanted to cry at the way the words made my chest go tight. It was like an overwhelming rush of affection mixed with an emotion I couldn't identify. Maybe it was vulnerability.

"You're pretty sweet when you want to be," I told him.

"I mean it, though." He ran his fingers down my arm, to the ends of my fingers, and back again.

"I'm glad I have you too."

"That's good, because I'm all in on this. And I don't know if you've noticed, but I can be pretty stubborn."

We lay still for another moment, tired and contented. Then his stomach growled insistently, breaking the silence.

He flashed me a sheepish grin. "I'm starving. Didn't eat after the game, then I worked up an appetite with you. What are you in the mood for?"

"Whatever you want." Though now that he mentioned it, I was starving too. Shiv and I had eaten a late lunch slash early dinner after apartment hunting, but that was hours ago.

"If it's okay with you," he said, "I'm going to veto pizza. I'm still annoyed with that fucking delivery guy."

I laughed. "Sure. And maybe we can actually watch that movie while we eat."

Chase unpacked the food on the kitchen counter and sorted through it. I surveyed the contents of the three paper bags, which were probably enough to feed ten people. Styrofoam containers of rice, silver trays of chow mein, stir-fry, beef with broccoli, cashew chicken with vegetables, spicy shrimp, more noodles, and a few other meat dishes. The common theme here? Meat.

"Do you think you ordered enough food?" I teased, tilting my head. "I'm afraid we might run out."

Opening the cupboard, I took out the plates and set them on the counter. While I was turned away from him, he swatted my behind with a kitchen towel playfully.

"I told you. I've had a physically taxing night. A man needs to eat."

"That's true. You did work hard," I said, turning back to face him.

Walking over to me, Chase gave me a crooked smile. He placed a hand on either side of me, fencing me in against the counter.

"You know what they say; hard work pays off."

"Oh, it did," I said. "It definitely did."

His eyes gleamed mischievously. "Speaking of that—when are we going toy shopping?"

Oh. So he hadn't forgotten.

"You were serious about that?"

"Of course," he said. "I can't think of anything hotter than seeing you using something like that."

I uttered a little involuntary gasp because that scenario had never even crossed my mind. Really?

"Or by yourself," he added.

I still wasn't convinced I could get used to it—ever—but I'd told him I would keep an open mind.

"We'll see..."

"Or I could go without you." He shrugged. "Make it a surprise."

Gulp. That would be worse than facing the sex boutique by myself.

"Maybe it's better I come with you."

"Great." He winked at me. "Let's make a date."

I woke up to the bed sagging under Chase's weight as he slid under the covers and draped a heavy arm around my waist. His body was warm and comforting wrapped against mine, the scent of his soap and cologne surrounding me.

I peeked through one eye to discover light seeping between the gaps in the curtains. It was morning, which meant he must have returned from dryland training.

Shifting, I moved closer, snuggling into him. This was the best imaginable way to wake up.

"Sorry. Didn't mean to wake you," he whispered, giving me a squeeze.

"It's okay."

Realizing I probably had horrible morning breath, I lifted my head and tried to wriggle out of his grip, but his arm held me tighter, keeping me in place.

"No way." His tone turned deep and gravelly. "I sped home for this."

I laughed, turning my head partway to face him. "I need to brush my teeth. Especially because you already did."

"Fine." Chase sighed, reluctantly releasing his hold. "But make it quick."

In a sleepy daze, I used the bathroom and brushed my teeth. When I opened the bathroom door again, he patted the mattress beside him, inclining his head.

"You. Here."

Pulling back the covers, I crawled in and faced him. "You sped home to snuggle?"

He shrugged. "I sped home to do whatever you want. But I have some ideas if you need suggestions."

CHAPTER 33
DOUBLE-EDGED
CHASE

AFTER SPENDING THE NIGHT—AND morning—with James, I was on cloud fucking nine. I drove her to class, popped back home for a few, then headed to campus, where I spent the day basking in a perfect post-sex high.

Okay, so I wasn't overly focused on my lectures. Economic theory was going in one ear and out the other while I daydreamed about various naughty scenarios—with the odd hockey-related tangent thrown in—but I was in a good mood, at least.

Dallas, on the other hand, was not so chipper. Like he was brooding underneath a massive black cloud. I'd seen him in passing on my way out the door, and he was grouchy as hell. When I'd said "see you later," he'd grunted. Snarled might have been a more accurate descriptor.

By the time practice rolled around in the late afternoon, his mood hadn't improved. He barreled into the dressing room and threw his bag down on the bench beside me like it had personally offended him.

I finished pulling on my socks and glanced up at him with a questioning look. "What's up?"

"Nothing," he said under his breath.

Right…

"Are you and Shiv okay?" I asked, trying to catch his eye. "I thought I heard you two arguing this morning."

Over Dallas's shoulder, Tyler widened his eyes, shaking his head emphatically. Whoops. Too late now.

Dallas avoided my gaze. "Dunno." He bent over and unzipped his bag, then pulled out his socks and base layers and worked on removing his street clothes.

"What do you mean you don't know?" I said, fastening my shin pads. "How can you not know?"

Ty cleared his throat loudly and shot me a *what the fuck* look. But subtlety had never been my strength, and it was a genuine question. My relationship experience was obviously pretty limited, but wouldn't one know if their relationship was okay or not? Didn't people talk to each other? Especially when they'd been together as long as Dallas and Shiv.

"Just worried about you," I added gingerly. "You've been off all day."

"Look," he said. "I take it that you finally got laid, and I'm happy for you, man. I really am. Shiv and I are not in a good place. We got into it at O'Connor's." Dallas yanked on his compression pants and stood, grabbing his base shirt. His jaw ticked. "Some dumb shit was hitting on her."

Dallas had, shall we say, a mild jealous streak. Shiv did attract a lot of attention. Combine that with her refusal to fully commit, and he got a little touchy at times.

Tyler made a show of turning away, silently exiting the conversation. They'd probably already been through this, and Tyler's usual blunt "just fucking deal with it" advice likely went over like a lead puck.

"Was she flirting back?" I asked.

"No. But she wouldn't even say she had a boyfriend. Just told the dude that she was there with 'someone.' Like, what the fuck? I'm 'someone'? So I told her, in or out. Decide."

"Holy shit." I pulled on my shorts, turning to face him. "Isn't that kind of awkward if she's staying with us?"

"Guess I'll crash on the couch."

"Are you serious?"

"I'm not sure." Dallas hung his head. He raked a hand through his hair and looked at me, expression tense. Then he ducked in closer, lowering his voice. "I'm just fed up. I mean, come on. I have chicks all up on my jock left and right. But the only one I want can't stomach calling me her boyfriend?"

It was ironic. Being hard to get was part of Shiv's appeal early on. While so many other girls tried to land Ward by any means possible, like nudity or offering up blowjobs, Shiv wasn't one of those chicks who liked the idea of landing a hockey player.

I understood the intrigue. I liked that about Bailey too. Being wanted for *what* I was rather than *who* I was had gotten old fast. But months later, Dallas only sort of had Shiv, and it wasn't enough. I could see both sides. On the one hand, it was just a label. On the other, the label was kinda nice.

"Has she said what her issue with that is?"

"Something about her ex," Dallas muttered. "Turned psycho and got possessive. She won't give me any details."

Bailey had sort of alluded to that too but hadn't gotten into it. All I'd gathered was the dude was worse than Morrison, which meant he must be pretty fucking terrible.

"That's rough."

"Sure," he agreed, stepping into his skates and lacing them up. "But obviously she knows I'm not a psycho by now."

"Except when it comes to video games."

Dallas made a face. "Ha ha. Fuck off."

"Doesn't really sound like a you problem." Which meant he couldn't fix it, but telling him that wouldn't be helpful.

"I know, but how long do I put up with this? It's been, like, five months. Almost six."

"What's the alternative?" I gestured. "Come on, man. Are you really going to end things with Shiv because you like her too much? You realize that sounds fucking stupid, right?"

Behind Dallas, Tyler snorted.

"Thanks, Ty." Dallas drew in a breath. "And your brutal honesty is refreshing as always, Carter."

Pulling on my shoulder pads, I shrugged. "I'm just saying."

"I like that you've had a girlfriend for like, twelve hours, and suddenly you're a goddamn relationship guru."

"To be fair," I said, "I've been calling out your stupidity for years."

Dallas rolled his eyes. "Yeah, I gave up on yours. That shit would be a part-time job."

"I'll have you know I haven't done anything stupid in at least a month or two."

Admittedly, the summer had been rocky, and I'd made more than a handful of regrettable decisions. But fall had been smooth sailing. Mostly because of Bailey. Okay, solely because of Bailey.

"Pretty sure that's a record," he said, pulling his red captain's jersey over his head.

"Yeah." I nodded. "Pretty sure it is."

I was amped up on testosterone and refueled sexual frustration during practice, which meant I had no shortage of energy. Yeah, I was frustrated again. It would take a while to work that out of my system. A long while.

"Carter!" Dallas shouted.

I snapped back to reality in the middle of the rink. "What?"

"The puck?" He gestured. "Go get it. We're done for today."

"Oh, right." I skated off to the side and retrieved it before hopping off the ice.

One would think finally having sex would temper some of my horniness, but instead, it fueled it. Now I was thinking about James twenty-four seven. That part wasn't new, but the scenarios had heated up significantly.

Though I was still trying to reconcile what she told me at XS with how she was in my bed, because they were like night and day. Seemed like actually paying attention to her needs went a long way.

Christ. I felt sorry for chicks. Sometimes I wanted to mail a map of the clitoris and a fucking clue to other guys.

On the plus side, it made me look good in comparison.

After hitting the showers, I got dressed quickly and headed for Coach Miller's office. I'd hoped weekly check-ins would go to the wayside now that my probation had ended, but I still had the pleasure of seeing his shiny bald head and stern, cranky face for one-on-ones every five to seven days.

"Hi, Coach." I set down my bag, flopping into the seat across from him.

Hopefully, this would be another in-and-out meeting so I could go do literally anything else. Maybe hit the library before my last class to write my economics paper or text James or think about James instead of writing my economics paper. Ooh, James as a sexy librarian…goddamn it.

"Carter." Coach Miller tented his fingers, furrowing his brow. "I'd like to talk to you about the game the other day. Tell me about the hit you made on that Morrison kid from Callingwood. The one where you got a charging penalty."

Well, this wasn't good. Last thing I needed was to get benched for our next game against Callingwood because Miller thought I was a liability.

I mean, I probably was. But I didn't need him to know that.

I kept my expression neutral, my tone to match. "What do you mean?"

Dodging the Bullet 101: When sensing trouble, keep the other person talking to determine what, exactly, they know. Thus avoiding incriminating oneself.

Learned this one the hard way. Several times.

"You're lucky they didn't call a major penalty on you for that," he said. "You went way out of position to hit him. Why?"

"Got carried away, I guess." I shrugged.

"You never get carried away." He narrowed his eyes, studying my face with the intensity of someone reviewing game tapes. "Don't think I missed your verbal altercation with him beforehand. That hit was clearly personal."

"Off day," I said. "Won't happen again."

The lie detector determined: that was a lie.

He harrumphed, leaning back in his reclining desk chair. "Make sure you keep your head on straight out there. Your game was a little uneven too."

He wasn't wrong. The rest of the team wasn't pulling their weight, either, but that didn't excuse my lapse in performance.

"Noted, Coach."

BAILEY

After the night with Chase, I spent the following day in a total daze. I'd phoned it in for my classes, squealed over the new developments with Zara and Noelle at the *Callingwood Daily* office, and thought about him way too often.

Then I had to meet Siobhan to discuss which apartment to go with and pretend like I had my brain together.

I did not.

And like I'd thought about apartments.

I had not.

Roughly speaking, I was about 90 percent ecstatic and 10 percent terrified. I had no reason to be terrified. No excuse for feeling that way. Things had been nothing but amazing. And that's what scared me.

Being so high meant there was so much farther to fall.

"So," Siobhan smiled at me expectantly across the table, "how are things?"

Heat creeped up my neck. Suddenly, the cafe felt like a sauna.

"Good."

"Things with Chase, I mean."

"Really good."

She grinned. "Dallas wanted to bring people back to the house last night, and I told him no way."

"I appreciate that," I said, hiding behind the menu to conceal my blushing. "The alone time was nice."

"Did I hear him call you his girlfriend before you guys left?"

I broke into a grin. "Yeah, he sure did."

"That is adorable." She made a puppy dog face.

"Right? It's nice to finally make it official." I set the menu down. "What about—I mean, you and Dallas. You guys still haven't had that talk? If I'm being nosy, just tell me, and I'll shut up. We can blame it on too much time with Chase."

Shiv laughed at my last comment, then her expression sobered. "We had a fight about that last night, actually." She pursed her lips, looking away.

"You did?"

"Yeah," she said. "Some guy hit on me, and Dallas got pissy over it. I turned the guy down, so what does it matter? But then he tried to give me an ultimatum. I mean, he didn't phrase it that way. It was more of an 'are you in or not' type of thing?"

I sucked in a breath. "How did you guys leave it?"

"A little frosty. But we've had this argument before. It'll probably blow over." She shrugged. "It's not like I want to date anyone else."

"But…" I prompted her.

She winced. "What if making it official changes things?"

"That doesn't mean it'll change for the worse," I said gently. "It could change things for the better."

At least that's what I was hoping for with Chase. Not that there was much to improve on. But I felt more secure in our relationship now. Hopefully, I could work through some of my residual trust hang-ups. Might take a while, though.

Shiv frowned at her Diet Coke. "This is going to sound stupid. Like, really stupid. But I honestly never thought of it that way."

"If Dallas was anything like your ex, you wouldn't still be with him."

"I know." She sighed, pinching the bridge of her nose. "I'm crazy about the guy. He's right there in front of me. The man's perfect. What the hell is wrong with me?"

I shrugged. "Once burned, twice shy. I get it."

"Honestly, I'm this close to taking the leap." She held her thumb and pointer finger an inch apart. "I just need to wrap my head around it."

After we ordered, our conversation turned to the reason we were here: living arrangements. At this point, we'd narrowed our apartment selections down to two. The unit I had liked initially, plus another new one that had come onto the market when its prospective tenant fell through at the last minute. It was one hundred dollars more per month, which wasn't totally make-or-break, but still a factor.

Shiv took a sip of her drink, then slumped over the table. "I hate making decisions," she said, muffled by her arm.

"Me too," I admitted. Between the both of us, it was a tough combination. "The possession date for the first one is in four weeks. But the new unit on Pine is available almost immediately."

"Right," she said, glancing up at me. "As soon as we clear reference checks, get the deposit, and all of that."

Shiv was fronting almost all of the deposit. She claimed not to care—Chase said her parents were loaded, which was probably why—but I hated feeling like I was freeloading.

Then my phone vibrated. I glanced down, expecting a text from Chase. But it was from Amelia: *Found someone who wants your room. They want to move in within two weeks.*

I wrote her back: *Fine*.

"Okay." I locked my phone and set it down again. "Sorry about that. What are your thoughts on going with the unit on Pine? That was Amelia, and they found someone to take my room. I need to be out in two weeks."

It wasn't about the money so much as getting the hell out of there. And this was the push I needed. Being away from that toxic environment would be a relief.

The server set down Shiv's chicken quesadilla, then my buffalo chicken sandwich.

"If it makes the decision for us, maybe all the better," she said, dipping her quesadilla into the little bowl of salsa. "Then we don't have to agonize over it."

"Do we have an agreement then?"

"Yep." She nodded, doing a little dance in her seat. "I'll email the rental agent. I'm excited!"

"Me too," I said honestly, grabbing my sandwich. With an escape plan solidified, food had never looked so good.

My phone vibrated again. I expected a snarky follow-up from Amelia, but it was a text from Zara.

Zara: Good news, bad news. Liam just quit. Sports section is all yours! But that means you need to cover that volleyball tournament out of town. Sorry, I know it's short notice.

I let out a gasp. "Oh my god."

Shiv frowned. "Everything okay?"

"Everything is great," I said, staring at the screen in giddy disbelief. "I just got a promotion at the school newspaper."

This was the experience I needed to build my portfolio for after college. If I landed the paid internship, the combination of the two would look seriously impressive to potential employers.

Except…this meant I'd be attending more Bulldogs games. And, like, interacting with the team to get quotes and conduct interviews.

Ugh. Talk about a double-edged hockey stick.

After finishing up dinner with Siobhan, I texted Chase about the volleyball tournament. Now that I was handling the entire sports section alone, it was even more imperative that I attend. Although I didn't mind having an excuse to take a day trip with him.

Bailey: What's your schedule like the Saturday after next?

Chase: Practice at eight Saturday, off Sunday.

Bailey: Perfect. I have an exciting proposition for you.

Chase: Keep talking.

Bailey: I've got my hands on a pair of super hot tickets to…

Bailey: Callingwood's volleyball game in Roseford.

Chase: And I have the text version of blue balls.

Chase: Just kidding. If it's with you, I'm down.

Bailey: It's our team's finals. But…it's 1.5 hours away, early Saturday afternoon. Does that work? I would give you gas money.

Chase: Of course, and not a chance.

Bailey: You never let me pay for things.

Chase: Never will. Sorry, James.

CHAPTER 34
PERSONAL SHOPPER
BAILEY

I PERCHED at the table in the *Callingwood Daily* office with Noelle and Zara, trying to finish my part of a group project for Ethical Issues in Journalism and Communications. Knowing I'd see Chase later always made it difficult to focus, but today was especially challenging because he was picking me up later for the volleyball game—followed by sex toy shopping.

What had I gotten myself into?

I hadn't even told Noelle or Zara, though I knew they'd cheer me on if I did.

"Bailey," Professor Johnson said, lingering in the doorway. "Can we chat quickly in my office for a moment?"

I glanced up from my laptop. "Sure." I shut it quickly and slid it into my bag, then followed her out of the room and down the hall to her office.

Professor Johnson was the epitome of laid-back, down to her untameable frizzy gray hair and colorful floor-length skirts. A hippie in her youth, she'd racked up countless journalism awards for her coverage of international affairs. As our faculty advisor for the paper, she tended to give us a long leash. But she did check in with us every now and then when we needed guidance or when something went truly off the rails.

She lowered herself into her desk chair, gesturing for me to have a seat. "I wanted to touch base with you about taking over for Liam. I know it was sudden."

"I'm excited," I said, sinking into the red cloth chair across from her. "I've always wanted to handle the sports coverage."

Professor Johnson raised her salt-and-pepper eyebrows. "Are you sure you can manage it on top of your other responsibilities? I know you have a heavy course load, and I don't want to overwhelm you."

"No, it won't be a problem."

I just might have to make a few sacrifices. Like sleep. Or possibly my sanity. You know, those minor negotiable things.

"Good." She nodded, sliding a piece of paper across the desk to me. It was a list of Liam's assignments until Christmas. "I wasn't sure what he passed along to you in terms of his current and future assignments. As you can see, he started a feature about how the assistant captain for the Bulldogs is stepping up to guide the team while their captain is injured."

I took a closer look at the list, and my stomach plummeted to the floor. Much to my dismay, there it was, second bullet from the top: *Bulldogs feature with assistant captain.*

The Bulldogs' assistant captain was Paul.

Would it be unprofessional of me to dry heave?

"Liam did an interview with him already?" I asked. "Does he have a recording or transcript I can review?"

"No," she said, folding her hands over top of the desk. "He hadn't completed it yet."

By "starting" the feature, she meant Liam had thought about it. Maybe.

Dread took root in my stomach and blossomed from there. A one-on-one interview with Paul wasn't exactly on my bucket list, even if it would add to my writing portfolio.

"Since you're familiar with the team," Professor Johnson added, "I knew it would be no problem for you to conduct the interview so you can write the article."

I nodded, but I wanted to scream. "Right. None at all."

"I can email you the guidelines for a feature article as well, since this is your first time writing one."

"Thanks," I said, "that would be great."

By the time I left her office, it was time to leave to meet Chase at the traffic roundabout. I made my way out of the center for communications and texted Amelia for Paul's number while I walked across campus. After receiving an exceptionally frosty response—almost like she thought I wanted it to hit on him or something, and um, not a freaking chance—she eventually passed it along.

Then I connected with him via text and arranged a time to meet at a coffee shop on campus Monday. Better to get it over with rather than have it looming over my head.

A few hours later, Callingwood had pulled off an impressive win, Chase and I had eaten more than our share of junk food at the game, and we were back in town.

He pulled into a parking spot in front of Lush Boutique and killed the ignition. The neon pink sign glowed accusatorially at us. Going in there would be like announcing to the world that I was having sex. Not just sex, freaky sex. Or that I was masturbating, which I wasn't keen on advertising, either.

"Ready?" He turned to face me, dark brown eyes glinting playfully.

Nerves seized hold of me, fight-or-flight response kicking in. The trepidation was like the first time I'd filled my birth control prescription amplified times a million.

"Nope." I shook my head, crossing my legs. "I changed my mind. I can't go in there."

Could I?

Chase lifted a shoulder, his expression neutral. "Okay. I won't make you. We can leave if you want."

Ambivalence simmered within me. In theory, I wanted to leave. But reality was a different story and he knew it. He was eerily good at reading me. But since he literally said what he was thinking all the time, I guess that evened out.

I bit my bottom lip. "I don't know."

"I'll be right with you." He rubbed my thigh and left his warm hand there. "In and out. Easy."

"But we have to pay before we can go home." I looked at him, cringing. "Like, I have to stand there and face another person while purchasing…that."

He cocked an eyebrow. "You think a sex shop cashier is going to judge you for buying a little vibrator? Trust me, James. Those people have seen some shit."

I glanced at the store through the windshield, back to him, then at the store again.

Part of me was curious. Most of me was intimidated.

It was just a store. A simple brick and glass structure, innocuous enough from the outside. But as for what it contained…

Chase squinted, leaning over the steering wheel. "Look," he nodded at the window, "Carl's working the register today. He's super nice."

"You know the cashiers *by name*?"

"It was a joke," he said, laughing. "How much of a perv do you think I am?"

I reached over and poked his arm. "I plead the fifth."

"If you join me, you have some input." He winked. "But I can go in without you if you want. We could make it a surprise like I said before."

"That sounds even scarier." I drew in a breath and held it for a beat before exhaling. To go, or not to go? The million-dollar question.

Chase held my gaze. "James." He lowered his voice, intentionally doing that thing that somehow massaged my brain—not to mention other parts of my body—and made it impossible to say no to.

"Yeah?"

"Come on."

"Fine," I grumbled, but I was a little thankful for the prodding.

What was the worst that could happen? Other than dying of embarrassment.

CHASE

I'd done my homework for this outing, and I'd intentionally chosen a nicer, chick-friendly store per the reviews and pictures online. The inside of this one looked more like a clothing boutique than a sex shop, finished with wood shelving and decked out in black and pink decor.

It was the opposite of the seedy, fluorescent-lit type of store one would picture when thinking "sex shop," which made it perfect. Hopefully.

We entered and made a beeline past the role play costumes, sex swings, and a BDSM section taking up an entire corner. Fortunately, no one else was in the store, so that was one less thing to potentially freak out James.

On the far wall stood an array of vibrators, butt plugs, and other battery-operated toys. I guided her over, maneuvering myself so I was blocking the adjacent shelf of massive suction-cup dildos from her line of sight. We were shooting for baby steps here. Hell, some of them even disturbed me a little. They were gigantic. I didn't even want to think about the amount of lube those would require.

I scanned the display, looking for something beginner friendly. They had a decent selection, at least. Rabbit vibrators, bullet vibrators, G-spot stimulators, massage wands, the works. I quickly ruled out anything too anatomically correct. I was pretty sure she had no desire for a veiny purple battery-operated cock. Ditto the low-end toys; this wasn't the type of purchase to cut corners on.

"I don't even know what most of these things are," Bailey said under her breath, fidgeting with the sleeve of her gray wool coat. "I can't believe I'm doing this."

I squeezed her hand. "It's pretty awesome that you are. Gonna be worth it." And I meant it on both counts.

"If you say so." She ran a hand through her loose blond waves, stealing another nervous glance at me. Then she turned her attention back to the display with a hint of curiosity on her face.

See? I knew she had a naughty side. It was just buried really, really deep.

And uncovering it would be half the fun.

My gaze fell to an app-operated turquoise vibrator, my interest piquing. Remote control. The display said the app worked remotely from different locations. Holy shit. If I could get James off while I was out of town for hockey, that would be the fucking sexiest thing ever. Definitely not happening today, but it was going on my shopping list for later.

"What about this?" I grabbed a hot pink silicone bullet vibe off the shelf and examined it. It looked and felt high-end, with a contoured shape, and it wasn't much larger than my thumb. It was about as cute and non-threatening as a sex toy could get.

Bailey eyed it warily, like it might bite. "I don't know."

Turning it over, I switched the button on the base to low. It hummed quietly, vibrating in a pulsing pattern. I pushed another button, and it moved in a slower, wavelike rhythm. Versatile. Nice.

"Look, it has different settings." I held it out to her, changing the pattern again to a steady vibration. "See? It's not scary."

She furrowed her brow and reached out, poking it with her finger. "Huh," she said. "It's softer than I thought it would be."

"Potential?"

"You tell me." Bailey shrugged. "I have no idea what I'm looking at."

"We can keep looking if you want." I switched it off and set it back on the shelf, scanning the other toys. "This one looks like a tube of lipstick. This one fits on your finger. This one has suction…"

"This first one sounds fine." She turned, surveying the store for onlookers—like she might randomly stumble upon a college classmate in a random sex toy boutique downtown. "Should we go pay?"

"Yeah. Let me look at the box for a second." Fifteen speeds, ten different rhythms, anatomically designed, made out of medical grade silicone with a USB charger. So theoretically, I could charge it in my truck. Handy. And a six-hour battery life, which I couldn't see using in one go, but good to know.

Bailey laughed. "You're acting like you're buying a car." Then her eyes fell to the price tag, widening. "Oh my god. You practically are. It's a hundred and twenty dollars."

"Good toys aren't cheap," I said. "Plus, think of where it's going." We'd already established that I was paying, and it wasn't up for discussion, so there wasn't much more she could say to that.

I held up the box. "You in agreement?"

"Sure."

I snagged a bottle of toy cleaner to go with it, and we made our way to the cash register by the doors. Contrary to my joke about Carl, the sales associate working the register was a chick. She was close to our age, heavily tattooed with a septum piercing, and a name tag that read Harriet. Weird. She did not look like a Harriet.

She glanced up from the worn paperback she was reading, bookmarking her spot and setting it aside. "Find everything you were looking for?"

"Sure did," I said, passing her the items.

Bailey gave her a polite, albeit uneasy, smile. I squeezed her hand again, and she squeezed it back. She'd actually come, and I was stoked that she did.

And eager to get her back to my place.

Harriet scanned the vibrator box and the bottle of toy cleaner, then I handed her my credit card. There was a display of massage candles beside the register that looked intriguing, but we could circle back to that one later too. My list kept getting longer and longer.

"Since you spent over thirty dollars today, you get a complimentary sample of flavored lube," she said, printing out my receipt and placing it in the small black and pink bag.

"Cool," I said.

The cashier pointed to the display. "Which flavor do you want?"

"You pick." I nudged Bailey.

"Huh?" She snapped out of her daze, glancing over at the bottles on display: mango, pink lemonade, strawberry, watermelon. "Um... strawberry?" she squeaked, cheeks turning pink. Adorable.

The salesclerk tossed a tiny sample bottle into the bag and slid it across the counter. Bailey grabbed it, which I took as a massive win.

"Next time, I'll pack sunglasses and a hat for you," I said, throwing an arm over her shoulders and kissing the top of her head as we headed for the door. "You can go incognito."

"Oh my god, no." She glanced up at me. "Next time we're ordering online."

"So you're open to expanding your toy collection down the road?"

Bailey laughed. "Never change, Carter."

"You wanna swing by the handcuffs on the way out, or...?"

"I'm good," she said. "Maybe next time."

Wait, *what*?

I turned to look at her. "Really?"

"I said maybe."

Pushing the door open, I held it for her, and we headed back outside into the chilly fall air. The weather had taken a turn, reminding us that winter was imminent.

"Food time?" My truck beeped from afar as I hit the remote start, the engine roaring to life.

"Yeah," she said. "I'm starving."

I guided her to the passenger-side door and backed her up against it. My hands found her waist and I leaned in, kissing her quickly. Had to keep it brief because I was already too worked up for my own good. Plus, she smelled delicious, like vanilla and Bailey. Good enough to eat. Literally.

Hmm. Maybe we could skip that meal.

We pulled apart and I studied her face. "What are you in the mood for?"

"I'm not sure." She shrugged, lips quirking. "What about you?"

Opening that box and test driving the toy, but I wasn't going to push my luck. She could take it home, and we'd see how that went. Fingers crossed.

"You," I said. "Sitting on my face."

Her eyes widened, and she looked over my shoulder, then back at me. "Carter." She gave me a look. "We're in public."

"Technically, we're in a parking lot. And I didn't mean here. Just, you know, later."

I opened the door and shut it behind her before walking around to the driver's side.

"What's the over/under on the timeline for opening that box?" I put the truck into reverse and backed out.

"I don't know," Bailey said evasively. "Depends on lots of things."

I stole a glance at her. "I give it four days, max."

My real bet was two, but I was being conservative.

"Aren't you optimistic?"

"Always," I said. "Gonna tell me when you do?"

Her expression shifted, a mixture of self-conscious and mischievous. "You want me to?"

"Hell, yeah."

Ideally, I wanted a play-by-play, pictures, video. A highly detailed review. But I'd settle for knowing. My imagination could do the rest.

She grinned. "We'll see."

CHAPTER 35
AN EXCUSE
CHASE

ON THE DRIVE TO DINNER, I managed to pull my mind out of the gutter enough to be out in public without risking arrest. As long as I didn't let my thoughts circle back to the errand we just completed.

That part took some self-control.

I ordered for both of us and handed the server the menus. We'd gotten a whack load of appetizers instead of meals—chicken wings, spinach-artichoke dip, pulled pork sliders, the works. Bailey was the opposite of picky, which complemented my less adventurous palate nicely. A.k.a., she let me pick all the food. She was the best.

"I meant to ask," I said. "Are you going home for Thanksgiving?"

"Still have to decide with Derek and my parents." Bailey pursed her lips. Her black sweater slid off her shoulder a little, revealing a glimpse of black bra strap underneath. I had to consciously clamp down on the thought spiral as she adjusted her neckline. "But I'll probably wait until Christmas. It's too expensive to fly home for both holidays."

"My mom's place is only an hour away. If you don't leave, I'm dragging you home with me. Just FYI."

"Really?" Her face brightened. "You'd want me to come?"

"Of course. I'd never let you spend a holiday alone." Was that even a question? "Plus, then you can meet my dysfunctional family."

Kidding not kidding on the dysfunctional part.

"I'm sure they're not that bad."

I grimaced. "You might want to temper those expectations. My mom's fine, and my younger sister, Seraphina, is cool. But in the interest of full disclosure, my stepdad, Rick, is kind of a douche. Neither my sister nor I get along with him."

Rick didn't respect professional sports as a valid career path and made no attempt to hide it. I guess it wasn't fancy enough for his snotty CPA ass. Too bad I would rather fucking die than stare at spreadsheets behind a desk all day.

Similarly, Rick thought Seraphina was a bit of an airhead and treated her accordingly, which pushed Sera's buttons, as well as mine.

Then there was my mom, who ran around like a chicken with her head cut off, trying to referee between all three parties. She was too soft-spoken to have much impact in that regard. Her quiet *tsks* and pleas to "be nice" did little.

Though having Bailey there as a buffer might be a good thing. Rick was probably less inclined to make his snide, passive-aggressive comments in the presence of outside company.

"Why don't you two get along?" Bailey took a sip of her ice water, studying my face.

Too many reasons to list.

"It's a long story."

"We have time," she said, raising her blond eyebrows. "If you want to tell me."

I shifted my weight in the booth, suddenly uncomfortable on every level. My big mouth strikes again. I'd brought it up in the first place. Might as well clear the air about some of those family skeletons.

The server returned, setting down our plates of food. I waited for her to finish before continuing.

"It goes back to when my dad died, ten years ago."

"Oh, gosh. You were so young." Bailey's hazel eyes brimmed

with sympathy. "I can't imagine how hard that must have been for all of you."

Breaking eye contact, I grabbed a slider and set it on my plate, giving myself a moment. While her intentions were pure, this was why I had dragged my feet on bringing this up—I hated the way people reacted. Being on the receiving end of pity never sat well with me. Although it shouldn't, it made me feel weak.

"Yeah, well …" I kept my gaze fixed on my pint of beer. "It was a helicopter crash. I meant to tell you about it sooner. Just hard to slip that one into casual conversation."

A sudden wave of guilt hit me. In addition to avoiding my dad as a topic of conversation, I avoided memories associated with him too. I had tons of his photos and NHL memorabilia at my mom's house. They should have been displayed in my bedroom, but it was too hard to look at it all every day.

Maybe I *was* weak.

Bailey reached across the table, taking my hand in hers. Being comforted by someone felt unfamiliar, but surprisingly, I didn't hate it. Probably because it was different with her. Everything was different with her.

"He was in Jersey, trying to make it back for my hockey game in Connecticut with his friend's private helicopter," I added. "His friend had an experienced pilot, but they hit an unexpected storm, and that was it. Chopper went down, and all that was left was the black box."

Followed by a swarm of predatory reporters climbing all over the crash site. I still hated the fucking press. That would probably become an issue someday when I had to actually talk to them.

Of course, he never would have been on that helicopter if I hadn't guilt-tripped him into coming home. It was my first season on a top-tier team, and all I'd been thinking about was myself. I never should have asked him to come.

I would never forget the way my mother had screamed when she received that phone call. The way she sank to her knees in the middle of our kitchen. The way a light went out inside her that never fully returned.

A knot formed in my stomach, and I drew in a deep breath, but it did little to quell the sensation.

"Why was he in New Jersey?" Bailey asked softly. "For work?"

I snapped back to reality. How long had I zoned out for?

"He played for them at the time. He had just been traded from New York, and we were still trying to sell our house."

Her thumb skated along my skin, easing some of the tension I was holding. "Did he play hockey with you when you were growing up?"

"All the time," I said, still avoiding her eyes. Talking about him made me feel nostalgic, sad, and uneasy all at once. "He's why I started playing."

"You must have loved watching him on TV."

"Sure did." I took a sip of my beer. Time to steer the conversation in another direction. It was easier to talk about my asshole stepdad.

"As far as Rick goes," I said, "I have to qualify this by saying that my mom's not a bad person. She never quite recovered after my dad died. It was like she was broken. Lost."

More specifically, my mom didn't get out of bed for a month and a half after the helicopter crash. After that, it was a merry-go-round of meds and therapy, a few good days sprinkled into a lot of bad. My happy, fun-loving mother disappeared and never returned. And my rebellious teenager stage did our relationship no favors—especially with Rick in the picture.

These days, we got along, even if we weren't close.

Bailey nodded. "I can imagine. It must have been devastating to your whole family."

She wasn't wrong. I think I'd been off-course ever since.

"Once she started dating again a year or so later, she dated a string of losers. Unemployed deadbeat types, probably after her for my dad's money. One guy, Mitch, was a straight-up alcoholic." I hesitated, weighing whether to continue.

Generally speaking, I hardly ever raised my voice. At my size, I didn't need to in order to get the point across. Even when I got into fights in hockey, I wasn't angry, per se. Annoyed maybe, or thinking someone needed sense knocked into them after a cheap hit, but not mad.

I could count the number of times I'd lost my temper on one hand.

But if I had a sore spot, it was men disrespecting or hurting women. Also see: Morrison.

"He pushed her against the fridge one night, and I beat the shit out of him."

James might worry that I had anger issues, but it happened; I couldn't rewrite history. Wouldn't want to, either. He deserved it.

Her eyes widened. "How old were you?"

"I was thirteen. But I was big for my age, and I was fucking pissed. He didn't know what hit him."

"I believe it," she said. "I've seen you fight."

"Anyway, having a difficult preteen the size of an adult wasn't a big selling point. I scared most of her boyfriends off, intentionally or not. Rick wasn't the worst of them by a long shot—he's decent to my mom, at least. But he didn't want kids, especially ones that weren't his. So he stuck around, but he made the rules. Which were basically, *don't be a pain in the ass and stay out of the way.*"

What looked like sadness mixed with a hint of anger flashed across Bailey's face. This was why I didn't get into things like this, though with her, it was tolerable.

"And you still don't get along?" she asked, tilting her head.

"I have a trust from my dad's insurance. Once I turned eighteen and gained access, I moved out, and things improved a little. We can sort of coexist now. He and Sera still butt heads a lot, though."

"What's your sister like?" Bailey looked at me playfully. "Is she trouble like you?"

"A bit of a party girl, which is probably why she's at ASU, but she's a sweetheart. You'll like her."

"I'm sure I will." She grabbed a chicken wing and took a bite, recoiling and setting it back down on her plate. "Holy crap. These aren't medium. They're more like extra-hot."

"I can send them back if you need, princess."

"Princess?" She narrowed her eyes. "I can handle them just fine."

"That's true. You're good at handling things."

"Oh my god, you"—she laughed, shaking her head—"never a missed innuendo."

"Now you know more than you ever wanted about my fucked-up family tree," I said. "What about your family? All I know is that your brother hates me." I bit into the barbecue pork slider, watching her reaction.

Bailey waved me off. "I wouldn't say he hates you..."

"Yeah." My lips quirked. "He definitely does."

Until recently, I would have said I wasn't a fan of his, either. But if it came down to it, I could get past it for her.

"My parents are your typical middle-class suburbanites. They'll be married for thirty years next spring. And I have two older brothers besides Derek."

"Oh good," I said cheerfully. "Then they can all gang up on me when I meet them."

"No, they aren't like that." Bailey picked up a blue corn tortilla chip and dipped it in the spinach-artichoke dip. "They aren't into hockey, so Derek's dumb grudge won't hold water. And Derek will come around—eventually." Her lips folded into a frown. "I don't know what's gotten into him, actually. We used to be close." She bit into her chip, expression clouding over.

"Maybe he's going through something with that whole Jillian mess. But it doesn't excuse him for being a crappy brother. Not to overstep."

Friend or not, Derek should have stood up to Morrison about Bailey a long time ago. More than that. Derek should have pummeled Morrison.

Ward was like a brother to me, but had they somehow dated, I would have never let him treat my sister like garbage.

"I don't disagree," she said. "But between classes, the paper, and you, I'll be so busy that I won't have time to worry about Derek anyway."

"That's right. You must be happy about getting the sports section all to yourself." I grinned.

"I am…Except it means more Bulldogs games." Bailey drew in a breath. "Maybe that's what I need to go incognito for."

My smile faded, my tone dropping. "Anyone gives you trouble, they answer to me."

It pissed me off that she was uncomfortable with the idea of being around these people, even in public. Especially when she'd never done anything to warrant their dislike. The way they treated her was fucking brutal. A bunch of spineless sheep.

"I think Jillian and Amelia already answered to Shiv."

"I heard she gave them a nice little verbal smackdown," I said. "But I meant the guys."

"Yeah." Her voice flattened, posture stiffening. "Speaking of that, I'm really dreading this interview with Paul."

My second least favorite person. Well, tied with Amelia and Jillian. They were all so terrible that it was hard to even rank them at this point.

"I can tag along if you want. Sit there and glare at his sorry ass to keep him in line."

I was 100 percent not kidding. I would enjoy nothing more than playing bodyguard around that idiot.

She paused with her hand in midair, reaching for a slider. "Probably not necessary, but I appreciate the thought."

"Are you sure?"

"I think I'll be okay," Bailey said, biting back a smile. "Your caveman act is cute as always, though."

And it was cute that she thought it was an act. This was how I was wired.

CHAPTER 36
DOING NOTHING
BAILEY

I TWISTED Chase's arm to get hot chocolates to go from the Uncommon Coffee Co. after dinner. Not that it took much twisting.

We made our way back to his truck, drinks in hand. The fall days were still reasonably pleasant, but once the sun set, the evenings turned bitingly chilly.

"How's packing coming?" he asked, taking my free hand in his.

I sipped my white hot chocolate. "I've got lots of the small stuff taken care of already. It's probably premature, but I'm excited to get the heck out of there."

"Me too. The new living arrangement will be way better for you." He paused, forehead creasing. "Though I don't love the idea of you on the train at night."

"It's a five-minute ride," I said. "Three stops."

He grunted but said nothing, which in Chase terms meant he didn't agree but didn't want to argue with me. Stubborn man.

I elbowed him gently. "I don't have any evening classes, anyway. The only time I stay late is when we're on deadline for the paper."

"Good," Chase said. "I'll pick you up on those days."

"What if you have a game?"

His eyes gleamed. "Then you'll be there watching me."

"Sometimes, Carter."

"All the time, James." He grinned. "Starting with our next game. We have to win this one. It's a male pride thing now."

I laughed. "I'll come. But honestly, you don't have to pick me up from campus every time I stay late."

"But I want to." His tone brooked no argument. "Besides," he added, "it would be a good excuse to squeeze in sleepovers."

"Do we need an excuse?"

"I guess not." We came to a stop by the truck, and he dipped, his lips meeting mine. A rush ran through me, electric and exhilarating. I curled my fingers around his coat and pulled him closer. He slanted his mouth against mine, deepening the kiss for a moment.

"Let's go," he said when he pulled back, nodding to the truck with a crooked grin. "I want to make good on what I said earlier."

No time was wasted once we got back to Chase's. We stumbled into his bedroom in a blur of kissing and groping, sighs and murmurs. Mouth still fused to mine, he shut the door behind us and locked it, then steered me over to his desk and switched on the lamp.

After another minute, we broke apart, breathless and dazed.

He gave me a slow, deliberate once-over in the dim light of his room. "You are wearing entirely too much clothing, James."

"Oh yeah? What are you gonna to do about it?" I asked, giving him a playful look.

"I'm not going to do anything." His voice turned dark and satin-smooth, like rich black coffee. "You're going to take it off for me."

Oh…my.

My pulse kickstarted, sending a surge of adrenaline through my veins.

"You want me to strip for you?"

"Uh-huh." He nodded, lips tugging into a rakish smile. "I'll make it worth your while."

"I might need a few drinks in me first," I said. "Like, approaching XS number of drinks."

Chase slipped his warm hands beneath the fabric of my sweater and ran them down the sides of my torso until they landed on my waist. Ducking his head, he skimmed his lips along the curve of my neck, alluding to kisses without delivering.

"I know you don't have a shirt under that sweater," he murmured against my skin, "so there are only two layers between me and you in a bra and underwear. And I can take those off with my teeth."

Heat unfurled between my legs at his offer. He planted a line of soft kisses starting below my ear, followed by a nip on the top of my shoulder. I drew in a soft breath of surprise, and a low chuckle rumbled from his chest.

"You are so beautiful." He kissed my neck again, featherlight. "And hot." He moved higher, kissing my jawline. "And sexy."

Winding his hand in the hair at my nape, he angled my face up to meet his, mouth crashing down on mine. I drew in a breath, parting my lips as his tongue slipped inside. Kissing him was like an instant kill switch for my brain. Everything else ceased to exist as the need in my core surged, growing nearly too great to ignore.

His other hand slid around to grip my behind, squeezing possessively. A wall of warm muscle pressed against my breasts as he drew our bodies close enough that I could feel exactly how much he wanted me. I splayed both palms on his chest, probing the muscle that lay beneath his shirt.

Then he slowly pulled away, pivoting us both half a turn. Still facing me, wearing a devilish smile, he took a few steps backward and lowered himself to sit on the edge of the bed.

Once in a while, I found myself awed by him. Surprised on some level that he was mine.

This was one of those moments.

Dark, tousled hair and a devastatingly perfect face. Eyes I could get lost in and a smile I couldn't say no to. And while he was still fully dressed, I knew the body that lay beneath that shirt and those jeans too. Smooth skin over taut muscle, power and prowess contained within.

Tipping forward, he placed his elbows on his thighs and gave me an expectant look. My attention fell to his powerful forearms for a beat before sliding down to his big hands. Strong, skillful hands that I very much wanted on my body again.

I toyed with the hem of my sweater, then paused, pretending to think. "You want me to take this off?"

"Very much so." Chase grinned.

Heart pounding, I took a step forward, watching the rise and fall of his chest quicken as I drew nearer. He observed me, rapt with desire. Although I felt self-conscious, having such an effect on him was empowering.

I came to a stop just out of reach.

"I guess I could." Crossing my arms over my chest, I slowly lifted the hem of the soft knit sweater and pulled it over my head before tossing it onto the floor.

His expression turned hungry, his eyes tracing my body from head to toe with such intensity that I could almost feel heat glide across my skin.

With another step closer, I was standing between his legs. Our gazes locked as he looked up at me, his eyes taking on a predatory gleam. Masculine energy radiated off him, carefully restrained but ready to pounce, to ravish.

I tilted my head questioningly. "Now what was I supposed to do?"

"Fuck it." He shook his head, letting out a low laugh. "This is a failed experiment. I can't keep my hands to myself." With nimble fingers, he unbuttoned my jeans, tugging down the zipper. He pulled them all the way to the floor, and I stepped out of them and nudged them aside with my foot.

A soft gasp escaped from the back of my throat as he gripped me from behind, yanking me up against him. His mouth landed on the sensitive skin below my navel before he kissed his way down my body. I let out a throaty sigh, running my hands through his soft, dark hair as he made good on all his promises.

The following days passed in a blur. Lectures, homework, the paper, and Chase occupied nearly all of my free time. Plus, a movie with Zara and Noelle on Friday and a Falcons game with Siobhan on Saturday. Unlike the game before, they won—including an assist from Chase. The win put him in a very *good* mood. We didn't get much sleep that night and slept in late on Sunday to make up for it.

But if I thought my average Sunday blues were bad, they were nothing compared to facing down a Monday when I had to see Paul —especially after a perfect weekend. Talk about a rough way to start a new week.

With no small amount of dread, I headed to meet Paul at a coffee shop on campus after my psych class. Hopefully, a public setting would ensure he wasn't too much of a jerk. But Paul was basically Diet Luke, so how he would behave was anyone's guess.

I arrived first, so I ordered a large vanilla latte at the front and tipped the barista with the change. Normally, I would have grabbed a berry muffin or banana bread to go along with it, but I had no appetite in light of my expected company. Then I grabbed a table off to the side, praying Paul would stand me up so I had an excuse to not write the article.

Not two minutes later, he crushed my hopes by appearing. Damn.

He pulled out a chair and eased into it, placing an elbow on the table. He nodded at me, oozing arrogance and self-satisfaction. "'Sup."

Objectively speaking, Paul was good-looking. Tall, athletic, pleasant if generic features. But the accompanying personality canceled out any appeal entirely.

I had never liked him, not even when Luke and I were dating.

"Hi." I reached for my coffee and took a gigantic gulp. This interaction was beyond awkward, but the sugar and caffeine cushioned the blow a bit. If only I'd packed a flask to spike my coffee with. Even if it wasn't yet noon.

This was literally the first time we had ever been one-on-one. And hopefully the last.

Working methodically through the list of ten questions I'd

written—because Liam hadn't done that, either—I tried to be as professional as possible. How did he start playing hockey? When did he know he wanted to play at the college level? Who were his role models? What did he intend to pursue after graduation? I took scrupulous, detailed notes to eliminate any possibility that I would have to contact him again for clarification or follow-up.

While I'd planned to keep our meeting brief, Paul was more than happy to talk about himself. Or rather, to drone on about himself. He kept spiraling off on unrelated tangents while I desperately tried to harness my interviewing skills and wrangle him back on course.

Paul was thirstier for the spotlight than I'd realized, and apparently, he viewed this temporary Luke-free window as his time to shine. Seemed like Chase had done him a favor.

Twenty-five painful minutes later, which was ten longer than I'd intended to spend with him, he concluded a long-winded tale about hockey training camp last summer. Or last spring. I didn't know; I'd tuned out. I glanced down, cross-referencing my notes with my list of questions and praying I hadn't missed anything. I was ready to end this nightmare of an interview.

"Okay, I think that covers everything." Standing, I pushed my chair back and closed my silver laptop. The massive tension I'd been holding in my shoulders eased as I gathered my things. "Thanks for meeting me."

"By the way." Paul leaned back in his chair, leisurely crossing an ankle over his knee. "I have a funny story for you."

I paused and glanced back up at him, bracing myself for another boring, self-promoting tale.

"My cousin is a server at O'Connor's, and she knows your boyfriend—you know, because he fucked one of her friends."

My stomach lurched, and I stifled a flinch, wishing more than anything that I could un-hear the information. Why had no one yet invented brain bleach to erase disturbing pieces of information like that? I didn't want to know, didn't need to know, didn't want to think about it.

He continued, "Anyway, she said some blond chick was all over Carter when he was there recently."

Thoughts spun in my mind, rotating faster than an F5 tornado.

First, Paul's comment about his cousin's friend had been wholly unnecessary. In theory, the past didn't matter. But that didn't mean I liked being slapped in the face with it—particularly when I had just slept with him and was feeling extra vulnerable as a result. It wasn't that I judged Chase's past; it was that I was scared of becoming part of it.

Then there was this girl who was supposedly all over him recently. What was that about? When was the last time Chase had even been at O'Connor's? Had he lied to me about where he was one night?

It was like being shot twice with one bullet.

Then again, Paul could be lying. Especially about the second part.

"Huh," I said. "Sounds like a misunderstanding." I tried to keep my voice steady, expression neutral.

"Doubtful." Paul smirked. "She was sitting in his lap."

Oh, so he had corroborating details. A sickening sense of déjà vu crashed over me. With Luke, I always heard it from someone else, always long after the fact, always with specifics to back it up. And he'd always deny it.

But Chase wasn't Luke. He was nothing like Luke.

At least, that's what I thought.

"I don't believe that." Shoving my laptop into my bag, I intentionally avoided Paul's prying gaze. I drew in a breath, trying to slow my speeding pulse.

Triggered would be putting it mildly. He'd hit me right where it hurt, like a sucker punch to the heart.

Paul shrugged. "Go ask my cousin. Tell her I sent you. Why would I lie? I might think Carter is an asshole, but I have no issue with you."

"Right." I zipped up my black leather shoulder bag, meeting his gaze evenly. Barely concealed triumph was etched in every line on his face. "I'm sure you're looking out for my best interests."

"Just thought you should know."

"That's cute," I said. "You were always more than happy to cover for Luke. Now you're pretending to be Mr. Honesty and Transparency?"

Paul had lied and provided alibis for Luke countless times. Of course, I hadn't known until Mendez got wasted last New Year's and basically confessed to being part of a three-person conspiracy that excluded my brother. But I never sold Mendez out, which meant I knew more than Paul or Luke even realized.

I knew more than Amelia did too—but people liked to shoot the messenger, and I didn't want to take that bullet. She preferred to exist in a state of intentional ignorance, anyway.

As for taking Luke back after that, I obviously had poor judgment. Maybe I still did.

Had I made the same mistake twice?

Paul's expression hardened, dark blue eyes taking on a malicious gleam. "All I'm saying is that if you're determined to be a puck bunny, there are probably better options."

"Excuse me?"

"Going straight from being Morrison's girlfriend to Carter's girlfriend is a bad look, don't you think?"

Asshole.

I glared at him, scrambling inwardly for something to say but coming up woefully empty-handed. Chase would have had something cutting and witty to fire back. Unfortunately, I wasn't as quick on my toes when it came to offering up retorts on the fly.

Especially when my brain was imploding.

"You can save your fake concern," I said. "As for the article, I've got all I need." Throwing my bag on my shoulder, I turned on my heel and stormed out of the coffee shop, narrowly missing two people standing near the door who threw themselves out of my way as I approached.

For the sake of my position with the paper and my portfolio, I would write the article diplomatically, even if I wanted to shred Paul and his bloated ego to pieces, word by word, paragraph by paragraph. Complete with a headline that read something like,

"Assistant Captain with Inferiority Complex Revels in Captain's Absence."

The title had a nice ring to it. Obviously, I couldn't publish that. But I might write it anyway for my own petty enjoyment.

Continuing my brisk pace, I sped down the tiled hallway and pushed open the glass door, exiting the student commons. Fresh, crisp air washed over me, and I sucked in a breath, but it didn't quell the nausea in my gut. And, of course, I'd forgotten my half-full coffee on the table. Clearly, even the smallest things would go wrong today.

I had planned to go to the *Callingwood Daily* office, but I couldn't face Zara and Noelle. My stomach was in my throat, and my hands were shaking—they would know something was up the instant they saw me, and I was in no condition to discuss the interview from hell. Instead, I turned right and cut across the quad, heading to the library to hide at a table somewhere deep in the stacks.

As I walked, I tried to see things objectively. Paul's intentions weren't sincere. That was a given. He was probably trying to mess with Chase by messing with me. But despite that, a small part of me wondered if what he said was true. If Chase had been flirting with some girl…or worse. I didn't want it to be true, and I wanted to rule it out, but I'd been wrong about these things before.

And was I just someone who went hockey player to hockey player? A *puck bunny*?

I told myself I would take a day to think. One day turned into two. Two days turned into three. And things with Chase were getting increasingly strained. I wasn't handling things well; I knew that. And in the past, any time I tried to resolve an issue, I inevitably made it worse. Somehow, I always tripped up. Things came out the wrong way, and everything blew up in my face.

It always turned into a fight, and I hated fighting.

Maybe I was being illogical, but it was like being scared of a spider—an irrational, physiological fear I could not seem to shake.

Was I overreacting? Probably. But I had been sucked into this vortex filled with horrible, familiar feelings, and I didn't know how to get back out. Like being trapped in a pinball machine, rebounding back and forth between fear, hope, mistrust, and guilt.

Paul's words played in my head like a broken record, setting off a vicious cycle of rumination. I'd waffle between dismissing it as ridiculous and second-guessing myself, wondering if it could be true. Sometimes, I considered talking to Chase about it, but if it was true, he would never admit it. And if it wasn't, I didn't want to upset—or insult—him.

I went over it again and again in my head.

The only conclusion I could come to was that I had no idea what to do.

CHASE

After days of heavy tension at home, one blowout fight, and tears I'd overheard while I was trying to sleep, Dallas and Siobhan finally made things official.

Ward was over the moon like a dopey puppy dog about the whole thing, and they'd been extra affectionate ever since.

I was happy for them. Really, I was.

Except something was going on with Bailey.

Holed up in my room after a disastrous practice, I stared at my phone like it would somehow reveal an answer. Rereading text messages for the tenth time didn't provide any insight. Restless energy seized me, and I went downstairs because I couldn't sit still.

As I hit the bottom step, I found Shiv curled up on the living room couch, highlighting something in a biology textbook. Asking her was worth a shot, I guessed.

"Have you talked to Bailey recently?" I propped myself up against the wall, trying and failing to sound casual.

She glanced up at me, yellow highlighter in midair. "Not a ton," she said, looking thoughtful. "We've texted a bit, but she's been busy with classes and packing."

"Ah." I nodded. That was the same line Bailey had fed me. Repeatedly.

"How come?" Shiv studied my face, dark brows crinkling.

"No reason."

Except she'd been replying with one- and two-word texts for days, making vague excuses when I tried to make plans, and blowing me off in general. A total one-eighty from less than a week ago.

At first, I assumed she was just having a bad day. We all had them. The second day, I gave her the benefit of the doubt. I didn't want to be unreasonable or demanding. But now it was after eight p.m. on the fourth day of this shit. I had still barely spoken to her, and not for lack of trying.

I hadn't understood when Ward didn't know what was up with him and Shiv. Now I was eating my words with a fucking fork because I had no idea what was going on with Bailey. I'd flat-out asked her, and she said everything was fine.

It clearly wasn't.

Worse still, I didn't know why.

All day, I'd been distracted as hell. School had been a wash, and practice was a tire fire. After I got off the ice, I'd received a stern reprimand from Coach Miller for botching nearly every drill. And some of them were incredibly straightforward. Skate straight and shoot, that kind of thing. It was downright embarrassing.

It didn't help that she was everywhere. In my brain, in my bed, in my truck, in the dressing room, in the corner of the goddamn rink.

Fuck this.

CHAPTER 37
COUNT ON IT
CHASE

IF SHE WOULDN'T COME to me, then I would go to her.

After blatantly disregarding the speed limit and one questionable four-way stop, I made it over to Bailey's complex and parked haphazardly in the visitor zone. I killed the engine and slammed the driver's side door, then speed-walked over to her place like a heat-seeking missile.

I sprinted up the steps and came to a screeching halt in front of the navy blue door, staring at the scattered scratches and scuffs in the paint. Doing my best to center myself, I drew in a deep breath and held it for a few seconds before exhaling heavily through my nose, getting my head on straight like I was heading onto the ice.

It didn't work. At all.

Rolling my shoulders back, I rang the bell and followed it up by pounding on the front door like a cop with a warrant. I hoped she was home studying like she said, because I needed an explanation. Stat.

The lock rattled, and the door opened a crack. A sliver of Jillian's face appeared. "What do you want, Carter?"

For you to get the fuck out of the way, but I couldn't use my outside voice for that sentiment.

"I need to talk to Bailey." I nodded at the door. "Let me in."

Jillian swung open the door, revealing Amelia standing beside her. They eyed me disdainfully, like two partners in snottiness. They didn't like me, and the feeling was more than mutual.

"B would let you know if she wanted to talk to you," Amelia said, giving me a death stare.

Jillian curled her upper lip. "Maybe she's come to her senses."

My teeth set on edge. I wasn't exactly the biggest fan of either to begin with, but my usual sense of hostility was amplified times a billion right now. They were meddling, and I didn't appreciate it.

I could not fucking wait for James to move. Counting down the days.

"You know what?" I said, using every shred of restraint I had to keep from raising my voice. "After the way the two of you have treated her, I'm not in the mood to watch you pretend to give a shit now."

Amelia huffed. "You can't talk to us like that."

Since when? Maybe a hockey player chewing out a hockey girlfriend violated some stupid bro code. Which meant I would probably hear about it from Paul and Mendez later. Whatever.

"Pretty sure I just did." They backed up as I took a step closer. I ducked my head through the doorway and leaned into the house. "James!"

A door creaked open, followed by the sound of footsteps. Bailey came down the stairs, wearing purple and gray plaid pajama pants with a matching purple sweater, bare feet, and messy hair loose around her shoulders.

She looked so perfect that something inside of me broke.

Possibly the last tether to my sanity.

When she made it halfway down the staircase, her gaze landed on me, her eyes widening. Probably because I looked like a madman running on adrenaline, frustration, and lust, which had combined to form some cocaine-like substance in my body. Something like that. I'd never done cocaine, but I was amped as fuck.

For all the pride I took in generally being calm and collected, I most certainly was not right now.

Bailey came to stand next to Jillian and Amelia at the door. "Chase." Her brow furrowed. "What are you—"

"We need to talk."

She froze. Her hazel eyes swung from me to Jillian and Amelia, then back to me. If she took their side on this, I might never get over it. No, I would definitely never get over it.

I raised my eyebrows. "Now."

"Okay." Bailey took a step closer and waved me inside. "Let's go talk in my room."

BAILEY

I may have made a slight miscalculation. Because now there was a very large, very angry caveman on my doorstep.

His black T-shirt hung off his broad shoulders, hinting at the muscles that lay beneath. And gray joggers sat low on his waist, wrapping around the V of his hips. He looked every single inch the heartbreaker I was scared he might be.

Chase stepped inside, and I took his hand. Waves of tension radiated off him with such intensity that they filled the room, palpable and heated.

Amelia rolled her eyes and turned away, heading into the kitchen, with Jillian trailing behind her. They pretended to be occupied with the fridge and dishwasher while I led Chase upstairs. In reality, they'd be up right behind us to eavesdrop. Then they could report the intimate details of my personal life back to everyone else. Super.

He followed me up the staircase and down the hall into my bedroom, lit by the yellow glow of the small bedside lamp. My iPad lay on my white comforter, still paused on the Netflix show I had been half watching instead of studying like I told him I had been—like I should have been. But I hadn't been able to focus on anything in days.

I didn't know if we were about to talk, fight, or break up.

He shut the door behind him quietly. Before I could sit down on my bed, he closed the distance between us, and his large hands landed on my hips, turning me to face him.

Eyes still locked on mine, he took a step forward, followed by another, until he backed me up against the wooden door. His divine, familiar scent enveloped me, going to my head and straight through my defenses. My eyes dropped to the pulse at the base of his throat for a beat, then traveled to the tense cords of his neck before snapping back up to his.

He pinned me to the spot and heated my skin with just a look. He had me cornered—figuratively and literally. I couldn't draw my attention away from him. I was victim to his commanding presence. Five extra inches was pretty significant when it was accompanied by an additional forty pounds of muscle.

Especially when he was pissed.

"What's going on, James?" he asked quietly.

"What do you mean?"

His jaw ticked. "Why are you ghosting me?"

"I'm not." At least, not on purpose. It started innocently enough, taking some time to think. But thinking had turned into catastrophizing, and now I was pretty sure I had blown things way, *way* out of proportion.

"You absolutely are," Chase said. "And I didn't work my ass off earning your trust only to have you throw it away without an explanation."

Desire, guilt, regret. They all slammed into me like a wrecking ball. I reached up to touch him, but he took hold of my wrists and pinned them against the door.

He shook his head. "No."

"Why not?"

"Why do you want to touch me when you don't want to be with me?"

I didn't know how to answer that. I did want to be with him. I wanted it so badly it hurt, and that was the problem.

This wasn't the kind of thing I'd walk away from in one piece.

"That's not it."

His pupils dilated as he considered me. "Then explain."

It was an order, not a request.

My breath grew shallow. "I don't know how."

Every time I had tried to talk to Luke, he gaslighted me into thinking I was crazy, or he twisted the narrative to make me the bad guy. Eventually, I stopped trying. I was letting that—the past—interfere with the future. But knowing that and overcoming it were two separate things.

"Try." He wedged a muscular thigh between my legs and brought his mouth down to hover above mine, almost touching.

I lifted my chin, and his lips crashed down against mine, his tongue pushing inside my mouth. The minute we kissed, every doubt I'd ever had, every question, every second-guess vanished.

Our mouths moved against each other, indomitable and wild, sending a wave of want surging through my body. He tore away from my lips, placing a trail of frenzied kisses down my neck and sending my desire into overdrive. I squirmed against his grip, trying to touch him, but all that did was make him press his thigh harder between my legs and hold my wrists tighter while I moved against him in response.

"If this is your idea of convincing me to talk," I said breathlessly, "I don't have a very good incentive to comply."

But I was in sensory overload. He was pressed up against me while I was unable to touch him back. I wanted to feel his body beneath my hands, to map the muscles beneath his skin, and to run my fingers through his dark, silky hair.

I hit the breaking point. "Chase."

"Stop?" He pulled back, looking at me pointedly like he was trying to prove something.

"No," I said. "Just let me touch you."

He released my wrists and cupped my chin, tilting my face up to his.

"Answer my question first," he said calmly.

I bit my bottom lip, searching his face. He slid his hand from my jawline to the side of my neck. With anyone else, I would have been scared, but he wasn't applying any pressure. It was a power move.

He would stop instantly if I said.

But I didn't want him to.

With his free hand, he dragged the pad of his thumb along my bottom lip, gaze focused intently on the movement. Then he traced down my cheek, along the curve of my neck. I drew in a shaky breath, eyes fluttering shut as goose bumps popped up all over my body.

"I missed you." He placed a kiss just below my ear.

I tilted my head, yielding to give him better access.

"It's only been a couple days, and I'm like an addict in need of a fix."

I'd missed him too, which was why I was melting like butter beneath his hands, unable to think clearly or form coherent sentences. He splayed his palm, cupping my breast and squeezing, and I melted a little more.

"Mm-hmm," I murmured, my brain going offline.

He skimmed lower, gliding down past my ribcage. My breath snagged as he toyed with the elastic waistband of my pajamas, but he didn't move any farther. He pulled back suddenly, removing his hands, and my eyes flew open.

"But I'm confused. Because here's what I think," Chase said, voice low. "You do want to be with me."

He was right. Not just wanted—in the moment, I needed him like air. But falling so hard, so fast for someone was terrifying. Scariest thing I had ever done. Hands down.

I wanted to believe it was a calculated risk, but in truth, I never had a choice.

"So tell me." He bracketed the wall above my head with his hands, towering over me. "What the hell is going on?"

My brain slowly kicked back into gear now that he wasn't touching me. "You realize Amelia and Jillian can hear all of this." I nodded to the door. "The walls in this place are paper thin."

"Don't care. I'm afraid I used up all my fucks worrying about you."

He nudged my legs apart with his knee, and I complied, pliant against his touch. Grabbing the backs of my thighs, he hiked me up and pinned the upper half of my body against the door. I drew in a ragged breath as the length of him pressed against the perfect spot between my legs, rock hard and ready.

I held on to his shoulders and pulled myself close, trying to kiss him.

"Explain first." He pulled away, expression stern. "You were in my bed a few mornings ago, kissed me goodbye like everything was fine when I dropped you off for class, and you've been dodging me ever since. Why?"

His tone was razor sharp, but there was hurt in his eyes. He tilted his hips, pressing against me again and creating a jolt of pleasure that radiated up through my core. Heat flooded my body, desire unraveling. I was about two seconds or one more thrust away from trying to take off his clothes. But the tiny part of my brain that was still functional knew he was right—we had to talk first.

"Was some girl sitting on your lap at O'Connor's recently?" I finally forced out. "Because that's what I heard."

Chase furrowed his dark brow. "What?"

Slowly, he lowered me until I was standing upright. I let my hands linger on his shoulders, soaking up the heat beneath his soft black T-shirt.

"I answered your question. Now answer mine, please."

"That's what this is about?" he asked, tilting his head incredulously. "That's why you've been avoiding me?"

"I need a yes or no, Carter." Now that he was here in front of me, I knew the answer, but I still wanted to hear it from him.

He slipped his hands beneath my sweater, rough fingers warm and reassuring against my waist. "That was for, like, two seconds. Lindsay plopped down into my lap from out of nowhere. I promptly turned her down, and she moved. The end."

"That's it?" My body relaxed, the ability to breathe returning to normal.

"That's it. Nothing happened," he said, voice gentle. "And it wasn't recently; it was before Ty's party."

The explanation was genuine. And I was a complete jerk. A jerk who'd been baited into overreacting by Luke's crony.

Chase narrowed his eyes. "Who told you this?"

"Paul..."

"Jesus Christ," he muttered, shaking his head. "Consider the source, James."

"But she did sit on your lap. Kind of." I didn't know why I was arguing that point, except to say I felt silly for having gotten upset in the first place. And even sillier for how I'd handled it after that.

"Paul twisted things around to suit his agenda and you know it. Please don't let that asshole get in your head."

"Thin walls." I lowered my voice and gestured behind me. "Amelia?"

Chase glanced over my shoulder at the door, raising his voice a level. "I said, Paul is an asshole. He can't fucking skate, either. Feel free to quote me."

Despite the situation, I laughed. He was an instigator to the bone. At some point along the way, it had become endearing. He was my instigator, at least.

Then he looked back down at me, and his tone softened. "Paul say anything else to you?"

"Um...Well." I drew in a breath. "He said that you slept with his cousin's friend." Oh, and then he called me a desperate puck bunny. But that would make Chase even more angry, and I wasn't sure I needed to fuel that fire.

He nodded, studying my face. "Is there any chance it's the sex thing that set you off?"

"Maybe a little," I admitted. But it wasn't fair to hold the past against him.

"Just because I have had meaningless sex in the past doesn't mean it's meaningless with you. It's definitely not. You know that, right?"

"Yeah," I said. "I do."

"As far as the other thing goes, I'll tell you when girls hit on me if you want, but it seems kind of pointless when I'd never act on it. Besides, I'm sure you shoot down guys all the time."

Not really. My little bubble of journalism classes, the school newspaper, and seeing Chase didn't lend itself to being on the receiving end of many pick-up attempts. It was sweet he thought that, though.

"Probably not nearly as much as the other way around."

"You're going to have to trust me for this to work," he said tersely.

"I'm trying to. If I didn't, I never would have slept with you." My voice wavered. Suddenly, I was dangerously close to tears. I tamped down on it with every ounce of self-control I had. "Maybe I'm a little off-kilter right now, but that was a huge deal to me."

His coffee-brown eyes softened, shining with affection. "I know. I don't take that lightly." He tucked my hair behind my ear, his lips tugging up at the corners. "I think, deep down, you know you can trust me. You just don't trust your own judgment."

Things clicked into place.

"Oh my god. I think you're right."

Chase leaned in and kissed me briefly, softly, sweetly. He pulled back and brushed my cheek with his fingers. "Then can you talk to me next time instead? Because this pushing me away thing sucks. If you don't talk to me, there's nothing I can do on my end."

Right. If I had been able to approach this like a rational person, that's probably what I would have done—talked to him. It's what I would do in the future. Even if it was difficult.

"I'll try. I'm not as good at talking about things as you are." I glanced down at the floor, then back up at him. "You might not have a filter, but I have an extra-strength industrial-grade one. With a spare for backup."

"You overthink, huh?" Chase gave me a half smile. "I've noticed."

I tugged his arm, pulling him toward the bed. It sagged under his weight as he sat and turned to face me. Shifting closer, I placed a hand on his sweatpants-clad thigh. "I know this is my baggage, and I'm trying not to take it out on you. It won't go away overnight, though."

"I get it," he said, rubbing my lower back. Warmth spread through the fabric of my shirt in the wake of his touch. "But I have feelings too, and that shit hurt."

Guilt settled in my stomach, heavy like a bag of pucks. For all my worrying about him, maybe I was the one who would ruin things.

I touched his muscular shoulder, fingertips resting softly on his T-shirt. "I'm sorry."

"I forgive you. But let's not handle things this way again, okay?"

"Okay."

We fell quiet for a moment. He dipped his head and caught my eye, forehead wrinkling. "I've been pretty open with you, but I feel like you're holding back."

"Holding back how?" I asked, deflecting.

Thing was, he was right. I'd been holding back a tiny piece of myself…just in case. Maybe that wasn't fair to either of us. It wasn't working very well anyway.

"I'm not sure where your head is at sometimes."

"I'm—" I faltered, trying to summon the courage to be vulnerable. He'd met me more than halfway. Multiple times. Warmth rushed to my face, and my nerves shot through the roof. "Crazy about you," I said. "Certifiable. I'm just scared."

Or, you know, terrified.

"Oh, I'm not going anywhere. That's why I'm here right now." He grinned, gesturing to the two of us. "Stubborn, remember?"

"Thank god for that." I picked up my phone and checked the time. My heart sank. "It's nine thirty, and you probably have to be up early tomorrow. Can you stay for a little longer?"

"I can give it another hour or so, but I should go move my truck first."

"Why?"

Chase laughed, standing and making his way to the door. "I'm parked the way you sleep. Diagonally."

"When you get back…" I said. "Can we pick up where we left off?" Thin walls be damned. I could turn on music or something. Or they could leave. I really didn't care.

He stopped and glanced back at me, a smile playing on his lips. "Count on it, baby."

CHAPTER 38
MISSED THIS
CHASE

IT TOOK some serious effort to park properly the second time around. I was so distracted that I had to reverse and straighten out my truck three times to get within the lines—laughable for someone whose livelihood literally depended on good aim and depth perception. But there was a decent chance I would stay longer than the hour I'd promised, so I took the time to get it right so I wouldn't get ticketed or towed.

Bolting back inside, I ignored Jillian and Amelia's poisonous glares and resisted the urge to flip them off. I'd consider it award-winning self-restraint and serious personal growth on my part.

When I walked into her room, Bailey was sitting cross-legged on her white comforter, long blond hair hanging in a curtain as she glanced at her phone. And my desire went into overdrive.

"Hey, beautiful." I shut the door to her bedroom behind me, quickly securing the lock and double-checking it for good measure.

She looked up from the screen and locked it, setting it aside on the nightstand. "Hi." Her lips curved into a small smile as her doe eyes raked over my body, expression a mixture of affection and lust.

Fuck.

"Just so you know," I said, sitting on the bed beside her, "your roommates are downstairs watching TV with the volume turned up excessively high."

Bailey smirked. "Probably trying to prove they aren't listening."

"Probably. But they're protesting a little too much for me to buy it." My gaze traveled around the room, scanning methodically. "Either way, got a speaker? We can throw on some music to muffle your screams."

Her eyes widened and she lowered her voice. "You're teasing me, right? I don't scream in bed…do I?" A pink flush crept across her cheeks.

I grinned, because she was adorable and, well, she kinda did. "You've come pretty close." I rubbed a hand over my cheek, thinking. "I feel like there's a good dirty joke in there somewhere. But there isn't enough blood going to my brain right now to connect those dots."

Bailey shook her head and huffed a cute, bashful laugh. She swiped at the iPad beside her and put on a random Spotify station without looking twice. Music poured out of a purple wireless speaker on her desk beside the bed. The volume was just high enough to create some background noise and afford us a little more privacy.

Music would only help so much, though—all teasing aside, she was pretty loud sometimes. But worst case, I could kiss her to muffle some of her cries. And my lips on hers put her over the edge when she was close to coming, which was both flattering and hot as hell.

Our eyes locked, and the energy shifted, the air turning heavy with anticipation. With a hand behind her neck, I pulled her closer. Her eyelids fluttered shut as our lips came together, our mouths exploring.

Shifting, I eased her onto her back beneath me and settled between her legs. I grabbed her hands and threaded her fingers in mine, pinning them to the bed. She let out a soft sigh, squeezing my hands and kissing me back more deeply.

A rush ran through my body, but it was more than physical. Every time we fooled around, I fell a little harder. Sex with her was next-level. All the casual hookups and one-night stands could never have prepared me for it.

I broke away from the kiss, catching her eye. "Hey, James? I'll stay over." I pulled one hand free and traced a finger along the side of her neck, down between her breasts over her soft knit sweater.

Her gold-flecked eyes studied me, watchful, blond hair spread out across the pillow beneath her.

"I'll set my alarm and make sure I'm up in time tomorrow morning."

Bailey's brow knit together. "But you don't have any of your stuff."

"I can get up early and swing by home first," I said. "If we're going to have sex, it feels wrong for me to leave after." Wrong was an understatement. I would feel like an asshole. I'd almost rather not fool around at all than do that to her.

"I kind of thought so too. But I didn't want to seem needy."

There was a tug in my stomach at hearing her say that.

I held her gaze. "I want you to ask for the things you need. Or, you know, demand them." I shrugged. "Because that would be pretty hot." I didn't mind the idea of a little role reversal with her bossing me around once in a while.

She pulled her lush bottom lip between her teeth for a beat and released it. "Well, I would like it if you stayed."

"Done." I glanced down at the mattress beneath us, which was significantly smaller than mine. For two tall people, it would be a tight squeeze. "Though your bed is pretty small, so I guess we'll be spooning all night."

And by spooning, I meant she was guaranteed to wake up with me pressing up against her perfect round ass. But that happened at my place anyway.

"That's okay. I like spooning."

"So do I," I admitted. And I never thought I would be saying that.

I grabbed the hem of my black T-shirt and pulled it over my head, then hovered over her again. Her eyelids grew heavy as her soft hands slid along my torso, fingers gripping the muscles. I hung my head and let out a groan, savoring the feeling of her touch. Four days felt like four years.

"Picking up where we left off," I said, glancing back up at her, "I think I was telling you how much I missed you."

"Yeah?" Bailey's lips tugged into a smile. "Keep talking."

"I missed this." Ducking my head, I nipped at the top of her neck below her jawline, alternating with soft kisses as I moved down the span of perfect, smooth skin.

She let out a hum, running her palms down my back.

"And this," I murmured, inhaling against her skin and savoring the vanilla spice of her perfume combined with a scent that was uniquely her. A massive surge of desire hit me, waging war between my need to take her immediately and the desire to take my time. But tonight she needed slow, and I was more than happy to comply.

I bracketed her jaw with my hand, angling her head so her eyes met mine. "Definitely this." I brought my lips down against hers, pushing into her mouth.

Bailey sighed, dragging her hands up to grip my shoulders and sending a wave of pleasure down my spine. I could kiss her all day, taking my time touching her and tasting her. In theory. With the current situation, I'd probably need some release eventually because I was wound pretty tightly after being apart.

Still kissing, still holding her face, I reached under her sweater with my other hand, caressing her ribcage to find nothing but a thin tank top over a span of uninterrupted skin—she wasn't wearing a bra. Fuck. So hot.

She slid her fingers beneath the waistband of my gray joggers, and I helped her drag them down. I was left in nothing but black boxer briefs. And she had some catching up to do.

Breaking apart from her mouth, I lifted her hips and tugged down her pants. I ran my hands along the curves of her thighs, down to her smooth, slender calves. "Missed these legs too."

Pulling off her pajamas one foot at a time, I glided my palms back up her warm skin. My hands came to rest on her hips, still clad in her little black cotton panties. Damn. They were simple but sexy as hell. She sat up partway, helping me pull off her purple sweater and tank top. In a flash, she was nearly naked, and I was in heaven.

I cupped her full, perky breasts, squeezing. "Can't forget these."

She tipped her head back as I brushed my lips along her collarbone, then skimmed lower to kiss the swell of her breasts.

My fingers traveled down her stomach, dipping below the waistband of her underwear. I moved lower, between her legs, where she was soaking wet already. "And you know I missed your pussy."

Bailey drew in a shaky inhale, hips tilting in response to my touch. I stroked her, and she grabbed me over my underwear, sending another swell of pleasure through my body. She squirmed beneath me, circling her pelvis against my hand. The way she was moving, like she knew exactly what she wanted, gave me an idea.

I grabbed her by the hips and lifted her up off the bed beneath me. "Hang tight, baby." Kissing her again, I placed a hand between her shoulder blades. She giggled against my mouth as I flipped us around in one sweeping movement, putting her on top of me so she was straddling my hips.

"Show off." Bailey arched an eyebrow playfully.

"Maybe a little," I said. "But this is a great view."

James on top of me, topless with nothing but that tiny black underwear. Hair falling around her shoulders, framing her perky tits. Perfection in every way.

She gave me a crooked smile, examining my torso. "I don't know. I think mine's better."

My fingers spanned her waist, pulling her down as I thrust up to meet her. She let out a small whimper and closed her eyes, moving her pelvis, grinding against me in response.

"I missed your sounds too."

"Mm-hmm." She nodded, biting her bottom lip.

I lifted my hips again, and her hands flew to my biceps, digging in with each undulation. I watched her, mesmerized. "You're so fucking hot."

Her eyes flew open, her expression verging on embarrassment. Probably because we were both still partially clothed, dry humping like teenagers. But that was what made it so awesome—I loved getting her going. And with our bodies lined up the way they were, the external stimulation was definitely there.

I sat up halfway, wrapping a hand around her neck and pulling her down to me. She leaned over me on her elbows, running a hand through my hair and tugging, kissing me again, rocking her pelvis, moving against me greedily.

"James." I lifted my hips against her, and she let out a breathy whimper. "Is this working for you?"

Her cheeks were pink, eyes glassy as she looked at me. "Maybe."

Man, if only I had the stamina to keep going. I bet I could get her off. But at this rate, we would both be finished before we got all the way undressed. Maybe next time, after I got this out of my system.

"Is that a yes to you being on top?" I asked.

Bailey froze. "You want me to be on top?"

"Oh yeah." I bit back a grin. "If you want to."

The idea of her riding me was one of the hottest things I could imagine, but I wouldn't push. If she was self-conscious about it, I probably didn't want to know why, because it would likely make me even more homicidal toward Morrison.

"Kind of…" Her brow wrinkled.

Yep, I knew what was happening here. I pulled us both upright, placing a hand against her back so that our bodies were pressed against each other.

"James." Resting my forehead against hers, I tucked a lock of hair behind her ear. "Look at me."

She gazed back at me, eyes soft and lips parted. Her breath was a little shallow, either from being turned on or nerves. Maybe both. I rubbed my palms up and down her arms, squeezing gently.

"Everything you do feels good to me when we're together," I said. "Don't worry. Like, ever. I just want you."

I mean, for fuck's sake. It was virtually impossible for a guy to *not* get off during sex. It was simple. Get her off first, then switch gears at the end if necessary. It wasn't fucking rocket science.

"Okay," she said hesitantly, looking away. Then her eyes snapped back up to mine. "But can you stay sitting up a little like this? So I can reach you better? And kiss you?"

"Of course." I shifted, rearranging the pillows behind me and sitting up against the headboard. "Better?"

Bailey gave me a small, sweet smile. "Yeah."

She crawled off me and slid her little black panties down her legs. Then she kneeled beside me, kissing me and tugging at the waistband of my boxer briefs as I pulled them off and tossed them aside.

"Condom?" I reached over to her nightstand.

Her brows drew together, and then her eyes widened. "I don't have any. Luke and I didn't..." Rosy pink crept across her cheeks. "I mean, we used them. I didn't trust him enough to go without. He never really came over here, though."

"That's okay. We don't have to—"

"I'm on the pill."

My cock twitched, and I suppressed a groan at the thought of being completely bare inside her. While it was incredibly tempting, I didn't want her to offer up something she wasn't comfortable with, either.

"I'm okay with it if you are," she added shyly.

"I'm clean," I told her. "We get tested at the start of every season, and I haven't been with anyone else."

"I trust you." Her teeth sank into her bottom lip as she watched me, waiting for a response.

"If you're sure."

"I'm sure."

Vulnerability flashed in her eyes as she climbed on top of me. I brushed her hair out of her face and watched her, mesmerized. Not because of the act, but because of who it was with.

All I knew was I was in over my head more than ever before.

Once she was straddling my thighs, I gripped her waist with one hand and wrapped the other around my shaft. Palms on my shoulders, she eased down onto my cock with a soft moan. When she'd taken me fully, she fell still.

Concern sparked within me, and I tilted her chin up so she was forced to look at me. "Are you okay, baby?"

"Yeah," she breathed. "Just need a sec. You're...big."

Likely, her nerves about being on top made her tense, which didn't help. I ran my hands up and down her back to soothe her, kissing her shoulder, and after only a moment, her muscles relaxed and she took over, circling her hips and letting out a breathy sigh.

"That's it." I pulled her closer against me. "You're so fucking perfect."

Angling forward, she brought her mouth to mine as she picked up her pace. She was hot and dripping wet, and I had to suck in a breath to keep it together.

"You feel so good," she whimpered against my lips.

I groaned, fingertips digging into the curve of her hips. "You have no idea." Skin to skin like this, with nothing between us? I was dangerously close to becoming a minute man. As long as I could get her off first, my pride could handle a shorter than usual performance.

Her movements grew more confident, and she found a steady rhythm. I watched her ride me, marveling at how her beautiful face contorted with pleasure.

"I'm close," she moaned, sinking down to take me even deeper. "Oh god. *Chase*."

The desperate way she cried out took me almost over the edge. I tensed, gritting my teeth to hold off my release.

Bailey gasped, throwing her head back. "I'm coming."

And that put me over the edge entirely. "Fuck, baby. Me too."

She kissed me as she came apart, her nails digging into the flesh of my shoulders as she found her release. I slid a hand up to her nape, fisting her hair, losing myself in her, coming right behind her. Pleasure spiked and overflowed as I grabbed her hips, pulling her down harder and thrusting into her. The moment intense, profound, consuming.

In sync, we slowed, kissing softly as the wave faded out.

Bailey dropped her forehead to my shoulder for a beat, sighing. Then she lifted her chin and peeked at me through her dark lashes. "Wow."

I kissed her cheek. "Can say that again."

Wrapping my arms around her torso, I held her still for another moment, our hearts thundering and our breaths slowly returning to normal.

After cleaning up quickly, we readjusted ourselves in her bed, snuggling beneath the covers. As she nestled against me, her hair tickling my bare chest, my brain worked overtime to process everything that had happened.

In the span of a few hours, I'd gone from fearing we might be over to being more fully invested than ever. Despite the blip on the radar, I knew, deep down, that we were on solid ground. And maybe the sex had helped reassure me, but it was deeper than that. It was in the way she looked at me tonight, in a combination of awe and adoration. In the way she touched me. In the way everything clicked when we lay here like we were right now, not saying a thing, knowing our world was right again.

She yawned, burrowing against my shoulder. "Oh my gosh, I'm tired."

"Me too." My heart picked up speed as I pulled her close. I wanted to say more, but I didn't know how to put my thoughts into words.

BAILEY

I woke up with a heavy, muscular arm draped around my waist and a big, warm body pressed up against me.

Oh no. I fumbled for my phone and frantically checked the time, squinting to read the display. It was almost six.

I elbowed Chase gently. "Hey."

"Hmph?" he mumbled sleepily. He squeezed me tighter, nuzzling against my neck before falling quiet again.

If only I could give in to the cozy lure of going back to sleep wrapped up in him in my warm bed. It was incredibly tempting. But he had training.

"It's morning," I said, nudging him again. "We must have fallen asleep before I set my alarm. What time is your dryland today?" He'd told me, but my brain wasn't exactly functional at that point.

He let out a low groan, rolling onto his back. "Uh…not until eight. What time is it?"

"Almost six. Is that enough time to go back to sleep if I set my alarm?"

"Probably not." His weight shifted beside me, and a broad hand landed on my hip, skimming lower. Soft, warm lips grazed my shoulder. "But it's definitely enough time to do something else."

CHAPTER 39
FAMILY AFFAIR
BAILEY

AFTER WAKING up earlier than usual with Chase, I took the opportunity to head to the *Callingwood Daily* to get some writing done and study.

But I caught up with—and maybe did a little gossiping with—Zara and Noelle instead. I couldn't help it; I was flying way too high to write a dry technical piece for Professional Communications.

"I haven't seen you much lately, B." Zara leaned over the table, eyes glinting mischievously. "Chase keeping you occupied?"

I peered up at her from over my laptop screen. "Oh, you know, I've been busy in general."

"Getting busy, more like," she said.

I dragged my attention back to the blank word processor screen, warmth spreading across my cheeks. Good thing no one else was in the office with us.

Hopefully, I didn't have *just had amazing morning sex* written all over my face. Or more accurately, *just had amazing night and morning sex, which I've been replaying in my mind for hours while thirsting to see him again and questioning my sanity because I can't focus on anything else*.

What was happening to me? I'd never felt like this before. Ever. I'd have to tame this before finals or I'd flunk out of college.

"Maybe a little." I cleared my throat, certain my face was as red as a Falcons jersey.

Zara and Noelle exchanged grins across the table.

"What about you? How are things with your guy?"

Zara had crushed more than her fair share of fragile male egos—and hearts. This was the longest she had ever dated someone without losing interest. And she seemed really happy.

Her glossy plum lips pulled into a wide grin. "They're great. He's amazing."

"Aww! I love that for you, Zar." I nudged her playfully.

Noelle frowned at her laptop screen. "Um…Huh." She drummed her fingers on the tabletop thoughtfully. "Professor Johnson wants you to cover the Bulldogs game tomorrow so we can move the arts feature to Saturday and fill that empty space. Sorry, I know that's short notice. Are you okay to do that?"

Did I want to? Not really. Should I do it anyway? Probably. Even though I was supposed to watch Chase's game that night.

"It'll be fine," I lied.

If anything was going to kill my Chase buzz, it was dealing with Derek.

We had hardly spoken in weeks, and when we did, things were strained. I'd tried to blow him off—again—when he texted asking to meet, but I finally relented when he insisted that it was important and promised it wasn't Chase- or Jill-related.

Coffee with my brother should be easy enough, right? Couldn't be any worse than the disastrous meeting with Paul.

I was having second thoughts now, though.

We settled into a table near the front of the campus Starbucks while I eyed him warily. It was sad and awkward and comforting all at once to be with him.

Derek was dressed the same as always, in athletic pants and a Bulldogs top—today it was a hoodie. His entire closet was a monochromatic blur of gray and navy blue.

He glanced down at his white cardboard cup before meeting my eyes again. I swore to God if he said one word about Chase, I would leave immediately and ignore him until Christmas.

"So…Mom and Dad are selling the house," Derek said.

My stomach pitched. "What? How come?"

The cozy brick two-story wasn't anything impressive. It was well lived-in, to be sure. The beige carpets needed replacing, the worn hardwood could have used refinishing, and the bathrooms were terribly outdated.

But it was the house I grew up in. The house we came back to for holidays. The place my mother loved more than anything, with the garden that she babied year after year, spending hours each day tending to the peonies and rose bushes.

It was warm and welcoming, comforting when I needed it. And one of my favorite places in the entire world.

"I guess Dad's been out of work for a little while. They can't afford to keep it."

Everything came crashing down. A wave of nausea slammed into me. Hard.

"Hold the phone," I said. "*Dad is out of work*? Since when?"

Why was it that when one thing went right in my life, something else immediately went off the rails?

He hesitated. "June. They didn't have him return this fall. Education budget cuts, I guess. They axed a bunch of the older, more experienced teachers in favor of hiring new graduates who are cheaper."

"Why are you only telling me this now?"

"I just found out, B."

Glowering at Derek from across the table, I took a sip of my vanilla latte. It held no appeal anymore, but I couldn't justify wasting it.

"Are you sure about that?" If he'd kept this from me, I was going to be so ticked.

"Yes," he insisted. "They didn't want either of us to worry."

I frowned, still pinning him with a stern glare. Something didn't add up. "Why am I hearing this from you instead of Mom and Dad?"

"Mom wanted me to tell you in person. She thought you'd take it hard," he said carefully.

She was right. Especially considering the house had been almost paid off until they refinanced it to cover my medical bills. This was basically my fault. Not just basically—it was. Literally all because of me.

Derek added, "It probably makes sense for them to downsize now that we're all gone anyway."

"I never heard them talk about downsizing before," I said. "As far as I know, they planned to stay there forever."

Pretty sure our mom had used those exact words—it was her "forever house."

"I don't know." He shrugged. "Things change."

Running out of money would do that. I scrambled mentally, searching for possible solutions or ways I could help, even though I only had about ten dollars to my name.

"What about Mitch and Steven? Can't they help them out?"

"They have been." Derek tilted his head, giving me a look that was meant to be sympathetic but came across as borderline condescending. Still pulling the older brother act. "That's why they've been able to keep the house this long. But neither of them has much money, either. Everyone is tapped."

"Right." I nodded, swallowing a massive lump in my throat. Now I wished we hadn't met somewhere so public. I kind of felt like crying. "So, they're going to sell it after Christmas?"

"Er, no. It's already been listed. But worst case, we'll do Christmas at Mitch's." Derek frowned and picked up his cup.

Right. My oldest brother lived in a small house with his wife and three kids. My second oldest brother, Steven, was a perpetual bachelor who lived in a one-bedroom apartment. And this scenario left Derek and me sleeping on couches, because we couldn't afford a hotel.

Not to mention my parents. Where were they going to live?

"Have Mom and Dad got a new placed lined up?"

"Not yet," he said, giving a one-shoulder shrug. "They can't buy anything until the house sells. Plus…I mean, their credit isn't great anymore with all this. They might have to rent something."

"Oh my god." I crushed the cup I was holding slightly. My parents weren't that young. They should have been thinking about retirement, not losing their home.

"It'll be okay, B."

But Derek was trying to convince himself as much as me.

"I don't see how," I said. "I hope the house sells if that's what they need. But I'll be really sad if we don't get to have Christmas there. Especially one last time." My breath snagged.

Derek nodded. "Yeah, me too." His throat bobbed, and he paused.

I used the lull in conversation to take some deep breaths, quelling the urge to cry. For now, anyway.

"On another note—"

My sibling senses tingled. *Alert, alert. Attack incoming.*

"Don't start." I was already keyed up emotionally, and I'd probably explode if he started in on the Chase issue.

"I'm not trying to," he said softly. "I wanted to know how you were doing."

I deflated, lowering my shields halfway, willing to give him a chance but still ready for a fight.

"I'm good. Things are good."

"Classes?"

"Going well. Straight As." Not like I had a choice if I wanted to keep my scholarships.

He studied me, brow furrowed. "Carter's good?"

"He's great." I felt a goofy smile emerge across my face. Couldn't help it; always happened when I talked about him.

"I'm glad," Derek said. "I mean, I still don't get it. But if he's good to you, I'll try."

It wasn't exactly a glowing endorsement, but it was progress. If they could start off by co-existing peacefully, I'd consider it a win.

"That's all I ask. If you guys kept an open mind and put all that other stuff aside, I'm sure you'd get along. At least off the ice."

He shot me a look that said he didn't believe me even a little, but he said nothing.

"What about…you?" I asked.

I was afraid to know the answer.

"I ended things with Jill."

"Oh, thank god." At least there was some good news coming from this. And Jill had been extra bitchy lately. Maybe that was why. "Are you okay?"

"Yeah." He drained his coffee and set down the empty cup. "Honestly, I don't know how I got sucked into something that messed up. It was like this weird slippery slope."

In a way, I got it. Not the whole affair part. But the slippery slope thing, for sure. It was like I woke up one day in a really terrible, controlling relationship with Luke, and I couldn't believe I'd let it get to that point. And I didn't fully grasp how bad it was until I was out of it.

"Good. You deserve better than that."

Now if Mendez would dump her, the karmic retribution would be complete.

"I'm going out with a chick from my finance class this weekend, so we'll see where that leads."

"Even being alone is better than being with someone toxic," I said. "I wish I had known that a long time ago."

He shifted his weight, looking uncomfortable. "Is Luke still contacting you?"

"Sometimes." I shrugged. It was hit or miss.

Chase wanted me to block him, but that kind of thing only made Luke escalate more. If Luke thought he was getting to me—he wasn't—it kept him on more of a leash.

Derek shook his head, his face clouding over. "I told him to stop."

Good to know he had tried for once, I guess. I wasn't sure if he knew about the untrue things Luke had texted to the team, but I wouldn't get into that right now.

"So did Chase. Repeatedly."

"That's what the hit was about, huh?"

"Little bit. Luke is a cheap shit anyway," I said. "He probably deserved it either way."

Derek laughed. "Probably."

My phone lit up with a reminder. I had an appointment with my academic advisor across campus in half an hour.

"Oh shoot. I should go." I stood up, pushing the chair back.

"I'm glad we got to talk," he said.

"Me too." We had more to work through, but it was a step in the right direction.

CHAPTER 40
TOLD YOU
BAILEY

A ONE-DAY BREAK TO sober up from intoxication via Chase probably wasn't the worst thing. After flying high all day yesterday, I needed to come back down to earth.

Just not today, apparently.

Best laid plans and all that.

Rain pelted against the glass rooftop of the atrium as Chase and I perched at a black metal table tucked away in the corner of the Callingwood campus food court, finishing the last of our burrito bowls. We hadn't planned to see each other today, and I'd planned to work on a few assignments during my break while Chase performed his usual pre-game routine after his last afternoon class. Later tonight, we would be at two different arenas for two different games.

But when one of Chase's profs called in sick at the last minute, he'd texted me to meet for lunch, and all the other stuff went right out the window. Finalizing the feature on the Callingwood Symphonic Chorus for the paper's weekend edition would have to wait because the lure of spending time with him was way too appealing.

So much for the self-discipline I prided myself on having.

I turned to face Chase, taking in the adorably awkward way he was trying to fit his oversized frame into the chair attached to the small table. His legs were far too long, forcing him to bend his knees out at an unwieldy angle.

"The world's not made for people your size, huh?"

Chase glanced down at his blue jean-clad legs, lips tugging up. "Nope." He nodded at me. "That's why I like that you're tall too. You know what it's like to tower over everyone else."

"I feel bad that you came all this way to see me when you have to turn around and go right back."

He threw his arm along the back of my chair, fingers grazing my upper back. "What else would I do with my free Friday afternoon? Study? *Alone*?"

"Well, yeah." I laughed, taking the last bite of my cilantro lime rice. "That would probably be a good idea. And what about your whole pre-game nap routine?"

"Why would I want to sleep when I could hang out with you here?"

I pointed at him with my fork. "You don't even go here."

"So?" Chase shrugged. "I'm still a student."

Fair enough. And at least he was wearing a black zip-up hoodie instead of his usual scarlet Falcons gear. The crimson bird was verboten around these parts.

"Okay, but as soon as we're done eating, we have to actually study." I tried—and failed—to keep a straight face, my tone stern. "And by we, I mean you. Study. Not flirt with me from across the table."

"How about both?" He flashed me a playful smile. "You know, compromise."

Impossibly charming and impossible to refuse.

"Whatever keeps you studying and off probation."

"I'll have you know I'm pulling straight Bs this semester." He took a sip of his bottled water, giving me an innocent look that I almost bought. "I've been a perfect angel."

"You mean replaced by an impostor?" I asked, gathering up my empty bowl, napkin, and cutlery, while Chase did the same.

"More like rehabilitated by your good influence."

We stood and took our garbage and recycling over to the bins by the pillar, then I steered him to the stairwell that led to my favorite study room on the second floor. It was cozy, with comfortable chairs and functioning heat, which was more than I could say for some of Callingwood's other study areas.

"Hmm." I hummed, pausing with my hand on the stainless-steel door handle. "If I'm your good influence, does that make you my bad influence?"

"Definitely." Chase brushed my hair off my shoulder. A shiver ran down my spine at his touch. He tucked my hair out of the way and moved in close, nuzzling my ear. "Speaking of that," he murmured. "I can't wait to get my hands on you tomorrow night."

My breath caught. I was expecting a kiss on the cheek, not dirty talk in the middle of the student commons. But this was Chase I was dealing with.

"Why's that?" I asked, voice breathy.

"Because I'm going to make you come so hard you wake up your new neighbors."

A jolt ran through me, and I whipped my head around to face him, eyes wide. "Oh my god. Chase. There are people everywhere."

"I know." He gave me a wolffish grin. "That's why I said it quietly."

"But now I feel..."

"Turned on?"

"In *public*." I scanned our surroundings for eavesdroppers. The seating area behind him was filled with students eating and milling around, carrying trays of food and talking on their phones. Of course none of them had noticed a thing. No one knew I was getting all hot and bothered. But still.

"That's the point, James. Anticipation is half the fun." He nudged me, opening the door and holding it for me.

I shook my head, lowering my voice. "You're such a tease."

"Of course," he said. "I love teasing you."

"I could tease you too, you know."

His gaze snared mine, warm brown eyes a mixture of amusement and desire. "Yes, please."

"Famous last words, Carter."

I would get him back someday. I just had to work up the nerve.

After spending an hour studying—or trying to while Chase took advantage of the otherwise empty room, doing his best to banter and play footsie with me—he walked me to class on the opposite side of campus.

We made our way across the quad with the wind gusting, a gloomy gray sky looming overhead. At least the rain had stopped. Usually, I loved fall, but the weather today was depressing, hinting of the winter to follow.

"Guess who called me the other day?" Chase said, taking a sip of his black coffee. His other hand was laced in mine, the heat of his skin warming it against the cold.

"Who?"

"The assistant GM for Los Angeles."

"What?" I froze with my cup halfway to my mouth. "That's huge. What did he want?"

"Checking in. How's school coming, training and nutrition, how are my coaches, talk about game tapes, things scouts have noticed."

Having been drafted before he started school, Chase was in the ideal situation for a college hockey player. A spot on the team was his to lose.

Conversely, Derek hadn't been drafted. He still didn't know who, if anyone, would pick him up after graduation. He might not know until well into next summer. And even then, it could be the NHL, AHL, or ECHL—or none of the above, which meant finding a regular job like everyone else. The last possibility scared him the most. He desperately wanted to play professionally after college.

"It's early in the season for them to be reaching out, isn't it?" I asked, my brow furrowed. I wasn't as familiar with the ins and outs of the signing process as I was with other aspects of hockey.

"Kind of, yeah. I think they're trying to feel me out."

"For next year?" My heart stuttered. I wanted to say it was

because I was happy for him, but my feelings weren't quite that altruistic.

"Maybe." Chase shrugged. "That or they know I'm trouble and they're keeping tabs. Could be both."

I laughed, but it died quickly. "Would you really leave school a year early? Without getting your degree?"

"Oh yeah." He nodded.

"This way." Making a left, I pulled him toward the brick social sciences building. Guess I knew why he was so unmotivated when it came to school. He had no plans to stay long enough to graduate.

"You would leave? Just like that?"

"One hundred percent."

I suddenly found myself winded. "That's a big decision."

"I know," he said. "But I've given it lots of thought. If it came down to it, I would jump ship. I could always finish my degree later if I needed to."

"Most people don't end up going back, though." Pretty hard to take the lifestyle hit that would entail.

"Probably not," he admitted.

A million things flew through my mind, but I wasn't sure it was my business.

"Speaking of hockey," Chase said, "I'm still leading in my fantasy hockey pool. Partly because of you." He squeezed my hand, rubbing the back of it with his rough thumb. He was trying to change the subject.

"That's awesome." But all I could think of was what would happen to us if he left. I knew it was too early to worry about that, but the thought of this being something temporary was gutting.

A few minutes later, we settled onto a wooden bench off to the side of the social science foyer, finishing the last of our coffees. In a twist of terrible timing, I had a lecture in less than ten minutes, and now we were locked in a disagreement about tonight.

"You didn't tell me you'd be at the Bulldogs game alone." Chase frowned. "I don't like it."

"It'll be fine," I said, placing a hand on his muscular thigh.

"Then I can finish packing after I get home, and we can move all of my stuff tomorrow."

"Still don't think you should be there without someone. Morrison gives me the creeps, James. Have you seen the way he looks at you? I feel like he's going to roll up and yank you into a white cube van one day. I'm not even kidding."

Luke was lots of things—lots of really crappy things—but he wasn't dangerous. He never physically hurt me. Though one could do a lot of damage to someone without laying a finger on them.

"You're being a little dramatic," I said. "There will be people everywhere in the arena. And Derek too."

"So?" he asked gruffly. "When was the last time Derek stood up for you?"

I gave him a withering look. "You don't think my own brother would stop someone from abducting me?"

"Who's to say he would even notice? He's pretty absorbed in whatever he's got going on."

It landed like a slap. Part of me knew he had a point, even if his delivery did sting. But Derek and I had made headway in mending the fence. Things weren't perfect by a long shot, and if I let myself think too hard about things, I might let my frustrations get the best of me.

"That's a little harsh," I said. "Besides, he ended things with Jill."

"Cool, now he can start making up for being shitty to you."

"Damn, Carter. Tell me what you really think."

Yes, he had a protective streak a mile wide, but sometimes he could stand to soften the blunt delivery a little.

"Remember when I said I'd always tell you the truth?" His tone was flat. "If the truth hurts, I'm not the one you should be mad at." He unzipped his hoodie, exposing the white tee underneath. He was always overheating. Arguing probably didn't help that.

Drawing in a breath, I blew it out slowly to calm the frustration brewing within me. "Back to the topic at hand. You're blowing this whole game thing way out of proportion."

Chase shook his head, the cords in his neck tight. "I'm not. You need someone there with you. I'd legit send Ward if he didn't have to be at the game with me."

"I'll be gone before the players even get out of the dressing room."

"It's not just Morrison. What about Amelia and Jillian? What if they corner you and give you a hard time? Not to mention that fucker Paul."

"I deal with Amelia and Jillian at home already, remember?" A sour taste filled my mouth. "Besides, Zara, Noelle, and Shiv are all busy."

I was borderline embarrassed that I had no one else to ask. In the past, I'd had an abundance of friends—until it turned out they weren't actually my friends.

"I guess we could hire a bodyguard. Unless you have another solution."

"I do, actually. A really easy one. Don't go."

"I'll be fine."

His jaw tensed. "What if you're not?"

I felt like pulling out my hair. Chase meant it when he said he was stubborn. I was quickly learning that meant he was impossible to argue with when he dug in his heels.

"Oh my god. It's one hockey game. In public. Why are you being so stubborn?"

"Because I'm right," he said, voice low. "He's a total fucking creep." I knew that voice. It was the end-of-discussion voice. I liked it in the bedroom—a lot—but it was frustrating as heck outside of it.

"Wait." I held up a hand, frowning. "Are you sure you aren't mad because I won't be at your game? My stuff is important too, you know."

"First of all, I'm not mad—I'm upset. There's a difference. And of course your stuff is important." His expression softened, his tone following suit. "It's got nothing to do with you watching me or not. But I'll be worried about you all night."

"Which will throw off your game."

"Which will throw off my sanity, James." He tucked a stray lock of hair behind my ear and rested his palm against my cheek. "I care about you more than the game."

My heart did another stutter for entirely different reasons this time.

"I care about you too. And it's super sweet that you're worried. But I'll be fine. Promise. I'll text you updates to prove I'm alive." I checked my watch. "Sorry, I've got to get to class."

We came to stand, face to face, and he wrapped his broad hands, warm and strong, around my waist. He dipped his head and touched his lips to mine, the tension between us evaporating. Smiling against my mouth, he let out a low chuckle as we broke apart.

"I think I needed that," he said. His smile faded and a frown ghosted his face. "Call me if anything happens."

"But you'll be on the ice."

"Do it anyway, okay?"

"Okay."

He leaned in, planting a soft kiss on my cheek. "See you tomorrow, beautiful."

Since the Bulldogs weren't playing the Falcons tonight, I didn't actively root against them—at least, not as much. In the end, they won three to two, which was good news for Derek.

I rooted against Paul, though. Enthusiastically. He didn't score any points, which I privately gloated about. Luke was still out with his knee injury too—an additional blessing since I didn't have to watch him on the ice.

The light was fading as I began my walk home. I was ten minutes into my twenty-minute walk, keeping a brisk pace to generate bodily warmth in the chilly evening air. Then, from out of nowhere, Luke's car pulled up beside me. It was like Chase's cube van prediction come to life, only with a navy blue BMW coupe.

My stomach pitched as Luke slowed the car to an idle and rolled down the window, leaning his head out. "Bailey. Can we talk?"

The universe had just given me the biggest I-told-you-so ever.

CHAPTER 41

WHIPPED

BAILEY

I IGNORED LUKE, picking up my pace to a near jog. The street was lined with tiny older houses, largely rented out by students, so there weren't any shops to duck into or other means of escape. Besides running, that is, but that probably wasn't warranted—I was fairly certain Luke was just being annoying.

Fairly.

Not positive.

"I said can we talk?" Luke raised his voice, his tone taking on a familiar sharp edge.

"No," I called over my shoulder. Why weren't there any other pedestrians around? If there were witnesses, he would probably leave. Luke wasn't prone to showing his ass to strangers. He had an image to maintain—or so he thought.

"I'll give you a ride home," he said, tempering his voice to appear calm. I knew this routine inside and out.

"Hard pass."

"Come on," he said, still easing the car down the street. "Don't make me park and get out."

And do what? Maybe I was wrong about him not being dangerous.

"Don't make me scream for help," I snapped.

With shaky hands, I fumbled in my pocket for my phone and

checked the time. It was 9:09. Chase was probably still on the ice. Maybe hitting the shower. Either way, not reachable. He said to call, but if I did and I couldn't reach him, he'd be even more upset.

"Bailey. Talk to me for a second."

Why? So we could fight? There was nothing to talk about. He loved nothing more than trying to suck me back into his cycle of drama.

I shook my head. "No."

Coming to a stop at the corner, I looked both ways before darting across. He rolled through the red light, keeping pace with me.

"After a year and a half, this is how you're going to leave things?"

"Yep. And Chase is about one minute away," I lied, "so leaving things would be in your best interest too." I shivered as the chill sank deeper into my bones, unsure of whether it was the cold or my flight-or-fight response kicking in.

"Why are you being such a bitch?"

And that was it. I finally snapped. If I'd been holding a rock, I think I would have thrown it through his windshield.

I stepped up onto the curb and came to a screeching halt. "I'm not a bitch. You're an asshole!" My voice climbed. "Leave me alone. Can't you take a hint?"

Unfortunately for me, engaging with him seemed to be what he wanted, because he stopped the car on the deserted street.

I should have known better.

Luke sneered, resting his forearm along the open window of the car. His silver Rolex glinted in the streetlight. "I was trying to make things right with you. But I don't know why I would even bother when you ended up in Carter's bed the moment after we ended things."

He didn't know how right he was. But it wasn't his business. Never mind the whole Sophie thing on his end, but at this point, I didn't care enough to volley back verbally.

"You're a slut," Luke added.

I shrugged, resuming walking. "Sure. Whatever."

"So you admit it?"

"I don't care what you think." I pretended to check my phone. "You should go. Chase will be here any minute. Don't think it'll end well for you."

"That guy isn't who you think he is," he said. "I'll prove it."

His tires squealed as he peeled away.

I had a good idea of who Chase was, for better or worse. The good, the bad, the stubborn. Luke's energy would have been better spent investing in some hardcore therapy of his own.

A short while later, I arrived home—my home for one last night, at least—to an empty house. Hands still trembling, I unlocked the door and quickly locked it again behind me. Leaning back against the door, I flipped on the hall light and sucked in a breath. Safe. Done. Over.

Once my heart resumed a more normal speed, I sent Chase a text to let him know I'd gotten home and left it at that. I didn't even know what to tell him about Luke. I should tell him. And I would, probably, tomorrow. I couldn't deal with it tonight.

After grabbing a drink, I went upstairs to finish packing. Moving out of the brownstone was bittersweet. I was mourning the loss of two friendships along the way. Even though it was harder and harder to remember, Amelia and Jillian hadn't always been the way they were now.

But I guessed it was never a real friendship, given how quickly they flipped the script on me. Sucked that I couldn't see that until it was too late.

A notification appeared on my phone as I folded the last of my clothes.

The Sideline: Rumor has it there's a hockey sex tape floating around with a girl from Callingwood. Offering a large monetary reward for anyone who can provide a copy.

Sex tape? My stomach twisted as my mind immediately jumped to the worst possible explanation, like it always did. Was the girl from Callingwood me? Luke wouldn't have secretly recorded us…would he?

That blind item could be referring to anyone. Could be Jillian or Amelia, even. Or one of the thousands of other students at Callingwood. I was being paranoid. Right?

—

CHASE

I'd had better games for sure. But we brought home a win, four-three, so it was all good.

Pushing past several of the guys in my way and receiving several fuck-yous in response, I barreled straight for my locker and grabbed my phone. I unlocked it as I sat on the bench, still in full equipment.

Dallas flopped down beside me and gave me a hard shove with his elbow. "Carter, what the fuck was that out there?"

"Hang on." I held up my hand, studying the screen. She'd texted me her last update ten minutes ago.

Bailey: Got home safe. All good. FaceTime when you're home too?

I quickly wrote her back.

Chase: Naked FaceTime?

Bailey: I thought you were teasing me until tomorrow.

Chases If you're actually game, I'll call off the teasing for now.

Bailey: We'll see...

I was pretty sure she was fucking with me—probably getting revenge for earlier—but hey, there was a chance she was for real.

And maybe I had overreacted a little. I still thought Morrison was a stalker, though.

"Earth to Carter."

I locked my phone and looked back up at Dallas. His light blue eyes pinned me to the spot, searing into mine, and his sharp jaw was tighter than the laces on my skates. He was more pissed with me than he'd been in a long time.

"What? We won, didn't we?" I tugged my jersey off over my head and unfastened my shoulder pads.

"Barely," he spat out. "And no thanks to you." Dallas lowered his voice, brow furrowed. "Where the hell was your head at? You almost skated the wrong way at one point."

"I told you; I was worried about Bailey. She was at the Bulldogs game alone."

And by worried, I mean imagining all kinds of disastrous scenarios. Usually, I used my imagination for good—a.k.a. dirty—things, but I was also incredibly good at picturing bad possible outcomes too. Hadn't realized that till recently, though.

"Did she get home okay?"

"Just now."

"Good." He slid off his elbow pads, giving me a withering look. "But you know worrying doesn't actually accomplish anything, right?"

This, coming from the guy who did things like check the weather three times before he left the house for fear it might rain on his designer suede sneakers. Cute.

"I guess."

I wasn't much of a worrier in general, so I hadn't given that idea much thought. What he said checked out, but somehow, I couldn't effectively apply that principle to Bailey.

Dallas leaned down, untying his skates. "You're gonna have to learn how to compartmentalize that shit."

"Easy for you to say. You've had way longer to figure out how to do that."

Not all of us had been training for this boyfriend thing for months in advance like it was the fucking relationship Olympics. Come on.

"I guess." He grunted. "But if you keep that up, Los Angeles will leave you here for another year."

"You've had off games because of Shiv too. Remember our season opener?" I pulled off my skates and wiped off the blades.

"Vaguely," he muttered.

Dallas couldn't argue that one and he knew it. That game was a fucking disaster. They'd had a blowout fight earlier in the day—probably about the boyfriend/girlfriend label; thank god that was settled now. Our alternate captain, Maxwell, had to assume control because Ward was a total space case the entire time. In fact, he'd been an outright liability on the ice. And unlike tonight, we'd lost that game.

"Besides," I said. "Miller already tore into me."

"Next time you miss a pass like that, I'll bench your ass myself."

"Fair enough."

After we showered, Dallas's mood improved. He tended to blow up quickly and cool off equally fast once he said his piece.

"Are we still good to move Bailey's stuff tomorrow afternoon?" I asked. "She doesn't have a ton, so it'll be pretty quick. Mostly it's the dresser, bed, and desk."

"Yeah. Around three or four or so? I'm taking Shiv to meet my parents for dinner at seven." He zipped up his jeans and paused. "Though I guess I could shower at the girls' place."

Then they'd probably never make it to dinner. We had our own bathrooms at home, luckily, but that didn't save me from the TMI knowledge that Shiv and Ward had a thing for shower sex. Unfortunately, while marble floor-to-ceiling tiles were nice to look at, the acoustics meant that sounds echoed. A lot.

"What's this, now? Shiv is meeting Maggie and Stewart?" I let out a low whistle. "Big step."

Dallas's parents were awesome. His dad was a typical old-school litigator, senior partner at one of the big four firms and a total dick in the courtroom. Chillest guy ever in his personal life, though. As long as you didn't fuck with him. There were very few people who actually scared me, but Stewart Ward was at the top of that list.

And Dallas's mom was the warm, motherly type who fussed over everyone. She was a *bit* of a trophy wife—he definitely got his looks from her; *not* his dad. Maggie always flirted with me too. Not in a creepy way, but in good fun. Drove Dallas crazy, which was extra hilarious.

"'Bout time, right?" he asked. "We're going to Allegro."

"Fancy."

That bill would clock in at five hundred dollars, easy. But that was the equivalent of a Chipotle bill for them.

"They're paying. Might as well milk it while I still can." Dallas shrugged.

"Yeah, once you make the league, they might actually make you pay your own rent."

His lips curled into a wry smile. "Like you pay market rent, jackass."

That was true. Our living arrangements were heavily subsidized by the Bank of Stewart Ward. I could easily afford to pay more, but his parents insisted on something "more reasonable for a student." I tried arguing with them, but they wouldn't hear it.

"I would if they'd let me," I said. "I can't help it if your parents have a soft spot for yours truly."

"They haven't gotten to know you well enough yet." Dallas pulled his navy long-sleeved T-shirt over his head.

Except I'd spent the majority of the last four summers at their beachfront cottage. Ward was an only child, so I was the closest thing he had to a brother.

"You're jealous because they like me better." I tugged my black hoodie on and straightened it.

"If that were actually true," Dallas said, "I'd go ahead and disown myself for being such an embarrassment."

I glanced up from buckling my belt and grinned. "Love you too, man."

"Who said I liked you?" He smirked. "You coming out for drinks?"

"Nah," I said. "Don't what to be tired for tomorrow. Big day of moving and whatever comes after that."

Plus, I was still hoping naked FaceTime could be a thing.

"You're so whipped."

"Yup."

CHAPTER 42
MOVING DAY
CHASE

I DIDN'T GET naked FaceTime, but I got cleavage FaceTime, and that's still pretty hot. And now Bailey was finally leaving her hellacious living situation with Satan's mistresses.

Saturday was off to a great start.

After a quick lunch, we headed back to her soon-to-be-former place. Bailey sat at her desk, meticulously itemizing the contents of each box because she was adorably and obsessively organized. She didn't even have much to keep track of, but hey, whatever worked.

Until Ward arrived to help move big things, I was taking care of the boxes of smaller items, stacking what I could fit in the back seat of the truck.

"Wow," I mused, picking up another medium-sized cardboard box. It was one of the last, then we could move on to the large furniture. "It'll be so weird for you to live somewhere I'm actually welcome."

"I know, right? I can't wait."

From beside her on the desk, her pale purple phone vibrated. Then it vibrated again. She glanced down and made a sound of disgust.

Oh, it better not be.

I set down the box I was holding. "Is that dick texting you again?"

"Yeah." She turned in her chair to face me, tugging on the drawstring of her turquoise hoodie. Her eyes were wide, her expression vaguely guilty. "I've been ignoring him."

She should have blocked his sorry ass, but Bailey was scared he would escalate if she did. We'd argued about that, but I eventually gave up because fighting about him wasn't worth it. Once she moved into her new place today—which he didn't have the address for—she would hopefully come around.

"Why is he bugging you now?"

Bailey inhaled and held her breath for a beat. "Because he's mad that I wouldn't talk to him last night."

My blood pressure shot through the roof, skyrocketing off into the atmosphere.

"*What*?"

I wasn't paranoid; I was *right*. I knew it. That fucking stalker.

"It wasn't a big deal," she said. "He wanted to talk, I said no, we had words. Then I called him an asshole, and he left."

Had words? Sure sounded like a big deal to me. I balled my hands into fists while I clamped down on the sour irritation brewing in my gut. I was only annoyed because I cared. Picking a fight wouldn't accomplish anything positive.

And yet. Dammit, James.

"But you didn't call me."

She scrunched up her mouth, which was cute enough to lessen my frustration. "You were still on the ice."

"You said you would either way." I raised my eyebrows.

"I would have if I needed to."

In my opinion, this incident fell firmly under the "needed to" category. Clearly, I wasn't the only stubborn one in this relationship.

I shook my head, my lips drawn in a thin line. "James."

Her phone vibrated again.

Easing down onto the foot of her bed, I nodded at it. "Mind if I see?"

I liked to keep tabs on what Morrison was saying and doing because he pinged my crazy radar—which, generally speaking, was pretty spot on. Taking the temperature of how he was behaving at any given time was important. Just in case.

Was this that worrying thing Ward was talking about last night? Whatever. It was necessary. Justified too.

Bailey shrugged. "Sure." She stood and came to sit beside me, handing me her phone. But her expression was off—almost like there was something she didn't want me to see. Weird.

The latest one said: *Answer me.*

My grip on the phone tightened. Oh, I'll fucking answer you.

I scrolled back to his previous string of messages.

Luke: It's rude to ignore texts, Bailey.

I scrolled again.

Luke: I could have taken care of you. And your family. Now your parents have to sell their house. They're going to lose everything because of you.

The blood in my veins turned to hot molten lava. What a piece of shit. The fucking nerve of this guy. I was too angry to read any more. Strong chance I'd break her phone if I did.

With a death grip on the device, I glanced up at her. "Can I please write this motherfucker back?"

"If you want to."

You bet I wanted to.

Bailey: Hey asshole. It's Carter. Text this number again, and I'll fuck up a lot more than your knee.

I hit send and locked her phone, handing it back to her. I doubted it would deter the creep anyway. Changing her number would probably be a whole lot more effective than blocking him.

With that said, there was a more urgent issue at hand.

"Not trying to pry," I said carefully, "but is it true that your parents are selling their house?" Or losing their house, from the sounds of it, but I was trying to be delicate. It wasn't my strong suit, so I was trying really, really hard.

"Yeah, they are."

"Morrison knew that, and I didn't?" I asked, putting my arm around her shoulders and pulling her closer. Her hair smelled like something tropical, maybe coconut and pineapple.

Bailey looked down, placing her palms on her dark jeans and refusing to meet my eyes. "Derek must have told him."

"Circling back to the me not knowing part," I said gently. "Why didn't you tell me?"

Probably why she looked at me funny when she gave me the phone. She didn't want me to know. But why?

"I don't know." She peered up at me, snagging her pink bottom lip between her teeth. "I found out the other day. My dad got laid off recently, and they can't afford to keep it."

My stomach sank. Well, fuck. I guess that was why.

"I'm sorry, James."

Bailey gave a little one-shoulder shrug that was anything but convincing. "It's not a big deal."

But it clearly was. I could tell from the way she talked about home that the house mattered to her. It was where she'd grown up. She said her mom had this crazy huge garden in the backyard; they did Christmas there every year; all of her and her brothers' heights were marked on the kitchen doorframe, all of those sentimental things.

"Where will they live?"

"They're downsizing somewhere nearby," Bailey said. "They

don't need as much space now that we're all grown, anyway. It probably makes sense."

Maybe, but making that choice and having it made for them were two different things.

"The market is terrible where they live, though, so the house isn't selling," she added.

And it kept getting worse.

"Will they be okay if the house doesn't sell for a while?"

"I think so," she said. "My brothers can help them out if they need money. I'm sure my dad will find another teaching position soon too."

I nodded. "Right."

For better or worse, Bailey wasn't a good liar. The way she nibbled at her lip and kept her head ducked told me things wouldn't be okay. And she wasn't giving me the full story, either, not with how Morrison's text was worded. Money was a touchy thing with her, though, so I didn't want to pry.

I needed to mull this one over a little. There was something to it, I just didn't know what.

We fell quiet for a moment. The room was nearly empty, save for a few boxes and bare furniture, but the air was heavy.

I nudged her with my elbow, trying to lighten the mood. "Are you excited about moving?"

"Yeah. Mostly."

"Mostly?"

If I were her, I would be wearing a shiny party hat and giving both Amelia and Jillian a gigantic "fuck you" on the way out.

"Well," Bailey hesitated, "I guess there's a small part of me that wonders if I'm letting my life revolve around yet another hockey player. You know, with the whole you-Dallas-Shiv connection. Feels a little…puck-bunny-ish."

Ouch. I had skin as thick as hockey equipment, but that one still stung.

"You think you're a puck bunny?" I gave her a pointed look until she made eye contact, trying to get a read on where this was coming from. "And I'm just another hockey player? We aren't cardboard cut-outs. We're real people."

And if, god forbid, things ended between us, I'd never be a crazy asshole like Morrison and make her living situation difficult. But I couldn't bring myself to think about that scenario in any greater detail. Wasn't going to happen, anyway.

Bailey took my hand, her skin cool and soft against mine. "Don't you think I'm a bit of a stereotype, though? I went from one hockey player straight to another."

"It's not like you went after me because I play hockey. I pursued you. In my own slightly misguided way."

A small smile peeked out on her lips. "Still…"

"Would you still like me if I quit the team tomorrow?"

Her hazel eyes widened, and her tone hushed. "Of course."

"Then you're not a puck bunny. Problem solved." I studied her. "Where's this coming from?"

She tucked a lock of hair behind her ear and shrugged, making a little "I dunno" sound.

"Did someone call you a puck bunny?"

"Paul may have. That one day."

A trail of expletives exploded in my brain.

My hit list had officially grown to two people.

We were due to play Callingwood again in a few weeks, and my entire team would be ready to clobber both of those dipshits. Repeatedly.

"Don't let him get in your head. It's exactly what he wants."

"But it's not wrong. First I was Luke Morrison's girlfriend, and now I'm Chase Carter's girlfriend."

Ouch again. But now I knew where this was coming from.

"You're not *just* my girlfriend. There's so much more to you than that label. Anyone with two brain cells to rub together knows that." Which ruled out Paul.

Plus, the way she worded that made it sound terrible. I would have 100 percent stayed friends with Bailey even if nothing had happened between us.

I would have had to deal with the insane attraction part somehow, sure. But I would have wanted her in my life.

"Do they?" She frowned.

"If they don't, they're too stupid to matter in the first place."

Bailey fell quiet again.

There were times when I swore I could see straight into her brain. Some of those times were good, but other times, it gutted me a little. Like right now.

I sighed. "I wish you could see yourself the way I see you."

"How's that?"

"You're a talented writer, a video game playing goddess, loyal to a fault, and so beautiful that sometimes it hurts a little."

"Do you really think that?" she whispered.

"Of course."

While Bailey packed up her bedding, I ran the last few loads of boxes out to the truck, ignoring Amelia and Jillian's glares as I went back and forth. Couldn't they have vacated the place for one goddamn day? It was like they'd purposely hung around so they could be relocation spectators.

Literal worst.

Vultures.

Returning to her room, I picked up one of the last boxes, but this one felt like it was full of bricks. "Holy shit, James. What's in here? A set of kettlebells or something?"

"No, some books. Mostly hardcovers…" She turned to look at me and trailed off, eyes turning a little glassy.

I knew that look.

I was a big fan of that look.

BAILEY

"Are you checking me out right now?" Chase set down the box, a smug grin playing on his lips.

I was. I totally was. I was biting my bottom lip in full-on thirst mode.

Busted.

"What? It's just…you know." I gestured with an outstretched arm, heat flooding my cheeks. "You're being all manly. Lifting heavy stuff. Muscles."

Apparently, my brain had decided to take a coffee break while other parts of my body seized control.

But, I mean, look at the guy. Black joggers slung low on his hips, white tee hanging perfectly off his athletic frame, sinewy muscle covered with smooth, taut skin…

He closed the door and took a few steps in my direction, grin intensifying as he drew closer. "So you want me for my body."

"It's definitely a selling point." I fought a sheepish smile.

Obviously, there were lots of other things I liked about him. But the view was pretty nice.

"Now who's got the dirty mind?"

"Too much time with you, I guess." I laughed softly, turning away from him to face the desk.

I attempted to look over my checklist again, but Chase's proximity made focusing on anything but him impossible. He was close enough that I could smell the intoxicating combination of him and his cologne, and my brain shut off completely.

An aura of warmth surrounded me as he pressed against me from behind, broad hands landing on my waist. He gathered up my hair and moved it to the opposite shoulder. Soft lips skirted along the arch of my neck, drawing a line of light kisses. Desire pooled between my legs, and a familiar throb pulsed in my core.

One hand tugged at the button of my jeans, nimbly unfastening it and tugging the zipper down.

"Speaking of dirty minds. I've been thinking about you." He slid his hand lower, past the waistband of my lacy white underwear.

"How's the toy, baby?" His skilled fingers moved against me, sending off a shockwave of pleasure.

"Um…" I arched my back, drawing in a ragged inhale in response to his touch. "It's good."

"You're so fucking hot," he murmured, lips pressing against my neck. "Think of me when you're using it?"

"Maybe," I breathed.

His voice rumbled in his chest. "That's not an answer."

"Y-Yes."

"Good girl."

His other hand slipped beneath my black T-shirt, his rough palm grazing the side of my ribcage. He squeezed overtop of the thin fabric of my bra. When he rolled my nipple between his thumb and finger, I couldn't stop the soft moan that escaped my lips.

Desire from moments before had surged into all-out need. Nothing else existed besides his body pressed up against mine and his hands coaxing my desire.

"Gonna let me watch you sometime?"

"If you want to." Then again, in the moment, I would have agreed to anything.

"Very badly," said Chase. "That falls into my top five fantasies."

He stroked me again, teasing. Heat flooded my body, and I drew in a soft gasp. "What are the other four?"

He didn't even miss a beat. "Tying you up, you in a skirt without underwear, truck sex, getting you to talk really dirty to me, and teasing you until you beg me to fuck you."

"Isn't that five?" Maybe it wasn't. Not sure I could count to three, let alone five, with what he was doing to me right now.

He slipped beneath my bra, palming the bare skin. "The last two are interrelated, so I'm counting them as one."

"You've given this a lot of thought."

"Sure have." His hand beneath my underwear wandered even lower, one finger sliding inside, followed by another.

My knees went soft, and I drew in a breath, steadying myself against him. "The walls are paper thin in this place, remember?"

"So? That didn't stop us before."

From downstairs, the doorbell rang.

Well, that sure would.

We froze, then broke apart.

Chase sighed. "That'll be Ward, half an hour early, which means he's right on cue to cockblock me. I swear he has the worst timing."

"I guess we'll have to make up for it in the new place."

"Later?" He grinned. "Absolutely. I meant what I said yesterday."

Oh my.

I quickly refastened my jeans, straightened my T-shirt, and smoothed down my hair. But I still worried that what we'd been doing was obvious.

Chase grabbed the heavy box from earlier. "I'll run this out while we let him in."

We descended the stairs, and halfway down, made the unpleasant discovery that it wasn't Dallas at the door—it was Paul. Here to either visit Amelia or simply to stir up shit.

I lingered awkwardly at the bottom of the stairs while Chase ignored Paul completely, making his way past him toward the front door.

He jutted his chin, his tone taking on an edge. "Heard you were shooting off your mouth about me, Carter."

Chase stopped and turned to face him with the box still in his arms. He smirked. "I said you can't fucking skate, in case your girlfriend failed to relay the entire message."

Paul paused like he had expected Chase to deny it.

"Fuck you."

He must have stolen this sad excuse for a comeback from Luke.

"Fuck you for talking shit to Bailey." Chase stepped closer, dark brow drawn into a harsh line.

"Nothing that wasn't true."

Chase's jaw tightened, and he glared at him, shaking his head. Pretty sure he was going to clobber his ass next time he was anywhere near the puck.

Or possibly now.

"Chase." I stepped closer, touching his arm.

"Brave words," Chase said. "Stupid, but brave. See how that plays out for you on the ice in a couple weeks."

Paul scoffed. "You didn't even hit me last game. I'm not scared of you." He probably should have been, but no one ever accused him of being smart.

"That's right." Chase snorted. "Why would I bother when you did such a good job of taking yourself out?"

Dallas strolled up to the open door then, giving me a friendly smile. It faded when he caught sight of Chase and Paul standing face to face. His hands fisted, square jaw tensing.

"What's up, Carter?" Dallas asked sharply. "Is there a problem?"

Chase glanced over at him and rolled his shoulders back. "Nothing worth your time. Let's get James moved the fuck out of here, shall we?"

CHAPTER 43
SAY IT
BAILEY

SEVERAL TRIPS UP and down the elevator later, I was moved into our new place. Not even remotely unpacked, but all my boxes were stowed away in my room, along with my bed, dresser, and desk. Siobhan had, thankfully, already purchased furniture for the shared areas with her rental insurance payout. It was a good thing too, because I didn't have any other furniture. Or money.

Everything Shiv purchased coordinated perfectly. A sleek navy blue sectional, modern light-colored wood kitchen table set, plus a few accent pieces. The pieces were stylish and looked distinctly grown-up; a definite improvement over the second-hand furnishing situation at my old place, complete with battered coffee table and worn, dirt-brown couch oozing stuffing at the seams.

Factoring in the much nicer roommate, significantly newer building, and the ability to finally have Chase over, the move was an upgrade in every sense of the word.

Including the monthly rent. *But who needs groceries*?

After we brought up the last set of boxes, Chase followed me into the kitchen to get a glass of water. I filled my cup under the fridge dispenser while he leaned against the counter, reading a text.

"Dallas and Shiv are going to Penner's for drinks." He locked his phone and slid it back into his pocket. "He's a guy on our team. Ty and a few other people will be there too. Do you want to go?"

"Sure. What time?" I set my empty glass on the black granite countertop, glancing up at him.

"Whenever. They're heading there now. But if you want to chill for a bit, we can leave in half an hour or something."

"I wonder what we should do till then." I tilted my head and smirked. "There's a game on. Chicago versus Boston?"

"Fuck the game. Let's circle back to my list." Chase pivoted to face me and took a step forward, eyes darkening. Warmth radiated from his body as he fenced me in against the cupboard with his arms, gripping the edge of the counter behind my back.

"Sadly, all my skirts are packed. And I don't think your truck will fit inside this apartment. Guess you're out of luck."

His smoldering expression cracked, his mouth tugging. "Watch it, or I'll make a point to tease you even longer."

"You already teased me once today."

"Oh, I was just getting started." He nudged my legs apart with his knee. I drew in a soft gasp as he pressed against me, igniting a flicker of desire within my core.

"Really?" I wasn't sure how much of that my brain could take. Or other parts of me.

"I've got all kinds of plans for you." He leisurely traced a finger along my collarbone, dipping over top of my dark green T-shirt between my breasts. A tingle ran down my spine. His tone softened, losing its edge. "But you can always tell me to stop if it's too much."

"I know." Never needed to, but I knew he would in a heartbeat.

"How about this? Say red if you want me to stop…" Chase ducked his head, and his soft lips met mine. I gripped his upper arms as his tongue pushed inside my mouth. One hand nimbly unbuttoned my jeans, and he pulled back slightly, breaking the kiss. "Yellow for wait or slow down," he murmured against my lips, tugging at my zipper. "And green for keep going."

"Mmm…" I ran a hand through his silky hair. "Green."

One rough palm skimmed down the side of my ribcage, then paused.

"You are so fucking gorgeous." He ran the pad of his thumb

along my cheek, tilting my chin up. His voice turned stern. "But you're still in trouble."

My breath caught. "For what?"

"Not calling me."

I should have known he wouldn't let it go so easily.

"I didn't want you to worry."

"I was worried anyway."

"Er…red?"

He shook his head, jaw tight. "Doesn't work for that, James." His deep brown eyes scanned my face. "You downplay things. Why?"

"I don't know." It was an instinct. I didn't know how not to. If I dug deep enough, I could probably come up with a few theories—but none that I particularly wanted to discuss.

"Turns out," he said, "I was right to worry."

"Guess so."

"I don't want anything to happen to you." Strong, broad hands spanned my hips, thumbs stroking the bare skin above my waistband.

"It won't."

He raised his dark eyebrows. "Sounds like it almost did."

It was hard to say. Did Luke actually pose a threat? He would never have bothered to show up and behave like he did when we were dating, so it made even less sense now that we weren't.

Chase watched me, waiting for a response. My tongue darted out, licking my lip, and his gaze fell to my mouth, his pupils dilating.

"Lucky for you," he said, eyes snapping back up to meet mine, "I'm way too worked up to get into this right now. But we're not done."

"Okay."

He pressed his body against me again and murmured in my ear. "You're wet for me already, aren't you, baby?"

"Maybe."

"Let's see." He slipped his hand beneath the waistband of my underwear and stroked me, setting off an explosion of pleasure. "Knew it. You're soaked."

I drew in a shuddering breath as he continued to touch me, pushing every button in exactly the right way.

"Do you like it when I touch you like this?"

"Mm-hmm." My eyelids drifted shut, and I whimpered again, hips tilting against his hand. I could barely stay upright, let alone dirty talk back to him.

Pressure built between my legs as he continued to tease me in the most exquisite form of torture. I leaned back against the counter, letting out another moan.

"Fuck. I love when you make sounds for me."

I grabbed his hand, hips arching against his touch. I was so close to an orgasm I could practically see it. Could almost reach out and touch it. Chase slowed down, keeping me on the verge, and a growl of frustration escaped the back of my throat in response.

"Not yet." His warm breath fanned across my neck.

I peeked up at him. "But I'm right there."

"I know." Chase grinned. "You have a tell."

I do?

"What is it?"

He shook his head, deep brown eyes gleaming. "Can't give away all my secrets. I just know."

I sucked in a sharp breath as his fingers slid against me again, holding me on the edge without release. Another growl of frustration followed.

"You're cute when you're frustrated."

"Oh my god." I whimpered. "You're mean." I wasn't used to being bothered in this way, either. Before Chase, it had been the frustration of trying to capture the ever-elusive orgasm. Now he was purposely keeping it away?

"You can say red and I'll stop teasing you. I'll let you have what you want right now. Otherwise, I'm not letting you come until I say so."

"When's that going to be?"

"When I fuck you. Later." He kissed me on the cheek. "But we should probably get going. I want to stop by my house to change."

I blew out a breath. How was it possible to be turned on and annoyed at the same time?

"I think I might hate you right now."

Chase smirked. "No, you don't."

"Let's swing by the liquor store," Chase said, signaling and making a left turn as we pulled away from his place.

"But you're driving."

"Not planning on drinking much. Just have a policy against showing up places empty-handed."

Minutes later, he pulled into the parking lot and scanned the rows of parking spaces with a frown. They were all occupied, probably because of the movie theater in the same commercial complex. Finally, he found a vacant spot nearly a block away.

The radio cut away from the sports talk show we were listening to.

"Breaking news on the sex tape scandal for NHL player Matthew Stevens," the announcer said. "Stevens allegedly recorded a second unidentified woman without her consent while they were engaged in sexual activity. Criminal charges are now pending."

Matthew Stevens was an up-and-coming hockey prodigy one year older than Chase. He was on track to be the next Sidney Crosby in terms of his skill and style of gameplay. Now it looked like his career might be over before it started.

"Yikes." I turned down the volume quickly. Definitely didn't need to think about that right now. Or ever.

"No kidding." Chase grimaced as he pulled into the lone vacant spot. "Something like that could end his career."

And hers too—whoever she was. The news was keeping her identity anonymous for now, but if criminal charges went ahead, it would be revealed eventually. Then his lawyers would probably drag her name and reputation through the mud any way possible.

Not to mention that everyone she knew could go to PornPlace—or whatever it was called—and watch her most intimate moments. Horrifying.

A prickle of anxiety crept back into the corner of my brain. I'd pushed the sex tape blind item to the back of my mind until now, but I was getting paranoid again.

There was no way that had anything to do with me.

Couldn't.

I hoped.

Fifteen minutes later, Chase pulled up in front of a blue two-story house in a newer development. It wasn't as impressive as the one he lived in with Dallas and Ty, but it was still nicer than the average college student accommodations.

He parked against the curb and killed the ignition. Unbuckling my seat belt, I shifted in my seat, moving closer to him and placing a hand on his thigh.

Payback time.

"Before we go in," I said, "tell me more about your truck sex fantasy."

His gaze fell to my hand, then lifted up to my face. He gave me a devilish smile. "What about it?"

"Where would this take place?" I slid my palm higher up his jean-clad leg. "I mean, in theory."

"Lots of quiet areas out where my mom lives. Maybe around Thanksgiving, we could take a little detour…"

"Mmm," I hummed, moving higher. "We should definitely do that."

Chase shifted his weight, drawing in a breath; now I had him going.

"Dammit." He shook his head.

"What?"

"You know what. You're making me horny before we have to go inside."

"Call it payback, Carter." I gave him a look. "Besides, you're always horny."

"Of course I am," he said. "Look at you."

Everyone was bombed by the time we showed up. Dallas and Siobhan had gotten drunk on expensive wine at dinner with his parents—Shiv in particular, and she was talking so loudly I could hear her from the next room. And reportedly, the majority of the guests had been playing beer pong for a good portion of the night. Based on the noise level, it showed.

Chase steered me into the kitchen and quickly introduced me to Kyle Penner. He had wavy, reddish-blond hair and didn't look familiar to me, but a lot of the guys looked different off the ice.

But the girl with him did look familiar. Dark hair, very pretty, petite. She was the girl hanging off Chase at the rink after the game against Callingwood. Kristen. I wasn't her biggest fan, and there was definitely history between her and Chase.

After an awkward exchange, we headed into the living room where a group of people was playing a drinking game with cards. Tyler and the girl he'd brought were making out on a couch in the corner while his hand crept dangerously high underneath her short skirt. I had to avert my eyes to avoid seeing straight up it.

"Bailey!" Shiv squealed, waving us over. We squeezed onto the couch beside her and Dallas. "Are we still going shopping for the gala this weekend?"

Right. The gala. In the chaos of the move, I had forgotten. It was a big charity event that the hockey community put on for the Children's Hospital Foundation. We were sharing a table with Dallas and Shiv, Ty and his date, and another couple.

It sounded nice—and fancy, which was a slight issue for me in terms of the dress code. But I would figure it out. Maybe via Zara or Noelle's closet.

"Yup."

By *we*, I meant I would accompany her and watch while spending zero dollars.

"I can't wait," she said. "I love dress shopping."

Dallas chortled. "You love shopping, period. Even grocery shopping with you is an event."

Shiv rolled her eyes, taking a sip of beer. "You have more shoes than I do, Dal."

Chase nudged me. "Are you going to buy something sexy for me?"

Yeah, with my negative-balance bank account.

"Uh, no." I cleared my throat. "I'm sure I have something. Just going for Shiv."

We joined in their drinking game, playing together and sharing a beer because I didn't understand the rules and didn't want to get drunk. A few rounds later, I excused myself to use the bathroom. The one on the main floor was occupied by someone throwing up, so Kyle directed me upstairs to the other bathroom.

After drying my hands, I opened the door and stepped out into the hallway. A wall of solid muscle with mischievous dark eyes stopped me.

Chase gave me a crooked smile. "Hi."

"Hi." My breath caught as he placed his hands on my hips and took a step forward, steering me into the bathroom. "What are you doing?"

"Getting you alone."

"Why?"

"Why do you think?" He closed the door behind him and locked it, then flipped on one set of lights, bathing the bathroom in a dim glow.

"But there are people downstairs."

"Not sure if you noticed, but they're all too plastered to even realize we're gone." His eyes danced. "Besides, that's what makes it hot."

I drew in a breath. "I—"

"Unless you don't want me to make good on all that teasing." Warm hands slid under my shirt, fingers digging into my skin.

Liquid heat pooled between my legs. "But teasing you gets me worked up too, so between that and the truck, I really need to fuck you. And I'm pretty sure you feel the same way."

I bit my bottom lip and nodded.

Chase backed me up against the counter. "Can you be quiet for me, baby?"

"I don't know if I can."

"Guess you're going to have to try."

With his lips on mine, he leveled me with a demanding kiss. Time sped up, our mouths and hands moving in a blur. Desire crashed over me as I fumbled with his belt, unfastening it and his jeans. His hands slid down the curve of my hips, taking my pants and underwear with them.

Grabbing the backs of my thighs, he set me on the counter and spread my legs. I splayed my hands across his lower back, trying to pull him closer to me, but he stopped short.

He dipped his head, mouth beside my ear. "Say it."

"Say what?"

"Say *fuck me, please*. Or maybe *I want your cock buried deep inside my pussy*. I need specific instructions about what you want me to do."

The throb between my legs verged on painful. I wanted those things. Very badly. Verbalizing them was another story.

"I can't say that," I breathed.

"Oh, I think you can." He palmed my breasts and squeezed. "Otherwise, we'll both be left hanging. And I don't think either of us wants that."

"I…want you."

His gaze held mine, predatory and expectant. "Want me to what?"

Breath coming out in tiny pants, I watched him for a beat. He placed his hands on my bare upper thighs, waiting. My heart pounded against my ribcage. I was too turned on to be self-conscious. I needed him.

"I want you to fuck me."

"Good girl." He gripped my hips roughly and pulled me closer to the edge of the counter, simultaneously pushing inside me. Pleasure instantly surged through my body, going from zero to sixty for the third time today.

"Oh god," I whispered, arching my back against him.

One hand spanned my lower back, holding me in place, while the other slid up the back of my neck and grabbed a fistful of hair at the roots. I tried to stifle a moan as he moved against me, staying deep and hitting the perfect spot.

"Can I pull your hair a little harder?" he asked, voice low.

"Mm-hmm."

His grip tightened, tugging in a way that pulled me deeper into him, into the ecstasy he created. At my ear, he murmured, "You take it so well for me."

Chase thrust harder, changing the angle and sending the pleasure past the limits of what I could tolerate. My vision turned fuzzy, and I buried my face in his shoulder to quiet myself.

As I hit the peak, he angled my face up to his and planted a scorching kiss on my lips, muffling my cries. My nails dug into his skin as pleasure spilled over in a wave. It was bright, blinding, all-consuming. I lost awareness of everything but what he was doing to my body.

Just as it was starting to recede, he thrust into me harder. Both of his hands flew to my waist, and he pulled me against him. "Fuck, fuck, fuck."

Then he stilled, dropping his forehead against mine. Drawing in a shaky breath, I placed my palms on his chest, feeling his heart pound against his ribcage. While not all that risqué, it was the most public thing I'd done—ever. And I'd liked it.

Pulling back, he studied me, biting his knuckle with a grin. "You look freshly fucked, baby."

"You might want to look in the mirror before you get too cocky there, Carter."

He glanced at his reflection and laughed. "Good point."

CHAPTER 44
SURE DOES
BAILEY

ON THE WAY home a few hours later, I curled up against the passenger door, eyelids heavy with looming sleep. But that didn't stop Chase from grilling me about my run-in with Luke.

As we drove, the streetlights cast flickers of shadows across Chase's profile. Reluctantly, I gave him the whole story, including the part where Luke called me a slut. The more I spoke, the more his face clouded over with anger. Not just anger—rage. His grip on the steering wheel got tighter and tighter, the cords in his neck tensing to match.

"Then he drove away," I finished.

"Fuck!" Chase smacked the steering wheel with his open palm. "I'm going to snap his neck like a twig."

He drew in a breath and let out a low growl. "Maybe break his legs first," he muttered, shaking his head. "Or his fingers. One at a time. Pull out some teeth with pliers too."

After his verbal rampage, he fell silent for several moments. I stole a glance at him but didn't know what to say. He was on a precariously short leash, especially given that he was operating a motor vehicle. It wasn't that he was flying off the handle. Just the opposite. An eerie, overly quiet calm had settled over him. The kind that meant something lethal was brewing beneath the surface.

"I hope you know I'm not mad at you," Chase said quietly. "Just at him and what he did."

"I know." But part of me felt strangely guilty that he was so upset.

"Has he texted you since I wrote him back from your phone?" His tone was unnaturally even. "I need the truth."

"No." Chase's threats tended to put Luke off temporarily. It just never stuck.

"Are you sure?"

"Promise. I can show you if you want."

"You need to block him, baby."

"Good call." I yawned. "I will now that I've moved."

Chase added, "Better yet, change your number so he can't contact you from someone else's phone. And for the love of god, no more attending games alone. Please."

"Deal. On both counts."

Getting a new number would be a hassle, which was why I'd been resistant initially, but Chase was right—Luke wasn't above using other people's phones to contact me. I knew that from experience. A clean slate was worth the inconvenience.

The game thing might be trickier, but I would make it work somehow. I wasn't eager to live through a repeat of what Luke did, either.

Chase turned onto the freeway entrance ramp. After shoulder-checking, he merged into the middle lane. I closed my eyes, snuggling against a black hoodie that I'd snagged from the back seat and folded into a makeshift pillow. It smelled like him. He probably wasn't getting it back. Sorry, Carter.

A few more seconds of silence passed, then he sucked in a sharp inhale. "I'm sorry, I can't get past this. Why the hell didn't you call me? What if he'd hurt you?"

"A few reasons," I said, eyes still closed.

"Like..."

"I guess part of me feels like it's my fault."

My fault for dating Luke in the first place; my fault for not handling him correctly and provoking him; my fault for going to the hockey game alone.

"James." His voice softened. "That's not even a little true."

"How is it not?"

"You're not responsible for anything that fucker does."

It didn't feel that way.

"That and I don't want you to get yourself into trouble," I said.

"One of these days I'm going to have to make good on my threats to him or they won't mean anything."

"Can you limit beating him to when you're on the ice so you don't go to jail?"

"Trust me when I say that I am trying very, very hard to do that. Counting down the days until I can demolish him," he said. "But if he pulls something like that car thing again, he's leaving in a body bag."

"Chase." I groaned.

"Don't worry," he said. "I can afford a top-notch lawyer. Call it self-defense or something, whatever."

He paused. "Or maybe I should hire a hit man. It would be money well spent."

I couldn't tell if he was serious.

CHASE

Bailey dozed off after she spilled the ugly truth, which gave me fifteen minutes to breathe deeply and cool down before we got home.

Or at least to shift into quietly planning Morrison's dismemberment while attempting to behave like a normal human, outwardly speaking.

I wasn't upset with her—especially after she told me she felt like it was her fault. That admission had guilt smashing me in the face like a slapshot.

I hated him that much more for making her think that.

And I really fucking hated him for scaring her.

Tomorrow was supposed to be my rest day, and now Morrison had fucked that up too, because I had serious amounts of aggression to work out on the ice or in the gym. Maybe both.

Or I could find his address and take it out on the source…

Also planned to consult Ward and Ty about orchestrating the most damaging on-ice hit possible that wouldn't land me a suspension or expulsion from the league. Still needed to mull that one over. Maybe get out the whiteboard and draw up some diagrams evaluating potential plans of action, optimizing speed, and leveraging angles. Watch some videos online, like compilations of the NHL's most devastating hits. You know, research that shit and really get it right.

I pulled into the visitor parking for Bailey's apartment building and shifted into park. As I did, the truck lurched slightly, causing her to stir. Bailey let out a tiny, adorable groan and pushed herself upright, stretching sleepily.

"Sorry," I said quietly. "We're home."

She unbuckled her seat belt and turned to me, still bleary-eyed with sleep. "Are you okay?"

"Yeah, I'm good." I had to put the Morrison thing on ice for the time being. I wouldn't let that creep ruin my night with her.

We headed upstairs to change and get ready for bed in a pattern that was nearly automatic by now. I knew everything down to the color of her toothbrush. She even had her own drawer at my place. I didn't recognize myself, but that was a good thing.

Climbing under the covers, I threw an arm around Bailey, and she nestled against me with a hand splayed on my stomach. She was wearing one of my shirts; she had a rotation of them now, and it was, as always, fucking adorable. And her blond hair smelled faintly of her fruity shampoo, which, oddly enough, was a turn-on for me. Probably because it brought about visions of her naked and wrapped around me while I pulled it.

God, I was in deep.

"I know we said we'd go for round two," she murmured, "but I'm pretty wiped out between the move and the late night."

"I figured after you fell asleep on the way home." I chuckled. "I'm bagged too, much as I hate to admit it."

All of today's heavy lifting had taken its toll. I could have rallied if she wanted—it wasn't like I'd turn her down, ever—but I was tired.

Bailey pulled the soft white comforter higher around her body, shivering. The room felt fine to me, but as usual, she was cold. Her bare feet told me as much, because they were pressed up against my calf like blocks of ice.

"Thanks for helping me today."

"Of course," I said. "I'm just glad you're moved."

She turned onto her stomach and propped herself up on one elbow to face me. Her blond hair fell in front of her face, and she brushed it away with her free hand.

Our eyes met, and her lips tugged at the corners, a small smile forming on her perfect mouth.

Everything shifted, like the earth moving on its axis.

It felt like the moment before our first kiss, before our first real sleepover, before we had sex for the first time. One of those slivers of time I'd remember forever, going into it as one person and leaving as someone else.

Her expression sobered as her green-gold eyes traced my face, lips slightly parted. She looked nervous for a split second, and her brow furrowed before she spoke.

"I love you," she said softly.

She beat me to it.

A rush ran through my body. The only time I'd ever felt something even remotely comparable was when I was drafted, but even that didn't compare—partly because, on some level, I always knew that would happen.

But in the scheme of my life, I never expected her.

"I love you, James. I've known that for a while."

For once in my life, I'd managed to filter something. I was fairly certain I'd gotten there first, although it took me a while to figure out what the hell was going on.

Her face brightened, her smile returning. "Really?" She shifted, moving closer to me and placing a soft, warm hand on my bare chest.

"Yeah." I tucked a stray piece of hair behind her ear. "I wanted to make sure you were there too before I said anything. But it's not a big secret, anyway. Pretty sure half the state knows how I feel by this point." I leaned in, my mouth hovering above hers. "Feels good to say it, though."

She smiled against my lips. "Sure does."

The week flew by in a blur of classes, practice, and dryland. In addition to her usual heavy workload, Bailey was consumed with completing some massive scholarship application that required an essay, references, and a million other time-intensive items. Between our conflicting schedules, we barely had time to see each other.

To make matters worse, Coach Miller was all over me again, which I couldn't understand because my grades were fine and so was my performance. I could barely breathe without him looking in my direction.

But even with staying busy, my thoughts weighed me down. It was like carrying a gigantic bag of hockey equipment around all week, metaphorically speaking.

I debated for several days over whether to do it. Weighed the pros and cons. Considered talking to Bailey first. Ruled that out. Tried to listen to my conscience. Wrestled with what my conscience said versus what my brain knew. Went back and forth several times. Asked Ward and promptly disregarded his advice because it didn't align with what I wanted to do.

Finally, I pulled the trigger.

After getting Palmer to pass along Derek's contact info, I had to do a shit ton of arm twisting via text to get him to meet me for a simple beer.

Dick.

I slid into the dark green vinyl booth, facing the front so I could watch for Derek when he arrived. Maybe this was a little hypocritical after giving Bailey a hard time about hiding the Morrison thing, but it was for a good cause. She'd understand.

Hopefully.

Plus, I did warn her that I was nosy.

Ten minutes later than we'd agreed, Derek pushed open the wooden double doors of O'Connor's and crossed the room to my table. He flopped down into the booth across from me, giving me a wary look. His head-to-toe uniform of blue and gray Bulldogs gear was probably intentional, meant to remind me that we were still firmly on opposite sides.

"What do you want, Carter? Is this about Bailey?"

Pretty cold reception from someone who—according to Bailey —was willing to give me a chance, but whatever. I guess he was singing a different tune when she was around.

"And here I thought Bailey said you were going to make nice."

"I still don't trust you," he said.

That was mutual. But, moving on. I was willing to be civil. We didn't have to be best friends.

Our server appeared, and we quickly ordered a pint of beer each. The same beer, actually—Half Moon Pale Ale from the local Rockwood Brewery.

Maybe he would chill out after he had a drink. Nah, probably not. Aside from Morrison and Paul, I didn't really hold grudges, but Derek took things much more personally than I did. Our bad blood went back pretty far too; right to the beginning of my freshman year, when I discovered how easy he was to rile up on the ice. Plus, he was really pissed after I got him thrown out of that game last spring.

I didn't want to jump right into it, so I made a half-assed attempt at conversation about hockey and the weather while we waited for our drinks to arrive. It was painful. I wasn't a fan of small talk at the best of times, let alone when the person across from me openly hated my guts.

My limited supply of patience dwindled quickly.

"What's going on with your parents?" I placed my forearms on the table and angled closer.

Derek frowned. "What do you mean?"

"The house and money situation," I said. "Your sister was pretty vague with me. How bad is it?"

"Well…it's not great."

Our server returned, setting down two cardboard coasters and placing the beers on top before leaving again.

"Elaborate."

Derek looked into his beer, hesitating. "I don't want to tell you anything Bailey doesn't want you to know."

"Tell me anyway. Maybe I can help."

He snorted. "What, do you have a money tree?"

I don't know, asshole. Does a hefty trust fund count? Christ. Was he always this salty or was I special?

"Maybe I do," I said. "How bad?"

Derek's expression shifted from overt hostility to poorly concealed embarrassment. "I don't know specifically. I just know they've fallen behind on everything." He shrugged, picking up his glass. "Living on one income for six months will do that."

So her dad hadn't been laid off recently. I wondered, given that he was a teacher, and it was partway through the school year. Dammit, James. Why was she trying to save face with me?

"Plus, they used up all their savings back when Bailey—" He caught himself.

Um, what's this now?

"When Bailey what?" I leaned over the table, elbows spread across the top, prompting him.

Derek looked at me, wide-eyed, like a goalie caught in the line of an oncoming puck without his pads. I guess an inability to lie well ran in the family. "Uh, nothing. Never mind."

I took a sip of my beer, pretending to let that Bailey thing slide. Even though I sure as hell wasn't.

"Are they in foreclosure?"

He shook his head. "Not yet."

"They're behind on the loan payments?"

"The mortgage is in default. They have a few more weeks before it goes into foreclosure."

In other words, right before Christmas. Fuck.

A sinking feeling settled in the pit of my stomach. I didn't even want to go home for Christmas to deal with my catastrophe of a family. And yet, it was all Bailey wanted—but might not get.

"So that's why they're selling the house."

"Yeah, they're hoping to sell before the bank takes it," he said.

Double fuck. I was no realtor, but even I knew hardly anyone was buying houses around Christmas. Especially in the midst of an economic recession.

"Can they get out of default before the deadline?" I asked. "Do they have anyone they can hit up for the cash?"

Derek sighed, avoiding my eyes. "Probably not. But they won't take your charity, if that's what you're trying to get at."

"Would they take an interest-free loan?"

"Doubt it," he said.

Did he actually doubt it, or did he just not want the help to come from *me*?

"They could pay me back once the house sells."

Assuming it did sell and assuming they could afford to pay me back once it did. Hopefully, they weren't underwater too. But I wouldn't offer anything I wasn't willing to part with permanently.

He looked at me warily, studying me with eyes that were a darker, duller version of Bailey's—more brown, less green. Then he shook his head slightly, like he was ruling it out.

"To be clear," I said, "unlike your dick friend Morrison, my help won't come with strings. I don't want Bailey to have to worry about this. And I definitely don't want her parents to lose their home at Christmas."

Derek's jaw tensed, probably because of the Morrison jab.

I wanted to ask him whether he was aware of the texts that fucker was sending his sister. Or the millions of other terrible things he'd done to Bailey. But covering that would take all night—and those were just the things she'd told me about. They were the tip of the hockey stick.

"B would be pissed at you for going behind her back about this," he said.

He was right, but the alternative was worse. I hoped Bailey would agree, at least once she forgave me. She'd never been really mad at me before; it was hard to say.

"Let me worry about that," I said. "How much is the mortgage, do you know?"

"Around three thousand a month."

"Do you think fifteen grand would help?"

His eyes widened. "You're going to cut a check for fifteen grand like it's nothing?"

Why did everyone think Morrison was the only person in the world with any cash? Because he rubbed it in their faces constantly? We weren't all tacky assholes. And fifteen thousand dollars wasn't that much money. It was well spent in this case, anyway.

"Would it help or not?" If it did, maybe they could hang on and sell the house in the new year. "Or do you need more?"

"I mean, yeah. Fifteen would help." Derek shifted his weight, clearly uncomfortable with the idea of accepting it.

"Okay," I said. "See if you can get them to take it."

"Where am I supposed to pretend I got it from?"

"Say you borrowed it from a friend. Or hit it big at the casino." I shrugged. "Tell them you won a fucking beauty pageant. I don't care. That's for you to figure out."

He actually had the nerve to glare at me. I glared back. Why were we having a pissing match over this?

"What's the alternative here?" I gestured with one hand. "Come on."

In the end, he might shoot me down, but I couldn't live with myself if I didn't at least try.

"If you're going to help, I think you should tell Bailey," he said. "It's only right."

Irritation sparked within me, and I clamped down on the urge to argue with Derek about what was right—like standing up for one's sister to a monster. Right now, my priority was the money. Arguing with Derek over Morrison wouldn't help get him on my side.

"Why? So she can say no?" I raised my eyebrows, waiting, but he didn't have a comeback to offer.

There was a weighty pause.

"Look," I said. "I'm going to lend you some money. Between us. Whatever you do with it after that is your business. Pay me back whenever you can. No rush."

His light brown eyebrows went wide. "You're serious."

"Dead serious. I can send you a transfer later today."

"Fine." Derek sighed, looking away briefly. "But this doesn't mean we're good. I'm doing it for my sister."

"And so am I. Give me your email address and banking information." I unlocked my phone and handed it to him over the table. He took it from my hands, tapping at the screen and handing it back to me with a sour look on his face.

"I'll send it when I get home."

"Thanks," he said.

CHAPTER 45
THE DIRTIEST
CHASE

WHAT A BULLSHIT CALL.

Eleven minutes into the second period against the Coastal U Sharks, I stepped into the penalty box. Serving two minutes in the sin bin. For what? Nothing. Gardiner hooked me on a breakaway, and somehow, I ended up with the penalty. Fuck that decision, and I not so politely told the refs as much. Then Miller reamed me out for beaking off to the officials.

Whatever.

Near the end of the third period, Gardiner got a hold of the puck again and sped straight for Ty. We were winning by two, but that didn't mean we could afford to give up our lead. Our defense was out to lunch, literally looking the other way, so I dug into the ice and barreled straight for him.

Seconds later, I crashed into him, shoulder to shoulder, freeing the puck while he flew into the boards. It was a perfectly clean—if brutal—hit.

Okay, fine. There may have been a slight element of retribution for the hooking.

Gardiner shook himself off, spun around, and skated after me. We raced for the puck, but when he caught up, he grabbed my jersey and yanked me toward him. He wasn't usually that aggressive on the ice, so it caught me off guard, and before I could react, he clocked me square in the face.

He landed that initial hit.

But I landed more.

Despite that, by the time the refs intervened, I had a nasty gash on my left eyebrow. The bleeding didn't last long, but I could feel it swelling with each second.

By the time the final buzzer sounded, I had blood on my jersey that wasn't mine and had set a season record for both penalties taken and drawn in one game. Maybe a career record.

Without getting a look at myself in a mirror, I could tell that my jaw was bruised too. That was probably going to hurt like a bitch when I kissed James later. And when I found myself between her legs, which was the plan.

For once, I was kind of glad she was at school trying to meet a deadline instead of watching in the stands. It wasn't my finest game. I'd gotten a goal and an assist, but I gave up the puck far more than I should have and botched a few basic passes.

Miller said my performance was uneven, and he was right.

After hitting the showers, I was a little more emotionally stable. But I still had this pervasive low-level irritation buried deep within me, like there was a tiny pebble in my shoe. Or in my skate, rather. Somehow, it made all the pressure I was constantly under a lot less tolerable.

I got dressed silently, mind swirling with a category five hurricane of thoughts and worries. Bailey, hockey, school, Coach Miller, our upcoming game with Callingwood, Bailey again, Los Angeles. Bailey *and* Los Angeles—fuck. Hadn't even begun to think about that.

"What's going on, Carter? Your fuse is way shorter than usual tonight." Dallas slipped into his charcoal suit pants and scanned my face with those glacial blue eyes. "You have for a while now. Things all good with Bailey?"

I dropped my gaze, buttoning my white dress shirt. "Things are fine. They're great, I mean. Guess I have some pent-up aggression after that shit Morrison pulled with her."

And by *some*, I meant a metric fuckton. Much as I tried to let it go, I couldn't. What Morrison did had been weighing on my mind since Bailey told me. That he got away with pulling that without any form of immediate consequence was making me insane.

"Still can't believe he did that. He's lucky you didn't show up." Dallas shook his head, square jaw set.

"Incredibly lucky." Though James was right; it was probably lucky for me too. Morrison couldn't fight for shit. I would have demolished him. Literally.

He thumped me on the back hard enough to almost wind me. "Don't worry. We're going to crush Callingwood next time we play. I'll make sure of it. Already laying the groundwork with the other guys."

"You're going to help me plan the perfect hit on that fucker too," I said. "Take him clean out of the game again."

I had been fantasizing about that more times than I cared to admit.

The impact, the crunch, the fall.

Maybe a light splatter of blood left on the ice.

It was going to be spectacular.

Dallas nodded. "Oh, I have a few ideas."

"I do too," Ty chimed in. "I saw this sick hit Stevens took from Younger last week. You should look up the replay. Younger fucking creamed him. He'll be out for weeks."

"Doubt Stevens will ever see the ice again anyway. He's suspended indefinitely because of that sex tape scandal. Did you guys hear about that?" Dallas let out a low whistle. "That's messed up, man."

"I know," I said. "What a fucking creep." Nothing worse than a guy taking advantage of women like that.

"No kidding." Ty snorted, slipping into his navy blue suit jacket. "And everyone knows if you're going to film shit, you have to make people sign a waiver."

Dallas glanced over at him. "Um, *what*?"

My phone pinged, and I glanced down, expecting a text from Bailey but seeing Derek's name instead.

Derek: FYI, had to tell Bailey the financial situation had improved. Didn't tell her why. Leaving that up to you.

Chase: Thanks, man. Appreciate it.

Well, shit. I'd been hoping to delay that talk, but now I'd probably have to come clean before she put the pieces together herself.

But maybe I could delay a little longer. Guess I could gauge the mood when I saw her.

"You still coming for dinner?" Ty asked.

"Yeah, just have to head out after to pick up James."

Halfway through my chicken club sandwich, Penner slid into the seat next to me at O'Connor's.

"Carter, haven't seen you out in ages."

"I saw you last weekend. Remember?" Maybe he didn't. He was blackout drunk with his tongue down Kristen's throat. When she wasn't making eyes at me, that is. Penner didn't seem to notice that part. Hopefully James didn't either.

I wished I could go back and erase everyone I'd slept with before her. It would simplify my life immensely.

His brow furrowed. "Oh yeah. Your girlfriend is fucking hot."

"I know." I picked up my pint glass and took a sip. "What about you and Kristen? Is that serious?" *Please say yes so she gets off my jock.*

"We'll see. Keeping it casual right now."

Yeah, good luck with that. I tried to do that too, and she went *Fatal Attraction* on my ass.

His attention slid to the door, where she'd just walked in. Speak of the she-devil. A group of her friends at another table across the room called her name, waving her over. With any luck, they'd stay over there. At least until I bailed.

"I'd better go," he said, "but we'll see you at the gala."

"The gala?"

Penner nodded. "Yeah. We're at your table."

I schooled my expression, pretending like I knew. I did not. And I was not pleased about this development.

"Oh, right. See you then."

As Penner walked away, I stood up, slid my plate down a few seats, and eased into an empty chair beside Ty.

"What the fuck, Ty? Penner was the only person you could come up with?" I hissed under my breath.

The table for eight cost five grand. It was for a good cause, so I didn't particularly mind. But with the steep ticket price, not all the guys could go, let alone bring a date—which made filling the last two seats at our table tricky. Ward and I let Ty handle it, and he said he would. But Kristen? Had Tyler lost his mind?

Ty set down his burger and raised his eyebrows, evidently miffed at my combative tone. "What?"

"Don't you think that's going to be a little awkward for me?" I stabbed my french fry into the ketchup and bit into it.

Guilt creeped into his expression. "Fuck, man. He didn't tell me she was his date."

Tyler paid approximately zero attention to the love lives of other people, so this excuse checked out.

Gripping my glass, I sucked in a breath. "Look, I know you don't do the whole dating thing, so you don't understand. But for future reference, sharing a table with someone who still tries to fuck you isn't ideal. Especially when your girlfriend will be in attendance too."

Should I warn Bailey about Kristen ahead of time? Or play it cool and pray? If I warned her, she'd be on edge all night. If I didn't, she might wonder what the fuck the deal was.

"Sorry." He let out a long breath and looked me in the eye. "I just wanted to unload the tickets. Do you want me to see if I can get them to switch with someone?"

I shook my head. "It's fine. That'll make it into an even bigger issue." Biting into my sandwich aggressively, I chewed and swallowed before continuing. "Truth is, I'm worried Morrison will be there too. He came last year. Between the two of them, I'm scared the night will turn into a clusterfuck."

It almost made me second-guess going. But the tickets had already been paid for and, in theory, it would be a nice night out with Dallas and Shiv, plus Ty and whoever he dragged up. As long as those other things didn't go off the rails.

"It's a classy affair," Ty said. "I think everyone will stay in line. But did you hear..." His voice grew quiet, and he furrowed his brow, dark eyes darting around the table to check for anyone listening.

"Hear what?"

"It's probably just a rumor. But someone told me Los Angeles was talking to him."

I almost blacked out.

What. The. Ever. Loving. Fuck?

"You're kidding me."

Los Angeles did have a need for some bodies to fill the fourth line. I sure as hell wasn't going to be playing down there.

But Morrison? If I ended up on the same team as that dipshit, I was going to get kicked off or arrested. Maybe both.

BAILEY

Two exams, one massive essay, and one disastrous group project later, I'd almost survived the week. Unfortunately, it meant I had barely seen Chase. We were both feeling the strain of that. His constant stream of spicy and sweet texts said as much.

My phone buzzed on the table in the *Callingwood Daily* office.

Chase: I'm going to strip off your clothes and devour you later.

Bailey: Is that a promise?

Chase: Absolutely.

Bailey: Can't wait to see you.

Chase: You have no idea.

Chase: Wrapping up dinner with the team. Be there in half an hour.

Biting back a smile, I shook my head and locked my phone, then flipped it facedown. I still had to finish a few tasks before I could let my mind wander in that direction. Even though the tug between my legs said other parts of my body already had.

I missed those big, strong hands. Those demanding lips. That low voice in my ear. That wall of muscle pressed against my body…

Oh god. Get it together, Bailey.

"Here." I clicked send, and my laptop chimed, letting me know the email had left my outbox. "I sent you the art show piece for your review, Noelle. I think it should be pretty clean, but let me know if it needs any edits or trimming."

"Thanks, B." Noelle didn't look up from the newspaper layout she was finalizing. When she was in the zone, she didn't switch gears for even a second. She raked a hand through her blunt, midnight bob, thick hair falling perfectly back into place.

I reached over and grabbed my now-cold coffee and gulped the rest of it back. I'd pushed through the week fueled by excessive caffeine, sheer determination, and copious amounts of unhealthy food. Probably pushing the upper limits of safe caffeine consumption at this point, but I needed to be functional for a few more hours.

I could start healthy habits another time—like after graduation.

Checking the time, I did a quick mental calculation and determined I could submit my internship application before Chase arrived. I already had a current resume because of the scholarship package, so all I had to add was a quick cover letter. After writing that up, I crossed my fingers and held my breath, then submitted it to the email address listed. Then I let out a heavy sigh, trying to calm my nerves. Between the internship and the scholarship, maybe one of them would work out.

Before I knew it, an innocent kiss hello turned into a full-on make-out session in the parking lot.

Chase tangled his fingers in my hair, pulling me closer. My chest fluttered as his lips slanted against mine, the kiss turning heated and demanding. He pushed deeper into my mouth as he grabbed me by the hips and picked me up, placing me on top of him.

I was literally straddling him, complete with the steering wheel digging into my backside. And something else digging in between my legs. It was exceedingly cramped, not to mention incredibly public.

I didn't care.

We were parked in the back corner of the lot, at least.

Mouth still latched to mine, he slid his palms down my sides and gripped my ass, crushing my body against his. The pull between my legs intensified, pleasure curling through my core. I dug my fingers into his shoulders, clutching the firm muscle to steady myself. Every touch, every movement he made, ramped up my desire, making me lightheaded, almost dizzy.

I only snapped back to reality when his hands slid under the hem of my shirt and crept up along my bare skin.

"Carter." I giggled and pulled back, grabbing hold of his large wrists.

He ducked his head, capturing my lips with his again. "Sorry," he murmured against my mouth, nipping at my bottom lip and releasing it. "Forgot where I was for a minute."

We pulled apart, and I studied his face, including the bright red gash above his eyebrow. Carefully, I cupped his chin and turned his head to find a fresh bruise blooming on the right side of his jaw. I caressed his skin with gentle fingers, afraid to push too hard and inflict more pain.

I winced. "Do those hurt?"

"A little." He gave me a lopsided grin. "But not as much as what I did to the other guys, probably."

"You didn't tell me you got into a fight."

Chase could definitely throw down gloves—and he didn't back away from it when someone else did—but he didn't fight all that frequently. He was more prone to trash talking and rattling the other side so they missed shots and made other stupid errors. Occasionally, he engaged in the odd shoving match or a scrum, generally falling short of an altercation.

College hockey was strict, which meant full-on fist fighting didn't happen nearly as often as it did in the NHL. If this was a glimpse into the crystal ball, I was a little worried about the future. I'd never seen him look so ragged after a game.

"Got into a few," he said. "But I figured you'd do the math when you saw me."

"Why? What's going on?"

"Nothing." Chase lifted a shoulder. He was being evasive. "I didn't start most of them."

I tried to fight a smile and failed. "You mean you didn't throw the first punch." We both knew fights started long before that.

"Close enough." One hand slid up the side of my neck, drawing my lips to his again. I melted a little, desire unraveling within me. "Maybe I was going through James withdrawal. I hear it's very serious. Life-threatening, potentially."

My heart stuttered. He knew how to work me inside and out.

"You're changing the subject," I said between kisses. "And it's working."

After another minute and another failed attempt of his to start removing my clothes, we grew too impatient to stay in the parking lot.

"Let's go home," I whispered, leaning my head on his shoulder. "Then we can pick up where we left off."

"Deal."

I climbed off him and buckled my seat belt while he adjusted himself before shifting the truck into reverse. At least I wasn't the only one who was hot and bothered.

"By the way," he said, glancing down at the backup camera, "did you get hit on while you were walking over to the truck?"

I shrugged. "I guess."

Chase laughed and shook his head. "And you said you never get hit on. What did that guy say?"

"He asked if I knew CPR…because I took his breath away." I rolled my eyes.

"Psh. Weak pickup line."

It was. You could tell the guy was just roaming campus, throwing that out to every solo girl he encountered.

"You're one to talk, Mr. Wannabe Air Traffic Controller." I reached over and poked him in the ribs.

He flinched and caught hold of my hand, placing it palm-down on his thigh. My mind instantly traveled back to our kiss moments ago and all the things that would happen in about twenty minutes.

"Hey, that kept you talking to me for a solid couple of minutes. Better than getting shot down out of the gate."

"Pretty sure I did shoot you down," I said, squeezing his leg. "You just kept talking. And talking."

"Which worked, because you fell for my charm."

Cocky bastard. Hot, cocky bastard. Yet he wasn't totally wrong.

"I believe my words to Zara and Noelle were something like 'he's a hot jerk.'"

"You also threatened to stab me with a cocktail stirrer." He smirked. "And yet you came back."

"True. But with the number of metaphors you threw out on the spot, I should have known you had a dirty mind."

He lowered his voice, his eyes raking over me and leaving a trail of heat across my body in their wake.

"When it comes to you? The dirtiest."

I bit my bottom lip. "Yeah? Prove it."

"Famous last words, James."

CHAPTER 46
THE FILTHIEST
BAILEY

AT SOME POINT during the drive back to my place, the mood shifted from playful to solemn. Something was weighing on Chase's mind, and whatever it was could probably explain his multiple altercations in the game earlier tonight. I was tempted to ask, but when he was reticent like this, prying wouldn't get me anywhere, so I held out.

After a few minutes of silence, Chase spoke up. "Have you talked to Derek lately?" He signaled and pulled onto my street. The veins in his forearms bulged as his hold on the steering wheel tightened. Suddenly, he was tense, and now I was too. We rarely discussed my brother, for obvious reasons.

"About what?"

"I met with him the other day."

Alarm bells sounded in my head. When Chase was vague about details and slow to get to the point, it was a fishing expedition to determine what I already knew. Which, in this case, was nothing, as I was taken completely by surprise by this revelation.

Though Derek had acted strangely when we last spoke.

"Why did you do that?"

Chase parallel parked against the curb and killed the engine. He unbuckled his seat belt, turning to face me, wearing an unreadable expression. If I had to guess, I might have said he looked nervous, which was a look I was unfamiliar with on him. Chase was always sure of himself, almost always forthcoming.

A wave of uneasiness engulfed me. Please tell me they didn't have some kind of argument about me or Luke.

He dropped his gaze to the steering wheel, his brow lowered. "I may have loaned him some money."

"You *what*?" I stared at him, unblinking. It wasn't remotely close to anything I expected him to say. "Why am I only hearing about this now?"

But…Everything came together then. This explained Derek's evasive behavior over the phone. He told me Christmas was back on at our parents' and said things were less dire financially, but he'd been unable to explain why. After several dodged attempts to get answers out of him, I'd given up. Derek was a terrible liar, but when he stonewalled me, he was impossible to crack.

"I asked Derek not to tell you. But it's progress, because we were able to get along. Right?" Chase raised his dark eyebrows, trying to affect a look of innocence. He was still in a charcoal gray suit from his game earlier, with his tie removed and the top buttons of his white dress shirt unbuttoned. It was hard as hell to get mad at him when he looked like this. And he knew it.

"Don't change the subject."

Then again, he did have a point. Derek and Chase agreed to meet, engaged in a discussion that must have been at least civil, and came to some kind of agreement. It was oddly encouraging—even if I wasn't sure how I felt about the money part.

I frowned, twisting my leather purse strap in my hands. "Is that why Christmas is back on at my parents' place? I've been racking my brain, trying to figure out how it's suddenly possible from a financial perspective. You're telling me that was you?"

"Possibly?" Chase gave me a sheepish look that cut through my defenses like a hot knife through butter.

He was great at evoking a specific combination of emotions in me—frustration mixed with amusement and affection. Lucky for him, it usually led to hot sex. If I wasn't careful, he'd seduce his way out of answering my questions and we'd skip straight to the sex part.

"Was it?" I repeated, trying to stay firm. Thank god we were in his truck and not yet inside; if this conversation was happening in my bedroom, it would be taking a dramatically different trajectory.

"Technically, I offered him a long-term loan. What he did with it after that, I can't say."

I nodded but said nothing. My mind was trying to process the situation, but I was going in circles without any resolution as to how I felt.

"James." Chase nudged me. "You mad?"

I turned to look at him. "I don't know?"

Mad wasn't the right word. Exasperated, maybe. And a war of other emotions raged in my mind in addition to that. The whole situation made me feel vulnerable, which was why I had hesitated to tell him in the first place.

Everything else aside, I'd forgiven Luke for doing so much worse—repeatedly. Thoughtless things, hurtful things, horrible things. It had my sense of right and wrong all kinds of skewed. I didn't know what was and wasn't worth getting upset over. Especially something with good intentions behind it from someone who'd been nothing but caring and thoughtful.

"I see what you were trying to do. But I can't believe you did that." The last words were harsh, but my tone wasn't. Raking a hand through my hair, I nervously combed through the tangles at the ends. I was overdue for a haircut I couldn't afford, which was ironic, given the topic at hand.

"For what it's worth, I'm sorry for going behind your back." Reaching across the center console, Chase took my hand in his. His skin was warm and rough as he stroked my palm with his thumb, moving back and forth.

"I appreciate the apology." My shoulders relaxed in response to the combination of his words and bodily contact. "How much did you give Derek, exactly?"

"Fifteen grand."

My breath snagged. As in, fifteen, followed by three zeros?

"Carter." I grimaced. "That's a lot of money." I could live off that amount for a long, long time. I lived on significantly less than that, in fact.

"I've spent money on worse things."

I widened my eyes. "Fifteen thousand dollars' worth?"

"Well, no," he admitted. "I know I joke about being an idiot, but I'm responsible when it comes to finances. I'm not going to be one of those athletes who blows through his paychecks and ends up broke. My dad drilled being frugal into my head before I even learned how to count."

"This isn't what I would call being frugal."

But the mention of his father made it that much harder to lean into being angry with him. Any time the subject came up, hints of vulnerability surfaced. And they so rarely did that I didn't want to risk shutting him down emotionally.

"Do you want to get into the money thing?" he asked, tone gentle. "Because we can. I'm fine with it, but I don't want to make you uncomfortable."

Make me uncomfortable? I was already there. Chewing my bottom lip, I scanned my apartment building. Most of the windows were dark. A chill was seeping into the truck interior now that the engine was off. I wasn't sure why we were still parked outside instead of going in, but it was difficult to pause the conversation now that we'd started.

"I don't need specifics," I said, glancing back over at him. "I'm just confused."

"Let's say that this amount of money isn't enough to worry over. Promise."

I shook my head. "Fifteen thousand dollars is *a lot*, no matter how you slice it."

Chase uttered a cross between a sigh and a frustrated growl, slumping back in his seat. "I have no way to counter that without getting into specifics."

I didn't want to look like I was asking for his bank account balance, because I definitely wasn't, so I changed the subject.

"Why didn't you come to me about helping?"

"You would have said no."

Defensiveness struck me, and I opened my mouth to protest.

But he gave me a look, cutting me off with his end-of-discussion voice. "Tell me it isn't true."

It was true. One hundred percent true. And we both knew it.

I pinched the bridge of my nose. "You're the most stubborn person I know. You literally do whatever you want, don't you?"

"Kind of, yeah. Been doing it for nearly a decade." He looked down at where our hands were entwined on the black leather console between us. His brow furrowed, and he took a deep breath before meeting my gaze again. "After my dad died, my mom checked out mentally. I was forging signatures on school permission slips and completing my own hockey registration online by the time I was twelve. I've been calling the shots for almost as long as I can remember."

My stomach pitched. More vulnerability, more difficulty staying angry with him. And honestly, this explained so much about the way Chase was. Stubborn, independent, and set in his own ways.

I knew, deep in my heart, that he'd done it because he cared and thought it was the right thing. It was the calling the shots without me part that was the issue.

"We have to be a team. You know, make big decisions together."

"I know." Chase tugged my hand and pulled me closer to him. "I guess some habits are hard to break. I'll do better."

"Okay." I nodded. "That's fair."

He tipped my chin up, and his deep brown eyes held mine, so full of affection that it nearly made my heart burst. "I love you."

"I love you."

He slanted over the console, brushing his lips against mine for a heartbeat. Just long enough to make me melt but brief enough to leave me wanting more. He knew what he was doing—that simple act made me that much less angry and that much more distracted. A shiver ran down my body, whether from the chill or his kiss, I wasn't sure. Probably both—the temperature inside the truck had dropped into unbearable territory, and my teeth were nearly chattering. Since Chase ran at a million degrees all the time, he hadn't noticed, but I was turning into an icicle.

"I'm freezing," I said. "Let's go inside and finish talking there."

Or not talking, as I suspected the case would soon be.

Once we were safely inside my apartment—with the luxury of insulation and central heating—I slid off my boots and started for the living room, expecting him to follow. Chase grabbed me by the hips instead, stopping me. He walked me a few steps backward so I was up against the wall in the front entry. His lips tugged into a grin that was impossible to resist.

"You know…" He dipped his head, planting soft kisses along the base of my throat. One hand slid down my backside and squeezed. A rush of heat ran through my body from head to toe, eliminating any remaining trace of chill as it went. "I could make it up to you."

"Oh? How's that?"

His lips traveled up the curve of my neck, hovering over the shell of my ear. "It requires getting you naked."

CHASE

Having Bailey on top of me in the truck was a tease in the best possible way, but now it was time for the real thing.

I shrugged off my suit jacket and tossed it onto the desk chair, followed by my tie. With my eyes locked on hers, I crossed the room to where she stood. Her pupils dilated as I placed a hand along her lower back, walking her over to the bed. The backs of her legs bumped the edge of the mattress, and we came to a stop.

She gave me a playful look, batting her eyes at me. "So, what did you have in mind?"

"I don't know. How mad are you?"

"Oh, pretty mad." She furrowed her brow and tried to glare, but her mouth tugged at the corners.

"Guess I have my work cut out for me, then." By the time I was finished with her, she'd forget all about what we'd talked about in the truck. I moved in to kiss her again but stopped as she halted in response, her smile fading.

"What about your"—she bit her bottom lip, cool fingers gingerly tracing from my forehead to my jaw—"your face. Does it hurt? I don't want to hurt you."

I shook my head. "Nah. I'm about to be so distracted I won't remember they're even there." In fact, I'd already long since forgotten about both injuries. And the game.

Right now, I was focused on one thing and one thing only.

Bailey unbuttoned my dress shirt, then moved on to unfasten my belt and pants. My fingers landed on the hem of her soft black sweater, and I tugged it up and over her head. Her lacy black bra showcased her small breasts perfectly and hinted that she might be wearing skimpy underwear that matched. In a blur, we were half-undressed and I was fully fucking hard, ready to bend her over the bed, but I had plans before I let things go that far. I undid the button of her jeans and kneeled to peel them off her body before tossing her pants and socks aside. I was right—she was wearing nothing but a hot-as-fuck tiny scrap of black lace that sat on her hips. How the hell did I get so lucky?

"I love undressing you," I murmured, still on my knees in front of her. "It's like unwrapping a present."

Slowly, I kissed my way back up the soft skin between her legs. Nudging them a little wider, I grasped her inner thighs and held them apart for access. She let out a soft, throaty sigh as my lips found the juncture of her inner thigh, and I circled the outer perimeter. Tension coiled in her body, and her breath grew shallow. She was waiting for me to move on to her most sensitive spot, but I took time. Teasing her was half the fun.

"These are very, very sexy." I ran a finger along the hem of her lace underwear.

My mouth landed on her center over the thin material, and she let out a soft gasp. She sank her hands into my hair, tugging and pulling me closer.

"I wore them for you," Bailey said, voice strained.

"In that case, we can keep them on for now." I dragged them aside and closed my mouth over her clit, sucking gently.

She moaned, throwing her head back as my tongue laved against her and I savored every minute. Being between her legs was one of my favorite things in the world.

"Chase..." My name was a shaky breath across her lips. "I don't think I can hold myself up if you're doing that."

With my hands on her hips, I pulled her down to sit on the edge of the bed, spreading her legs apart. She leaned on her elbows, watching me with a dazed expression. There was a point in time where she would have felt self-conscious fully on display like this. Now she was completely confident in front of me, and I loved it. Sometimes, I couldn't believe how lucky I was.

My gaze fell to my belt lying on the floor next to my knees, and I grabbed it.

"Trust me?" I asked her, gripping the strip of leather in both hands.

Bailey studied it for a beat, and her eyes lifted to meet mine. "Always."

Glancing down, I threaded the tail end through the buckle to make the first cuff, looping back again to make a second. In a flash, we had a makeshift set of restraints, and I was about to have some fun.

"Impressive," she said.

"I did my homework."

She watched as I pushed to stand, looking up at me with a mixture of desire and adoration in her eyes. I scooped her up and repositioned her at the head of the bed before taking her wrists in my hands and pinning them above her head.

"Green?" I asked before I went any further.

Her mouth pulled into a smile. "Green."

One at a time, I slipped her wrists into the belt, then tightened it until she couldn't escape. Once her wrists were secured, I kneeled beside her. "Is your toy charged?"

Bailey's eyes widened slightly. "Yes."

I retrieved the silicone vibrator from her nightstand and

switched it on, adjusting the intensity to one of the low settings. That meant I had room to increase it, gradually driving her more and more wild.

Fingers, tongue, and toy, I teased her until she was shaking. Bailey cried out, straining against the leather handcuffs. I slid a finger inside her soaking wet heat, followed by another. She moved in rhythm with my strokes, pelvis tilting, and her walls clenched around my fingers as she neared the peak.

She let out a gasp. "Yellow."

My head snapped up in alarm. I immediately shut off the vibrator, crawling up her body to check on her. "Are you okay?"

Bailey's bottom lip poked out in a pout. "I want a kiss."

I suppressed a laugh. How could someone be so cute and so disobedient at the same time?

"I thought you were getting overstimulated."

"No, I was getting lonely up here."

"Well, we can't have that." Dipping my head, I brought my lips to hers. She sighed as my tongue slipped into her mouth, the two of us falling into a deep kiss.

"Do you want me to untie you?" I murmured, planting a trail of open-mouthed kisses down her neck.

"Not yet. But I need you to make good on all this teasing soon, or I'm going to lose my mind."

Oh, now she was trying to call the shots? Cute.

I pressed a thumb where my tongue had been and worked it in small circles. "You want to come?"

"Yes." She whimpered, cheeks flushed pink and eyes glassy.

"Say please."

"*Please*."

Switching the vibrator back on, I placed it to her center, and her body jolted. I brought my lips to her swollen bundle of nerves, devouring her with the aid of the toy. With another few strokes of my tongue, her back arched and her legs shook uncontrollably. She cried out, louder this time, pleading for me not to stop, coming apart in my mouth. Her hips swayed against me over and over again. Eventually, she slowed, little by little, until she stopped moving against me entirely. I eased off her once I'd pulled every available ounce of pleasure from her, pulling away and giving her a break before she got too sensitive.

Leaning on one elbow beside her, I studied her face. "Still mad?"

Her skin was dewy, her expression dazed, and her hair a tangled mess. She always looked so fucking hot after an orgasm.

She laughed. "No, but I feel a little weird about how noisy I was."

"Don't. That was so hot that I'll think back on it daily."

Reaching up, I unfastened the belt and freed her wrists. I stroked the delicate skin, carefully inspecting for any signs of abrasion or bruising and finding none.

"But what about you?" She brushed her fingers down my body and beneath my waistband, then wrapped her hand around me. Pleasure shot through me in response to her touch.

"I want to bend you over this bed and make you come again."

Bailey gave me a wicked smile and pushed me onto my back. Her breasts brushed my skin while she planted a trail of kisses down my chest and abs and worked herself lower as I helped her tug off my black boxer briefs.

"But I'm liking the idea of a detour along the way, if that's what you're suggesting."

She gripped me with one hand and took me into her mouth, her tongue sliding over the tip in a way that sent an agonizing bolt of euphoria rocketing through me.

"Fuck." I sucked in a sharp breath, threading my hand in her long hair. "Your mouth feels so fucking good."

She hummed a low laugh, her mouth vibrating against me. After another minute or two of watching her, I was dangerously close to losing it.

"Baby." I squeezed her shoulder. "You're going to have to stop if you want me to make good on the rest."

Bailey looked up with a sexy little smirk. "Okay."

She crawled up to the head of the bed beside me, and I yanked down her underwear with a renewed sense of urgency. I came to hover over her again, our mouths crashing together. My plan had been to fuck her from behind, but suddenly, I wanted nothing more than to see her face when I made her come again.

Emotion overtook me, and I slid a hand up the side of her throat, pulling back from our kiss. "Look at me."

Bailey opened her eyes and blinked up at me. Her gaze stayed locked on mine, and she drew in a breath as I pushed inside her. I thrust once, twice, and she let out a throaty moan; the sound was feminine and vulnerable, and somehow, it almost undid me.

I stilled above her, watching her, countless thoughts swirling in my mind.

"What's wrong?" she whispered.

Nothing was wrong. Everything was right. Everything.

"I just love you." I dipped my head and bit her neck gently. "And I love fucking you."

CHAPTER 47

ENDGAME

CHASE

MY PLAN WAS to crawl back into bed with Bailey and catch a few more hours of sleep. We had a nice little routine going, and it usually involved waking up for a second time in the best possible way. But there was no hope of going back to sleep today. Despite the grueling workout and innumerable burpees I'd been subjected to, I was buzzing.

When I got home, I briefly debated waking her to fill her in, but she'd been working overtime on classes, the paper, and her scholarship application, so in the end, I decided to let her sleep.

This led to a spur-of-the-moment decision to make breakfast. Only problem was, between being amped up and ravenously hungry from training, I got carried away and greatly overestimated the quantity of food required—even with my enormous appetite. I could count on Dallas to eat something when he got up, though. And Shiv was probably still here too, so one more mouth to feed would help make a dent in this massive spread.

I took the bacon out of the oven and set it on a potholder to protect the counter. As I turned around, Bailey came down the stairs, still in pale blue pajamas with her wavy golden hair rumpled from sleep. I loved seeing her first thing in the morning. She was a lot more pleasant than I was upon waking, not to mention far cuter.

Bailey yawned, groggily surveying the kitchen. "You made

breakfast?" Her gaze landed on the waffle iron, her eyes widening. "Oh my god. I love waffles."

"Then you're in luck because I make the best waffles around. I'm a man of many talents. Not just on the ice—or in the bedroom."

Her mouth tugged into a wry grin. "I'm starting to see that." She padded over to stand beside me and peeked around me to see the waffles in progress. I wrapped my hands around her waist, ducking in for a quick mint toothpaste-flavored kiss.

"Plus," I said, "I was too wired to go back to sleep."

"Rough session?" She took a few steps and hopped up onto a clear span of countertop beside me. Sliding an elastic band off her wrist, she watched me, waiting for a response, and gathered up her hair and tied it up in a messy bun.

"Not overly. But I talked to the AGM for Los Angeles on the way home, and then I was pretty pumped, so…here we are." I gestured to the food lining the counters. Waffles, thick-cut bacon, whipped cream, strawberries, and blueberries. And a bottle of real maple syrup, because my dad was Canadian and taught me how to do things right.

"Oh." Her voice climbed in pitch, but it was strained. "So the call went well?"

She was feigning excitement for my benefit, that was obvious, but her tone held a hint of unease the minute the topic came up, same as the day we talked about it when I met her for lunch at Callingwood.

"It did."

The waffle iron beeped, and I turned so I could remove the last waffle and set it on a plate. Once I switched off the iron and set down the white dish towel, I took a few steps to close the distance between us. I stood in front of where Bailey was perched on the counter and rested my hands on her thighs.

She looked at me, her expression unnaturally neutral. But she wasn't good at concealing her feelings. Her eyelids fluttered as I skimmed my fingers along her jawline until I was cupping her face.

"Are you worried about what will happen to us if I leave, James?"

"Kinda." Her eyes flashed with uncertainty. "Aren't you?"

"I guess I figured we would make it work."

Maybe it was stupid of me to assume, but it hadn't occurred to me that there might be an alternative. I didn't see her presence in my life as optional. Hopefully, she felt the same way.

Bailey's forehead crinkled and her voice was quiet, hesitant. "How?"

Good question. I hadn't thought through the specifics yet. I'd been too focused on all the things that would come before that. But it didn't seem that hard—we could visit each other when our schedules allowed, and we could talk all the time. Maybe that line of thinking was naïve, though, given that the vast majority of guys I knew who'd attempted long-distance said differently. I'd heard horror stories about everything from constant fights to cheating. One of my former teammates found out by seeing a picture of his girlfriend kissing another guy on Instagram. But we were different; neither of us would even consider doing something like that. That was my theory and I was sticking to it, anyway.

"Racking up lots of reward miles flying back and forth? FaceTime? Sheer stubbornness? You know I've got lots of the last one; it must count for something."

"Okay." She looked down at the counter and gave a one-shoulder shrug. Because she didn't believe me about making it work? Or she didn't want to try?

Would choosing to leave early be the equivalent of signing a death warrant for our relationship? Maybe I was wrong about her inability to hide her feelings, because suddenly, I couldn't tell what was going through her head.

I raised my eyebrows, trying to read her face. "Unless you don't want to do that."

"No." Bailey shook her head and squeezed her eyes shut for a beat before reopening them. Her hazel eyes focused on me, still unreadable, and her posture was rigid, like she had an invisible wall up. "I just…didn't know if you would. Long-distance seems difficult."

"Who else is going to put up with me?" I teased, smoothing my hands up and down her arms. Touching her may have been a mistake, though, because now my mind was going in a different direction. *Focus, Carter*.

She bit back a smile. "Good point."

"Jokes aside, I would rather have you than not, no matter what that looks like. Why let a temporary situation ruin what we have? I want to be with you for a lot longer than the nine or ten months we would be apart."

There I went again, assuming. But she didn't object, only nodded, so maybe I was on track.

I ducked my head, catching her eye. "We're endgame. Right?" My parents were crazy in love. I never thought I would find that until I met her. And now that I had, I'd fight for it.

The tension in her body eased, and I finally won a full, genuine smile. "You think?"

"I know it." I glanced at my watch. "If we're fast, we might have time to get back in bed for a different reason."

Minutes later, I had enough food to feed a small army loaded onto my plate. Bailey sat across from me with a more reasonable quantity, but she didn't judge me for eating the equivalent of three meals in one sitting.

"Still going shopping with Siobhan?"

"Yup." Bailey speared a strawberry with her fork and topped it with whipped cream. "I have to work on that scholarship application first, though. It's due Monday. The process is killing me. Essay, references, transcript review, and then if I make it to the final stage, I have to do an interview with an entire panel of people." She paused, mouth pulling into a tiny frown. "I should stop talking about it. I don't want to jinx it."

I bit into a piece of bacon and swallowed. "I think you'll get it." If anyone could, it would be her. She was great on paper, great in person, and had the grades. Obviously, I was biased, but even factoring that in, I was confident she would be in the top group of applicants.

She pressed her lips together. "You're sweet, but you're not exactly objective."

"If there are that many hoops to jump through, most other people don't stand a chance. Have you met the average student?"

"Here's hoping," she said. "It's going to be a long day at the mall, I think. I have a feeling Shiv is a marathon shopper."

Spoiler alert: she was, according to Dallas. And the dude liked to shop, so if he was whining, then it had to be dire. Plus, back when Shiv stayed with us, she'd come home loaded with shopping bags more times than I could count. I tripped on them in the entryway frequently.

"Are you excited about the gala, though?"

"Yeah." Bailey nodded. Then she pursed her lips and gave me a thoughtful look. "Who's Ty's date?"

"His friend Zoe. She's in the same major as him."

Bailey arched a brow. "Are they 'friends' as in the way we were friends?"

At one point, I wondered this myself, but the constant rotation of different women in his bedroom suggested otherwise.

"Nah. Ty isn't the commitment type. But it'll be fun. It's a nice event, and the food is always good. Plus, I'll have the hottest date there, so bonus." I paused, thinking back on last year's gala. "You didn't go with Morrison last year, did you?"

"No." She scoffed like there was a story behind that, but she didn't elaborate, and I didn't really want to ask. There's no way it didn't involve him being a total and complete piece of shit.

"I figured. I would have remembered you if you had."

Bailey gave me a crooked grin. "Would you have hit on me?"

Is ice cold? I mean, come on.

"The minute I saw you."

I wasn't just flattering her, either. That was a forgone conclusion regardless of where I encountered her for the first time—the gala, XS, a game—hell, I'd have hit on her at the doctor's office. With someone like her, you shoot your shot no matter what the setting.

"To piss off Luke?"

"No, because you're fucking hot."

"Ah. But your date probably wouldn't have appreciated that." She bit into her waffle, eyeing me teasingly.

"Who do you think you're talking to? I didn't bring a date," I said. "Ward and I went together."

At that point, Dallas hadn't met Siobhan yet. And until Bailey, I hadn't met a girl I liked enough to bring along to that type of thing—or to any type of thing. The gala's $625 per head price tag further cemented that. Definitely wasn't letting Bailey know about that—she'd faint. Or try to argue with me about paying. Didn't need to revisit the money issue.

"I'm sure you made a handsome couple."

"Obviously." I winked at her, pushing my chair back and returning to the counter to refill my plate. "But it'll be more fun with you there. Last year, we went to put in face time and support a good cause." It was always nice to see Boyd alumni and to meet players from the league, as well as coaches, managers, and other people in the industry.

"And to get drunk on premium liquor at the fancy open bar?"

"Who, me?" I scoffed, slathering butter onto a waffle and drenching it in syrup. "Never."

Bailey raised an eyebrow. She knew me too well. Pre-Bailey me spent every weekend—and many weekdays—getting obliterated. My liver was probably thankful I'd met her. And my lungs. My stats were better for it too. I rallied pretty well before, but it was amazing the difference not being perpetually hungover made.

"Ward may have had to drag my drunk ass out of the Uber." I gave her a sheepish smile. "I won't do that this year."

Bailey looked at me over the top of her glass of orange juice, fighting back a grin. "I hope not. I don't think I could get you up the front steps. You'd end up sleeping in the yard."

"Don't worry, I want to be sober for what happens after the gala." I pulled out my chair and eased back into it, keeping my focus on her. Dammit. I shouldn't have let my mind wander back in the direction the conversation was heading.

"What's that?" She leaned over the table expectantly, one elbow on the table, and rested her chin in her hand.

"Dressy sex."

Her brow furrowed slightly. "What's dressy sex?"

"What it sounds like. Sex after we're all dressed up," I said, waggling my eyebrows. "I get to rip off your clothes and mess up your perfect hair and makeup."

"You have quite the brain."

"That's not where those ideas come from."

She laughed. "I know."

BAILEY

All week, I worked to complete the scholarship application, and by the time Saturday morning rolled around, every form was filled out, essays were complete, and letters of reference obtained. Perfect or not, I had to pull the trigger and submit it at some point rather than edit it for the umpteenth time.

As a reward for completing it, I allowed myself to deviate from budget a little. After all, if I'd splurged on a dress for my disastrous birthday dinner with Luke, I could justify buying something for the gala.

Before hitting the shops, Siobhan and I stopped by Starbucks for a requisite caffeine and sugar fix.

"It's freezing outside," Shiv said, nodding to my drink—an iced caramel macchiato—once the barista slid it across the counter. "How can you drink something cold right now?"

"It just tastes better this way." I shrugged. Cold caramel coffee trumped warm caramel coffee no matter what the outside temperature. I didn't make the rules.

"I don't get it." Siobhan shivered dramatically. "I practically need to carry a personal space heater everywhere I go to survive the winter."

"That's the Florida in you," I said. "You'll adapt to winters here eventually."

She snorted. "Or freeze to death trying."

We collected our coffees and made our way out of Starbucks and into the mall. It had just opened for the day, and it was already filling with weekend shoppers. Shopping with crowds was the worst —crowds in general, really—hopefully we wouldn't be too long. Chase had led me to believe that probably wouldn't be the case, though, so I'd mentally prepared myself for the possibility that I'd be here all day.

"I know I said I wouldn't buy anything, but I think I'm going to cave on that point."

Shiv turned to me, her eyes alight and a huge smile spread across her face. "*Really*? Yes! It'll be way more fun if we're both trying stuff on."

Her definition of fun was wildly different from mine in this situation. Finding clothes that fit properly and didn't make me look like even more of a giant was always a challenge, but items like dresses were somehow always hopelessly out of proportion in either length or width.

"But I have a strict budget," I said. "Like, hard stop. I can't go over that amount." I really shouldn't be spending any money, but we only live once, right? Even if it means I have to live on a bargain basement food budget as a result.

Her blue-green eyes sparkled. "I love a challenge. This is what I live for. It's like a reality TV show where we have to compete to find the best deal."

Good, because the idea of navigating the sales racks alone was incredibly daunting.

Coming to a stop by the mall's directory, Siobhan scanned the list of stores, frowning in concentration.

"Okay, let's make a battle plan." She pointed to the screen, tracing out a path in the air with a well-manicured purple fingernail. "We should hit the department stores first. Find dresses. Then circle back for shoes."

"Sounds good. I need shoes too." My monthly budget was going to be blown to bits, but I could re-wear both the shoes and the dress. Or at least that's what I told myself. Repeatedly.

"To be fair, I don't know if I *need* them. My parents might kill me if they see another shoe store on the credit card statement. But Dal put in a request." Shiv huffed a laugh, raking a hand through her dark hair. "More specifically, he asked that I buy 'slutty' shoes."

I sipped my macchiato, trying to translate. "What does that even mean?"

"Probably a stiletto." She shrugged. "You know, fuck-me heels."

"That's a thing?" Now I was seriously questioning my own shoe wardrobe. Did I own said fuck-me heels? Did I want to? I wasn't sure on either count. I knew where Chase would stand on the second question, though.

Siobhan's cherry-red lips pulled into a bemused smile. "How are you this innocent? I thought Chase would have corrupted you by now."

"Oh, that's well underway."

She nodded behind me. "Let's start at Nordstrom and work our way over to Bloomingdales."

"That sounds expensive." I sucked in a breath between my teeth, grimacing.

"You're talking to the sales rack queen. Give me your budget and I'll deliver."

We navigated through the throngs of shoppers over to Nordstrom. Siobhan glanced down at her navy Apple Watch, scrunching her face up in thought.

"By the way, are you, um, coming to the game against Callingwood next week?" She hedged. "It's totally fine if you don't want to. Just wondering if I should talk to some of the other girls so I have someone to sit with."

Walking into the department store, we headed to the escalators off to the back. "Yeah, I plan to." And I'd pray beforehand.

"Awesome." Siobhan drained the last of her mocha and tossed it into a garbage can as we passed by. "Moving out probably helped put a damper on some of that stuff. There's no way it'll be as dramatic as last time, right?"

"Right." At least, I hoped so.

CHAPTER 48

FIND OUT

BAILEY

THE WEEK FLEW by in a blur of classes, newspaper, dinner with Zara and Noelle, and trying to squeeze in some time with Chase. Emphasis on trying, because the universe seemed perpetually determined to make our schedules incompatible. If we didn't have sleepovers, we'd never see each other.

Getting ready for the gala consumed a good half of my Saturday. Probably because Siobhan made an event out of it. We ordered takeout for lunch, we pre-gamed—in my case, that consisted of only one drink, because I had zero alcohol tolerance—and we listened to music while we got ready. I even curled my hair, which was a momentous twice-a-year event. Shiv had to swoop in and help me with my makeup because I still hadn't mastered the fine motor skills necessary to make a straight line with liquid eyeliner. Probably never would.

When it was time to leave, Chase strolled through the door, and his jaw literally dropped. "I definitely should have tried to squeeze in a quickie with you earlier, because now I might die waiting."

"Well, hello to you too."

"Do you think there is any chance we still—"

His phone chimed, and he glanced down, brow furrowing. "Guess not. Ward's timing strikes again."

When Chase said the gala "nice," that was a massive understatement. It was by far the most lavish event I'd ever attended. To be fair, that list mostly consisted of family weddings, which, in my middle-class suburban circle, meant they were held at a community center and were sometimes potluck. They were nice in their own way, but they weren't high-end like this.

On top of feeling out of place at such a formal event, I was beyond starstruck. The banquet hall was stacked with college players, AHL players, NHL players, and management from teams at all levels. I had to stop myself from fangirling multiple times.

And the food? It was freaking filet mignon. Siobhan's salmon looked amazing too, though I would pick steak over seafood any day.

After dinner wrapped up, Chase excused himself to go to the bathroom and get us another round of drinks, leaving me behind with Siobhan, Zoe, and Kristen. Siobhan and Zoe were immersed in a heated debate about purse designers, which left Kristen and me to our own devices.

Awkward.

We sat in silence for a few moments, and I scanned the hall for familiar faces, hoping I could find an excuse to make an exit. To my dismay, the only people I recognized were Luke and Paul. I quickly looked away, a jolt of nausea shooting through my stomach when I noticed Luke's gaze on me from across the room, but I could still feel his attention linger on me.

Guess I was out of options. Something about Kristen made me uneasy, but she was still better than Luke. Given the circumstances, I'd make an effort to be friendly.

"Kristen, right?"

She glanced up at me, and the slightest frown grazed her face before she assumed a more neutral expression. "Yeah. You're Hailey? Hannah?"

"Bailey." I'd met her multiple times. At this point, the attitude came across as nothing but passive-aggressive.

"Right."

"You go to Boyd with the guys?"

"Yup."

Unfortunately, the rest of my attempts to make conversation were just as stilted. I'd have been better off talking to the orchid centerpiece at our table.

Blessedly, Siobhan and Zoe wrapped up their fashion chat a minute after and started a table-wide conversation about the guys' last game, which I had unfortunately missed. From there, the conversation flowed much more smoothly and eased most of the tension.

Then Shiv started recounting the guys' funniest and most noteworthy hockey moments. There were some real gems, like the time a guy from an opposing team tried to pick a fight with Chase, then tripped and fell flat on his butt before the fight even started. Another time, Dallas's shot hit the backboards, rebounded, and bounced into the net against the other team's goalie. And Ty got himself thrown out of a game last season after getting into a shoving match with a player who took a dirty hit on Dallas.

While I did my best to listen attentively, the skin on the back of my neck prickled. I glanced up, expecting to see Chase watching me from nearby. But it was Luke. Again. I immediately dropped my gaze, pretending I hadn't seen him. Because I wish I hadn't. I couldn't wait for him to graduate this spring so I'd never have to see him again.

CHASE

Halfway through the night, I'd successfully avoided any run-ins with Morrison. Things were moderately weird with Kristen, but she was being friendly enough to Bailey. I had hopes that things would continue smoothly.

On my way back from the bathroom, I got roped into a conversation with a few guys from the Bulldogs—Palmer and Reed, plus a few others who weren't total pieces of shit. We started talking stats, which turned into a lively debate about which NHL player was the biggest disappointment so far this season. It was Hancock, obviously. But try telling that to those guys.

By the time I excused myself, Bailey was at our table talking to Shiv and Kiara. Shiv tilted her head back, howling, while Bailey covered her mouth, her shoulders shaking with laughter. Bailey was more than nice to look at in that black dress. Damn. Who knew backs could be so sexy? But the way it dipped low, revealing all that bare skin, put very dirty thoughts in my head. Then again, she always made me think dirty things.

Maybe I could get her to keep those heels on later.

My gaze lingered on Bailey for another beat. Then I remembered I was supposed to be getting drinks. *Stay on task, Carter*.

I continued past the clusters of tables, heading over to the corner bar. As I drew closer, I caught sight of Morrison with a drink in his hand, watching my girlfriend like some kind of fucking stalker. He was angled away from the counter, pretending to look at his phone and fooling absolutely no one because his gaze was blatantly glued to Bailey.

You've got to be kidding me.

Didn't he have a date? Sophie or Sophia or something? Then again, I doubted her company would stop him from being such a creep. He'd probably ogle James right in front of his own girlfriend.

I caught the bartender's eye, ordered, and stuffed a couple of bills in the tip jar while I waited.

Then I set a motherfucker straight.

"Don't even think about it." I leaned against the wooden countertop, facing Morrison's back.

He swiveled in my direction and gave me a haughty once-over. "What are you talking about? Are you a psychic now or something?"

Didn't need to be a psychic to know he was a cretin.

"My girlfriend." I nodded at Bailey. "Do yourself a favor and stay the hell away."

"Last I checked, this was a free country."

I shook my head. "Not for you, it isn't."

"Calm down, psycho." He scoffed, but a hint of fear shone in his pale blue eyes. He pretended to brush off his navy suit to avoid my searing glare. "Maybe I want to make things right with her."

"And maybe I'm Mary fucking Poppins."

He only wanted one of two things: to hurt Bailey or to hoover her back in. The first one wasn't happening on my watch and the second one wasn't happening in this lifetime or the next. Which meant he had zero reason to interact with her ever again.

Luke's eyes darted over to the left, where Paul was standing with a few of their teammates—dirtbag ones. His posture straightened, shoulders squaring then. Right. He was feeling brave now that he knew there were reinforcements nearby. Too bad I didn't care about that.

"Best mind our own business."

"Bro." I laughed. "Bailey is the definition of my business."

The bartender returned with my beer and Bailey's vodka seven and handed them to me. I thanked him before turning to face Morrison again.

"Pretend she has a restraining order against you. Because she really should. Do you follow?" I asked, raising my eyebrows. "I know you're a little slow, so I want to make sure."

He took a sip of his dark drink. I suspected the alcohol was making him even more obnoxious than usual. Hard to say, I guess, when that bar was already set so high.

"Last I checked, Bailey was an adult who could make her own decisions." His voice oozed with an arrogance that matched his smug face. I'd bet good money that was the way he spoke to servers at restaurants too. What a douche.

"And she has made her own decisions. Repeatedly. You just don't respect them." My knuckles turned white as I tightened my grip on the drinks I was holding.

He was always a punk in settings where he thought he was safe from my wrath. With every word he uttered, every breath he took, every second he continued to exist, my constant low-level anger toward him crept closer to incandescent rage.

Having him within grabbing distance wasn't helping my self-control. I wanted to pummel him. Had wanted to for some time now. But I needed to keep it in check until the next game. It would be sweet satisfaction to demolish him like I did last time.

Taking a step closer, I lowered my voice. "I know about your little car stunt, you piece of shit. I should drag your ass outside right now for that alone."

"You know, your whole tough guy act is really lowbrow," Luke said. "But I guess it matches your cheap suit."

Pretty sure he wouldn't know a Brioni if I strangled him with it. Morrison was a walking example of how money couldn't buy taste—or class. But whatever. Quibbling over designer clothing with him would be a waste of time. I wasn't going to let him ruin my night. Or hers. So I would keep it on a leash for now. As long as he didn't go near Bailey.

I drew in a breath, steadying myself. "Just be smart and steer clear of her. Neither of us wants a scene. After all, we're here for the kids."

"Exactly." Luke smirked, taking another pull of his highball. "Even you wouldn't be crass enough to start something tonight."

"See, that's where you're confused," I said. "I don't start things. I finish them."

He made a face. "What the hell is that supposed to mean?"

"Fuck around and find out." I turned, then, and strode toward my girl.

CHAPTER 49
EXTRA LUCKY
CHASE

MY HOPE that the night would continue to go smoothly may have been unrealistic. First, my conversation with that lowlife Morrison, then Kristen ran smack into me. Literally. As I turned to leave the bar, she walked right into my chest. Given that I'd been standing there all along and I wasn't exactly easy to miss, it was suspect.

"Kristen. Hey…" I took a step back to put some distance between us. Bailey was still at our table with her back turned to me, engrossed in a conversation with Shiv and Zoe. Where the hell was Penner?

She was making eyes at me—and I was trying hard to miss them. "How are you?" she purred.

"Good." It was difficult, but I vowed I would make an effort to be civil. "You?"

"Great." She took a sip of her drink, wrapping her cherry-red lips around the straw in a way that was intended to be suggestive and made me infinitely more uneasy.

"So, you and Penner, huh? Good for you guys." Penner was a decent enough guy, which probably meant she'd eat him alive. I thought about warning him, but he probably wouldn't listen anyway, and getting involved like that had the potential to stir up drama I didn't need. Easier to steer clear of that tire fire in the making altogether.

Kristen glanced over to where he was standing with a group of guys from our team. Her face was impassive. "Yeah, I guess he's all right."

Damn, that was cold. Considering he brought her as his date tonight, I hoped she at least liked him a little.

"How are things with your girlfriend? Hailey?" Her arched brows knit together. "Kailey?"

"Bailey," I said, for the millionth time. "They're great."

A frown glanced across her face, and she quickly forced a bland smile. "Oh, that's nice."

There was an awkward pause. It was uncomfortable even for me, and I had a lofty threshold for feeling uncomfortable. It happened about as often as I was wrong, which was basically never.

Behind Kristen, Luke stood in front of his table with Paul and the other Bulldogs. His eyes were on us, and he watched for a beat, wearing a chilling expression. Great. That's what I need—Morrison thinking I'm chatting up other chicks in front of Bailey.

Already in motion, I pivoted around Kristen. "I should get back with these drinks. See you later." Unfortunately.

Mental note to kill Ty for putting them at our table.

By the time I finally returned to our table, Dallas and Ty were there too. Ty had his arm slung around Zoe's chair while she and Siobhan were locked deep in conversation.

I set down our drinks and pulled out my chair, then sank down beside Bailey. Briefly, I wondered if she would ask me about my Morrison or Kristen run-ins.

"Thanks." Bailey grabbed her vodka seven and took a sip. "I heard about the time you took a guy out without touching him."

"You mean Paul?" Hopefully, that idiot would give a repeat performance when we played them in a couple of days.

"No," Shiv said. "When you played the Blizzards last season and that guy trying to fight you slipped and bailed."

I laughed. "Oh, yeah. That was awesome." The guy speared me

and skated away without being called for it. When I made a hit on him in response—which was a perfectly reasonable thing to do—he got salty and started a fight. But before we could actually throw down, he lost his balance, fell on the ice, and gave himself a concussion. I loved when people did my dirty work for me. Avoiding the fighting penalties was great too.

Bailey gave me a wry smile, shaking her head. "I always said you were devious, even before I met you."

"I think you mean genius."

Bailey huffed a soft laugh. From across the table, Dallas snorted and rolled his eyes but said nothing.

"Actually, I need to run to the bathroom." Bailey stood and pushed her chair away. "Be right back."

With Morrison here, I was half-tempted to escort her there, but that would probably be overkill. I would watch her from afar like a totally normal, not at all overprotective boyfriend would. As she weaved her way through the room, I scanned the crowd but couldn't locate Morrison.

While I waited for Bailey to return, I turned away to talk to Ward for a moment. "What time do you want to take off?"

"Up to Shiv." Dallas shrugged.

Ty nodded behind me. "Uh, pretty sure Greenfield is hitting on your girlfriend."

I craned my neck, scanning the banquet hall in the dim glow of the crystal chandeliers. Off to the side, beside an artificial tree covered with twinkle lights, I spotted endless legs, long blond hair, and that dress I wanted to tear off later. Bailey was being chatted up by Mason Greenfield, power forward for the NHL's Boston Storm.

He was sporting dark, slicked back hair, a ridiculously flashy, expensive suit, and a gold watch so big I could almost make out the time from across the room. A walking new money cliché designed to pull chicks which, frankly, worked most of the time. It was easy enough being a professional athlete; the window dressing was just gravy.

And yes, he was definitely hitting on Bailey. He was probably fully aware that she was here as someone else's date—he just didn't care. Greenfield had graduated from Boyd last spring, and he made me look like a fucking saint.

"Looks that way."

Guess I wasn't the only one who liked the way she looked in that little black dress.

"She thinks he's being nice, doesn't she?" Shiv murmured, watching them.

I took a sip of my beer. "Probably."

Bailey told me she didn't get hit on very often. But—my obvious bias aside—Bailey was attractive. She had long legs, gorgeous hair, a killer smile, captivating eyes. She was the whole package.

Then I spent more time with her and discovered that, more often than not, she didn't realize when guys were trying to pick her up. She thought they were being friendly.

My beautiful, sweet, oblivious girlfriend.

"You gonna rescue her?" Dallas asked.

"I'll give it a sec to see how this plays out."

I didn't want to be a helicopter boyfriend who got crazy jealous at every turn, even though, inwardly, I kind of was. Whether or not Bailey knew it, she attracted a lot of male attention. I didn't love it, but at the end of the day, I trusted her. She would never cheat, and she could generally handle herself. The only time I intervened was with her creeper ex or when she looked uncomfortable.

Greenfield leaned in a little too close for my liking and said something to her. Bailey shook her head, and what looked like the word *boyfriend* passed her lips, although I couldn't hear the conversation from here. He cocked his head and responded. Knowing Greenfield, the retort was probably something classy about how his dick was bigger. She glanced away and scanned the crowd, eyes locking on to mine. We'd hit uncomfortable.

"That's my cue." I pushed off from the table and strolled across the room to join them.

Bailey watched me approach with relief written all over her pretty face. I probably should have stepped in sooner. Hard to gauge sometimes when I was trying not to go full caveman. If I let myself,

I'd never leave her side. Or let any other guys look at her. Hence my holding back.

I nodded at him. "Nice to see you." Jesus, man. I could smell his cologne from where I stood.

"Carter," he said. "Long time no see." He extended his hand, offering me a firm handshake—way firmer than necessary. Were we doing this now? Maybe we could pull out a ruler next.

"I see you've already met my girlfriend." I slid an arm around the curve of Bailey's waist, giving her a little squeeze.

Understanding dawned on his face. "I have. You're a lucky guy."

"The luckiest."

His gaze darted back and forth between us like he was trying to find his way out of a dead-end street. And, for him, this absolutely was.

"Well," he said, "I should go mingle. But it was nice meeting you, Bailey. Good to see you again, Carter."

He didn't mean that last part one bit.

"Same to you." And neither did I.

With a nod, Greenfield turned and walked around us, making his way to the bar to find his next potential target. I had to admit, I was curious about whether he would succeed at pulling someone else's date tonight. Hell, maybe he could rescue Morrison's date.

"Thanks." Bailey glanced up at me with a little smile. Her eyelashes looked impossibly long, framing her round hazel eyes in a way that I couldn't tear my attention from. Sometimes, like right now, I got a little lost in her.

She shifted her weight, wincing and bringing me back to reality. "My feet are getting tired. Not used to heels. Can we sit down?"

"Sure." With my hand on her lower back—a little lower than was probably appropriate—I guided her around the tables until we reached ours in the middle. Everyone had left, probably to dance or get drinks, leaving it vacant. I pulled out Bailey's chair and pushed it in for her before sinking into mine beside her.

I slung my arm along the back of her chair, resting my hand on her shoulder. She leaned in closer, nestling against me, and her vanilla-spice perfume hit me like a drug, doing bad things to my self-control. That dress wasn't helping, either. It hugged every curve in a way that made me jealous of the fabric. I wanted to hike it up and bend her over the table.

"What did Greenfield say to you?"

"Um…He asked me to leave with him."

Yup. Pretty on-brand for Greenfield.

I nodded. "I figured."

"Why?" She angled her head, giving me a questioning look.

"Because I saw the look on your face, and I know what he's like." I slid my arm off her shoulders and rested my palm on her thigh. Warmth from her skin radiated through the thin fabric, melting away the rest of my self-control.

"Don't worry." Her lips quirked. "It was nothing compared to the things you whisper in my ear in public all the time."

I should fucking hope not. I'd said some pretty filthy things to her. If another guy talked to her like that, I would cut out his tongue.

"Better not be."

Beneath the white linen tablecloth, I skimmed my hand down her leg and dipped under the hemline of her dress. Bailey drew in a soft breath as I walked my fingers up the smooth, silky skin of her inner thigh. Too bad it wasn't my mouth. But later…

"Jealous, Carter?" Her voice turned breathy, taking my mind to even dirtier places.

"Just making sure he was somewhat respectful."

My fingers traveled another inch, close to reaching my desired target. Bailey bit her bottom lip, crossing her legs and clamping down on my hand with her thighs so that I couldn't move any higher. She shot me a sidelong glance, fighting a smile. I definitely had her going, and I'd gotten myself worked up in the process too. Was there a coat closet somewhere nearby, or…?

"For the record, Mr. Caveman, I've caught multiple girls checking you out tonight. One practically undressed you with her eyes."

Probably Kristen. She basically eye-fucked me. Awkward.

Bailey took that in stride, though. I wouldn't have been thrilled in her shoes. Hell, I wasn't thrilled myself.

"There are other chicks here?"

"Well played." She smirked. "You must want to get lucky tonight."

"Wasn't I going to get lucky before?"

"Oh, I meant extra lucky."

Fuck me. I would be surprised if I left this event without getting arrested for doing something indecent.

"What does extra lucky mean?" I lowered my voice, ducking to catch her gaze. Anyone who came back to our table before I found out the answer to this was going to be on the receiving end of a galvanized death stare.

Bailey's eyes danced in the warm light. "I don't know. What do you want it to mean?"

"Are you sure you want to know the answer to that?"

What *don't* I want it to mean? That list is probably shorter.

"Tell me and we'll see." She inclined her head, bringing her ear closer to my mouth. God, she smelled good. Maybe we could call it a night early. Like right now.

"I picked up those Velcro cuffs we talked about the other day."

"Hmm." She shrugged. "Maybe if you're nice."

"I'm always nice, baby."

Unfortunately for me, several hours and three drinks later, Bailey was in no condition to be tied up—or do much of anything other than pass out.

When Siobhan handed Bailey that last drink, I had a hunch it might put her over the edge. I didn't say anything, but maybe I should have, because by the time we got out of the cab, the drink had worked its way into her system and she could barely walk a straight line. And she tripped on the sidewalk. Twice.

I steadied her with an arm around her lower back as we climbed the staircase. "Are you feeling okay?"

"Yeah, why?" Bailey stumbled as we scaled the last stair.

"Easy." I was having some vague déjà vu from the night at XS, though the circumstances were dramatically different. Better in every way—I was with her now and also, no one was throwing up. Not yet at least.

"I'm fine," she insisted.

I steered her over to my dresser and released her once I was confident she'd regained her footing. "You will be once you sleep it off, my little lightweight."

"Sleep it off?" She looked up, making a pouty face that was both adorable and sad. "I didn't think we were going to sleep. You said we could…"

"I love you, but you're minutes away from having the spins, and that won't be a good time for either of us."

Bailey harrumphed a little sound of annoyance, like she knew I was right but didn't want to admit it. I kissed the top of her head and turned toward the bathroom to brush my teeth. While she got ready for bed, I went down to the kitchen to grab two glasses of water. When I returned, Bailey was in bed with the covers pulled up to her chin, looking pitiful.

She rolled onto her side, and the blanket shifted, revealing a sliver of my red Falcons T-shirt. "I feel gross."

"You'll feel better in the morning." I set the water on the nightstand and slid into bed beside her.

"Then I'll be hungover."

"Drink something. It'll help." I picked up her a glass from my nightstand and handed it to her. She drained half of it before placing it on her side of the bed. When she settled under the blankets again, I pulled her closer, and she slipped beneath my arm, nestling against my chest.

"I ruined our night."

"Not at all. Obviously, you're not getting out of being tied up another time, but that can wait. Did you have fun?"

"I did…" She groaned, covering her eyes. "But why am I so drunk? I didn't even drink very much."

"You don't drink very often, though."

"Neither do you."

Not anymore. Probably a handful of times since we'd been together. Maybe I still had some leftover tolerance.

"I'm also, like, twice your size."

Bailey laughed. "Not even."

"Fine. One and a half times your size."

She snuggled closer to me, letting out a long sigh. As she fell quiet, her breaths grew slower and more even, like she'd drifted off, but a moment later, she spoke up again.

"My academic advisor is going to put in a good word for me with the scholarship committee. She has a lot of sway as the department head. Plus, I got a call about videoconference interview for that internship…" She trailed off. "I wasn't going to tell you about either of those because I was scared of jinxing them. But if you do leave, maybe at least those things will work out."

My chest tightened, and there was a sharp pang in my gut. She was obviously spinning in circles about this, but I didn't know what I could do to help. It wasn't even a surefire thing yet.

"Don't worry about the leaving thing for now, James."

"It's hard not to."

I kissed the top of her head, giving her a squeeze. "I'm here now, right?"

"I know."

CHAPTER 50

GAME DAY

CHASE

SLIVERS of golden afternoon light filtered in from the gaps between my blinds, rudely reminding me it was the middle of the day and I was wide awake. I let out a heavy sigh of frustration, staring at the stark white ceiling. The house was silent, the air still. Both of the guys were probably out cold—like I should have been. Like I wanted to be.

Unfortunately, I'd been vibrating with excess energy from the moment I woke up this morning. My long-standing, low-level rage toward Morrison had mingled with an unpleasant tinge of anxiety, making it impossible to relax, let alone fall asleep. I hated worrying, rarely ever did it, and thoroughly resented that I was. But this was personal in a way no matchup had ever been before.

I was going to win or die trying.

Was probably going to hit the wall something fierce after the game was over too, but as long as we emerged victorious, I didn't care.

Because of classes and pre-game prep after, I didn't get to see Bailey. I'd loosened up on my rigid pre-game routine lately, but I couldn't take any chances today. Ty, Dallas, and I religiously executed every single superstitious ritual we had, no matter how small or how silly. Even the dumb ones, like Dallas wearing his pair of lucky socks and which one of was driving to the rink.

If there was any chance it would tip the scales in our favor, we were doing it.

Well, except for my pre-game nap—and not for lack of trying. I loved sleeping, never struggled with insomnia, and normally, I would have been sound asleep twenty minutes ago. Instead, I was obsessing over plays and daydreaming about inflicting severe bodily harm on Morrison. Would it be another open-ice check, or would I smash him into the boards like the pest he was? I'd planned for either scenario so I'd be ready when either opportunity arose. Hopefully, I'd take him clean out of the game again so I didn't have to see his stupid, smug face a moment longer than necessary.

Sleep crept farther out of reach as my rage climbed another notch. *Fuck.* Morrison was living in my head rent-free when I should have been resting and recharging. Or fantasizing about Bailey naked, at the very least.

Finally, I slid out of bed and sank down into my desk chair, grabbing my Urban Economics textbook. Studying was the last thing I wanted to do before a game—and was something I'd *never* done—but I didn't know what else to do with myself.

That lasted all of three minutes before I gave up and looked up hockey stats online, rearranging my fantasy hockey lines. I was still in the lead, and I wanted to keep it that way. This occupied my restless brain for a while, but the low hum of resentment lingered in the back if my mind, nevertheless.

Footsteps sounded in the hall, snapping me back to reality.

"Ready?" Dallas pounded on my door.

I glanced at the clock on my desk, electricity shooting through my veins. Go time. "Yeah," I called. "Be right down."

Body buzzing, I stood, pushed in my chair, and grabbed my stuff on the way out. I jogged down the stairs and found the guys waiting in the hallway, their faces tight. The atmosphere was so heavy it was like we were heading to a funeral rather than a game.

"Are you ready to fuck some shit up?" I asked.

Dallas nodded. "You know it."

Tyler eyed me warily. "I know you want to crush Morrison, but don't let him take your head out of the game."

"I won't," I said.

Bailey: Good luck tonight. I love you.

Chase: I love you too. See you after.

As the clock ticked down to puck drop, Miller gave us a legendary pep talk in the dressing room that none of us needed—we were more than amped to play our biggest rival. By the time we we burst out of the dressing room, we were ready for a bloodbath.

Another overdose of adrenaline hit my veins as soon as the ice came into view. So much so that I feared going into cardiac arrest before the game even started. Knowing Bailey was watching made me want to win that much more too.

Scratch that. I didn't *want* to win—I needed to.

Dallas and I hopped on for a shift against Callingwood's first line. Morrison, of course, was nowhere to be found because he was down on Callingwood's third line again. As the game went on, though, we would inevitably cross paths, and I wouldn't waste a single opportunity to destroy him.

The first ten minutes were painfully tight, with several scoring opportunities for both sides without success. Ty was holding his own, but so was Mendez. With each minute that passed without a goal, the tension in the stands and on our bench ratcheted up. It could be a one-goal game at the rate things were going, and that goal needed to be ours.

A few shifts later, Morrison and I were on the ice together for the first time. The moment I'd been waiting for. The puck sailed loose, heading into their zone, and we both barreled straight for it. Arguably, he should have stayed higher and let one of their defensemen cover me instead, but he wanted to bait me, and I was more than happy to bite.

We battled for control of the puck against the boards. Morrison pushed me, and I shoved him back twice as hard. Normally, I wasn't one to take cheap, sneaky shots, but I'd make an exception for him and spear him right in the ribs where the refs wouldn't see.

Before I could lay a glove on him, his skate caught on his own stick and he lost his balance. When he realized he was going down, he embellished his fall, arms flailing, and flopped flat onto the ice. He remained there, pretending he'd been laid out.

Dive, much?

Did my job for me, I guess. I shook my head and pivoted, racing Derek for the puck that was now behind the net, but Derek had a significant head start and beat me to it. Winded as hell, I dug into the ice and pushed off to catch up with him. I stole a glance back at Luke, who was skating off to their bench while holding his shoulder, feigning injury.

To my shock, a whistle sounded a split second later, and the ref called a delayed penalty. On me. Morrison tripped himself, and I got called for it. He should receive a fucking Academy Award for that performance. Maybe he could go into acting when his hockey aspirations didn't pan out.

Jaw clenched, I glided over to the penalty box to serve my time. Convicted of a crime I didn't commit. Usually, I would have argued with the officials, but I managed to hold my tongue. I couldn't risk pissing off the refs when the stakes were so high. A few bad calls could make or break a game.

I watched helplessly from the box while the game continued with us at a one-man disadvantage. A line change later, Morrison had mysteriously recovered and was back on the ice. Suddenly, our penalty kill fell apart, and we lost possession of the puck. Penner looked the wrong way, searching for it in vain, because evidently, he needed a fucking eye exam.

Paul passed to Morrison while our defense was still on the other side of the ice, giving Morrison a good lead—and, unfortunately, a breakaway. My stomach flew into my throat.

No. Anyone but this jackass.

Our defense scrambled to catch up while I held my breath, watching and praying. Morrison's shots had been garbage lately, so we had that working in our favor.

With our players hot on his heels, Morrison skated up to our net and deked the puck, trying to fake out Ty. Ty wasn't fooled by his maneuver and reacted lightning-fast, grabbing the puck in time, but it deflected off his glove and tipped into the net. Some goals were pure dumb luck, and this was one of them.

The buzzer sounded, and the scoreboard changed to one-nothing, Callingwood, with 8:06 left in the period.

Luke hollered, doing an obnoxious celebratory dance on the ice before fist bumping his entire team.

I slapped my thigh in frustration. "God dammit."

With the power play converted and penalty now over, I was freed from the box and headed back to our bench. Dallas and I exchanged a terse look as I flopped down beside him, taking a drink of water.

"We have to turn this around."

I hadn't done anything to instigate my penalty, but I was still frustrated as fuck. Ending this period down a goal would make it that much easier for Callingwood to maintain their lead.

"We will," Dallas said. "They don't have any stamina. We'll wear them down."

Two minutes later, Derek took an unwarranted penalty. He'd barely looked at Penner, let alone touched him. It wasn't justified, but I breathed out a relieved breath. Looked like the refs were being equal opportunity with their shitty calls.

Miller sent Dallas and me out for the power play, accompanied by a not-so-veiled threat to even the score or else. And I fully intended to. With Derek in the box, the Bulldogs were missing one of their better defensemen, and it gave us the perfect scoring opportunity.

After a beautifully executed play on our part, I got possession of the puck and barreled for Mendez like a freight train. One of their sophomore defensemen swooped in, trying to stop me. He put up a good fight, but with a quick toe drag, I transitioned from forehand to backhand and fooled him into attacking the wrong side. His confusion gave me a window to pass to Dallas, who was wide open in front of the net.

Dallas caught the pass and faked a shot, convincing Mendez he was aiming for the bottom corner, but then he shifted toward his backhand side while pulling the puck laterally. Dallas, who had some of the best hands in the division, moved so quickly that Mendez couldn't recover in time. No goalie could have. Dallas sank the puck deep into the opposite corner, evening out the score.

The buzzer was music to my ears.

"Nice one." I gave Dallas a fist bump as we skated back to our bench.

"It's a start," he said, "but now we have to demolish them."

As the second period began, we emerged fired up and ready to battle. Evening out the score had reinvigorated us and had shaken Callingwood's confidence.

Strangely, after being whistle-happy in the first, the refs were letting more and more slide. Infractions piled up without being called. Subtly at first, but it became increasingly blatant as the game went on. Hit, hook, slash, spear, trip. Nothing.

Miller went off script and split the lines, separating me from Dallas. But maybe he knew what he was doing, because Dallas sank another goal past Mendez on his first shift without me. Then I added to the score with a goal of my own shortly after, a slapshot that brought the score to three-one.

With each goal, the Bulldogs looked incrementally more defeated.

Couldn't happen to a more deserving team.

I watched from the bench while Dallas assumed possession of the puck and brought it up the side, looking for an opportunity to pass to Martin in front of the net. Hope surged through me as Dallas wound up and shot it over to Martin. Four-one would look great up on the board.

Martin took a quick wrist shot that bounced off Mendez's glove. A nice attempt, but no dice.

A good five seconds after Dallas executed the pass, Luke skated up and checked him from behind. Hard. Dallas crashed into the boards, shoulder first, and bounced off before falling onto the ice.

I nearly snapped my stick in two.

That dirty motherfucking Morrison.

My gaze cut to the refs, and I waited for them to call it, but they didn't. What the fuck? The hit was so blatant, there was no way none of them saw it. Clearly interference, at a minimum, and possibly boarding if Dallas was injured.

Chest tight, I watched Dallas stand and shake himself off, then slowly skate to the net. He seemed mostly unharmed by the cheap hit, but that wasn't the point. In addition to the official rules and regulations of the game, there were a number of unwritten rules that were implicitly understood—a major one being, we didn't take dirty hits on clean players. And if we did, we expected to answer for it.

I was coming for those answers.

Minutes crept by without penalties, even though infractions were flying left and right from both sides. The tension between the teams was at an all-time high. We were dangerously close to a full-on line brawl.

Luke's game was less garbage than usual, which meant the Bulldogs were putting up a decent fight. But it also gave me opportunities to hit him every time he had the puck, and I took full advantage. I'd checked him three times since the second period began, though none were the devastating collision I'd been aiming for. Even though we were ahead, I wouldn't be satisfied until I flattened him.

Thirteen minutes in, I made a fourth hit on Morrison—a nice shoulder-check into the boards. He bounced into the glass but remained upright, steadying himself. Then he threw his arms up, whining to the officials about "boarding" and pointing at me. The ref closest to us shook his head and waved him off.

Luke skated back up to where I was positioned, like he was going to cover me. "Cheap hit," he spat.

"You'd know about those." I looked away, clamping down on the ever-present urge to ragdoll him. I couldn't punch him outright, no matter how much I wanted to.

"Fuck you."

Knowing it would piss him off more than engaging, I laughed. "No thanks."

Before I turned to skate away, I knocked Luke's stick from his hand. It clattered to the ice as I started for our bench. Petty? Sure. Better than beating his ass like I wanted to and getting ejected from the game, though. He shouted something I couldn't decipher, but I didn't look back.

Four line changes later, the score was still stuck at three-one. Bulldogs were moments from losing their shit, taking cheap hits left and right on our smallest, least confrontational players. One of our freshmen, a gangly kid, left the game missing a tooth after a run-in with Paul, and still the Bulldogs received no consequence for drawing blood.

Despite my attempts to remain calm, my leash was dangerously close to snapping. Even Dallas was pissed off, and it took a lot to get him worked up emotionally during a game. An all-out fight was imminent.

I was in the offensive zone when Paul grabbed the puck and wound up, taking a shot on Ty. Ty successfully deflected it, and the puck bounced off his pads, ricocheting out of the crease. Penner turned on a dime and skated right for it. From the other side of the ice, Morrison switched directions and headed for the net.

Morrison didn't have a chance in hell of beating Penner to the puck. He knew it too. But what he was doing was obvious—he was taking a run at our goalie.

The lowest of the low moves.

Apparently, their new motto was *if you can't beat 'em, cheat.*

Much as I tried, I couldn't cross the ice in time. I watched it happen like it was in slow motion. Morrison sped to the net and made a half-assed attempt to stop inches before he hit the crease. He slammed into Ty, bringing him down as he toppled over.

I waited for a penalty call that didn't come. He was going to get away with it.

Not on my watch.

CHAPTER 51

BAD BLOOD

BAILEY

I HADN'T WANTED to take my eyes off the game, but I couldn't wait any longer. I'd rushed to the bathroom and couldn't have been gone for more than two minutes. But when I returned, every member of both teams on the ice was involved in a massive altercation. They yelled and pointed and gestured at each other while the referees stood in the middle, holding players back.

One of those players was Chase. He and Luke were having words—again. Other guys sniped back and forth, not all that worked up, but Chase's face was twisted in anger, and he was gesturing wildly.

Heart racing, I hurried down the stairs and sank back into my seat beside Siobhan. I tried to time my bathroom break with Chase's shift change, but apparently, I'd fallen short.

"What happened?" I grabbed my half of the blue and purple plaid blanket we huddled under together for warmth, covering my legs with it.

Shiv nodded to the scrum. "Your ex took a run at Ty."

My stomach clenched. Of course he did.

"Is Ty okay?" I asked, eyes still glued to Chase. My chest was tight, my breath shallow. What would he do? There was no way he'd let Luke get away with lowbrow action like that.

The ref leaned in and said something to him. Chase shook his head and responded with what looked like a no.

"Yeah, he got knocked for a loop, but he seems fine." She pointed to the far corner of the ice, where Ty was trash talking Mendez.

Goalies answered to other goalies, but Mendez was soft-spoken and probably not to blame for anything. While some of the players were amped up and reveling in the chaos, Mendez was mostly still and speaking calmly, like he just wanted to get back in the net.

My gaze snapped back to Chase, whose movements weren't quite so irate. He was still yelling at Luke, but the referee wasn't straining to hold him back anymore.

"But it's the principle at this point," Siobhan added, pulling her hands into the sleeves of her red Falcons hoodie.

"It really is," I agreed with a nod.

Goalies were off limits. Everyone knew that. Add that to the cheap hit on Dallas, and it wasn't surprising that Chase wanted to tear off Luke's head.

The silver lining was that Derek wasn't on the ice, so I had one less person to worry about.

"Think anyone's going to take a penalty?"

"Nah," Shiv said. "No one threw any hits."

Eventually, the referees negotiated some kind of peace, and the players filtered back to their respective benches. One steered Chase toward the Falcons bench, but Chase shrugged off the ref's arm and headed off the ice on his own.

My breathing resumed a more normal pattern and the tightness in my shoulders relaxed a notch. It was almost the end of the second period, so maybe things would cool down during the break. Then there would only be twenty minutes of game time to get through without bloodshed. God willing.

Instead of heading to the Bulldogs' bench, though, Luke made a sharp turn and skated over to Chase, who was halfway to the Falcons bench. They were side by side on open ice, separated from their teammates and the officials.

My heart leapt into my throat.

Luke leaned in close and made a comment. Chase shook his head, and they had a quick verbal back and forth. In a flash, Chase's expression went from irritated to homicidal. He threw his stick, dropped his gloves, and clocked Luke square in the face. Before Luke could so much as react to the hit, Chase grabbed him by the jersey and tossed him onto the ice like he was weightless.

No, no, no.

I watched as the official blew his whistle and sped over to them, wedging himself between their bodies while holding Chase back. Or attempting to, anyway, as Chase pushed against him to get to Luke. A second linesman skated up, trying to help him restrain Chase with limited success.

Luke scrambled to his feet and backed up a few strides, stumbling as he went. He didn't fight. Ever. Hell, he didn't know *how* to fight. Which meant Chase would destroy him and get himself into serious trouble in the process.

Dallas hopped over the boards and joined the linemen, trying to talk Chase down while restraining him. Chase shook his head, all the while yelling at Luke. I had never seen Chase look that mad. There was no way they wouldn't kick him out of the game. Maybe suspend him for multiple games.

After another split second of watching and praying, I couldn't take it anymore.

I stood and ran down the stairs to ice-level. "Stop it!" I banged on the glass. I couldn't get his attention, but I didn't stop. "Carter!"

Finally, Chase turned and looked in my direction. Our eyes locked, and I made a "cut it out" gesture. "Please?" I mouthed.

He nodded, and he stopped resisting the linesman. Head down and shoulders slumped, he skated off the side and headed for the locker rooms. I climbed the stairs back up to our seats, exchanging a look with Siobhan.

"What the hell just happened?" she asked.

"I have no idea."

Waiting for Chase to emerge from the dressing room was torture. Like time was moving in reverse.

I'd spent the intermission pacing the concourse with poor Shiv in tow, who had to work double-time to keep up with my strides. I couldn't help it; I was too wired with worry over Chase.

Siobhan and I were still on the concourse—mostly alone, thankfully—when the buzzer sounded, announcing the start of the third period. Shiv looked at me uncertainly, deep teal eyes studying my face.

"Go watch," I said. "It's okay. I'll wait for him here."

"You sure?"

"Yeah, Chase could be a while." He was probably getting reamed out, or he'd been forced to sit in on the intermission pep talk with the rest of the team.

It wasn't nearly as cold in the concourse, so I unzipped my puffy black coat and perched on an uncomfortable blue metal bench, killing time by texting back and forth with Zara and Noelle about everyday stuff. I couldn't fill them in on what had just gone down because I still didn't understand it.

Two minutes later, Chase appeared in the hallway. His face was tight, and his posture was even more stiff. I locked my phone and shoved it into my purse, then stood to greet him.

Chase leaned in, giving me a half-hearted kiss on the lips, then pulling back again quickly. His expression was stormy, a mixture of emotions I couldn't read. He grabbed my hand, but he was silent as we walked to a quieter, more secluded area by the doors and sat at a small table.

"What happened out there?" I dipped my chin in hopes of catching his eye, but he looked away, his attention fixed on the speckled white table between us. Like usual, Chase was too tall for the furniture, and his knees were angled out awkwardly.

"Game stuff."

"Looked like more than just game stuff. Why did you get so mad?" I asked, voice low so we wouldn't be overheard, although we were alone since the third period had begun and the fans were all in the arena again. "I was scared you were going to slit Luke's throat with a skate or something."

Chase shook his head. "Morrison shot off his mouth again. He's been needling me for a while, and I finally snapped. That's all."

I stretched my arm across the table and took his hand in mine. He stroked my fingers with his thumb, but he didn't look up at me.

"What did he say?"

"It's nothing, James." If it was possible, he went even more tense then, the cords in his neck tight. "Don't worry about it."

His deflection ramped up my worry. "Why are you being so weird?"

"I don't want to repeat it," Chase said, dark eyes snapping up to mine. His tone took on an edge that he never used with me. "Let it go, okay?"

"Why? Was it about me?" *Of course it was*. I didn't really need to ask.

His jawline turned to granite. "Bailey." Now I knew it was serious because he never used my real name. "I don't want to repeat it to you. It's gross and it's disrespectful."

What the hell did Luke say?

"Now you *have* to tell me."

Chase's brow knit together, but he didn't reply. Stubborn as always. But I had a right to know what Luke was saying about me, especially if it was that offensive.

I squeezed his hand, tamping down my frustration. "Carter. Tell me, please."

"Fine." He loosened his tie and shifted his weight in his seat. "But I want it on the record that I'm only telling you so you're not upset with me."

"Stop stalling."

Chase swallowed. "Luke told me he broke up with Sophie, so I said, 'why the fuck would I care?' and he said…"

"He said…?"

"Then he said, and I quote…" Chase drew in a breath, nostrils flaring. "Because I seemed to like his sloppy seconds."

I felt like I'd been punched in the stomach.

"*What*?"

"Yeah, so my plan is to break both of his knees with a crowbar next time I see him off the ice." He paused. "If you could give me his address, that would really help move things along."

I opened my mouth to reply, but no words would come.

"Carter!" a deep voice barked. Coach Miller was standing with his hands on his hips at the dressing room entrance.

My heart sank at the very sight of him. His face was redder than the Falcons cap he was wearing, and fury radiated off his body.

"I have to go back and talk to Coach."

"Okay," I said. "I'll wait for you. Good luck."

CHASE

"Carter!" Coach Miller barked, storming into the office. He threw himself into his chair, leveling me with a poisonous glare. "What the *hell* was that about?"

"Nothing, Coach. I just lost my cool," I said, sinking into the seat opposite him. "Won't happen again."

Technically, it was true. Next time, I would be calm and methodical when I tore Morrison apart. I wouldn't make the mistake of snapping and giving him a warning signal.

"You were about to commit a felony out there." He pinned me with his beady eyes, his expression stern. Then he softened a fraction. "What did that Morrison kid say to you?"

I folded my arms and did my best to keep my voice level. "I'd rather not discuss it. It was personal."

Coach Miller frowned. "If it was a slur or another inappropriate comment, it can be reported to the league, and the schools will get involved."

"Sorry. Can't say."

"I can take the three-game suspension down to two if I demonstrate mitigating circumstances to the league."

"I appreciate it, but I'll take the three."

Even if my stats would tank.

He sighed and stared at his steepled fingers on the surface of his desk. After a long moment, he blew out a breath and brought his attention back to me. "I'm going easy on you because I think you've really turned a corner this year."

"Thank you."

"I'll let this go for now. But if you look at this Morrison again, the suspension will be a lot longer than three games."

"Understood, Coach."

"And if you start a fight with him again, you're out for the rest of the season."

Fucking hell. We both knew I couldn't afford that.

"I won't," I said. "You have my word."

Fine, so I couldn't go after him on the ice.

And my teammates had my back.

Getting reamed out by Miller didn't take long. But Bailey and I had to wait for the game to end before we could leave because Siobhan had driven Bailey and I gotten a ride with Dallas.

We killed time talking about anything but hockey. Or trying to talk, because Bailey was unusually quiet after I came back out. She was obviously upset by what I told her—which was why I didn't want to in the first place.

Relief washed over me as players from both teams filtered out of the dressing rooms. All I wanted to do was get the hell out of here.

Suddenly, Bailey stiffened, her focus fixed in the direction of the concession stand. I swiveled in the direction she was looking.

Morrison.

My vision tunneled, and every promise I made to Coach Miller flew straight out the window.

I clenched my fists. "If you'll excuse me, I'm gonna annihilate that motherfu—"

"No." Bailey put a firm hand on my chest. "Let me handle him."

I grunted, pressing my lips into a thin line, breath shallow and jagged. Morrison was so close I could practically see my fist hitting his face. It was going to feel so good. The crunch would be music to my ears.

"Carter," she said. "Look at me."

I turned back and focused on her calm hazel eyes. My blood pressure dropped a few notches at the sight.

"I love you," she said. "And I appreciate that you want to stand up for me, but I don't want you to get in trouble over Luke. He isn't worth it. I got this."

I sighed. "Fine." I wouldn't argue with her because of this asshole.

She looped her arms around my neck and pulled me closer. I went willingly until our mouths came together, lips parting. I was already hopped up on adrenaline and testosterone, and the contact made me want to bend her over the nearest hard surface and fuck her right here. But I could hold off on that until we were at home.

Then she took me by the hand and pulled me halfway to where Luke stood with his friends.

"Wait here a sec, okay?"

"Okay," I muttered.

Uneasy and without an inkling of what she planned to do, I propped myself against a pillar and watched Bailey march up to Morrison. She wound up and slapped him so hard it echoed through the concourse.

Oh snap. I wasn't expecting that. And neither was he. Sucker.

God, I fucking loved her.

Luke put a palm to his cheek, mouth hanging open in shock. He looked over Bailey's shoulder, and our eyes met. Her back was still turned to me.

"You're dead," I mouthed, making a throat-slitting gesture.

Sorry, James. I only had so much restraint.

He paled, turning his gaze back to Bailey.

"Don't talk to me ever again." She spun on her heel and strode my way.

Luke dropped his hand, exposing a red handprint on his face. It was beautiful. Really suited him. I had to admit, seeing Bailey lay the smackdown on Morrison might have been more satisfying than getting to do it myself.

"Bailey! What the hell was that?" Derek called, jogging to catch up with her. But she didn't stop.

"Luke knows," Bailey said over her shoulder, long blond hair bouncing, "why don't you ask him?" She grabbed my hand and pulled, inclining her head to the doors. "Let's go."

"No." Derek caught up to us. He touched her on the arm, ducking to meet her gaze. "B, tell me what's going on."

Bailey and I exchanged a look. She bit her bottom lip and raised her eyebrows as if in question. I shrugged. This wasn't my place.

"Fine." She sighed. "Actually, why don't you tell him, Chase?"

So I did.

When I was finished, Derek's face contorted with rage. "What in the actual fuck?"

He stormed back over to Morrison and shoved him, sending him flying onto his ass.

"What the hell is wrong with you?" Derek said, looming over him.

Paul watched the confrontation from a few feet away, his expression torn. Probably because, at the end of the day, although he was good friends with both guys, Paul was a little bitch who didn't want to get into a tussle.

Luke got up, dusting himself off. "What are you talking about?"

"What you said to Carter about my sister. You're a fucking asshole, man." Derek shoved him again, but this time, he kept his footing. "Bailey never did anything to you."

I watched, barely fighting back laughter. I could not contain my glee at this turn of events. Both people in the James family were beating on Morrison this evening. It was fantastic.

But if one of those other idiots stepped in to defend Morrison and touched Derek, I'd wipe the fucking floor with all of them.

"What?" Luke scoffed. "Why would you trust Carter? He's fucking lying."

Mendez cleared his throat. "Actually, dude…I heard you say that in the locker room too."

Oh, how the turn tables. My night was improving by the second.

Amelia and Jillian looked at each other, eyes wide like they didn't know what to make of everyone turning on their leader. Now which way would Paul land?

Luke's face reddened, and he glared at Mendez. "Obviously, you misheard."

"Fuck you, man." Derek shook his head. "And to think I gave you the benefit of the doubt over and over again because we've been friends for so long."

Fucking finally. It was long overdue, but Derek was taking Bailey's side.

"Derek," Luke said. "Come on—"

"We're done," Derek fumed. "Better watch your ass on the ice against Boyd next time, because I won't do shit if they come for you. And neither will the rest of our D."

Derek made his way to us again, and the three of us walked away from the crowd. When we stopped at the front entrance, he shook his head, exhaling heavily.

"I am so sorry, Bailey. I had no idea…" He trailed off. "Why didn't you tell me?"

She tangled her fingers together, her head dipped low.

"Do you want me to leave you two?" I asked Bailey, thinking the siblings might need some privacy for this conversation. "I can look for Ward."

"No, it's fine." Bailey grabbed my hand and laced her fingers in mine. "We can talk about it another time. Okay, Derek? I just want to get home."

"Okay." He nodded, turning his gaze to me. "Thanks for sticking up for her. I'll see you guys." He turned and weaved back through the crowd.

A pretty redhead came up to him, and he leaned in, giving her a kiss. Bailey's eyebrows shot up a notch.

"New girlfriend?" I asked.

"I'm not sure," she murmured. "But I'm happy he's moved on."

Bailey turned to me again, studying my face. The low thrum of people milling about in the background filled the silence. Neither of us said anything for a minute.

"That slap was pretty badass," I told her, unable to hide a smile.

Her lips tugged. "It was, wasn't it?"

"Hey," Dallas said as he and Shiv approached tentatively. No doubt he wanted to grill me about what happened with Miller, but he wouldn't do it in front of the girls.

"Are you okay?" Shiv asked, her eyes darting back and forth between Bailey and me.

"Fine," I said. "Let's get out of here."

CHAPTER 52
OWN ME
BAILEY

THE AIR WAS BITTERLY COLD, making my breath come out in little white puffs as I weaved through the quad on the way to the library. After the most dramatic hockey game of my life, attending classes like normal the following day was almost a relief.

My mind was spinning, and I was still struggling to process last night's events. Had I really meant so little to Luke? Then again, he'd done lots of things when we were still together that were also disrespectful. Things that had been normalized at the time. Strange how one can be in the thick of such a plight and not see it for what it is.

And what about Derek's relationship with the team after his fallout with Luke? It sounded like he wasn't the only one sick of Luke's shit, though. Paul was still in his corner, but not many others. Luke was captain in name only at this point.

Halfway to the library, I ducked into the student commons to use the bathroom. When I pushed open the door, my stomach twisted and I froze.

Sophie was standing at the sink, sobbing. Like, someone-died ugly-crying. She dabbed at her eyes with a tissue, but she was still bawling, so fixing her makeup was an exercise in futility.

After the two coffees I'd had earlier, my bladder was on the verge of exploding. But seeing Sophie was awkward enough. But crying? What should I do? Continue my mission? Find another bathroom? If she noticed me, though, turning around and leaving would look weird.

"Um, are you okay?" I asked, tentatively walking closer.

There was relationship overlap between the two of us with Luke, if not flat-out cheating. And Sophie was likely a knowing accomplice. But breaking up with Luke was the best thing that ever happened to me, and that made it hard to muster up anger right now. Plus, she looked so…sad. The dated pinkish-brown tile backdrop and dim fluorescent lighting made the whole scene extra tragic.

Sophie startled, turning to face me. "Bailey?" She placed a hand on her chest and heaved a sigh. "Oh my gosh, you scared me."

A tear trickled down her cheek, taking her mascara with it and leaving a gray trail in its wake. Her long blond hair was perfectly curled, and her trendy outfit perfectly assembled, but her once impeccably applied makeup was now a perfect wreck.

"Sorry, I didn't mean to. Are you—are you all right?"

A jagged sob slipped out before she pulled her shoulders back and cleared her throat. "You don't have to be nice to me. I know you hate me. And you should." She turned and dabbed at her eyes in the mirror again, working to clean up her running mascara.

"Luke's the one I hate. But at least we both dodged that bullet, right?" I said, trying to lighten the mood. I cringed a second later, though. She was probably crying about their breakup.

"Not both of us." She let out a shaky laugh that echoed through the empty bathroom. "I'm pregnant."

Oh my god.

"I don't know why I'm telling you this," Sophie said. "I literally just found out. I bought a test, and I took it in here because I was sure it would be negative. And then I found out I was pregnant in a goddamn public bathroom at school." Her voice climbed, and she clutched the edge of the sink, bursting into tears again.

A long, heavy pause followed. I hovered near her awkwardly, scrabbling for words that would soothe her. *I'm sure Luke will support you* wasn't it—that was a given. Luke only cared about himself and his career.

"It'll be okay," I said. "It's just a big shock right now."

"Luke already told me he wants me to get an abortion." Sophie raked a hand through her hair frantically. "And that was just when I told him I was late. He's going to freak out."

What an asshole. That was low even for Luke.

I shifted my weight, adjusting the strap of my book bag on my shoulder. Between my laptop and my textbooks, it was starting to dig in something fierce. "That isn't his choice to make. It's your body."

"He made it pretty clear where he stands. What am I supposed to do, handle it all it on my own?"

"He'd have to pay child support," I pointed out. And if he made the NHL, he'd have more than enough to do that comfortably. "Don't let him strong-arm you into making a decision you don't want."

"I don't want to have to fight about it."

I didn't blame her. Luke was a miserable person to fight with; he went for the jugular every time.

"That's what lawyers are for, though."

"Yeah, I guess." Sophie blew her nose loudly, sounding more like an elephant than a tiny college girl. She glanced back up at me. "I don't know why you're being so nice to me. I don't deserve it."

It was Luke's bullshit she didn't deserve. But now she was stuck with him, and I felt extra sorry for her because of that.

"Please don't tell anyone," she added.

"I won't," I said. "Why don't you call one of your friends? Don't worry about Luke for now. Talk to someone you can trust."

She sniffled. "Thanks, Bailey. I'm really sorry about the way things happened."

"It worked out for the best. I hope it does for you too." I pulled the door open and stepped into the hall. It wasn't until I was outside that I realized I hadn't used the bathroom, but going back inside was not an option.

CHASE

Suspension sucked.

And the game against AWU tonight marked the first of three games I had to watch from the bench.

It was torture.

No matter what Coach Miller tried, the team couldn't get their shit together. In the end, we lost five-two. Maybe I wouldn't have made a difference, but not knowing was beyond frustrating.

It was freezing outside, so after the game, I ducked out of the locker room and went over to the entrance. I hit the remote start on my truck keys, watching through the window. In the far corner of the parking lot, the lights turned on as the engine roared to life.

Turning, I threaded my way back through the crowd to find Dallas, Shiv, and Ty. Normally, Bailey would have been here too, but she'd been busy preparing for her internship interview, and I wasn't allowed on the ice, so the timing wasn't the worst.

In the distance, Dallas and Ty stood with a few guys from the team. I was about ten feet away from the group when Kristen appeared from out of nowhere.

Jesus.

She was in heavy makeup and a short black skirt, her long brown hair curled. More appropriate for a club than the rink, and more than likely intended for me. Was she ever going to take the hint?

My usually spot-on crazy radar had been defective when I met her, and about a year ago, I'd picked a sociopath for a fuck buddy. Somehow, I had missed all the red flags. Should have stuck to my one and done policy until Bailey.

"Hey." She placed a hand on my forearm. I yanked my arm away and took a step back, glancing over to see if anyone was watching. Fortunately, they were all huddled around Dallas, listening to him recount his breakaway goal. It was about the only good thing that had happened tonight.

"You've got to stop this shit, Kristen. Penner will be out any minute. And you know I have a girlfriend."

Even if I didn't, there was no chance I'd go there again. Kristen had burned that bridge to a crisp. Doused it in kerosene and lit the match herself.

Kristen shrugged, stroking her dark hair. "That never stopped you when you were with me."

Like comparing apples and pucks, Kristen.

"You were never my girlfriend." I took another step back, keeping my voice low.

"We could still share…like we did with Nikki at your party."

"It's not like that with Bailey." I lowered my voice. "Plus, that night doesn't exactly bring back fond memories."

She smirked. "Come on, Chase. It was hot."

I balled my hands into fists, my blood pressure rising. "You didn't even fucking ask me."

Because she knew I'd say no if she did. I was dumb, but not dumb enough to leave behind evidence, especially with a random hookup.

"Whatever." Her dark red lips folded into a pouty frown. "Nikki was cool with it."

This conversation struck me as off. Why was she bringing this up now? And then it clicked.

Holy fuck.

Did Kristen plan that?

More importantly, did she delete the video?

My heart rate skyrocketed. Suddenly, my lungs couldn't take in oxygen fast enough.

I took Kristen by the elbow and pulled her farther away from the group, ducking my head to catch her gaze. "You did erase that, right?"

Kristen batted her long, dark eyelashes at me. "You saw me delete it."

I thought I did, but I was tanked. I couldn't see straight, let alone verify whether she had deleted a file in her phone correctly.

"You sure you didn't text it to someone first?" I asked, raising my eyebrows. "Email yourself a copy?"

"I'm sure. Since when are you so uptight?"

"Since the start of the school year when Coach gave me the gears about pictures he'd heard rumors about. Said they were taken at my end-of-school party last spring. Kind of fucking fits, don't you think?"

Kristen waved me off with her pointy red fingernails. "He said pictures, not a video. He was probably trying to scare you."

In hindsight, his lecture was too specific to be a scare tactic. I'd written it off as a rumor and forgotten about it. Ignorance was bliss. It hadn't come back to haunt me—yet. But the way Kristen was acting now sent a wave unease rolling through me. I might have a serious problem.

Not to mention that when Coach brought that up, I barely knew Bailey. It didn't faze me because, at that point, I didn't give a shit about, well, anything. Now, though, this was a catastrophic problem.

This was a wrecking ball about to demolish my life—a life that looked nothing like it did last spring. I had so much more to lose now than I did back then.

If I could go back to last April and punch myself in the face, I would.

"Then why are there rumors about a sex tape flying around both schools?"

"Why are you so paranoid?" She scoffed. "That could be anyone."

Could be, but all signs pointed to me, her, and Nikki.

"None of us need that shit getting out. Ever think about how that might look on your med school applications?" I raised my eyebrows. "Or about how Nikki's boyfriend might react?"

I hadn't known Nikki was dating one of the guys from the Bulldogs at the time. Didn't need that, among other things, coming back around on me. Plus, Nikki went to Callingwood, so the odds of this getting back to Bailey were that much higher.

"Relax." Kristen glanced down, adjusting her cleavage. "There's nothing to get out."

"There better not be."

She gave me a bored look. "You wanna frisk me, officer?"

Like this was some kind of game? I'd never been so mad at a chick.

"That doesn't prove dick. It could be in the fucking cloud somewhere."

"It's not." Kristen rolled her eyes. "Calm down. You don't have anything to worry about."

I stole a glance at my friends again, but they were laughing about something Ty said. Penner was nowhere to be found, either, which, in this case, was a good thing.

"How can I know that for sure?" I stepped closer, pinning her with a searing glare. She stared back at me, dark blue eyes wide in feigned innocence. I didn't buy it.

"Guess you'll just have to trust me."

Right. Trusting her was what got me into this mess in the first place. Then she'd pulled out a phone and recorded without my permission.

I shook my head, my teeth set on edge. "You'd better be telling the truth."

"If you're so worried," Kristen said, "maybe you should be nicer to me."

"Don't threaten me."

Spinning on my heel, I stormed over to my friends. I was so fucked. If this got out, it would be like throwing napalm on my life. No contract, no girlfriend, nothing.

Fuck. Fuck. *Fuck.*

Shiv turned to face me with a frown. Her hands were pulled into the sleeves of her oversized white Falcons hoodie.

Fear and anger mingled, turning into rocket fuel via chemical reaction. The arena lobby was frigid, as always, but I was literally sweating where I stood.

"Everything okay?" She looked up, blue-green eyes studying me.

"Yep. Just fine," I gritted out. The rage was impossible to hide.

Her voice turned hushed. "Are you sure?"

"Kristen wasn't taking no for an answer, that's all." I tugged at my tie. Its hold on me felt like a noose.

Shiv huffed a sigh of disgust. "Ah. She's a persistent one."

"Yeah," I said. "I'll tell the guys she's not allowed to come by our house. This has gotten way out of hand."

Though I risked poking the bear if I did that. Did Kristen really have a copy? If so, I didn't want to piss her off. I needed to get a hold of it somehow and destroy it.

"Fine by me." She nodded. "Never liked her. Do you want to come with us to O'Connor's for a drink?"

Not a chance. My head was spinning too much to make small talk. Would Bailey dump my ass if this got out? Who'd want to date a guy who had a sex tape circulating everywhere? Especially one like that. A threesome while I was getting high? Good look, Carter.

"Thanks, but I think I'll take it easy tonight."

"Okay." Her brow furrowed and she lingered, still studying my face with concern. "Let me know if you need anything, all right?"

Like a time machine?

"I will. Thanks, Shiv."

CHAPTER 53

CAN'T HAVE BOTH

CHASE

AT THE ASS crack of dawn the next day, I drove nearly three hours to meet with Stewart, Dallas's litigator father. He not only fit me in last minute, but he refused to charge me for his time. Hell, I'd gladly pay his insane thousand dollars-an-hour rate or whatever he charged if he had a legal magic wand to make this all go away.

I needed to talk to Bailey. Would talk to Bailey eventually. But first I needed to get a handle on the situation and what the possible fallout could be. At least then I'd have more information when I did tell her.

After barely squeezing my truck into the heated underground parking garage, I took the elevator up to the thirty-first floor. A stainless-steel sign mounted on the wall that read Ward, Myers, and Trenton LLP greeted me.

I hadn't been to a lawyer's office since we had to handle all the legal matters relating to my dad's death. It had been a media shit-storm back then. Paparazzi camped outside our house, my school, even my friends' houses.

The constant, low-level nausea I'd had since last night surged. I didn't want to relive that again, but I might if this got out.

Fuck. Maybe I should talk to my mom, but that conversation had the possibility of being even worse than the one I needed to have with Bailey.

Stewart's assistant led me into his massive corner office. Floor-to-ceiling windows displayed a panoramic view of the city and beyond. Clad in a suit, Stewart's imposing figure was seated behind his glass desk. He waved me in without glancing up from the paperwork fanned out in front of him.

"Thanks for meeting me on such short notice." I settled into the sleek leather chair across from his desk and crossed an ankle over my knee.

"Not a problem." Stewart shuffled the papers on his desk and set them aside. He glanced up at me and steepled his thick fingers, leaning over the desk with his brow furrowed. "Dallas said you had a nine-one-one situation on your hands. What's going on?"

If only I knew.

"I'm not sure. There might be…pictures. Of me. Compromising pictures. Or a video maybe." My stomach lurched, like speaking the words somehow made it more real.

He nodded. "Do they contain any non-consensual acts? Because if they do, you'll need a different kind of lawyer. I can refer you out to a criminal attorney."

I flinched. Was he seriously asking me that? At my physical response, his expression softened, turning from businesslike to sympathetic.

"I have to ask," Stewart placated. "Covering the bases. It's nothing against you, son. I would ask Dallas the same thing."

"Nothing like that," I said. "But I didn't consent to the recording, if that counts."

My phone chimed in my hand. It was a text from Bailey. Guilt flooded me. I dismissed the message and flipped the ringer to silent.

"Were you aware of it at the time?"

"Kind of. I caught the girl with her phone's camera on and got mad. She said she deleted it. I thought she did. But I was pretty, uh, intoxicated."

Stewart made notes on a pad of paper in front of him, then looked back up. "It's a criminal offense to record someone engaging in sexual acts without their permission."

This confirmed what I had gathered based on my internet

research, but it was of little comfort right now. I didn't want to press charges after my life exploded; I wanted to defuse the bomb.

"What if they pass it around?" I swallowed, mouth suddenly desert dry.

"The state doesn't have specific laws that govern revenge porn. But blackmailing you about releasing would be an offense. Those are criminal matters. For those, you'd have to go to the police and file a statement to press charges."

Cops. Great. If there was a group of people that didn't like me, it was them.

And like a big-ass hockey player filing charges against a chick half his size would go over well. Great optics there in terms of my career.

"Okay."

"I have to caution you, though, that it would be messy and public. If a civil suit arises, or you want to initiate one, that's where I come in. Also messy and public." He scanned my face. "But I assume you don't want to poke the hornet's nest right now."

"Correct."

"Generally speaking, that is what I would advise," Stewart said. "Wait until we have a better handle on what the situation is."

"I'm trying to figure it out, but I think she's lying to me. She says the video doesn't exist, but there are rumors circulating that have me worried. Seems like a smoke-fire kind of thing."

"We work with excellent private investigators. It might be worth seeing what they can dig up."

How was this my life? Hiring a fucking PI?

"As long as they don't draw more attention to it."

"They won't." Stewart shook his head. "They won't approach anyone without your okay, but they'll do a lot of legwork—discreetly—and background research." He paused, giving me a meaningful look. "And maybe some electronic device investigation, for the right price."

"Electronic device investigation?" What the hell did that mean?

He lowered his voice. "Hacking. But that would be illegal, so I never said that, nor do I condone it. This is all alleged, hypothetical, you get the drift."

There's an idea. Hack into Kristen's phone. Maybe her email too.

"Problem is, I think she sent it to someone else."

"For the sake of argument, let's say there is something out there. What would it contain? I know it's an uncomfortable subject, but give me the gist so I can gauge the extent of the damage. How compromising are we talking?" He picked up his mug and sipped, watching me over the top.

"I don't know when Kristen took out her phone." I sighed. "I was having sex with this girl, Nikki. She was on top of me. Then I stopped her, and she was blowing me while we smoked a joint."

"So the consent should be pretty easy to establish."

"I should hope so." Consent hadn't even occurred to me as a potential issue.

"That's positive, as it's one of your biggest potential problems. A sex scandal isn't nearly as bad as sexual assault allegations."

Bile climbed up the back of my throat. He was right; the video was better than a fake rape charge. If we were comparing the lesser of the evils, anyway.

"What about the joint?"

"That's the least of your problems right now," he said. "It could be a homemade cigarette. Really neither here nor there in the scheme of things. But there was a third party who took the photos?"

"Right. Kristen. We were fooling around too, but as far as I know, it isn't on camera." But fuck if I knew at this point. Kristen may have had her phone out for a while before I realized it. I was obliterated.

"Unlike that situation, recording audio with one-party consent is legal. If you speak to anyone about this, record the conversation and get them to talk as much as possible. Then we can gauge whether there is any evidence you can use for criminal or civil proceedings."

Great. But what I really wanted was to avoid proceedings altogether.

"Will do," I said. "What about my contract with the league? Do you think…?" I trailed off, unable to force out the rest of the words. Would they drop me? There were morality clauses in my contract.

"This is entirely different from when that NHL player taped women without their consent. I don't think they'll be inclined to punish you, the victim, in this scenario. Especially not with me in the picture." His voice took on an edge.

I hoped not. If this tanked my career, my life was over. There was no plan B.

"What if it does leak?"

"One step at a time," he said. "But if it does, the parties responsible will wish it hadn't. I assure you."

Not as much as I will.

He looked at me sympathetically. "Take some time. I never want my clients to act when they're under acute distress. Sleep on it. Spend some time with your girlfriend. Talk it over with someone you can trust."

That wouldn't work. No one else knew. I wanted to keep it that way.

I swallowed. "What would you tell Dallas to do?"

"Bury it." Stewart gestured emphatically with his pudgy hands. "Find it, bury it, and throw a fucking funeral."

"How?"

"We find out whether there's a copy, and if there is, get some NDAs in place immediately. Then we properly destroy the files."

I sighed. "Okay. That makes sense."

"Look," he said, "ninety-five percent of the time, clients throw money at this type of thing to sweeten the NDAs, and the issues disappear completely. We both know you can afford to do that."

Yeah. But I shouldn't fucking have to.

"You want me to pay to keep it quiet? Even though I wasn't in the wrong here? You said what she did was a crime."

"Speaking as both a lawyer and your friend, in situations like this, I recommend you do what you need to do." He raised his eyebrows. "Think about how much it could cost you if you don't."

I shook my head, gaze fixed on the glossy black tile flooring. "This is brutal."

Christ. Not exactly what my dad expected when he set me up financially, I'm sure. That I'd have to use the money for something like this. Fucking awesome. He would be so proud.

If he were still here, I could talk to him. Get his advice. I wanted him back more than anything. The ever-present ache of missing him was almost intolerable right now. I was lost. I needed him. Needed someone in my corner more than anything—someone to tell me what the fuck to do, because I sure as hell didn't know.

"I know, son." Stewart planted his elbows on the desk, fixing me with a fatherly look—stern but somehow gentle. "Do you want to be right, or do you want to make this go away?"

"Guessing I can't have both."

"No." He shook his head. "You can't."

My mind was spinning on the drive home. Song after song played on the radio, but I didn't hear a single word.

I'd quickly responded to Bailey's text when I got into my truck, but we had plans tonight and I had no idea how to drop this bomb on her. I was still processing it myself.

Once I got back into town, I made a quick detour. Didn't want to, but I needed to know for sure.

I walked up the sidewalk to the townhouse with green siding and rang the doorbell of unit twenty-two. Then I switched on my phone's voice recorder.

Forgive me, James.

Kristen opened her front door wearing a coy smile. "Hi." She was in a tank top so low-cut I could almost see nipple and yoga pants that were nearly painted on. Had she changed when I texted her, or did she always lounge around dressed like that? Fuck if I knew.

"I have practice soon, so I can't stay long," I said, stepping inside the entry. "I wanted to talk to you about last night."

"What about it?" She looked at me suspiciously as she shut the door behind me and locked it.

I leaned against the wall, trying hard to affect calm. "Maybe I was too hasty. I was in a bad mood. But you were right. That night with you and Nikki was pretty hot." I choked down my nausea so I didn't dry heave in front of her.

"I know, right?" Kristen batted her lashes at me.

God, she was easy to play.

"Too bad I never got to see the video for myself," I added.

She sniffed. "I thought you were all about your girlfriend these days."

"Doesn't mean I can't reminisce about the past a little." The words were hard to force out, bitter in my mouth.

"Guess you shouldn't have made me delete it."

In the background, her roommate Charlotte walked by. Did she know?

I lowered my voice in hopes that Charlotte couldn't hear. "Come on, Kristen. I bet you could find it for me."

"Hmm." She shrugged, playing with a strand of her dark hair. "I might be able to dig it up if I tried."

I knew it. I fucking *knew* it.

"Try?" I gave her a flirty smile while hating myself inside. "For old times' sake?"

"Fine." Kristen rolled her eyes. "Hang on." She pulled out her phone and tapped at the screen.

My heart raced while I waited. After a minute, she handed her phone to me—and there it was. I watched the whole clip with the volume on low, feigning interest. I fought the instinct to smash her phone into pieces. I couldn't show my hand. Not yet.

As I had suspected, the video was four minutes of me banging Nikki, then her blowing me while we smoked a joint. The clip stopped before the moment I'd caught Kristen and told her to stop recording, conveniently painting me as a willing participant and eliminating all references to her.

She'd cropped the video. Shit. I needed the original. Somehow. It was the only thing that might exonerate my ass.

"Is this it?" I glanced up at her, eyebrows raised, and passed the phone back. Her hand brushed mine in the process, and I fought the urge to yank it away.

Her perfectly arched brows pulled together. “What do you mean?”

Careful, Carter.

“I was hoping it would be longer.” I shrugged. “You’re not in the video.”

“Maybe next time.”

“Maybe.” Never fucking ever. “No one else knows about this, do they?”

She blinked rapidly, taking a small step back. “No…”

Lie.

“Do me a solid and keep it that way, okay? It’s hotter that way anyway, right?”

“Totally.” She smirked.

“Thanks, Kris. I have to get to practice, but I’ll text you,” I lied.

I stalked back to my truck, climbed inside, and turned the ignition. Then I slumped against the leather-wrapped steering wheel. My thoughts were a tangled mess. How would I break this to Bailey? What could I even say to her?

Part of me thought she might hear me out. But what if she didn’t? The contents of the video were damning—me with two girls, one of whom was someone else’s girlfriend. At the time, I didn’t know she had a boyfriend, but it still looked bad. Bailey had been so upset about Derek and Jillian. Would she lose respect for me over this? Decide I wasn’t who she thought I was after all?

Not to mention the catastrophic effect this could have on my life—and Bailey’s, by association. Her reputation as the girlfriend of *that* guy could jeopardize her scholarship, her internship, her *career*. Would she resent me for dragging her into the vicious gossip and the trash talk?

Good god, I hadn’t even met her parents, and now they would hate me. And so much for any headway I’d made with Derek.

A sharp rap on my window startled me. I glanced up, expecting to find Kristen.

It wasn’t.

CHAPTER 54
24 HOURS
CHASE

I ROLLED DOWN THE WINDOW. "What do you want?"

"Let's chat." Luke flashed me a shit-eating grin.

Without hesitation, I unlocked the door. Why not? My day was already fucked. My life was fucked, really. Plus, he'd caught me leaving Kristen's, so he had the upper hand.

But I had a few tricks up my sleeve too. My phone was still in my palm, so I quickly switched on the voice recording app and set it on the center console, screen down.

Luke pulled open the door and hopped into the passenger seat. The overwhelming stench of his cologne wafted over to me, further amplifying my queasiness. He gave my truck a disdainful once-over. "Very pedestrian choice of vehicle. Fitting." Leaning over, he handed me a folded piece of white paper.

I snatched it out of his hand. "What the hell is this?"

"You tell me."

Transcript of video recording
— RECORDING BEGINS —
[music, background noise]
CHASE: Fuck. Hang on. Where's the lighter?
FEMALE 1: Are you seriously stopping right now? What the hell?
CHASE: Chill out, Nikki. Just let me light this.
[background noise]
[coughing]
FEMALE 1: Oh my god. (coughs) That's strong.
CHASE: I know. My dealer is the shit.
FEMALE 2: Gonna save some for me?
FEMALE 1: The joint or Chase?
FEMALE 2: (laughs) Both.
CHASE: Don't worry, I can go all night. Can't say the same for this spliff.
[laughter, background noise]
— RECORDING ENDS —

Ice ran through my veins. Spelled out like that, the encounter looked even worse. The world tilted around me, and I came closer than ever to emptying the meager contents of my stomach onto the floor of the truck. I'd barely eaten all day, so at least there wouldn't be much.

And it was still only an excerpt from the video. Even with his apparent digging, Luke hadn't been able to uncover the whole thing, either.

Gripping the paper, I read the transcript twice more. It was like reading a story about someone else. I wasn't the person in that video anymore, and I barely remembered that night. When I tried to play it back in my head, it was all a blur. My hangover had lasted for two days after.

"Wonder if *Callingwood Daily* would want to run a story. Front page, maybe."

I glanced up, keeping my expression neutral. "Where did you get this?"

"Fell into my lap. Kind of like that skank, Nikki, huh?" He snorted. "Or *Female One*, I should say."

"What do you want?" I tossed the transcript onto the console between us.

"My private investigator does good work," he said, ignoring my question. "I have a copy of the video too, but I'm sure you've already seen it."

At this point, I wondered who hadn't.

"In case you're curious," he added, "I only had to pay Kristen three grand to sell you out. I bet you're willing to cough up a lot more than that to keep it quiet, huh?"

A hundred times over.

"Get to the point."

Luke tilted his head and stroked his chin with an arrogant look on his face. "Isn't Bailey up for a big scholarship package right now? I thought I heard something about an important internship too. Sounds like the kind of thing that could really set her up after graduation."

My stomach did a nosedive. Bailey was one of five finalists who'd been selected to meet with the scholarship adjudication panel. *Penalty Box Online* had contacted her references and invited her for another interview on Friday, too. She'd been over the moon about both things all week.

If Luke had managed to track down the video, I guess I shouldn't have been too surprised he knew other intimate details about not only my life, but Bailey's.

"What does that have to do with anything?"

He paused and adjusted the collar of his pale yellow polo beneath his jacket. Oppressive silence filled the vehicle while he intentionally delayed, relishing in my fear. I looked at him blankly, refusing to give him the satisfaction of asking again.

"That video is interesting, you know. Female Two is off-camera the whole time. It would be a shame if people thought that voice belonged to Bailey." Luke gave me a pitying look. "Making sex tapes with her boyfriend could really hurt her chances of landing those opportunities. Would hurt her future career prospects too."

Panic gripped me by the throat, putting me in a chokehold. It took every ounce of strength I had to keep my voice level. "You know damn well that voice doesn't belong to Bailey. I didn't even know her then. And she was still dating you."

Luke shrugged. "Good luck proving that. There's no time stamp shown on that video. She's with you now, and she'll be guilty by association. And once the rumor gets out, they'll always believe it on some level."

Regret churned in my stomach. All this time, I'd worried about shielding her from Luke, but I was the one she needed protection from. Guilty by association because of me and my choices. About to pay the price for something I did before I even knew her. Something done *to* me.

"Again, what the fuck do you want? I know it isn't cash."

"End it."

The words stabbed me in the gut like a rusty blade.

"What?" I should have been expecting it, but a small, desperate part of me hoped for something else. Anything else.

His blue eyes held mine, cold with malice. "Did I stutter?"

"She'll never get back together with you." My pulse roared in my ears. "This is about control. You don't even love her. If you did, you wouldn't do this."

He waved me off. "We could play armchair psychologist all day. It doesn't matter. Question is, are you willing to blow up her life?"

The knife in my gut twisted and tore me apart from the inside, disemboweling me all over the inside of my truck. It killed me to think of Bailey losing out on something she clearly deserved. But it devastated me to think of losing her.

Luke held her future in his hands and he knew it.

I needed the other half of the video, the part where I'd gotten mad and called Kristen by her name. If nothing else, it would exonerate Bailey. Stewart's PI would start digging, but who knew how long it would take to find it—if he found it at all? But then what? Leak it myself to prove it wasn't Bailey? Even if I did locate it, the solutions were all shitty.

"Why would you do that to Bailey?" I asked, desperately

searching for a shred of humanity hidden deep within him. "And Nikki?"

I could deal with the fallout in my own life, but the collateral damage in this scenario was criminal. The guilt I was feeling was off the fucking charts.

Luke scoffed. "Who gives a fuck about Nikki? As far as Bailey goes, if you make the right call, I won't."

"If I say no?" I asked hoarsely.

"I'll make sure that a search for her name will imply she directs amateur porn. Potential employers, prospective boyfriends—because let's face it, we know you two won't last—even the teachers of her future children." He leaned back, leisurely placing an ankle over his knee like we were old pals shooting the breeze.

Denial seized hold of my brain. "That can be scrubbed."

"Not fully." Luke smirked, his tone even more condescending than usual. "The internet never forgets, Carter."

Neither did I. Somehow, I'd get even for this. But first I had to stop my life from imploding. Or minimize the damage, at least.

Morrison was nothing if not a coward, so I changed tactics. "You realize blackmail is a crime, right? A felony, in fact."

"Eh. I'm not concerned about that."

Holy fuck, he'd lost his mind.

"Why not?" I snapped. "You think your lawyer parents will bail you out?" I ran the risk of provoking him, but I was filled with so much rage, I could barely contain myself.

Luke remained eerily calm like the psychopath he was. "Speaking of parents, have you met Bailey's? Lovely people." He frowned, studying me with disapproval. "Not sure they'll say the same about you if this video makes its way into their hands."

"Are you willing to risk jail to take me down?" I spat out. "I could call the cops right now."

"You can't be stupid enough to think I have the only copy. If you do that, it blows up immediately. Putting me in jail won't fix her reputation. Are you willing to gamble with her future?"

The answer was no—and he knew it. At least I now had his

threats on tape. Problem was that wouldn't stop him from going nuclear on Bailey's entire life first.

"If you drag Bailey into this, jail will be the least of your concerns. I won't have anything left to lose."

Despite my violent fantasies about Morrison, I'd never seriously contemplated killing him. Until now.

"Oh, I don't know about that. You have lots of other things on the line. Deluca and I have been chatting lately. Maybe he would be interested in seeing your film debut."

"Go ahead," I ground out. Tom Deluca was part of Los Angeles's management team, and I spoke to him regularly too. "Do that and leave Bailey out of this."

"Nah."

I gripped the steering wheel, my knuckles turning white. "Why not? It's me you want to punish."

"You ruined my life." He sneered.

Presumably, he was referring to the backlash against him after the last game. He'd never owned up to a thing in his entire miserable existence; that sure as hell wouldn't change now. "It's only fair I return the favor."

"You ruined your own life."

Luke barked a caustic laugh. "I could say the same for you."

He wasn't wrong, though I never consented to that fucking video in the first place.

"Anyway." Luke feigned a yawn, shifting his weight. "I've drafted a detailed email to everyone Bailey knows, complete with video attached. Break it off, or I'm hitting send."

Heartache rocked through me like never before, mingled with pure, unmitigated rage. My brain went into lizard mode, rendering me speechless.

"Other people have copies, so don't try anything cute. And don't even think about trying to fake a breakup and pull one over on me. I have eyes everywhere," he said. "That's how I found you here."

My heart wrenched as I forced out the words. "If I agree, will you leave her alone?"

"I will." He opened the door and slid out but lingered. "You have twenty-four hours to do it."

BAILEY

I glanced away from the article I was working on, checking the time in the bottom corner of the laptop screen. Chase was over half an hour late. It was out of character for him not to text to let me know, but he'd been acting strange for the past two days. Distant and despondent, not like his usual self. No flirty or sexy texts, either, which we usually exchanged multiple times a day.

When I'd texted to ask him what was wrong, he'd shut me down completely. I could only assume he was stewing over his three-game suspension. He seemed to take it in stride at the time, but I could tell being benched really bothered him. Especially when they'd lost their last game in a brutal defeat.

Still, I couldn't shake the feeling that something else was going on.

Unease settled in my gut, and I returned my attention to my write-up about the school's art fair. From beside me on my desk, my phone vibrated and lit up with a new text.

999-855-5955: Where was your boyfriend this afternoon?

Bailey: I changed my number for a reason, Luke.

999-855-5955: Oh, I think you'll be happy I tracked you down.

A photo attachment followed. Fear creeped in as I dragged my fingers across the screen, zooming in. It was Chase on the porch of a green house. The door was open, and Kristen was standing in the doorway.

No.

A familiar form of agony settled in: betrayal. Just like with Luke. Learning about this from him was beyond ironic, like everything was coming full circle. My mind backpedaled, frantically searching for a reasonable explanation. Maybe the picture was old, from before. But then why would Luke even have it?

From inside my bedroom, I heard Shiv answer the door and let Chase in. When he crossed the threshold into my room, his posture was stiff, and his eyes were haunted. He even *looked* guilty.

"Hi." He stuffed his hands into the pockets of his jeans, leaning against the doorframe.

More alarm bells went off in my head when he didn't come close and give me a hug or kiss hello.

"Where were you earlier?" I was too upset to be strategic about how I approached what was going on, and his standoffish behavior was only causing me further panic.

"Practice," he said. "Look, we need to—"

My heart sank. Strike one. He lied.

I cut him off, giving him a sharp look. "You sure about that?"

"What do you mean?" Chase frowned, but guilt swam in his eyes.

"Did you make any other stops along the way?"

Please tell me the truth. Please own up to it.

"I had to do a few things, yeah."

Pushing my desk chair back, I stood, watching his face carefully. My pulse revved. "Was Kristen one of them?"

Chase broke eye contact and looked at the floor, shaking his head. Almost inaudibly, he muttered, "Of course."

"What the hell is going on, Carter?"

There had to be an explanation for this. There had to be a good reason he was there, and he was going to tell me what it was. I trusted him. I believed in him.

He looked back up at me with so much anguish in his eyes that tears welled up in my own. "Nothing happened with her. I swear."

Yeah, I'd heard that line before—a few too many times. But never from him. None of this made sense.

And the worst part was that it felt like he was telling the truth.

I sucked in a jagged breath and sank my teeth into my bottom lip to stop myself from crying. "Then why were you there?"

"I—" He faltered, shaking his head. "Can't."

My voice cracked. "Please tell me. I want the truth."

This was not happening. Could not be happening. This was the guy who'd been there for me unconditionally, even when I pushed him away. Who'd been nothing but patient and kind and—most of all—honest with me. Sometimes brutally so.

"No," he said more firmly. A flicker of his usual self-assured demeanor appeared, but it disappeared almost as quickly. "I haven't even looked at anyone else since I met you. I think you know that."

"I thought I did too, but I need an alternate explanation."

I took a step, followed by another, and drew closer to him until we were within arm's reach. His jaw ticked as he watched me, but he didn't move. Neither of us moved. I searched his face, probing, like I might see into his brain if I tried hard enough.

"I need you to trust me, James." The muscles in his neck were strained, his voice matching.

A strangled sob escaped from the back of my throat. "How can I trust you when you won't give me an answer?"

"I love you more than anything in this world, but I can't give you that." His eyes held mine, pained but unreadable. "And we can't…" He let out a heavy sigh. "I can't be with you right now."

My world shattered at my feet.

"*What*?" I shuffled back, putting space between us like it would somehow protect my heart. "How can you—how can you say you love me and then turn around and do this? You don't want to be with me anymore? Just like that?"

Chase started to reach for me and caught himself, dropping his hands to his sides. He balled his hands into fists, flexing and releasing. "That's not—I want to be with you more than I want anything."

"Right," I retorted angrily. "Except you're choosing not to." An ache erupted in my chest, so consuming that I thought I might literally be having a heart attack. I loved him. He loved me. I knew both of those things to be true, so how could this be happening?

It was like learning everything I thought to be true was a lie.

"I'm sorry," he said. "This is what's best."

I opened my mouth to respond, but the words didn't appear. We stared at each other, bathed in unspoken words and unanswered questions. The silence stretched on and on while my heart bled out on the bedroom floor, one beat at a time.

Finally, he cleared his throat. "I should go."

With another pained look, he turned and started for my bedroom door. Still frozen to the spot with disbelief, I watched him disappear into the hall. Moments later, the sound of the front door shutting quietly behind him followed.

Tears erupted in earnest, accompanied by huge, gulping sobs. I couldn't stop the tears, couldn't catch my breath, couldn't make sense of what Chase had said. Everything we had was gone. And I still didn't understand why.

"Bailey?" Shiv called. "Are you okay?"

"No."

Seconds later, she stepped into my room. When she caught sight of me, she rushed over and threw her arms around me. "What happened?"

My voice cracked. "I don't know."

CHAPTER 55
48 HOURS
CHASE

Fuck my life.
I guess I just did.

"Think about it, James. We would have really tall kids. They would be giants."

"You're drunk, Carter. Cute, but drunk."

BAILEY

BLINKING IN DISBELIEF, I reread the email on my screen.

Dear Ms. James, we are delighted to inform you that you have been selected to receive full tuition funding for the upcoming academic year...

My chest pulled tight as the words blurred. I got it. I got the scholarship.

It was a hollow victory when Chase had blown up my world recently. I still couldn't wrap my head around what happened. He showed up looking like someone died, broke things off with zero warning, gave me no explanation, and left. Just walked out the door without looking back.

Since then, radio silence. No calls, no texts, nothing.

I'd been going in circles ever since, trying to figure out what went wrong, what to do now, and how to make sense of it. I'd picked up the phone and selected his contact at least a dozen times —either out of sheer habit or because a surge of resentment would hit me and I wanted answers. Hell, I *deserved* answers, far better ones than the half-assed excuses he gave me. But every time my finger hovered over his name, I'd freeze. Hurt, anger, confusion, pride…a million things held me back.

I grabbed my coffee off the nightstand, draining my second cup of the morning. I hadn't gotten more than three or four broken hours since it happened, and those were punctuated with nightmares and crying fits. Eating held zero appeal, either. At this point, I was surviving on caffeine, sadness, and air.

After huddling beneath the covers with my laptop for another half an hour, I dragged myself out of bed and into the shower. I turned the water temperature up almost as hot as it could go, scrubbed the grease out of my hair, and had a nice, long cry under the stream of water. Once my throat was hoarse and my skin was wrinkled, I grabbed a towel and dried off, then changed into a set of clean pajamas. I wasn't leaving the apartment today, so why bother with real clothes? I was showered, and that was a major improvement over the previous two days.

Even though I still felt dead inside.

Looked it on the outside too. All the crying had left my skin blotchy and my eyes red and puffy. I had barely eaten in the past few days. Not for lack of trying, but looking at food turned my stomach, and actually consuming it was worse.

My friends were rallying around me, but somehow, their efforts were the opposite of comforting. I wanted to be left alone. Siobhan had cooked and tried to entice me into eating. Derek wouldn't stop sending *are you okay?* texts. And Zara and Noelle had kindly stepped in and offered to take over my newspaper duties for a while. Taking them up on it had been gut-wrenching, but I didn't have much choice. I wasn't fit to be out in public, let alone attending games and taking notes.

And later this week, I had a second interview for the *Penalty Box* internship via videoconference. How was I supposed to keep it together when I was dying on the inside?

When I emerged from my bedroom, Siobhan was settled on the couch watching a true crime documentary. Seemed like an odd choice for nine thirty in the morning, but I'd learned by now that her media tastes skewed eclectic, to say the least.

Crying for two days straight had taken its toll, and even after the hot shower, I ached all over. I shuffled into the kitchen and refilled my coffee. Breakfast was probably a good idea, but it held zero appeal.

Standing behind the counter, I debated whether I should talk to her about what I'd been mulling over. What more did I have to lose? Chase was already gone.

I went into the living room and sank onto the couch next to her. "Can I ask you something?"

"Of course." Shiv hit pause on the remote and shifted to face me. She scanned my face, her expression softening. "Are you okay?"

"Not really," I admitted. A lump formed in my throat, and I swallowed, willing it away. "But I have a question. Only if you can keep this between us, though. If you and Dallas don't keep secrets from each other, that's okay. I just won't ask."

"Ask away. I won't tell him, promise."

I trusted her. Unlike Amelia or Jillian, who were incapable of keeping secrets from each other or their boyfriends, I believed that Shiv would honor my request.

"Can you get me Kristen's number? Or maybe figure out where I could find her on campus? I need to talk to her."

Siobhan's brow creased. "I can probably track her down. Why?"

"This." I unlocked my phone and showed her the picture Luke

sent me. Only then did it hit me how strange it was that Luke had this picture in the first place. Between his texts and Chase's arrival —and subsequent implosion of my life—I'd been in such deep shock that I hadn't considered the implications until now. Was Luke following Chase? Was he following me too? My stomach turned at the thought.

Shiv frowned, studying the screen. "That's weird."

"Right?"

I hit the button on the side of my phone and held it in my lap, trying not to look at the lock screen, which was still a picture of Chase and me from the hockey gala. I couldn't bring myself to change it. But every time I saw it, a thousand papercuts tore at my heart. I set my phone aside and took a sip of scalding hot coffee, praying the caffeine would compensate for the lack of sleep and massive emotional hangover. At the rate I was going, I'd need an entire pot to make a dent in my exhaustion.

Siobhan rested her chin in her hand and drew in a breath, hesitating before she spoke. "I don't want to insert myself into something that isn't my business or cause more problems, but I did see—well, I saw Chase and Kristen having an argument after the last game. When I asked him about it, he said she wouldn't take no for an answer. Maybe he went over there to tell her to back off."

Another thing I'd been kept in the dark about. Chase hadn't told me about an argument with Kristen. We'd spoken on the phone that night, and he'd seemed different—distant. His argument with Kristen coincided perfectly with when he'd started to behave strangely. Like a switch had flipped.

But…

"Why would he go to her place to do that, though? And why wouldn't he tell me? When I asked him, he couldn't explain why he was there."

The more I thought about it, the less I thought there was any chance Chase had done something with Kristen. Unlike with Luke. I might have tried to sell myself on his lies, but deep down, part of me had known when Luke cheated and lied about it. This sick, uneasy feeling always rolled in my gut. A disloyalty radar of sorts.

Chase had never given me that feeling, even now. Something was definitely wrong, but cheating wasn't it.

Or maybe I was in denial. I still hadn't come to terms with the end of us. It couldn't be real. It went against everything I thought I knew.

Shiv hummed. "I don't know." Her gaze fell to her pale pink nails, then back up at me. "I'm worried about Chase. Especially with the way he broke up with you and peaced out of here. It makes zero sense."

"Glad I'm not the only one who thought that was out of left field." I huffed and took another sip of coffee.

She bit her bottom lip, blue-green eyes turning serious. "I'm probably breaking all kinds of rules in the girlfriend handbook, but I'm going to tell you this, anyway."

"Tell me what?" My heart skittered.

"After the game the other night, I went to bed early. The guys stayed up playing video games and drinking. When I got up to use the bathroom, Chase and Dal were talking in the hallway. Chase said he needed to meet with Dallas's dad about something urgent."

"Dallas's father? I don't follow."

"Well…he's a lawyer."

Worry seized me. "Why would Chase need a lawyer?" Was he in trouble?

"I'm not sure," she said. "I was half-asleep. Didn't think much of it at the time and didn't stick around to listen."

"What kind of law does Dallas's dad practice?"

"Litigation. But maybe Chase needed general legal advice." She rolled her lips into a line. "The timing is odd, don't you think?"

What kind of trouble could he be in? He hadn't been arrested for anything—as far as I knew. Luke was still alive, so it wasn't *that*. Chase wasn't suing anyone or being sued. And he didn't engage in anything too far outside of the law, aside from dabbling in occasional marijuana use.

Could he have failed a drug test for the team? Or could he have been using performance-enhancing drugs? That last one was doubtful.

Kristen didn't fit into any of those scenarios, either, unless she was a drug pusher.

None of it fit.

Then again, neither did Chase ending things out of the blue. Things between us hadn't been just fine, they'd been great. We'd been talking about the future. We'd been talking about *forever*. My heart tugged, and tears pricked my eyes. I inhaled slowly, trying to blink them away.

"Dallas didn't mention this to you at all?" I clarified.

"No." Siobhan shook her head. "I didn't ask because it was pretty clear I wasn't supposed to hear. They were talking quietly."

"Maybe it's good you didn't. This way Chase doesn't know that I know."

"What are you going to do?"

I wasn't sure, specifically. Something. Anything.

"Find out what the hell is going on."

"What are the stakes?"

"If I win, you have to watch The Royal Boyfriend.*"*

"And if I win, you have to watch Operation Vengeance.*"*

Ten minutes later...

"Nice, Carter. You beat me for once."

"Sure did."

"Fine. Operation Vengeance *it is."*

"Nah, we can watch your movie."

"Really? We don't have to."

"I know."

CHASE

I stared at my Sports Economics textbook blankly. Our exam was this week, but every time I opened the book to review the material, the words blurred.

All I could think about was Bailey. Missing her, wondering if she was okay, hoping she didn't hate me…even though she should.

I wanted to call her. No, I wanted to go over there and tell her everything. But I couldn't risk her getting caught in the crossfire.

If I could get through the next week or two without ruining her life, maybe I could find a way out of this chasm I'd dug myself into.

A sharp knock at the door jolted me back to reality. Dallas didn't wait for me to respond before strolling in like a man on a mission. He sat on the edge of my bed across from my desk, facing me. I shut my textbook before thinking better of it, then immediately flipped it back open to a random section. I needed to focus on something other than what I could only assume was an imminent interrogation.

"What's up, man?" His icy-blue eyes bored into me.

I dropped my gaze, avoiding eye contact by pretending to be fascinated with a random graph on page 256.

I turned the page. "Nothing. Just studying."

"Sure you are." His tone turned gruff. "Now that we've gotten the bullshit out of the way, what's really going on?"

Without looking up, I shrugged. It was difficult to lie to Dallas, because he knew me so well. But I didn't want to tell him the truth, either. The fewer people who knew, the better.

He snatched the textbook out of my hands and slammed it shut. I lifted my chin reluctantly, and when I finally made eye contact, he leveled me with a reproachful glare.

"You haven't left the house in three days," he pointed out. "If you don't resurface soon, Miller is going to come over here and drag your ass to practice himself. And at this point, I'll help him."

"I'll go tomorrow," I lied.

"We have a game in two days."

"I know." I didn't, actually. Our schedule had been the last thing on my mind. "I'll be ready." Another lie, but I was doing a lot of that lately. After barely eating or sleeping, I'd be useless on the ice. A liability, in fact.

Dallas rested his elbows on his knees, giving me a stern look that was all too reminiscent of his father. "You know, Shiv has been texting to check up on you every few hours."

"She has? Why?"

"Gee, I don't know, Carter." He threw his arms out. "Maybe because we're concerned about the status of your mental health since you dumped Bailey for no apparent reason."

An invisible hand wrapped around my throat. "Is she okay?"

"What do you think?" He gave me a hard look.

Guilt came crashing down on me like a ton of bricks. I was buried so deep I might never get out. And I'd never forgive myself for how this went down.

Dallas's voice took on a gentler tone. "Does this have to do with why you went to see my dad?"

I let out a long breath. He wasn't going to let this go. "Yeah."

"Why won't you talk to me?" he asked. "You know you can. I won't tell anyone. Not even Shiv."

"Because I fucked up, Ward."

"You know I'm going to ask you to marry me one day, right?"

"You are?"

"Count on it. Are you going to say yes?"

"Of course."

CHAPTER 56

THE BLAST ZONE

CHASE

THE MORE I TOLD DALLAS, the more tense his posture grew.

Halfway through the recap of my conversation with Luke, he leapt off my bed. "Holy shit," he said, interrupting me. "Why didn't you tell me this sooner?"

Good question.

"Uh, kind of been in shock over here. My life went from normal to a living nightmare in the span of twenty-four hours. Still not thinking clearly, in case it wasn't obvious."

I circled back to detailing the sordid chain of events. By the end of my story, Dallas was pacing the floor of my room, nearly as distressed as I was.

"You didn't do anything wrong." He turned on his heel and made another lap. "I remember how upset you were the next day when you told me Kristen pulled that stunt."

He was right. But I was still pissed at myself for trusting her in the first place.

"That doesn't change the situation I'm in now."

Dallas shook his head, raking a hand through his dark hair. "You have to tell Bailey."

"Didn't you hear what I said? Morrison is going to blow up her entire world."

He meant well, but I'd been second-guessing and agonizing

over that very decision for the better part of the last three days. If it was as simple as telling her, I would have already done it.

"How would he know if you told her the truth?"

That was the million-dollar question. But the price if he did was far too high—Bailey losing everything she'd worked three years for. Her future. Her shot at a career she deserved. Being financially independent, which mattered to her more than she'd ever admit.

Not to mention the blowback in her personal life. I had skin thicker than an alligator hide, but Bailey didn't.

"I don't know," I said, prickly unease washing over me. "Morrison knows all kinds of shit he shouldn't. How does he even know about her internship? It's creepy as hell."

When I met Stewart's PI, Vincent, yesterday, the first thing I asked him to do was make sure Luke didn't have a tail on Bailey. Vincent told me to sit tight, so I'd been obsessively watching my phone and waiting for an update since. Waiting to hear whether he'd gotten a hold of the full tape, knew who else might have it, anything.

So far, no word. I couldn't even contact Stewart again until Vincent gave me the all-clear.

Sitting, waiting, losing my goddamn mind.

"Maybe you should let Bailey decide what she wants to do," Dallas said.

"You don't think I want to? Giving her the choice might be the same thing as making it for her. If I tell her, and Morrison finds out, he'll go nuclear. Game over."

The fallout played in my head like a horror movie on repeat: that fucking email going to her friends, her family, everyone affiliated with her scholarship and internship. Bailey's life falling apart like a house of cards, all because of me.

Morrison could pull the trigger at some point anyway, with or without dragging Bailey into it. God willing, it would be without. At the end of the day, I could own up to the things I'd done, even if I hadn't intended them to be public knowledge.

Whether Bailey would want to be with me once she knew about the tape, though? The answer to that question scared me.

"If you don't tell her," Dallas said, his voice quiet, "you could lose her."

It winded me like a hockey stick to the stomach. Again, he was right, but I couldn't accept that as a possibility. I couldn't be the reason her dreams went up in smoke, either. Hence the hellish purgatory I was trapped in.

I itched to pick up the phone. Better yet, to go over there and see her. I missed her more than anything in the world. The distance I'd put between us was literal torture. Like I was missing a limb, and it had only been days. How much more of this could I take?

"I'm trying to keep her out of the blast zone. I don't care what happens to me, but I can't let her get dragged into this shit. What would you do if it was Shiv?"

"I'd protect her," Dallas admitted. "At all costs."

"Exactly. Priority number one was pushing her out of the path of an oncoming freight train. If you have any ideas beyond that, I'm all ears."

Beside me on my bed, my phone lit up.

"You going to come to my first NHL game?"

"Wouldn't miss it for the world."

The hours I had to wait to meet with Vincent felt like a fucking eternity. Dallas tried to stay with me, but his anxiety level was feeding into mine, so I finally forced him to leave the house and keep his original plans with Shiv.

In the meantime, Vincent gave me the go-ahead to talk to Stewart. What I'd hoped would be a constructive conversation turned out to be *destructive*, because Stewart and I agreed that he'd preemptively inform Los Angeles about the situation. There was a chance I was about to blow my contract to bits and ruin my future hockey career, but Stewart assured me that getting ahead of it was the best way to go. I had no choice but to trust him.

It was after eight by the time I met Vincent. The grimy pub we were meeting at for the second time was located on the other end of town in an industrial park. Vincent claimed it was "a secure location," but the area was more than a little shady. He obviously knew what he was doing, though, so I kept my mouth shut. Maybe the cockroaches moonlighted as security.

I headed to the back corner and slid into the booth across from him. He was dressed in head-to-toe black, with hard features amplified by a jagged scar down his left cheek. How he blended in easily enough to be a PI was a mystery, but Stewart said his nickname was *the Ghost.* Hopefully, he'd live up to it.

Vincent laced his fingers on the table, looking at me over his half-empty pint of beer with a grim expression. He was a brand-new addition to my shortlist of terrifying people—one notch below Stewart. I got the feeling if I asked Vincent to have Morrison offed, he'd give me a price and initiate plans.

I'd be lying if I said I hadn't considered it.

"Before we go any further," Vincent said, "we have a don't ask, don't tell policy with sources. Which means it's not admissible in court."

"That's fine." My foot landed on something sticky on the floor beneath the table, and it made a ripping sound as I repositioned my legs. "I need to know."

"As we discussed, I have a copy of the full video," Vincent said. "Or rather, I have both clips, as it was digitally split into two."

Nausea brimmed in the pit of my stomach. "Can I see the second one?"

From across the table, he stretched his arm out, offering me his phone. I accepted and adjusted the volume to its lowest setting, hesitating briefly. Revulsion bowled into me as I hit Play.

Clip 2 of 2
Location: Private residence, 9516 32nd Ave

Date saved: Saturday, April 21st at 1:27 AM

— RECORDING STARTS —

[1:35:02 AM]
Nicole: Come on already.
Chase: Wait, I need to grab another—what the fuck, Kristen? How long have you had that out? Put that shit away.
[background noise]
Chase: Get off me, Nikki.
Nicole: (unintelligible)
Kristen: It's not on, Chase. I'm just messing around.
Chase: I don't care. Let me see your phone.
Kristen: But you look so good on camera.
Chase: What? You better not be recording this.
[background noise]
Kristen: (laughs) Or what?
Chase: I'm not fucking around. Give me the phone.
Chase: Now, Kristen. I don't need Coach seeing this.
Kristen: You're such a downer. Relax, I'll delete it. See?
[1:36:09AM]

— RECORDING ENDS —

The video ended, and I stared at the frozen screen without blinking.

Just like I'd thought.

A murky mixture of feelings swirled within me. Vindication, anger, regret. I'd been so focused on funneling my rage toward Morrison that I hadn't even begun to think about what to do with Kristen. First, she made the recording—and edited the clip to fuck me extra hard—then she sold me out for practically pennies.

At least I had the other half, time stamp and all. Should this hit worst-case scenario, at least Bailey would be spared some of the fallout. There was no way anyone could plausibly link her to the tape now.

"If you give the police probable cause when you press

charges, sometimes they dig up this stuff themselves." Vincent nodded at his phone, still in my hand, the screen having gone black. "Your audio recording, which was legally obtained, gives them a good starting point to go hunting for this. It shouldn't be too hard to find unless the cop working the case is a total fucking moron." He heaved a weary sigh. "Though, unfortunately, many of them are."

With my luck, I'd end up with the fucking moron variety working my case. Problem for another time, though.

I handed his phone back to him. "Was anyone following Bailey?"

"No. But I assume you're aware that you were being followed."

An icy sensation trickled down my spine. "I had an inkling." Confirming it didn't make it any less disturbing, though.

"Another PI firm. Travers Mill. Top shelf prices, bottom tier, sloppy work. They were retained by"—he glanced down and checked his notes—"Lucas Morrison."

No surprise there.

"How long have they been following me?"

"A month."

Holy shit. Since he pulled the car stunt with Bailey.

He shrugged, bringing his beer to his mouth. "Like I said, they're sloppy. Practically left behind a trail of breadcrumbs."

"Are they still tailing me?"

"No." The mug clanged against the table with an ominous finality. His thin lips quirked. "And they won't be again. I've seen to that."

"Wait, if no one was following Bailey, how did Morrison know all that stuff about her life?"

"Oh, Travers Mill was definitely poking around in her life."

Another arctic blast filled my body at the idea of Luke's minions snooping into Bailey's personal affairs. I tried to push it out of mind, focusing on the takeaway message. They were gone now.

"But they weren't following her like they were you," he added. "They won't be snooping around in her life anymore, either. Their investigator broke several laws and was too careless to conceal it properly. With that sort of leverage, you can expect them to leave you alone going forward."

"Does that mean it's safe for me to talk to her?"

"Yes," he said. "Travers Mill have to let Luke know they were exposed, but you have a small window of opportunity before that happens. I'm going to tail you myself for the next few days to be sure they've backed off."

A rush of air flooded my lungs, like I'd been holding my breath without realizing it.

I could see her. Talk to her. Tell her everything. Beg for her forgiveness, or at least try.

"Stewart is handling the legal end of things as we speak," he added.

In addition to talking to the management for Los Angeles, Stewart planned to "leash that sorry excuse for a shit stain" by going straight to the source of said stain—Luke's parents. He felt that, as lawyers, they'd be pretty receptive in light of the recording from the truck and the threat of a messy, public lawsuit. Not to mention criminal charges on top of that.

Either it would work or it wouldn't. I couldn't wait any longer to find out. If the coast was clear, nothing would keep me from seeing Bailey.

"Yellow."

"Are you okay?"

"I want a kiss."

"I thought you were getting overstimulated."

"No, I was getting lonely up here."

"We can't have that. Do you want me to untie you?"

"Not yet. But I need you to make good on all this teasing soon, or I'm going to lose my mind."

BAILEY

I'd insisted that Siobhan have Dallas over as planned, realizing too late how weird it would be to see him.

Cracking open my bedroom door, I listened for any signs of life. When all that greeted me was silence, I tiptoed into the kitchen and grabbed a glass from the cupboard. Crying non-stop was shockingly dehydrating. I hadn't ever drunk as much water as I had in the past few days.

To add to my stress, Shiv had gotten a hold of Kristen's number for me earlier today. I was trying to formulate the right thing to say before I called. Was there really a right thing to say in this situation?

As I turned to fill my glass from the dispenser in the fridge, a text popped up on my home screen. Luke again. This was why I'd hesitated to change my number in the first place—it was a pain, and I knew he'd track me down sooner or later. Turns out I was right.

I stared at the display. Irritation sparked within me, along with another flicker of heartache. The knife was already buried so deep —the twisting of the blade was uncalled for.

With my phone unlocked, I navigated into my texts to delete the message. My intention was to erase it without opening it, but the message preview sucked me in, and I took the bait.

Luke: Trouble in paradise?

Bailey: Stop texting me, stalker.

Luke: Don't be angry with me because Carter dumped you.

Bailey: How do you even know that?

Luke: I know everything.

Bailey: From what I hear, you have problems of your own to worry about.

Luke: What are you talking about?

Bailey: Guess I know everything too.

Luke: Everything? Did you know about his sex tape?

Luke: Told you he wasn't who you thought he was.

[attachment]

My heart roared in my ears as I stared at his message.

Sex tape? *What?*

The photo thumbnail told me all I needed to know. It was of a guy with dark hair, kissing a girl while holding a joint in one hand. His face was mostly obscured by smoke.

But I knew that side profile—that jawline and that nose. I knew that hair. And those hands.

An ear-splitting crash reverberated around me then. When I looked around for the source, I spotted the remains of my empty cup covering the dark gray tile floor. My bare feet were surrounded by a glittering sea of pale blue glass. It didn't just break. It shattered.

"Oh my god." Siobhan ran into the kitchen, frantically scanning the room. "I heard you scream. What happened?"

Had I screamed?

Her focus fell to the floor in front of me and she winced. "Are you okay?"

"I—" I shook my head. "The—no."

Shockwaves resonated through my brain. Nothing made sense. Why didn't he tell me?

Still clutching my phone, I lifted one foot and started for the hall.

"No, don't move." She held up a hand as she skirted the edges of the mess, surveying how far the shards had traveled. "There's glass everywhere. Let me clean this up first."

My stomach balled into a fist. "There's a video, Shiv."

"What video?" She glanced up, confused.

"Chase." I tried to verbalize what happened and failed. "There's a video."

Dallas rushed through the doorway. "Shit." He froze, blue eyes wide. "Where's the broom?"

"There's a brush and dustpan in the hall closet. Can you grab the vacuum too?" Shiv turned back to me. "Just stay put. Let me sweep it up so Dal can vacuum."

A moment later, Dallas returned with the necessary supplies. He handed the brush and dustpan to Shiv once she'd gathered up the larger pieces. Shiv kneeled and swept shards of glass into the dustpan.

The room threatened to turn sideways while I stood glued to the spot, drawing in shallow breaths. Everything turned a little fuzzy, my vision tunneling gray at the outer edges.

My phone rang in my hand. The minute I saw it wasn't Chase's number, I hit Decline. It rang again, and I sent it straight to voice mail. It immediately blew up with a slew of texts and non-stop incoming calls. Derek, Zara, Noelle, their names on the readout blurred. I hit Decline over and over, not even checking the display any longer. Finally, I responded to my brother and best friends so they knew I was okay but told them that I couldn't talk. Then I switched my phone into Do Not Disturb.

As Siobhan swept up the larger pieces, I caught Dallas's eye. "Did you know about the video?"

His face fell. "Uh…"

"Dallas," I pleaded, desperation rising to the surface. "Please tell me what's going on."

"If there's anything like that floating around, it's old. From well before Carter met you. That's all I can say."

I nodded slowly. What Dallas was saying made sense—in the photo, Chase's hair was longer than I'd ever seen it. But that wasn't my main concern. Why hadn't Chase told me? Did he know it was about to leak?

Then it hit me. He did know. And that was why he'd ended our relationship.

The dull ache in my heart turned into a searing, stabbing pain.

Did he think I wouldn't love him anymore?

How alone must he have felt to do something like that?

"What video?" Shiv asked, turning to him as she stood.

Dallas shook his head, giving her a terse look.

"Bailey." She gasped, her attention fixed on my feet. "You're bleeding."

"Huh?" I followed her gaze. Sure enough, a pool of crimson had formed beneath my left heel. "Oh."

"Do you need help bandaging it up?"

"No, I can get it. Once I get out of here."

Dallas switched on the vacuum, and it hummed to life. Once he'd created a clear pathway, I hopped over to the paper towels on one foot and grabbed a sheet for my cut and another for the floor. A bottle of all-purpose cleaner I'd retrieved from the cabinet in one hand, I kneeled and sprayed down the tile. At least the blood hadn't gotten into the grout. The literal only silver lining to my week.

With a piece of paper towel awkwardly wrapped around my heel, I opened the cupboard under the sink and stashed the bottle of cleaner, then threw the used paper towels in the garbage.

Keeping my weight on my uninjured foot, I straightened and faced Dallas and Siobhan. All I could think of was getting to Chase.

"Is Chase home?"

"Should be," Dallas said. "Hasn't gone anywhere besides practice and school." He scratched the back of his neck. "Hasn't really gone to those, either. Hasn't been in a great state of mind since…everything."

"Can someone take me to see him, please?"

Shiv gestured to us with an open palm. "You two go. I'll finish cleaning up."

A hush fell. From opposite sides of the room, Shiv and Dallas exchanged a silent look. She widened her eyes at him, as if to urge him into action.

Dallas hesitated for a beat, dark brow furrowed, and scrubbed a hand down his face. “Right. Uh, I can. I just need to—”

A knock at the door interrupted us. Shiv frowned, walking over and looking through the peephole. She turned back to face us.

“It’s Chase.”

CHAPTER 57
THE REASON
BAILEY

MY BRAIN WAS SCRAMBLING to catch up. "Chase?" I asked.

I thought I'd have time on the drive over to compose my thoughts, formulate the right things to say, and plan how to say them.

Right now, I was reeling. Like I was standing in the aftermath of a high-speed collision, surveying the damage left behind. Smoke in the air, broken glass on the ground, and horns still blaring. Learning about the video, Chase seemingly having known about it but not telling me, Luke sending it to my friends and family—and god knows who else—was giving me mental whiplash.

Protectiveness gripped me, laced with an undercurrent of sour guilt. No matter what animosity existed between the two of them before, there was no denying that it escalated sharply after Chase and I got together. Did Luke circulate that video because I provoked him in our conversation just now? Was he punishing Chase because he was angry with me? I ground my molars as a dizzying anger ignited. It was the lowest of the low, even for Luke.

Placing a hand on the counter to steady myself, I opened my mouth, but I closed it again without speaking. Words failed me. A million things both did and didn't make sense. Siobhan stood by the door, offering me an encouraging look as she waited for my direction. Slowly, my ability to think rebooted.

"Can you let him in?" I nodded to the bathroom behind me and hobbled in that direction, trying to keep from smearing blood on the beige carpet. "I need to put a Band-Aid on this cut."

"Sure," she said. "We were about to head out, anyway. To get, uh, some late dinner. Right, Dal?"

His light blue eyes flicked over to her, and he nodded. "Right."

It was a blatant lie. They'd planned to stay in to have a movie marathon with *Murder Mayhem* films one through five. She'd stocked up on snacks, and they were both in veg mode. Her long espresso hair was piled into a messy bun, and instead of contacts, she was wearing her tortoiseshell glasses, which she never wore outside the house. Plus, Dallas was in gray sweats. And Dallas didn't wear sweats in public.

I was essentially evicting them with zero notice, but I appreciated the privacy, especially when I had no idea why Chase was here. We were either about to make up…or end things for good. Every fiber of my being hoped I was right and that he'd broken things off so abruptly because of the video, but I wouldn't know until we talked.

I was scared to get my hopes up, and I refused to assume or take anything for granted.

As I shut the bathroom door behind me, the deadbolt rattled and the front door creaked open. From the front of the apartment, there was a hushed exchange between Chase and Dallas, but all I caught was one of the guys saying "fuck."

With trembling hands, I fumbled around in the first aid kit, tearing open a new box of Band-Aids and rummaging around for the right size. My thoughts circled back to the video, and a sick feeling swirled in the pit of my stomach. I had been terrified when I thought the rumored video might have had to do with me because of Luke. Now that it was real and about Chase, I was devastated. More than anything, I wished I could make it go away for him.

By the time I stepped out of the bathroom, Dallas and Shiv were gone. Chase was leaning against the wall beside the kitchen, frowning at his phone with his jaw tightly set. He was so preoccupied that he didn't notice me watching him.

I drank in the sight of him from head to toe, like he was water and I was dying of thirst. Tall frame, rumpled hair, perfect profile. But beneath that, when I looked a little closer, his face was drawn, his normally golden-toned skin was wan, and his posture was stiff.

A wave of heartache and longing crashed over me, bringing with it the inexplicable urge to smile and cry all at once. All I wanted was to be in his arms with my face buried in his neck. To touch him, kiss him, breathe him in.

I drew in a slow inhale to steady myself, taking a few tentative strides in his direction. "Hi."

Chase locked his phone and slid it into his back pocket. He looked up, and when our eyes met, my heart slammed into my ribcage. The sorrow in his expression made me ache. I froze on the spot, halfway across the room from him. A handful of steps were all that separated us, but the distance was like a chasm.

He ran a hand through his coffee-brown hair, expression pained. "I tried to call you."

I glanced down at my phone, unlocked the screen, and scrolled through the missed call log. He did. Six times.

"Sorry, my ringer was off. I wasn't avoiding you."

"That video," he said. "It's old. From before—"

"I know."

His throat bobbed, and his dark eyes lingered on me uncertainly. We regarded one another for a few heartbeats, my pulse escalating with each second that passed, but neither of us moved. Then, finally, adrenaline surged through my veins, kickstarting me into action. Heart pounding in my chest, I took a step, followed by another, and came to stand before him.

I didn't have a plan. Didn't have one when I'd asked Dallas to take me to see him, other than forcing a conversation. But right now, I didn't want to talk.

I wanted him.

Strong jawline tense, Chase watched me, cautious hope mingled with fear on his face. With a final step, I stood before him, chin tipped so I could study him. Beneath his black shirt, his broad chest moved up and down with each breath. Neither of us reached out to bridge the remaining gap between us. Only then did I notice the dark circles under his eyes, which matched the ones beneath my own. It had only been a handful of days, but we both looked like we hadn't slept in weeks.

Everything hurt.

We weren't supposed to be apart.

I rested my hands on his muscular shoulders, and he blinked slowly, letting out a small shudder at the contact. His cologne wafted over me, soothing me while simultaneously feeding my heartache. He was solid and heavy beneath my fingertips, the warmth of his body radiating through his cotton T-shirt. Just touching him again was a gift.

I drew in a jagged breath. "Carter." Hot tears welled in my eyes, nearly overflowing.

Now that he was here in front of me, I could breathe again, but it also made the contrast of missing him that much worse. I needed him. He was my home, my heart, my person.

"I'm sorry, James." Chase pressed his forehead to mine. "So fucking sorry."

He cupped my face and caressed my cheek with the pad of his thumb. I closed my eyes, fighting to hold back the gasping sobs that threatened to break through.

"I missed you," he murmured. "I couldn't sleep. Couldn't eat. Couldn't breathe without you."

At that, my hold on him tightened. "I missed you too."

As we soaked in the feel of one another, the apartment turned so quiet I could hear the heat kick on, warm air whirring through the floor vent beside us. The urge to cry ebbed and flowed, then finally faded away. I opened my eyes after several long moments, pulling back to look at him. Despite my appearance—messy hair, blotchy skin, pajamas—he looked back at me with such softness and reverence that I could almost forget.

His other hand found my waist with a grip so tender he barely grazed the fabric of my gray top. Every movement he made was tinged with uncertainty, like he didn't know whether I wanted him to touch me.

I looped my arms around his neck, drawing him tighter against me, and tilted my head. He did the same, angling closer cautiously. His mouth met mine, soft and tentative. With a sigh, I parted my lips in response, letting his tongue slip inside. Tension melted from my body, replaced by the feeling of completeness.

The kiss said more than words could. Making up for tears, for lost time, for the fear that I would never kiss him like this again.

His grip on my waist dug in as he moved his mouth against mine, deepening the kiss. Heat flooded my body, and the dull ache within me exploded into desperate need. He drew in a deep breath, rough hands sliding beneath my shirt. Somehow, his fingers on my bare skin soothed us both, and the frantic, needy edge to our kissing eased. Lips still together, we slowed, lingering.

Finally, he pulled back, surveying me, his deep brown eyes full of regret. "I'm sorry," he said, stroking my hair. "I love you more than anything in the world."

"I love you, but I need you to tell me what's going on."

Chase nodded, but his apprehensive expression returned. "I will."

Taking him by the hand, I tugged him into the living room. He shuffled to the couch at a glacial pace. For someone who was usually willing to spill anything and everything, the trepidation in every step he took was a marked departure from normal.

We sank onto the cushions, angling our bodies to face one another. Picking up my legs, he tugged them into his lap and pulled me closer to him.

He ran a hand along his jawline, shaking his head. "I don't know where to start."

Instead of continuing like I hoped he would, he looked away and fell silent. Seconds ticked by. Nothing. This was the first time I'd ever seen Chase look scared.

"I don't want to fight." I squeezed his hand, doing my best to keep my expression open and nonthreatening. "I just want to know why you didn't tell me. Did you think I'd be mad at you? Judge you?"

Chase focused his attention on our intertwined hands and shrugged. "Yes and no. I mean, yes. But that wasn't the main problem. I was trying to protect you."

My stomach rolled over as a flood of conflicting feelings surged within me. In all of this, he was trying to protect *me*? Why? And why didn't he talk to me?

"From what?"

"From me and my dumbass decision," he muttered.

"By breaking my heart?"

His expression crumpled, and he buried his face in his palm. "No. By distancing you from this clusterfuck so you don't get dragged down with me."

"You're calling the shots without me again, Carter." The words were harsh, but my tone wasn't.

"Look…" He trailed off. "Did you watch the video?"

"No," I said. Queasiness swirled in my stomach at the very thought. "God, no. I don't plan to."

"You might feel differently once you know what's in it."

CHASE

James beside me, holding my hand. I didn't deserve it, not one bit, but I was so fucking thankful she was here with me.

For now, at least.

"I doubt it." Bailey's brows knit together, her hazel eyes soft. "When did this happen, exactly?"

"Last April." Not even a year ago, though it felt like a lifetime ago. Or another lifetime completely. Like someone else's life. I wished it was.

"That was way before I met you."

"Yeah." I gritted my teeth, searching for the courage to spill the ugly details, but the words stuck in my throat. Would this change the way she saw me forever?

Her expression turned thoughtful. "*The Sideline* had a blind item a while ago about a hockey sex tape, but they said it was someone at Callingwood." Bailey grabbed her phone and navigated to the website. She scanned the screen, her mouth twisting into a frown. "They claimed it was a girl from Callingwood. Didn't say anything about who the other person was, I guess."

"I knew about that, but I wasn't sure if you did." I rubbed her thigh with my free hand, savoring the contact I'd missed so damn much.

She kept her gaze fixed on her phone instead of meeting my eyes when she responded. "I didn't want to bring it up because I was worried it was something Luke did without my knowledge."

My hand froze on her leg. "Oh my god, that would be the end of his sorry life." The very idea made me homicidal. It would have had me taking Vincent up on that hitjob immediately. Or doing it myself.

"Do you think they meant—" Bailey faltered.

Me.

"Maybe," I said. "One of the girls goes to Callingwood."

Her phone slipped out of her hand and landed on the cushion beside her. "*One of them*?" She blinked slowly, shaking her head. "Sorry. I don't mean to sound—to judge—I'm just confused."

"There were two girls in the video, James." I rubbed the back of my neck.

Hearing the words from me might have been worse than watching the video herself. When Dallas said she knew, I thought she'd seen it already.

Then again, if there was a video of her, I wouldn't have been able to stomach watching it.

"Okay." Bailey drew in a shaky breath. "Okay…okay. Can you, um, provide a little context?" She quickly added, "I don't want to know everything. Please don't give me your usual blunt honesty. Can you give me a high-level idea of what happened?"

I let out a long breath. "The video doesn't paint me in the best light. I was fucked up out of my tree, like every year on the anniversary of my dad's death. This girl Nikki and I were fooling around and smoking a joint. And Kristen was there too."

Her brow crinkled. "Nikki? Like Kevin Richmond's girlfriend?"

"Yeah. I didn't know they were together then."

Bailey nodded, her expression neutral and her demeanor far more understanding than I deserved. She watched me silently, so I pushed through the discomfort and forced the words out.

"Then Kristen pulled out her phone and started recording without my permission. I got mad and told her to stop. She said she was just messing around and told me she would erase it. Then she pretended to, but I was too out of it to realize she didn't." What a fucking idiot. How could I not have known?

"So you were violated." Bailey's voice was skate-edge sharp.

"I mean…I guess."

"You were, Chase. Are you hesitant to admit that because you're a guy or because there were three people involved? Do you think you deserved it?" Her gold-flecked eyes searched mine. "You still had the right to privacy."

"That's what I thought. I guess Kristen had other ideas."

"That crazy bitch," she said under her breath. "When did you find out?"

"After our last game. Then I met with Dallas's dad to talk through legal issues. My plan was to bury it and find the courage to tell you once it was taken care of." I swallowed, dread surging.

"But…" she prompted me.

I swallowed hard. This was going to be like dropping a bomb on her head all over again.

According to the texts Vincent sent while I waited for Bailey, it didn't look like Luke had dragged her into things the way he'd threatened to. So far, he'd sent the clip to people she knew simply to make me look bad—and, presumably, to put the final nail in the coffin of our relationship. But that didn't make telling her about how her world nearly got destroyed because of me any easier.

"Luke got a hold of a copy. Told me if I didn't end things with you, he'd send it to your advisors and the scholarship committee and tell them you were the other girl on the tape. Kristen is offscreen in the clip he has. She's just a voice on camera."

Bailey's body turned bolt stiff. "Luke did *what*?" Her eyes widened and her hands balled into fists. "Oh my god, I'm going to kill him *and* Kristen."

I'd never heard Bailey threaten bodily harm to someone else. That probably meant she'd spent too much time with me.

"I finally tracked down the second half of the clip today," I said. "In it, I call Kristen by her name, so everyone would know it wasn't you. There's a time and date stamp in the metadata too, along with the geolocation. That should take the teeth out of his threats regarding you."

She shifted her weight, scooting closer to me, and stroked my face.

"But why didn't you tell me? We could have faked a breakup. We could have figured it out." Her eyes were so wide and full of sadness, expressions so earnest, that another fresh shot of regret hit me. Maybe she was right. But I wasn't thinking clearly, and my only priority was shielding her. The stakes were astronomically high, and I didn't want to gamble with her future.

"I panicked, James. I was afraid Luke would know. I didn't want him to derail everything you'd worked so hard for. Turns out, he had a PI tailing me, so he probably would have found out if we faked it. Plus…" I trailed off and cleared my throat, forcing out the words. "Honestly, I wasn't sure you'd want to be with me once you found out. I thought you would be better off without me and this mess I created." The last part was the hardest to admit, but I wanted to give her the honesty she'd asked for.

"Chase," she said. "You have to know that isn't true. There is no scenario where I am better off without you. Ever."

"Are you sure? Whether or not I agreed to being recorded, there's a video circulating of me getting high while having a threesome. That would be a deal breaker for a lot of people. I would understand if that's how you feel."

It would kill me inside. But I wouldn't blame her. One bit.

"Kristen took advantage of you," Bailey said firmly. "You didn't consent to that. Imagine how you'd react to this situation if I were in your shoes."

I huffed. "I wouldn't be here. I'd be sitting in jail. Literally." I'd have been cuffed and placed in a holding cell within hours of finding out, and the guy would be six feet under.

With her fingers on my jaw, she turned my face to hers and fixed me with a loving gaze, her eyes serious.

"I don't understand how you can see that side of it and not extend the same sympathy to yourself. I love you," she said. "This doesn't change that. You're the same person you were yesterday. Or five minutes ago, for that matter."

The more understanding she was, the worse I felt. "I hope you know I was only trying to protect you."

Bailey nodded slowly. "I see that now, even if I don't agree with your tactics."

"I couldn't live with myself if you lost out on that scholarship because you were connected to me."

"I don't want that scholarship if it means I can't have you. I'll take out student loans. I don't care. That's fixable. Losing you isn't." Her voice wavered, breaking something inside me with it.

"What about the internship? You said it was the kind of thing that could make or break the start of your career."

"There would be others."

"It would still be my fault if you lost this one."

Her brows knit. "First of all, it wouldn't be your fault. And if anyone blames you after what Kristen did, I don't want to be associated with them." Bailey's bottom lip trembled, and she skimmed her fingertips along my cheek. My heart swelled at the love brimming in her eyes. "Those other things are replaceable, Chase. There's only one you. I need you."

"What if this blows up?" I asked. "There's a good chance it'll get even more ugly now. Lawsuits, criminal charges, bad publicity. You know Luke is going to come out swinging. If I get dragged through the mud, I don't want to bring you down with me."

Who knew what other skeletons Luke might unearth. Nothing else would be as damaging as this, but I was sure the laundry list of girls I'd slept with was a bad enough look in and of itself. I wouldn't put it past him to hire people to straight up lie, either.

"Loyal to a fault, remember?" She kissed my cheek. "You're not the only one who's stubborn. If it comes down to it, I'll jump into that mud myself."

CHAPTER 58

AS I AM

CHASE

THE NEXT MORNING, I reluctantly dragged myself out of bed to attend an early morning ice time. After crashing hard and sleeping for the first time in a week, leaving the comfort of Bailey's body beneath warm, cozy blankets was a struggle. I'd regressed to the phase when things were new with us, and I was actively trying not to be a stage-five clinger. Except right now, I wasn't trying to fight it. I was straight-up, unapologetically clinging. I didn't want to let her out of my sight.

With practice finally over, I swung back over to her place to pick her up. Because, again, I was static cling city.

After hopping out to open her door and give her a quick hello kiss, I slid back into the driver's side. We planned to grab an early lunch once we took care of an unpleasant but completely necessary task. Then I'd do my best to forget about everything for a while.

I waited with the truck idling while Bailey buckled her seat belt.

Lifting her chin, she gave me a small smile. "How was practice?"

She was trying a little too hard to sound casual, like it was another ordinary day.

"It was okay."

That was a white lie. Or a big fat lie, rather, because practice was a tire fire. I hadn't been on the ice in almost seven days, and it showed. It had been *years* since I'd gone that long without putting on skates.

To make matters worse, Coach Miller worked me until I nearly keeled over on the ice—probably as payback for my disappearing act. Things went downhill from there when I was hauled into his office afterward and grilled like a goddamn steak over an open flame. Like everyone else in the world, Coach Miller heard about the video, but it was clear he didn't have the whole story. His interrogation was so invasive, I was surprised he didn't a strip search me or stick a needle in my arm right then and there to drug test me for good measure. Though I wouldn't be surprised if I got a call in the next few days for the latter.

He started citing morality clauses, behavior expectations for the school's varsity athletes, and our team's code of conduct. Our conversation made a drastic detour when I explained the non-consensual nature of the tape, and then he was more sympathetic than I'd expected. I cut the conversation short and gave him Stewart's contact information in case he had any more questions. Presumably, dropping the *attorney* word would put the issue to rest with him and the school's administration.

"But are you okay?" Bailey prodded, concern across her face.

I met her gaze briefly before breaking away again and gave a one-shouldered shrug. "Yeah, sure. I'm fine."

Her lips rolled together, making it clear she didn't believe that, but she said nothing. She knew when and when not to push me, and I loved her for that.

Our drive was largely silent, mostly because I was exhausted on every level imaginable. Between having Stewart in my corner and the fact that, frankly, the team needed me, I wasn't overly concerned about my spot on the Falcons roster. Los Angeles was another story. My future for next year was up in the air.

While being on a Division I hockey team was like being under a magnifying glass, playing professionally was like living under a high-performance microscope. The scrutiny was next-level. The media, the public, everyone was constantly all over the athletes. I knew that firsthand from my dad. They camped out in front of our house for weeks after he died, shoving their cameras in our faces and yelling at us, trying to get quotes and soundbites. Vultures. I was having flashbacks to that time with all the attention this tape was getting.

On top of all that, I had mixed feelings about the possibility of staying, but I knew it could have been a lot worse. Realistically, keeping my contract and getting to spend another year with Bailey was the best-case scenario.

Ten minutes sped by like ten seconds, and we arrived at our destination before I was ready. I pulled into a vacant visitor space and switched off the ignition. The squat gray brick building stared back at me through the windshield like an insurmountable mountain.

Apprehension bowled me over, and I set my jaw. My hands stuck to the steering wheel like they were being held in place by an invisible force.

"Chase." Bailey unfastened her seat belt and scooted closer to me. "It'll be all right." She covered my hand with hers, her skin soft and cool against mine. "Stewart said it's straightforward. We'll go in, give our statements, hand over copies of the text messages and recordings, and we'll be done in no time."

"Yeah," I said. "Let's get this over with."

She grabbed her tan purse off the console and held it in her lap, waiting for me. I shifted in my seat but didn't release my death grip on the leather steering wheel. My brain knew I should get out, but my body wouldn't cooperate.

Frustration surged through my veins, further fueled by the unfairness of the situation. Today wouldn't be the end of it by a long shot. This was merely setting the wheels in motion for criminal proceedings to come. Seeking justice meant I would be forced to relive last April and the past week over and over again, like a nightmare stuck on repeat. Worst of all, the minute we filed our reports, Bailey would be dragged even deeper into this mess—the very thing I'd been trying to avoid all along.

In addition, there was the civil suit being spearheaded by Dallas's father. I was going to take Morrison and his trust fund to the fucking cleaners, and then I'd donate all the proceeds to whatever charity he hated most—which was probably any of them, because he was a piece of shit.

Bailey wrapped her arms around my neck and gave me a squeeze. I turned my head and buried my face in her hair, inhaling her familiar scent. My anxiety lowered a notch, and my breathing deepened, resuming a more normal pattern.

"I got you," she murmured.

"I know." And I was lucky for it.

Curled up under a blanket on the couch in my living room, we idly watched the New York vs. Boston game. It was in sudden-death overtime, but I couldn't garner even an ounce of excitement. It had been less than twenty-four hours, but the video had already exploded all over the internet. Luke had been muzzled a few hours too late, and the genie was out of the bottle.

I hadn't even talked to my mom yet. At the rate things were going, she'd hear about it herself—which would be so much worse —if I didn't tell her soon. Still, it was a conversation I sorely did not want to have.

Bailey leaned forward, bracing her hands on her knees. "Holy crap. Did you see that shot? That was insane."

"Huh?" I said absently. "Oh, yeah. Crazy."

With that goal, the game was over. I had no idea what had happened or who'd won. My mind kept circling back to how things had gone down today.

Stewart's firm was working overtime on damage control, sending menacing cease and desist letters to companies and individuals, contacting search engines to have it de-indexed in their databases, and dealing directly with hosting providers to have the content removed, but it was like a goddamn game of whack-a-mole. And all that did nothing to stop the copies circulating privately via text message and social media.

Everyone knew my business. And I do mean *everyone*. My

phone had been inundated with a steady stream of calls and texts from people I hadn't spoken to in ages or had never spoken to in the first place. I'd have to change my number first thing in the morning. I hadn't logged into social media, either, and I was considering deleting my accounts without even checking.

At least Derek had been understanding once Bailey confirmed that I didn't cheat on her with two girls. After she explained, he was almost as angry as I was. According to him, Luke had been placed on an indefinite suspension from the team. It was a small victory, but at this point, I'd take any I could get, no matter the size.

The biggest positive was that Luke hadn't dragged Bailey into it like he'd threatened—maybe his parents reined him in before he could, or maybe it had been an empty threat all along. Either way, I was thankful as hell.

Still, Bailey would be known as the girlfriend of *that guy* from now on. While she insisted that she didn't care, *I did.*

She wordlessly grabbed the remote and turned the volume down. Then she climbed onto my lap, straddling me, and ducked her head. When she failed to catch my eye, she poked my abs.

"Carter."

I gave in eventually and looked up at her, sulking.

Her pupils dilated and her expression softened. "I wish you saw yourself the way I see you."

Despite my crappy mood, I couldn't fight back the smile. "Now you're stealing my lines?"

"Maybe." She tipped closer. The cherry-vanilla of her lip balm drifted over as she brushed her lips against mine. "But it's true. I think you're pretty great."

At the moment, I felt like a million things. Great wasn't one of them.

"You're a little biased, James."

Bailey flattened a palm against my chest. My heart drummed against her hand, the pervasive tension in my body easing with each beat. She'd had that effect on me from the day I met her, like a superpower meant for me only.

"You saying my opinion doesn't count?" Lips parted, she

watched me. In the moment, she looked perfect. I couldn't believe she was mine. I didn't know how I got so lucky, but I'd do everything in my power to keep her.

"Of course it does, but..." I didn't have a response that didn't make me sound like a dick. Obviously, her opinion counted. But she was wrong in this case.

She traced my jawline with the pad of her thumb, studying my face intently. "My opinion counts the most, because I know who you are inside." Her hazel eyes held mine, patterned with a kaleidoscope of green and gold I knew by heart. "You've been nothing but patient and kind with me. No one has ever made me feel cared for the way you do."

At least I got one thing right.

"Of course," I said, rubbing her lower back. "I love you. I think part of me always knew I would."

I never cared about anything before Bailey—not even myself. I was sort of existing. Coasting through life on autopilot, playing hockey, half-assing school, and getting fucked up every weekend. I figured that was it until the league. Even then, I'd probably have done the same thing, just with a bigger budget.

Her breath snagged, and her eyes glittered with unshed tears. She looked up, trying to blink them away.

"Dammit." Guilt swirled in my stomach. "I didn't mean to make you cry." I grabbed a tissue from the box on the end table and handed it to her.

Bailey sobbed a laugh, dabbing at her eyes. "It's not the bad kind of crying. But it's messing with my attempt to seduce you."

"I'll stop talking." I sat back. "Seduce away." I wasn't worthy, would never be worthy. But I wasn't dumb enough to argue with that.

"Yeah?" Her lips curled into a lopsided grin that was somehow sexy and adorable all at once. Damn, I loved those lips. I wanted to kiss them for the rest of my life.

"Hell yeah."

We'd been so tired the night before that we fell into a near-coma without even having makeup sex. At this point, I wanted her so bad it hurt. Literally. And having her on top of me was compounding that significantly.

I missed her. Needed her. Loved her.

Eyelids heavy, Bailey tilted her head, and her mouth met mine, soft and sweet. A rush ran through my body, and everything clicked back into place.

I drew in a breath, deepening the kiss, and she parted her lips for me, her slender fingers digging into my shoulders. With my hands on the soft, bare skin of her waist, I pulled a soft sigh from her. Then I was sliding under her tank top and exploring her body like it was the first time. Savoring every smooth inch beneath my fingers, every curve beneath my palms—shoulders, breasts, stomach, hips.

I slid my hands down to grip her from behind and pulled her tighter. She fit in my hold perfectly, fit against my body perfectly, like she always did. Letting out a small moan, she moved against me and sent a surge of pleasure through my body. My craving for her kicked into overdrive in response. Suddenly, I was torn between the frantic need to touch her, taste her, claim every part of her, and the desire to draw it out and make up for lost time. More than anything, I wanted to be close to her, to have her body pressed up against mine with nothing between us.

Bailey ground against me again, and I grabbed the hem of her tank top and slid it up her torso.

She froze. "Roommates?" It was a breath against my lips.

"Good point." Dallas was at the girls' apartment, but I had no idea what Ty's plans were. I ducked my head and planted a kiss on the hollow of her neck. "Let's go upstairs."

CHAPTER 59
FOR YOU
BAILEY

WE BLINDLY STARTED up the stairs, mouths locked together and hands groping in a frantic, needy blur. Mistakenly thinking I had reached the landing, I took a step backward and nearly lost my balance on the final stair.

Chase's hand flew to my lower back, steadying me before I fell. He chuckled quietly, breaking our kiss.

"Still clumsy," he said. "And as adorable as always."

"Or maybe you have me flustered." Flustered was putting it mildly—I was overcome. My level of desire had sped off the charts, like he'd floored the gas pedal and cut the brakes at the same time. It hadn't been long, but being without him was torture.

"That's the goal." With his hands spanning my waist, he squeezed me, his tone teasing. "Without the falling down part, that is."

With another, more careful step, we reached the top of the staircase, and Chase steered me toward his bedroom, then slammed the door behind us. He tugged my soft pink sweater over my head and tossed it aside, then spun me around. My shoulders hit the bedroom door, and I drew in a breath as its cool surface pressed against my skin.

"Got a thing for doors, Carter?" I peered up at him, biting back a smile. “There’s a bit of a theme going on here. Car doors, bedroom doors…”

He grinned. “I can’t help it if they’re the perfect thing to pin you against.”

The air was pulled from my lungs as his lips crashed down on mine again. He kissed me like it was the first time, like it was the last time, like we were the only people in existence. I lost myself in him, my yearning intensifying with every sweep of his tongue.

He crushed me against the door with his broad frame, curving his hands down the small of my back and splaying them to grip me roughly from behind. With my palms under the hem of his black T-shirt, I soaked up the heat of his smooth skin. Now that I had my hands on him, I couldn’t stop touching. I was making up for lost time, my fingertips greedily mapping every inch of firm muscle. He was solid under my touch, heavy and immovable.

Still pressed against me, he nimbly unfastened my jeans, then took a step back only to peel them down past my hips, leaving me in nothing but a pale yellow lace bralette and panty set. The bralette had thin straps and plunged to a deep V in the front, and the underwear was little more than a flimsy scrap of fabric.

“Fuck me,” he murmured, more to himself than to me. His gaze flicked back up to meet mine, his mouth tugging into a wolfish smile. “Is this new?”

With his fingertips, he traced my hipbone, skimming beneath the delicate material. Goose bumps popped up in the wake of his touch, my body crying out for his hands to move lower.

“Sure is.” I’d bought the set two weeks before, and it had sat in my drawer waiting to be put to good use. A few days ago, I wasn’t sure it ever would be. I’d never been so happy to be wrong.

Chase let out a low rumble of approval, his attention lingering on my body. “It’s hot.”

He walked his fingers up my stomach, stopping momentarily at the band of my bra, then continuing higher. With my nipples between his thumbs and index fingers, he pinched them gently through the pale yellow fabric. They hardened beneath his touch, the need growing between my legs. All his attention—and he knew *exactly* how to work me—had me two seconds away from melting into a puddle.

"This too." He slid the straps of the bralette off my shoulders. "Very sexy. Going to look great on my floor." He slid his hand behind my back and unfastened the clasp, then let it fall to my feet. With both hands, he skimmed the sides of my ribcage and palmed my bare breasts. "God, you're so perfect."

With a hand behind my back, he turned us around and took a few steps, then eased me onto his bed. He placed a soft kiss on my lips before standing up and relieving himself of his clothing.

I swallowed and scanned his body leisurely, marveling at every sculpted inch of mouth-watering perfection. Planes of muscle beneath smooth, perfect skin. V-shaped indents in his torso that I wanted to sink my teeth into. And a light trail of hair leading to the waistband of his black boxer briefs, which barely contained his erection. Liquid heat pooled between my legs, my impatience growing by the second.

Chase cocked a brow, his lips forming a smirk. "Are you checking me out, James?"

Checking out, ogling, gawking, in giddy disbelief that he was mine. Same thing.

"Absolutely." My voice was breathy.

He kneeled on the bed, the mattress dipping beneath his weight. Once he'd settled between my legs, he hovered over me, his muscular arms fencing me in. His fresh, clean fragrance invaded my senses, comforting me and stoking the inferno within me all at once. I'd never felt so crazed and so calm at the same time.

Chase tucked a strand of hair behind my ear. "I missed you, baby."

"I missed you more."

The days we'd spent apart felt like an eternity—likely because I was scared it would be an actual eternity. Thinking back on it made my heart ache all over again, even with him here on top of me.

"Impossible," he murmured, planting a kiss below my ear. Goose bumps formed on my upper arms in response. He dragged his lips down my skin and landed on my collarbone, placing another soft kiss. "I'm sorry I was in a bad mood earlier."

My heart tugged. After what he'd been through, apologizing was the last thing he needed to do.

"Don't apologize. There's a lot going on," I said. "I understand."

"Good news is, I feel better now." He curled his fingers around the waistband of my underwear and slowly dragged them down. I lifted my hips slightly, helping him pull them off, and he set them aside.

"Because you've got me naked?" I whispered.

He pulled himself upright and kneeled before me, his eyes blazing a path down my body. "Because I'm with you."

Our gazes met, and his expression turned tender, his lips tugging into a smile.

Despite how exhausted I was after the past few days—and how tired I looked, based on what I saw in the bathroom mirror earlier—I felt beautiful because of the way he was looking at me. Because of the way always looked at me.

Reverently.

Chase grabbed the backs of my thighs, pulling me down so I was wrapped even more tightly around his body. The only thing separating us was the single layer of his boxer briefs. Once upon a time, I would have felt self-conscious, exposed. But right now, all I felt was wanted in the best possible way.

He nuzzled my neck and drew in a slow, indulgent inhale. "Have you noticed that we fit together perfectly?"

I pressed back against the pillow and sank my fingers into his silky hair, tugging gently. He hummed quietly in response, a smile breaking out against the skin over my clavicle.

"Mm-hmm." I nodded. "Almost like it's a sign."

"Oh, it's definitely a sign."

Chase clasped my hands in his and guided them over my head. Strong fingers handcuffed my wrists, pinning my hands to the mattress. I wriggled against his grip in mock resistance, but he didn't give an inch.

"Red?" He eyed me, expression playful.

"Green."

He leaned closer, and our lips came together again in a brief, chaste kiss.

"Bright green," I added, lifting up an inch and kissing him again. "Or dark green. Whatever the greenest green is."

Chase huffed a low, husky laugh, but then he furrowed his brow, his expression going serious. Shifting his weight, he dropped his chin and let out a cross between a growl and a sigh.

"What's wrong?"

"Nothing. At all." He shook his head and peered up at me, flashing me an utterly devastating smile. "Just have some conflicting feelings."

"Why?"

Chase pulled my hand up to his lips, kissing my fingertips. "Because on the one hand, I want to take my time with you." He grinned, sinking the softest of bites into my index finger. "But I also want to bend you over and fuck you into the mattress."

I could see his dilemma—both of those options sounded highly appealing. Part of me wanted him to go slow, to be loving and gentle. The other part wanted to be claimed, taken, his.

"I vote both."

"Yeah?" His eyes danced.

"Yeah." My voice turned breathy. "Definitely both."

"We do have all night."

He captured my mouth with his, then drew in a ragged breath and fisted my hair at my nape and tugged. I let out a whimper, and a fireworks display of desire went off in my body in response. His tongue swept deeper into my mouth, working with an intentional precision that reminded me of all the other things his mouth could do.

His other hand traveled past my waistband but came to a stop at my stomach. The flutter between my legs intensified, growing into a delicious, agonizing throb. Heat flooded my veins, and my skin grew feverish despite the cool air of the room.

Chase's eyes turned midnight dark as I dragged my fingers down the stacked muscle of his torso. I continued my travels until I reached beneath the waistband of his boxer briefs. Pulling his hand from my stomach, he helped me work them down his hips. I grabbed the hard length of him, eliciting a low groan from the back of his throat.

He returned the favor by sliding his fingers against my slick entrance. I drew in a soft gasp, a shimmering veil of pleasure falling over me. He slid one finger inside me, then another, and stroked me in a slow, tortuously divine pattern. Whimpering, I tightened my grip on him, causing him to utter another feral sound in response.

It quickly turned into a game of who could tease the other person most, and he was winning.

A shiver ran through my body, causing my legs to tremble. "You're such a tease." His touch had me so intoxicated, my words left me with a slur.

"I know," he said, voice husky. "I love teasing you. But right now, I need to be inside you."

"Yes," I sobbed. My hips swayed against his hand as another needy sound escaped me. "Please. I need you."

"I love you." He dipped his head and placed a kiss on the hollow of my throat. "More than you'll ever know."

"I love you."

We collided again, lips searing together, breathing the same air. My body buzzed with anticipation. I was desperate for his skin against mine, the feeling of him inside me, the way he sounded when he said my name when he was on the brink.

When he pressed into me, we both drew in a breath. A paradoxical mix of relief and longing coursed through me at the sensation being of filled by him. He came to a halt, and I shifted beneath him impatiently, encouraging him to move.

Chase pressed his temple to mine, his inhalations and exhalations shallow. "Give me a sec," he said, laughing a little. "I was already way too fucking turned on going into this."

I smoothed my hands up and down his shoulders, giving him time to compose himself. After a few seconds, he pulled out partway and thrust back into me, nudging the perfect spot only he'd ever found. A strong dose of pleasure shut my brain down completely. All that existed was this moment. His body in mine, us together.

The pressure in my core started to build immediately, turning everything a little hazy. I matched his movements, the two of us falling into a perfect rhythm.

"I could do this all day." Chase rocked against me again, deeper, pulling a soft moan from my lips. "Especially when you make sounds like that."

With his next thrust, pleasure overtook me. I closed my eyes and sank my teeth into my bottom lip, giving in to the sensation. He stilled again, and I forced my lids to flutter open, finding him studying my face, dark brown eyes serious.

"Are you mine, James?"

My chest tightened, and the deluge of feelings that hit me had nothing to do with sex.

"Completely," I said. "Are you mine?" I cupped his square jaw.

He leaned against my hand, his expression softening, the tenderness only I got to see shining in his eyes. "For as long as you'll have me."

"You're going to be stuck with me for a long time, then."

I let out a gasp as he flexed his hips, sending off another surge of pleasure.

"That's the idea." His voice was strained.

Chase moved one hand beneath my thigh, lifting me off the bed slightly. The angle made everything intensify a thousandfold. He hit the right spot again, making my back arch and my lungs take in a sharp, involuntary breath. With each rolling thrust, I drew closer and closer to oblivion.

I whimpered, scrambling to pull him tighter against me. "I'm so close."

"Fuck." Chase growled. "Me too."

Reaching up, he slid a hand to the side of my neck. He ducked his head, grazing my ear with his lips, his warm breath fanning my skin. "Be good and come for me first."

His words alone nearly sent me over the edge. I tensed around him, digging my nails into his back as he thrust again, causing everything but him and the way he worked himself over me to fade. He moved against me relentlessly, over and over, until I was a babbling, squirming mess.

The sensations became too much, too intense, too pleasurable. A string of words left my lips that might have been a prayer or plea, I wasn't sure. All I knew was that if he stopped, I'd die. It made no sense, but I knew it with a certainty.

"*Chase*."

Just as the world around us exploded, I looked up and locked eyes with him.

He slammed against me, his body shaking in release before falling still. With a groan, he collapsed, draping his heavy body on top of mine. His heartbeat hammered against his ribcage so hard I could feel it against my own.

"You're too hot." Chase buried his face in my hair spread out on the pillow. "That should have lasted way longer."

"No way. That was perfect. I love when we finish together." I ran my hands up and down his arms, tracing the defined swells of his muscles.

He huffed a low laugh and kissed my cheek. "It is a good way to go."

After another beat, we reluctantly pulled apart, and I darted to the bathroom to clean up. When I returned, he was sitting up against the headboard with the sheet draped low around his waist. I stepped closer, and he tugged me back into bed, wrapping his warm body around me.

Soft lips landed on my shoulder and traveled up the curve of my neck. I sighed, melting against his body. His rough, warm palm smoothed down the side of my ribs, to my upper thigh, and back again. Suddenly, he paused, releasing his hold on me.

"Look at me for a sec."

I rose onto my forearm and turned to face him. His fingers bracketed my jaw, tilting up my chin. Something that looked like worry skirted his face for a split second.

"Losing you would have been the biggest mistake of my life," he said. "I'm never letting you go again."

"Perfect. Then I'll never have to leave this bed. It's comfy."

It really was. Plush duvet, crisp sheets, pillows that were a perfect mix of fluffy and firm. The company was a bonus too. Hell, I'd have slept on the ground as long as I was with him.

His expression shifted, and he gave me a mischievous half smile. "That aligns nicely with my plans for round two. And maybe round three later tonight, after some food."

"At that rate, I won't be able to walk tomorrow."

"Also part of the plan to keep you in my bed. Can't leave if you can't walk."

I nestled into the crook of his neck, breathing in his scent. A low, satisfied hum rumbled in his chest.

I closed my eyes, relishing in the comfort he always brought me. When I opened them again, my gaze fell to his phone where it sat on the nightstand. The small spiderweb crack in the corner was gone. "Is that a new phone?"

"Yeah," he said. "Broke the old one."

I peered up at him. "Dropped it?" Maybe I wasn't the only clumsy one.

"Uh..." Chase trailed off, looking sheepish. "Threw it against a wall, actually."

I raised my eyebrows, waiting for him to elaborate. I'd never seen him lose his temper and take it out on an inanimate object like that. It was difficult to imagine.

He shrugged. "Told you. I have a low tolerance for frustration, which includes being apart from you."

CHAPTER 60

EASY LOVE

BAILEY

I LEANED against a pillar in Northview Arena's concourse, waiting for Chase to come out of the dressing room while excited Falcons fans poured out the doors, chatting excitedly about the three-one win. One of the goals had been Chase's—luckily, his time off during his suspension hadn't hurt his game any.

Coincidentally, Chase's first game back was at home and against none other than Callingwood. The game was significantly less dramatic than previous matches between the two schools, mostly because Luke was gone. Within a few days of the video leak, his parents flew up and hauled his sorry ass back to Texas. Apparently, they had to make a deal with the district attorney to get permission for him to leave the state.

With his departure, an invisible weight had lifted off my shoulders. I hadn't realized how keyed up I was about the ever-present chance of running into him until it was no longer a possibility.

Derek told me there were rumors Luke's parents had him working at one of the fast-food restaurants they'd invested in. It was poetic justice, given how Luke looked down on service jobs. That was in addition to being expelled from Callingwood and essentially shunned by the NHL. No team would even talk to him.

Kristen was gone too—suspended indefinitely, which would surely turn into an expulsion after her hearing.

The scandal was slowly losing its legs, probably because Stewart's team had been relatively successful in tamping down on the video. Over the past week, things had started to return to normal. Today almost felt like an ordinary day. Almost.

None of it erased the pain, but it was a start.

Scanning the lobby, I found a vacant red bench and made my way over to it. I checked my phone for a status update from Shiv, who was at home scrambling to finish a sociology paper due at midnight. She was the queen of procrastination. It had to be an incredibly stressful way to live, but her grades were solid, so I guess it worked for her. I, on the other hand, would have flunked out of college and been committed for a nervous breakdown if I tried that strategy.

Her latest text reported that she was nearly done and would commence packing for our weekend trip to Dallas's parents' cabin shortly. How she'd managed to write a ten-page paper in one day, I'd never know.

I strongly suspected Shiv wasn't a light packer, though, and that it would be a while before she and Dallas were ready to leave.

I glanced up just as Derek rounded the corner. His gaze fell on me, his expression brightening. Locking my phone, I pushed to stand and met him in the crowd.

"Hey," I said. "How was your first game as captain?"

The minute Luke got in trouble for the video debacle, he implicated Paul. It wasn't clear whether Paul had been involved or whether Luke was shirking responsibility. Derek had been asked to step in and assume Luke's previous role.

"Good." Derek shrugged. "Team is still adjusting, but we're pulling through. The energy is a lot less toxic, uh, now that he's gone."

I didn't doubt that.

"You guys played well, considering all the upheaval."

"Yeah, not bad." Derek gave me a half-hearted smile. His warm brown eyes scanned my face, and his mouth twisted into a frown that was eerily reminiscent of our father. "I wanted to apologize again, though." He rubbed the back of his neck and cleared his throat. "I was wrong."

Hold up. I blinked, doing a double- and triple-take. Derek admitting to being wrong? And apologizing? Hell had officially frozen over.

"About what?"

Of course I already knew, but I'd make him say it anyway.

"Carter," he said. "You were right; he's good to you. You seem happy."

Happy was an understatement.

"Crazy happy." A goofy grin broke out across my face. I couldn't even attempt to hide it. "He's my person."

"That's great, B."

I nudged him with my foot. "You'll find your person someday."

Someone bumped into me from behind, jostling me slightly. Derek grabbed my elbow and steadied me, giving me an uncharacteristically bashful smile.

"Actually, it is getting kind of serious with this girl Kim I've been seeing."

My mouth dropped open. "Shut up. And you've been hiding this? When do I get to meet her?"

"Whenever you want." He shrugged. He was making an effort to seem casual, but it was obvious that he was nervous.

"Tomorrow? Name a place and time." I laced my fingers together, stretching out my hands and rolling my shoulders. "I'll bring a list of questions. I have to play the role of protective little sister."

Derek laughed. "Think you've got that backward."

"Nope." I shook my head. "After Jill, I want to be sure this one is legit. Or she'll have to answer to me."

I was still grinning at my brother when Chase strolled up from the other direction and threw an arm around my shoulders. He was running hot like a furnace on full blast, like he always did after games, and the comforting warmth of his body radiated through his dress shirt.

"It's true," Chase said. "James is pretty terrifying."

Derek pursed his lips and looked off into the distance, pretending to give it some thought. "Well, she did have a biting phase in preschool."

Oh my god. It was one time. Jenny Martin started it when she stole my Barbie and shoved me to the ground. I was merely defending myself.

Okay, maybe I escalated the level of aggression a little. I was four, after all.

Chase squeezed my shoulders, barely fighting back laughter. "You don't say."

"I'm going to kill you, Derek." I narrowed my eyes at him, then at Chase.

Chase straightened his expression, feigning innocence, but it was futile. I could see the gears turning in Chase's brain.

"No. Nope. Nuh-uh," I said. "Don't think you two are going to get chummy and start to conspire against me."

Chase winked. "Too late."

"Oh, it's definitely happening," Derek said.

"Absolutely not."

Clearly, I'd have to become friendly with Derek's new girlfriend and exact my revenge.

"Does this mean you can show me old pictures of her now?" Chase rubbed his chin thoughtfully. "Specifically, the ones from junior high? She's never let me see any of those; claims they're too embarrassing."

And for good reason. I had braces, acne, and the worst haircut known to girlkind. My hair was cut in a blunt bob above the shoulders, and the natural waves made it stick out at the ends like a triangle. As far as I was concerned, pictures from that time period should be disposed of permanently—preferably with fire.

I'd seen Chase's childhood photos, and he'd *never* had an awkward phase. He went from adorable chubby baby to cute toddler to nice-looking kid to hot teenager. It was patently unfair, and quite honestly, it seemed impossible. *Everyone* had an awkward phase; that's what kept people humble.

Then again, the lack of one explained a lot about Chase.

"I'll kill you both," I threatened.

Derek excused himself to catch up with his team, and Chase dipped his head, nuzzling my cheek with his nose. "You can bite me any time you want."

CHASE

With my arm still around Bailey's shoulders, we navigated through the parking lot over to my truck. I held the door open, waiting for her to climb in, feeling lighter than I had in days. Maybe weeks. I was back on the ice, we'd won our game, and now Bailey and I were heading out of town to spend the weekend with Dallas and Siobhan at his parents' cabin.

My plans consisted of doing sweet, sweet nothing aside from eating, drinking, and trying to convince James to skinny dip in the hot tub with me. The cabin was in the middle of nowhere, so neighbors weren't an issue. And we could make a schedule or something with Dallas and Shiv, right? Book some time slots?

"What's their cabin like?" Bailey asked, buckling her seat belt.

I pulled out of the parking space and braked to let a group of Falcons fans pass. Their faces were painted crimson. It was awesome. I loved super fans.

"More of a mansion than a cabin, to be honest. Four bedrooms and five bathrooms, I think. It backs up to the lake, sick hot tub. You know, the works."

Their "weekend getaway" home was ten times nicer than the house we lived in. And our place was pretty damn nice.

"Why am I not surprised?" She laughed, then her expression turned wistful. "Ah, to be rich."

If I had it my way, she'd at least be comfortable someday. If she ever let me pay for things. It was still a battle with her most days. At this rate, I'd be stuffing money under her pillow like the fucking tooth fairy.

I signaled left out of the parking lot. "Ward texted and said Shiv was going to take a quick shower before they headed out too."

"Really?" Bailey groaned. We both knew there was no way she'd be showering alone. And their two-person showers weren't exactly quick or water-conserving. "She hasn't even finished packing yet. You said it's, what, a two-hour drive? They'll be a while."

Bailey was right—we planned to make dinner once we were all there. Their scheduling would make for a late evening, but that meant more time for the two of us alone.

"Looks like we have time to kill." I put my hand on her knee. "Want to take a little detour along the way?"

Bailey eyed me suspiciously. "Are you still trying to get truck sex?"

That wasn't my original plan. *But if she was offering…*

"I'm always trying to get truck sex, but I was thinking hot chocolate."

Half an hour later, we made our way up the staircase to End of the World with two cups of salted caramel hot chocolate in hand. Naturally, I had converted Bailey to the only appropriate flavor choice. Though her blowjobs were better than the salted caramel by a mile.

It was a brisk, chilly day and no one else was around, which afforded us our choice of benches. We grabbed the one with the best view, but the instant we got settled, my phone vibrated from inside my coat pocket. I pulled it out, expecting it to be Ward, but it was his father instead.

Bailey stared at my phone. I swiped the screen and put Stewart on speaker. It was easier than giving Bailey a replay after.

"Hi, Stewart."

"Chase," he boomed. "How are you doing?"

Bailey's attention snapped to my face as if she'd been wondering the same thing.

"Decent." All things considering. My life hadn't totally fallen apart. People were talking about me, but they always had. It was just amplified temporarily.

"I have some news," he said. "I just got off the phone with Los Angeles."

My body went rigid. Bailey's grip on her cup of hot chocolate tightened, and her breath stilled. We both froze, waiting for Stewart to continue.

"They'd like to see you stay and finish out your fourth year of college."

I must have been holding my breath too, because I let out a heavy exhale. "Okay." Then I nodded. Stewart, of course, couldn't see me, but it was more of a reflex than anything.

After several conversations with Stewart, I'd been expecting it and had made peace with it already.

Sure, I was disappointed. My future was veering in a direction I hadn't planned for, but a small part of me was relieved by this outcome. I liked my life the way it was now, so I'd welcome another year of it.

I stole a glance at Bailey, and for once, I couldn't read her expression. But I had a hunch she felt much the same way I did.

"It's not a punishment," he stressed. "They want to shield you from negative attention while the case is ongoing. As a rookie, the media would eat you alive over this. Waiting a year gives things a chance to cool down."

He was right. The last thing I wanted was to be known for a scandal instead of my gameplay. It would probably always follow me, but by the following year, at least it would be old news.

After I ended the call, I shifted my weight and turned to face Bailey.

She touched my arm, studying me with concern. "How are you feeling about that?"

"It could be worse." I shrugged. I could have been dropped from my contract altogether, so this was a win. "And it means more time with you."

If not for James, I probably would have been devastated. But I could keep playing high-level hockey, and I could still live with Dallas and Ty next year. And best of all—I'd be here with her.

"Still," she said, "it's okay to be disappointed. I wouldn't take it personally if you were."

"Maybe a little, but I'm good, I promise."

Bailey scanned my face and sucked in a breath like she was going to speak. Instead, she slowly let the air out and gave me a soft smile. She didn't believe me.

"Promise, James. When have I ever hidden how I felt?"

She laughed. "Fair point."

CHAPTER 61
THE MOON
CHASE

JUST AS I'D SUSPECTED, we beat Dallas and Siobhan to his parents' place. We had time to pick up takeout and eat said takeout once we got to the cabin. I even had time to eat Bailey for dessert and get her into the hot tub after.

Naked.

With, of course, the caveat that Ward would text me when they were fifteen minutes out so we had time to get decent.

Steam from the water rose in the cool night air, and stars blanketed the sky above us, far more vibrant than in the city. The colored light in the hot tub changed in a slow, continuous pattern, tinting the water all the shades of the rainbow and back again. It was silent aside from the jets of the hot tub bubbling.

Bailey nestled against my chest, and we fell into an easy, comfortable silence. I was relaxed beyond belief…until today's date hit me. I'd been so absorbed in hockey, the tape scandal, and all my own shit from the past week that I hadn't connected the dots.

Shifting, I set my amber bottle of beer in the drink holder beside me. "Weren't you supposed to hear about the internship this week?" True to my brand, the words slipped out before I could think them through, and regret hit me square in the face immediately after. Was it a mistake to bring it up now, when the moment was so perfect otherwise? In this case, I guessed that no news was bad news and Bailey didn't want to tell me.

"Um, I did hear, actually." Bailey reached over and turned down the jets. She peered up at me, her eyes dancing in the twilight. "I got it."

Cool relief washed over me. Fucking finally, we had something to celebrate for a change.

"James, that's incredible." I kissed her temple, smelling the hint of chlorine from the water on her skin. "Why didn't you tell me?"

She gave a one-shoulder shrug and tucked a stray strand of hair back into her bun. "I found out this afternoon. I was waiting until after the game to tell you. But then Stewart called, and it didn't seem like the right time in light of the news he gave you, so…"

"Are you kidding?" I tilted her chin up so we were eye to eye. "I always want to hear your good news. Though I knew you'd get it."

Bailey broke away from my gaze and ducked her head. She was so much more modest than she should have been. If I could slice off a chunk of my ego and give it to her, we'd both be set. But I'd settle for pumping her tires any chance I got.

"Yeah, they were sold when I pitched my article about toxic masculinity in team sports. They want to run it as a front-page feature on the site."

My chest swelled with an irrational sense of pride then, even though I'd done nothing more than cheer her on and be her occasional sounding board.

"That's awesome."

"Yup." She grinned. "They want it by the end of next week. I should start working on it soon, but I figured we both needed the weekend off."

"At a minimum." A month off—together—would have been even better. Maybe this summer.

"Can I interview you as a source?" Bailey took a sip of her beer, watching me from the corner of her eye. I tried not to get distracted by the way her lush lips looked wrapped around the glass bottle. And failed.

"Absolutely not."

Her face fell. "Really?"

"Kidding." I put my hand on her thigh beneath the water and stroked my thumb over her soft skin. "I'll make all the guys on the team tell you anything you want to know too."

She arched a blond brow, clearly fighting to keep a straight face. "Not sure coercion is the best way to get sources, Carter."

"Psh, no one needs to know."

From beside my drink, my cell phone lit up with an update from Ward. At least his trademark terrible timing hadn't struck again.

"They're twenty minutes away," I said. "Want to get out and hit the shower?" We'd been in for a while, anyway, and the heat was going to my head. But all the knots in my muscles had finally melted away.

"Sure."

Once I'd hauled myself out of the water, I grabbed two thick white towels from the nearby chair and handed one to her. Bailey climbed out and wrapped it around her chest. The heat had caused her cheeks to flush so deeply it was visible even in the dim glow from the tub's light. The sight of her like that paralyzed me in awe, and all I could do was stare. How did I get so lucky?

"What?" Her lips curled into a half smile.

Busted.

"You're just beautiful, that's all."

After we got cleaned up, we played several rounds of Cards Against Humanity with Ward and Siobhan, where he defended his reigning title as Worst Loser Ever.

"You guys have no taste," he grumbled, putting the cards away.

From behind him, Shiv rolled her eyes. She padded into the kitchen and returned moments later with a bottle of champagne in hand.

Dallas glanced up. "Where'd you find that?"

"Wine fridge," she said. "Is Stewart going to be mad if we open it?"

"Nah, they have parties here all the time, and people bring more booze than they could ever drink." He opened his palm, gesturing for her to pass it to him. "Just let me make sure it's not crazy expensive." He scanned the label, brow furrowed. "We're good. Go nuts."

"What are we celebrating?" Bailey asked, following her into the kitchen. She retrieved four champagne glasses from a high cabinet.

To be fair, we were all half-cut and probably didn't need the extra alcohol. But YOLO.

"You never need an excuse for champagne." Shiv pointed to her with the bottle. "But you did get the scholarship, which is a big deal, right?"

"Need help with that, Shiv?" Dallas asked, eyeing her warily. I drained the last of my beer, weighing the odds of this going wrong.

"I'm an old pro."

Somehow, that didn't inspire a lot of confidence in me. Loved Shiv, but she was four drinks deep and built like Tinkerbell.

Shiv cut away the foil from around the neck of the bottle, then grabbed a white kitchen towel and pulled on the cork.

"Are you sur—" At the same time Dallas asked, her hand slipped, and the cork shot out of the bottle, sailing clear across the room. With a crash, it shattered a turquoise pendant light over the island.

Luckily, the four of us remained unscathed.

Siobhan turned, eyes wide, then looked back at the broken light fixture. Bailey's expression was much the same. Champagne foam poured out of the bottle, spilling onto the floor, but she was too focused on the broken light dangling awkwardly from the ceiling.

"Um…is Stewart going be mad about *that*?"

Dallas shook his head, giving her a rueful smile as he fought back laughter. "No, that one's on me. No more tipsy Siobhan opening champagne bottles."

Bailey walked out of the bathroom in a set of dark gray pajama shorts and a tank top. She was all legs and all kinds of hot. Maybe we didn't need to go right to bed.

"I know it's late," she said, "but I'm kind of wired. Can we stay up and snuggle for a bit?"

"Sure." I slid over to make room for her beside me in the bed and wrapped my arm around her. Then a thought popped into my head, probably fueled by too many drinks and a long-standing, nagging curiosity.

"James?" I stroked her hair gently.

"Yeah?"

"This will sound a little out of left field, but I keep thinking about it. What happened when you were younger? Your brother said something about medical bills. I don't want to pry, but you usually tell me everything."

Bailey squirmed beside me like she was suddenly uncomfortable. There was a pause. "A bad car accident."

My gut twisted at the thought. She had already dealt with so much in her life. I hated knowing this happened to her. "How bad?"

"Um…" She drew in a breath. "I had a concussion. Bruised ribs. Broke my femur."

"Holy shit." My hand froze. "A broken femur is a big deal."

"Yeah, I was in a wheelchair for a while. My dad took a leave of absence from work to take care of me. But the person who hit us was underinsured, so it was an issue financially."

Damn, she'd had so many bad breaks—no pun intended—that sometimes I couldn't stand it. I wanted to fix every one, even when it wasn't possible.

"Is that why you stopped playing hockey?" I asked carefully.

"No, that was a money thing…before the accident."

My chest tightened like it was in a vise. "I'm sorry."

"That's how I ended up at Callingwood. Wanted to go to USC. Got accepted. Couldn't afford it. Even with loans, it wasn't workable." Bailey cleared her throat the way she always did when emotions hit her and she was trying to hide it. "It's a really prestigious program too. Kind of disappointing."

She was downplaying that.

"Bet they have a good grad program."

"They do." She nodded thoughtfully and sat up, turning to face me. Uncertainty stretched across her face. "I've been thinking about grad school lately. If I can get in, I mean."

See, there she went again with the misplaced modesty. If she couldn't get into a good grad program, there was no hope in hell for anyone else.

"You know you have the grades for it, James."

Her lips pulled into a tiny smile. "Maybe. But USC's grad program is even harder to get into than their undergrad."

"Either way, I'm sure there are lots of good journalism schools in California. Especially within the greater Los Angeles area."

"That's true," she murmured, her smile broadening. "There are a few."

"I wonder if there are any other selling points to California."

Bailey shifted her weight and rose onto her knees. Placing her palms on my shoulders, she straddled my waist. "Hmm, I wonder. Warm weather is a plus. No more shoveling snow or dealing with snow boots would be nice."

"The weather, huh?" I squeezed her ass, and she giggled.

"Good shopping? Rodeo Drive or whatever it's called?"

"I can't remember the last time you went shopping."

"Celebrity sightings…? I hear they have tour buses that take you to see the Kardashians' house."

My hands bracketed her waist, sneaking under the hem of her shirt. "Keep digging, James."

"What else?" She sighed and pursed her lips, staring off like she was deep in thought. Her focus landed back on me, her expression turning shy. "Well, I do know this cute guy who's moving to California after graduation."

"Just cute?"

"Handsome. Sweet. Dynamite in bed." She paused. "He's one in a million, really."

"Question is, will you be coming with me?"

A rush of nerves ran through me like never before. I held my breath, waiting for her response.

Bailey ducked her head, bringing her mouth to hover over mine. "One hundred percent."

EPILOGUE - LIFETIME

BAILEY

Three years later
Los Angeles, California

GRAD SCHOOL WAS BRUTAL. Every student in my cohort was cultured, experienced, and basically brilliant. With impressive professional backgrounds covering topics like foreign affairs abroad, reporting from the campaign trail, and even medical journalism. I was no slouch—I'd carved out a respectable niche for myself in the sports writing world—but it was intimidating. The pressure to keep up was insane. And not just to keep up; I wanted to be at the top of my class like I had been in undergrad.

Possible in theory; grueling in practice.

I groaned, slumping over my open Numbers, Statistics, and Data Journalism textbook. I'd been studying for so long that the words were blurring together. The more I reread it, the less sense it made. Like staring at a word so long that it no longer looked like a real word.

And sadly, schoolwork waited for no woman—or her birthday, which was today.

Downstairs, the front door slammed. I glanced at my phone to discover I'd completely lost track of time. Chase was a couple of minutes late, and I wasn't even dressed. Footsteps sounded on the hardwood, and moments later, he appeared in the doorway to my office, his keys in one hand.

He flashed me a heart-stopping smile. "Sorry I'm late. I had to make a quick stop." His smile faded, and he studied me with a frown. "Have you been studying all day?"

"Maybe." I hated to admit it, because he already felt bad about being gone all day for training camp.

"James." He crossed his arms, leaning against the doorframe. "Did you at least eat something? Take a break?"

Chase had left for the arena early, and I'd rolled out of bed not long after, taking a quick shower before shuffling directly to my office down the hall. I'd even set up a Keurig machine on a side table near my desk so I didn't have to leave to make coffee. It was a brilliant, if dangerous, move on my part.

And I hadn't exactly eaten breakfast. But I did eat lunch, so that counted as "something," right?

"Don't worry," I said. "I ate lunch on the deck and studied out there for a bit."

Or I tried to until our neighbor's kids and their friends got into their pool and yelled *Marco* and *Polo* at the top of their lungs. After moving out of an apartment complex full of people in their twenties who threw ragers every weekend, I thought we'd be guaranteed some peace and quiet in the suburbs. I never imagined it would be noisier here, but that was absolutely the case between the hours of three and eight p.m. Guess that's what we got for buying in a family friendly neighborhood.

Chase always laughed and said it'd be our kids making a racket soon enough. Fair point. Especially if our kids were anything like him—based on what his mother said, I was going to have my hands full.

Or maybe our kids would end up being quiet and studious like I was a child. But probably not.

"Did you take a break?" Chase repeated, raising his dark eyebrows.

"Yeah, I took a few study breaks in between."

He narrowed his eyes. "Uh-huh."

Chase, still standing in the doorway, was freshly showered post-training and wore a fitted black tee and newer jeans. I, on the other hand, was barefoot in black yoga pants and a random pink tank top, with wild, wavy hair. He'd kept my birthday present a secret, but regardless of what it was, my current hair and outfit situation probably wouldn't cut it.

I flashed him an apologetic look and stood. "Can you give me a few minutes to change? I'm a mess."

"You look cute." He stepped in front of me and put his hands on my waist, angling in for a brief kiss. "But I've gotta grab something to eat anyway."

No surprise there. The man was always eating. Our grocery bill was astronomical.

"Oka—"

Instead of releasing me, he ducked his head, captured my lips, and kissed me again, deeper. I dug my fingertips into his shoulders, my breath turning shallow. Just as I was starting to lose myself in the kiss, he pulled back, giving me a knowing look. If we kept going, we wouldn't be leaving the house anytime soon, if at all.

"Now," he said, steering me out of the office and into the hallway. "Go get ready. I'll give you fifteen minutes." He smacked me on the butt before turning and strolling away.

I paused for a moment, my burned-out brain trying to catch up from the kiss and a full day of studying. It wasn't until he was out of sight that I remembered my question.

"Can you give me a hint about how to dress?" I called.

His voice echoed from in the kitchen. "Wear pants."

Pants. Okay. Vague, but better than nothing.

I headed into the all-white master bathroom and quickly washed my face before applying a little makeup and a spray of my new perfume. Then I stood in the middle of our oversized walk-in closet, staring at the rows of clothes aimlessly. After changing three times, I finally settled on broken-in jeans, a white tank top, and a lightweight tan knit sweater—it was fall, and I had turned into such a wimp about cool weather that I could pass as a native Californian.

Inside his black SUV, the air conditioning blasted full force—as always—and I quickly turned the fan down and the passenger-side temperature up so I didn't freeze to death en route to our destination. Chase shifted into reverse and placed a hand on the back of my seat, shoulder-checking before he backed out of the driveway.

"How was camp?" I asked, sliding on my tortoiseshell sunglasses. They were another early birthday present from him. It was like birthday week in our house.

Chase shrugged. "It was good. Always a little rough to get back into the swing of things."

"A little rough?" Now he was the one telling white lies about his day. He was tired, and he looked it.

"Fucking brutal," he admitted. "But I hate to complain when you've been working so hard and I've barely seen you."

Between his pre-season training and the start of my journalism grad program, quality time together had been scarce. It was an abrupt change from our leisurely summer, the majority of which we had spent lounging lakeside a few doors down from Dallas and Shiv, taking out the boat, and sleeping in late. Having zero real-life responsibilities to worry about had been a nice reprieve, but they'd come crashing down again in full force lately.

Plus, now that we were back in LA, and Dallas and Shiv were in Colorado, I was going through best friend withdrawal. I'd made some friends in LA, especially other girlfriends and wives from the team, but it wasn't the same. Neither was drinking wine via video call.

"This program is intense." I raked a hand through my hair, which I'd recently cut to shoulder-length. It still felt bizarrely short, like I was missing a limb. "It's already kicking my butt."

"Hey." He placed his hand on my knee, warmth from his skin radiating through the denim fabric. "I understand the little fish, big pond feeling. But you're there for a reason."

"You have to say that."

Chase had been intimidated for all of five minutes during his first NHL game. Then he skated around the ice like he owned it and had ever since.

"Doesn't make it less true."

Outside the window of the SUV, the freeway sped by, but I still had no idea where we were going.

"When are you going to tell me where you're taking me?"

Chase shot me a sidelong glance, his lips tugging. "You'll see soon enough."

Three exits later, a huge gray structure appeared in the distance. The lettering on its oversized red sign grew clearer as we drew closer. We were headed to the same place he'd been only hours earlier.

"Are we going to the arena?"

"Skating," he said. "Birthday tradition."

The new arena in downtown Los Angeles—a modern architectural marvel comprised of steel and glass—had been completed two years prior.

Chase held the door open to the players' entrance and followed behind me. The enormous facility was almost eerily quiet, save for the distant echoes of the custodial staff. He navigated us through the winding hallways like it was his second home, brought us to a stop in front of a metal door, and keyed in the pin code.

In keeping with the rest of the world-class facility, the Los Angeles Blades' dressing room put the one at Boyd to shame. Solid wood benches filled the players' changing area, with long windows placed high along the outside walls to let in natural light.

Down an attached hallway to the left, there was a players' lounge, complete with leather couches, fireplace, and a snack bar. To the right was a video room with black leather seats for thirty, and a second-story mezzanine held a track and training area, plus hot and cold immersion tubs.

It was a one-stop shop for recovery, meals, and workouts. There were only one or two others like it in the league—I couldn't imagine the disappointment players who'd been traded must have felt when stepping into a standard facility after calling this their home. I'd seen it before, but it still wowed me every time I stepped foot inside.

Chase led me over to his cubby and set our bags on the floor in front of it. I sank onto the bench and watched him expectantly.

The sight of Chase on his knees, rooting through his black equipment bag, brought about a memory of the time he took me skating at the Boyd arena. Things were so new between us then. It felt like a lifetime ago. I was nervous just being around him then. Those butterflies were still there now, but in a comfortable, easy way.

"We aren't going to get busted like last time, are we? There's no Roy lurking in the wings?"

"This time, I got permission."

"Did you, though?" I nudged him with my foot.

He glanced up at me with a grin, messy dark hair tumbling in his face. "For real."

Still kneeling, he handed me my skates. I slipped my foot into the left, but when I put my foot into the right, my toes hit a solid barricade. Probably a roll of tape that had been floating loose in his bag.

"Hang on." I stuck my hand into the skate, finding a small square object wedged in the toe. "There's something stuck in my—" I tugged it free, revealing a small polished wooden box.

My heart skipped a beat or three. *Was this what I thought it was*? I didn't want to get ahead of myself, so I sucked in a deep breath to compose myself.

"There it is," Chase said. "I was looking for that."

He took the box from my hand and opened the hinged lid. I let out a woosh of air when my eyes landed on what was inside. The center stone from his mother's ring, re-set into a plain gold band.

"Carter," I whispered. My breath snagged, and tears flooded my eyes, threatening to overflow. This was it. My love, my life, my future. My everything.

The slightest hint of nervousness crossed his face, so faint that no one but me would have noticed it.

"I've made lots of mistakes along the way, but you're the one thing that's always been right. Will you marry me, James?"

"Yes." A warm tear escaped and traveled down my cheek. I sniffled, wiping it away with the back of my hand. "Of course I will."

He slipped the ring onto my left ring finger, and only then did I notice his hands were trembling. Cupping my face, he leaned in and kissed me like I had never, ever been kissed before. It was gentle but firm, asking but claiming, a promise of forever.

We pulled apart, and he rested his forehead on mine, dragging his thumb along my jawline. My heart was speeding, violating some law of nature. Time stopped, like a flashbulb moment I'd remember forever.

"I'm so fucking pumped," he said. "I can't wait to marry you."

"Won't that make me a Carter, though?" I teased.

"You'll always be my James." He heaved a heavy sigh, and his posture relaxed, his broad hands still wrapped around my waist.

"Were you nervous?" I whispered.

Chase's lips tugged into a half smile, his dark eyes holding mine. "Little bit. You're my once in a lifetime."

He was right. I never thought I'd find someone like him.

"You knew I'd say yes."

"Yeah." He broke into a full grin. "Like I've always said—we're endgame."

THE END

Want to see more of Chase and Bailey's happily ever after? Sign up for my newsletter and receive five exclusive bonus chapters as well as sneak peeks at upcoming books!

BONUS CHAPTER #1 - JAMES

BAILEY

Eight months later
Los Angeles, California - May

Nerves shot through me as I stood in front of the full-length mirror in our master bedroom. In less than three hours, I'd stand in front of eighty people and exchange wedding vows. I was terrified.

Not about the marriage part; the eighty people part. Sure, they were our friends and family, but that did little to ease my nerves. I had never been a fan of being the center of attention.

I'd probably flub my vows by saying something like "infidelity" instead of "fidelity" or by forgetting Chase's name.

Oh my god, I was totally going to forget his name.

We should have eloped.

I held up the front of my lace wedding dress with both hands while Siobhan tugged the zipper and fastened the row of decorative buttons over top.

"There," she said, patting my shoulder. "Perfect."

"Look at you." My mother scurried over and held me at arm's length, inspecting me fondly. She sniffled as she started to tear up. "You look so beautiful."

I looked up, blinking away tears. "Don't make me cry, Mom."

Siobhan rushed to my side and pressed a tissue into the palm of my hand. I carefully dabbed at my eyes. I'd spent the better part of the morning being fussed over by a team of hair and makeup professionals. If I ruined any of it, I had no idea how to fix it myself.

"I'm sorry. It's just…" My mother released her hold on me, forcing a sad smile. "My little girl is all grown up."

Seraphina stepped into the master bedroom and turned to shut the door behind her. Her dark hair was pulled into a perfect, elegant chignon. She regarded her reflection and smoothed the lines of her dusky plum bridesmaid dress, then her gaze fell to me through the mirror.

"Bailey." She spun around, and her hand flew to her mouth. "Oh my god. That dress. Chase is going to fall over when he sees you."

I laughed. "Thanks, Ser."

Though I suspected Chase would simply try to get the dress *off*. We'd spent last night apart, and he'd already texted me, outlining his highly detailed and predictably dirty plans for after the reception.

"Have you looked outside?" She nodded to the bedroom window behind me. "The backyard looks like something out of a fairy tale."

It kind of felt like a fairy tale, so that fit.

I pulled back the sheer fabric curtains to reveal a yard full of people bustling around. Twinkle lights adorned the trees, ready to light the evening reception. Chairs formed rows on either side of the aisle that led to the rustic wooden ceremony arch. And a cocktail bar had been set up off to the side by the pool. It was simple and low-key, at least by Los Angeles standards.

My sister-in-law, Kim, poked her head through the door, expression apologetic. "I'm sorry. I have to go get Mateo from Derek before my boobs explode. I don't want to leak all over this dress. But I'll see you out there."

"Sounds good," I called.

I now had a grand total of four nephews and four nieces. My mother had her hands full when it came to grandchildren, and Chase and I hadn't even started growing our family.

Shiv, Sera, and my mom did a quick sweep of the master en

suite, tidying empty champagne glasses and other items left behind after our morning primp-a-thon. I tried to help, but they waved me off.

While my mother's back was turned, Shiv nudged me, lowering her voice. "Speaking of babies, have you guys talked more about pulling the goalie?"

"I don't know how serious he is about that," I said. "I think he's just got baby fever because of Mateo."

I kind of did too. At three months old, Mateo was at peak baby cuteness. He had tiny baby hands, downy baby hair, and made the most adorable little sighs when he fell asleep curled against whomever was lucky enough to hold him—because we all fought for the honor. My ovaries practically seized control of my brain when he was around.

"Of course. He's adorable." Shiv's expression turned wistful. "Plus, that baby smell is..."

I raised an eyebrow. "Who's the one with baby fever now?"

"We're not *not* trying. Pregnant brides are very in these days." She shrugged, enormous emerald-cut engagement ring glinting in the light as she tucked a lock of dark hair behind her ear.

"You two will make beautiful babies." I paused. "Actually, have you talked to Dallas? How's the groom?" The question was pointless, though; Chase wouldn't be nearly as nervous as me.

"Dallas said Chase had the best golf game of the season this morning. Now they're chilling in the man cave." Shiv tipped back the last of her champagne.

Of course they were. Their morning had been full of lounging and leisure while I was being poked and primped. Chase would shower and throw on a suit and look like he walked out of a photoshoot. Lucky, frustratingly beautiful man.

Another knock at the door interrupted us. Our wedding planner, Janice, strolled into the room. She scanned us all, giving a nod of approval.

"Photos are in half an hour," she said. "Should we shoo everyone else out and grab the groom?"

Janice had suggested we do a "first look" before the ceremony.

It was a little unorthodox, but she said many of her couples found it helped ease their nerves, and I needed all the help I could get in that department. Once I saw Chase, I had no doubt I would feel a million times more at ease.

Plus, I kind of liked the idea of seeing each other alone first. It seemed more intimate that way.

"Okay," I said, my nerves giving way to excitement. "Send him in."

CHASE

I adjusted my shirt sleeves under my navy suit jacket, wondering what James was doing at that moment. Whether she was nervous or doing okay. Or whether she was even dressed yet. Still in sexy bridal underwear, maybe?

Dammit.

The whole *not spending the night together before the wedding* tradition was such a scam.

Don't get me wrong, the time I'd spent with my groomsmen had been great, but waking up next to Bailey beat waking up in a hotel suite with them by a thousand to one. And being on the road so often meant I didn't get to wake up next to her nearly enough as it was.

Dallas and Ty leaned against the pool table, beers in hand and shooting the breeze. For lack of a basement and a real man cave, we'd made the rec room and adjoining spare bedroom our home base to get ready for the ceremony. Bailey's two oldest brothers had ducked out to take the kids off their wives' hands so they could finish getting ready.

I glanced over at Derek. "Think Bailey is nervous?" Or worse yet, missing her dad. But I kept that question to myself.

"Probably a little." He shrugged, adjusting his tie. "She's not the biggest fan of being the center of attention."

True. One big reason why she went into writing instead of

sportscasting—even though she was more than attractive enough to be on screen.

Dallas strode over to me and gestured to his phone. "You're being summoned, Carter."

Finally.

"Good luck." Derek slapped me on the back. "We'll see you out there."

"Thanks." I turned and headed down the hallway over to the hardwood staircase. A handful of friends and family milled about the kitchen, lost in conversations, and I quickly stepped around them, trying to avoid drawing their attention so I didn't get waylaid. I'd already waited long enough.

The twelve or so stairs felt like ten times that. I'd never admit it, but I may have been a little nervous.

But that vanished the moment I saw her.

I stepped through the doorway, and Bailey turned to face me. She looked up at me expectantly with hazel eyes I still got a little lost in. Her hair was curled and loose around her shoulders, and her backless off-white dress hugged her frame perfectly, accentuating every dip and every curve of her body.

Perfection. Not just on the outside, either.

And I'd get to wake up to her for the rest of my life.

"Wow," I grinned, stepping closer. "You look…wow."

She gave me a coy smile as I set my hands on her waist. "You don't look so shabby yourself."

I regarded her for a few more moments but failed to find the words to do her justice. "I'm so lucky."

I was. I really was. The English language didn't have a word to describe how fortunate I was to have won this woman over.

Bailey made me a better person. She stuck with me through the worst of it, no matter what. And she made every day that much better simply by being part of my life.

Never imagined I'd find someone like her. Sometimes I still couldn't believe I had. And I'd spend the rest of my life making sure I deserved her.

"I'm the lucky one," she said, running her hands down my shoulders. "You look like you stepped out of a magazine spread."

"I clean up okay." I squeezed her. "I love you."

Her gaze softened. "I love you."

I tilted my head, and she did the same, our mouths drawn together by an invisible force. Bailey let out a soft sigh, parting her lips. I slid my hands around to her backside and pulled her up against me. When I deepened the kiss, she dug her fingertips into my shoulders, gripping and exploring every inch I could reach over top her dress.

Kissing her may have been a bad idea, because now I couldn't stop. She was addictive. Better still, she was mine.

Finally, Bailey pulled away, biting back a smile. "Gotta watch the makeup." Her eyes danced.

I leaned in, planting a row of kisses along the smooth skin on her neck.

"Don't worry," I murmured. "Plenty of time to mess that up later tonight."

"Mmm," she said, arching her neck. "Can't wait."

"Your dress is beautiful, by the way." I trailed my fingers up and down the ivory lace covering her ribcage. "But I'm especially excited to see what's underneath."

"Never change, Carter."

"What?" I gave her a wolffish grin. "Can't I be curious about my wife-to-be's wedding night attire? Good husbands take an interest in things, right?"

"I think they mean things like their careers, not their panties."

I cupped her chin. "You've already got the career part nailed. I'm marrying the sexiest sportswriter in the biz. So let's circle back to your panties."

"Can't spoil the surprise," Bailey said, batting my hand away playfully. "But I can assure you that you're in for a treat."

Oh god. How would I survive the ceremony and the reception? Would people notice if we disappeared for half an hour?

"*That* I know for sure."

There was a gentle rap at the door. “Hey guys?” Siobhan called. “Photographer wants to start in a second.”

I glanced down at Bailey, raising my eyebrows. “Ready, James?”

Her lips tugged into a smile. “So ready.”

“Let’s do this.” I held out my hand.

She reached over and laced her fingers in mine. This was it. Forever.

BONUS CHAPTER #2 - TWO PINK LINES

BAILEY

Two months later

Los Angeles, California - July

BAILEY

One nice thing about having several bathrooms? The ability to pee in private and freak out accordingly.

I placed the cap back on the pregnancy test and shoved it into my pocket. Three more tests sat in the garbage beside the vanity, but by the fourth test, I was reasonably certain the positives weren't evaporation lines.

Washing and drying my hands, I studied my reflection in the mirror. I smoothed my hair, drawing in a deep, calming breath like I did in yoga class. This was a happy surprise. Not even a surprise, really. A predictable outcome, given the sequence of events—honeymoon sex, and lots of it, without birth control. Not the biggest shock, either, since I'd been experiencing something like PMS on steroids all week. My boobs were so sore that a light breeze was painful; I was bloated like never before; and I'd cried at four different, entirely random commercials.

We'd talked about this. We were married. Stable in every way possible. And Chase would be thrilled.

But I hadn't expected it to happen immediately.

At least it was the off-season, and he was home. I couldn't imagine finding out while he was on the road.

When I stepped into the hall, the house was silent, save for the rumble of the garbage truck heading down the street. I headed to our bedroom to check on Chase. I'd already been up for an hour, drinking coffee and peeing on sticks, but I hadn't wanted to bother him on one of the rare days he got to sleep in.

The bed was empty, the white duvet pulled taut and the king-sized pillows straightened. The sound of water hitting the tiles echoed from inside the master bathroom. I sank onto the edge of the mattress, nervously destroying my cuticles. Chase always said to reframe nervousness as excitement, but right now, I was undoubtedly experiencing hefty amounts of both.

A moment later, the shower turned off, and the glass door slammed shut. Chase winked at me as he strolled out of the bathroom wearing nothing but a towel.

I drank in the sight of him as he headed into the closet, then I followed, lingering in the doorway while he pulled on black boxer briefs and a pair of gray sweats.

"Remember our honeymoon?" I asked, one shoulder propped against the doorjamb.

Chase tugged a black T-shirt over his head and shot me a questioning look as he straightened the hem. "Which part?" He raked his damp hair out of his face. His expression darkened, his signature wolffish smile emerging as he stepped closer and wrapped his big hands around my waist. "If this is your way of telling me that lacy garter belt is under your clothes right now, consider me sold."

Odds were I didn't have on elaborate lingerie beneath my Lululemon joggers, but I couldn't blame him for being an optimist.

"The part where we decided to throw caution to the wind and said whatever happens, happens?"

Chase's dark brow furrowed. "The part..." His eyes widened and his mouth formed a surprised *O*, realization dawning on his face. "Are you saying you're pregnant?"

"Yup." I slid the pregnancy test out of my pocket and handed it to him.

He gaped at the white plastic stick, then watched me for a beat before breaking into a massive grin. "That's fucking awesome." He set the test aside and wrapped his arms around me, burying his face in my neck.

The look on his face was more than I ever could have hoped for. It was pure happiness. Warmth spread through my body, and the heaviness of my worries evaporated. The deep, secure contentedness I felt in that moment was indescribable.

I had him, and together we could do anything; even take this big, life-changing step.

We looked at each other, falling silent. His expression softened, so full of warmth and caring that I felt like my heart might burst.

"I love you, James."

"I love you."

He leaned in, gently planting a kiss on my mouth. I parted my lips in response, and he tightened his hold on me, drawing me closer in a way that somehow felt like so much more than a simple touch. It was gentle but territorial; protective. It said a thousand things without a single word.

We slowly pulled apart, and he let out a sigh, leaning his forehead against mine.

"A mini-Carter. I'm pretty stoked." He tucked a lock of hair behind my ear, a smug smirk playing on his lips. "First try too."

Of course he would want to take credit for that part.

"I'm still kind of in shock," I said. "We weren't even really trying."

He claimed my lips again for another brief kiss. "Guess I'm just that good."

Pivoting, he steered me to the bed and sat, pulling me into his lap. I looped my arms around his neck, nestling against his skin and breathing in the familiar scent of his cologne. Sometimes I sprayed it on the sheets while he was gone, but on him, mixed with his natural scent, was so much more delicious.

"You're going to make the most adorable pregnant chick ever," he mused, nuzzling my hair.

"Here's to hoping."

I feared it might be the opposite. Seemed like it was a real roll of the dice, and I wasn't convinced I'd land on the "cute pregnant" square. Chase would probably think so either way, though, because he was lovingly biased.

"Where do you want to go celebrate?" he asked. "Teatro? Nobu? We've gotta make it somewhere good. This is huge."

"I don't know," I said, stomach doing a flip-flop at the idea of eating. "Food isn't exactly my friend these days. I thought I was stressed out over exams. But turns out, it was a little more than that."

Chase rubbed my back, making slow circles back and forth. "Morning sickness? That was brutal for Sera."

"Morning sickness, noon sickness, afternoon sickness, night sickness…" Or nausea, at least. No actual vomiting yet, and I dearly hoped it stayed that way.

"That bad, huh?" He hummed. "Sorry, baby. Guess I'll have to spoil you to help make up for it."

I laughed, angling in to kiss his cheek. "You already spoil me."

"Oh, that was nothing. I'm spoiling for two now."

Six months later

Seattle, Washington - November

Some parts of pregnancy were great. Baby kicks, for example. Foot rubs from Chase too. But getting winded after climbing one flight of stairs kind of sucked. I felt like I'd climbed Mount Everest when all I had done was haul myself up to the second floor of our house.

"Chase?" I called, walking into the spare bedroom we were converting into a nursery. "Oh my goodness." I came to a halt in the doorway, surveying the destruction.

We'd had it painted last week after finally settled on a light blue to go with the white furniture. Depending on whether the baby was a boy or a girl, I'd pick up some accent pieces to tie it all together later. But right now, it looked like a construction zone.

Boxes. Boxes everywhere. Packing peanuts. Furniture parts. Plastic bags with screws and pieces. Piles of instruction manuals. And one hot husband.

Chase stood and ran his fingers through his shaggy dark hair. He was overdue for a cut and rocking hockey hair to the extreme. His attention landed on me, and he flashed me a sheepish smile.

"You weren't supposed to be home yet." He sidled up to me and pulled me into a warm hug.

"My prenatal yoga teacher called in sick. But I can leave if you want." I poked his abs, vaguely remembering what it was like to have a flat stomach.

Now I could balance a glass on my belly, waddled when I walked, and wore stretchy pants twenty-four seven. I guess I wore stretchy pants before this too, but back then, it was by choice.

"I wanted to surprise you," he said.

It was sweet, but entirely unnecessary. Chase worked hard enough as it was. And after being traded to a new team, he was crushing it in on- and off-ice, training more than ever lately. In fact, the overtraining was more than a contributing factor to his recent minor knee injury. He wasn't at the surgery stage yet, but I wanted to keep it that way. *This* was not helping his situation.

"I appreciate it; I really do. But I don't want you to have to bust your butt on your days off. I could hire someone to help if it comes down to it."

Or I could attempt to assemble things myself, but that generally ended in Chase having to disassemble it and re-do everything from scratch. I had lots of strengths. Putting together furniture wasn't one of them.

He released me and held me at arm's length, fixing me with a stern look. "First of all, I'm not hiring someone to put together furniture when I can easily do it myself. Second of all, what if the baby comes early?"

I'd never seen the man worry more in his whole life. He fretted over what I ate, whether I slept enough, and my stress levels with the move. He wouldn't let me lift even the light boxes. And there was no way I could forget my prenatal vitamins, because he reminded me every day, even when he was on the road.

Of course, that didn't stop him from being his usual horny self. It was an explosive combination with my raging second-trimester hormones. We'd had sex against every single surface of our new house—including most of the walls.

Even looking at him now, I was tempted. Every part of my body was called out "mine" when he was around. In my defense, the man was gorgeous… and good with his hands.

"We still have time," I said, trying to focus on the conversation. Talk about a role-reversal.

His calm exterior faltered, and a hint of uncharacteristic panic crept in. "Sera was a month early. I had to be evicted from my own crib because my parents weren't ready for her." Like Derek and I, Chase and Sera were less than two years apart in age.

"Are you stressed, Carter?" I skimmed my fingertips along his forearms, moving up to his biceps and stopping on his shoulders, squeezing gently.

He let out a sigh, and the tension in his body eased. "I just want everything to be perfect," he said. "Still wish we knew whether the baby was a boy or girl so we could plan better."

"Nope, no way. The surprise is the best part." I took his hand and shuffled over to the gray-upholstered glider in the corner.

I eased into it, and Chase sank down onto the matching footstool and turned to face me, placing his elbows on his knees. He gave me a puppy dog face that almost always worked—almost.

"But how will I know what color skates I should buy?" There was a cute undertone of sulkiness in his voice. This wasn't the first time we'd had this discussion. I was team waiting to find out, and since I had to birth this gigantic baby, I won.

"We're a few years off from that. Besides, I hated pink when I was a child. Even if we have a daughter, there is no guarantee she'll like girly colors or girly things in general."

"Still…" He frowned, evidently troubled by this lack of ability to pre-purchase tiny hockey equipment. Knowing him, he'd buy skates in every color just to cover his bases. I was kind of surprised he hadn't already.

I nudged his foot with my toe. "You shouldn't be doing all this with your knee anyway."

"Huh?" He glanced down like he'd forgotten, then back up at me. "No, it's fine. My physical therapist told me to get up and walk every hour. Some light activity is good for it."

"Repetitive bending and lifting? Carrying heavy objects?" I tilted my head skeptically.

He gave me a guilty look. Here he was, on injured reserve, and he was doing physical labor. Stubborn, stubborn man.

"I'm the one who should be fussing over you," he said, rubbing my round stomach. He let his palm rest along the curve of my belly and regarded it thoughtfully. "Not the other way around."

"I'm not sure you could fuss over me more if you tried."

I tried to return the favor, but it was hard to spoil the man who could buy himself everything, was almost entirely self-sufficient, and had unwavering self-confidence. Hopefully, my undying love and affection would cut it. And, you know, what he claimed were world-class blowjobs.

"I hit the store earlier and bought ice cream. Strawberry and chocolate." He paused and gave me a playful half smile. "The dark chocolate looked better than the regular, so I got both. Plus chips. Salsa. Guac. Artichoke dip. Sparkling water." He went back to rubbing my belly, watching the movement of his hand as he did so. "That juice you like… and a couple of steaks for dinner, now that you can stand meat again."

"You make a fine househusband." With great effort, I hoisted myself up and scooted forward in the chair, snuggling up against his muscular shoulder.

He stroked my hair and rested his cheek on the top of my head. "Damn right."

"I feel bad saying this, because I don't like that you're injured… but I kind of like having you home."

During the season, we were always trying to make up for lost time—especially now that I was pregnant and weirdly emotional twenty-four seven. It was probably hormonal, but I wanted to be with him constantly, and that made for lonely nights when he was on the road. My pregnancy pillow didn't cut it as a snuggle substitute.

"I like it too," he said, putting his arm around me and pulling me closer. "You are my home."

BONUS CHAPTER #3 - BABY CARTER

CHASE

Three months later

Seattle, Washington - February

After hearing all the jokes, pregnancy anecdotes, and parenting advice from our friends and family, I was prepared to wake up sixty times per night, to wait a bajillion weeks to have sex again, and to change more diapers than I'd ever imagined. For unpredictable postpartum hormones, for changes to our marriage—both good and bad—and for hefty amounts of tears from all three of us.

But no one told me how helpless I would feel.

I propped my elbows on my knees, leaning closer to Bailey's hospital bed. "Are you doing okay?"

It was ten thirty in the morning, and neither of us had slept. I was exhausted both mentally and physically; I could only imagine how she was feeling.

"Yeah," Bailey said. "I'm fine." She toyed with the sleeve of her blue hospital gown absentmindedly, watching her obstetrician speak to the resident in the far corner of the room. They were huddled together beside the door, conversing in low voices as they reviewed Bailey's chart.

Unease settled into my gut when, not for the first time, her doctor shook her head in response to something the resident asked.

More than thirteen hours in, Bailey had agreed to an epidural, but her labor still wasn't progressing. She was stuck at seven centimeters.

After reaching some kind of consensus, her obstetrician approached the hospital bed and studied the fetal heart rate monitor with a frown. "Bailey," Dr. Harris said, adjusting her wire-rimmed glasses. "If the baby doesn't come soon, we're going to need to discuss a C-section."

Judging by her tone of voice, it didn't sound like there would be much to discuss.

"But—" Bailey's gaze cut over to me, her expression crestfallen. The look on her face gutted me.

I took her hand and stroked the back of it with my thumb, desperately wishing I could do something more useful.

She fisted the white sheet draped over her lap with her other hand. "That wasn't part of the birth plan."

Dr. Harris nodded sympathetically, her lips pursed. "I understand, but at some point, you'll both be too tired for labor to continue. There's also an infection concern since your water has been broken for some time now. We'll get you started on Pitocin to see if that can help move things along first, okay?"

Bailey sank her teeth into her lower lip. "Okay." She didn't want Pitocin either, but it was a last resort.

Moments later, a nurse appeared. She added a bag to the IV stand and adjusted settings on the monitors. As the door clicked shut behind her, Bailey drew in a breath and let out a long sigh. She rolled halfway onto her side to face me, wearing an expression of utter defeat that made my stomach twist.

"Hey." I stood and leaned over the bed, brushing her blond hair off her forehead. "You're doing great."

Bailey had been so strong these past nine months. Or forty weeks, as she liked to remind me, emphasizing that it was actually more than nine months. She barely complained—even through morning sickness that lasted all day, leaving her so sick she could hardly finish her articles at times.

She gazed back up at me, sadness behind her gold-flecked eyes. "I'm going to end up with a C-section, aren't I?"

Ever the perfectionist, Bailey had done a deep-dive into birthing practices almost as soon as the test turned positive. She had been determined to avoid what she said was "the cascade of interventions during birth." And she'd been especially hell-bent on not getting pushed into a C-section unnecessarily. Unfortunately, it looked like it might be necessary.

"I know you had your heart set on things going the way you planned. But like Dr. Harris said, what matters most is keeping both of you safe."

At this point, I didn't care if the baby came by literal stork. I just wanted her and the baby to be okay. But I wanted to respect her feelings, especially since it wasn't my body being poked and prodded.

Time slowed to a crawl. Even with the Pitocin, Bailey's labor wasn't progressing. When we first arrived at the hospital, Bailey had been skittish, but I'd been fairly calm, all things considered. Now, between the lack of sleep and the stress and the worry, my nerves were through the fucking roof.

Suddenly, the fetal monitor beeped wildly. A second alarm sounded, buzzing in an even more alarming manner. Bailey's attention rocketed over to me, and my heart clenched. Good thing we were already in a hospital, because I might need one myself if things went badly and I had a heart attack.

"Something's wrong," Bailey said, panic rising in her voice. "Something is wrong with the baby."

I swallowed. "I'm sure it'll be okay."

Dr. Harris burst into the room, accompanied by a handful of medical staff. They checked the monitors and examined Bailey, exchanging a rapid-fire dialogue of medical terminology that meant next to nothing to me.

A split second later, she turned to face us, expression solemn. "The baby is in distress and needs to come out now."

And in a flash, I was the only one left in the room.

After scrubbing up for surgery like I'd been told to, I paced in front of the double-doors outside the operating room, losing my mind. Who was I kidding? I'd already lost it. It had been at least a couple minutes without any update. Five, ten, maybe more. There was no clock, so I didn't know. All I knew was that Bailey was in there without me, and I had no idea what was going on.

Whether she was okay. Whether the baby was okay.

My entire life was on the other side of that goddamn swinging door.

Seven and a half laps later, the glass-and-metal door swept open, and a red-headed male resident rushed out, looking frazzled. Combined with the fact that he looked about seventeen, it didn't exactly inspire confidence.

"I'm sorry," he said breathlessly. "They forgot to come get you."

They fucking what?

I must have looked as furious as I felt, because his expression immediately shifted to one of terror.

"Sometimes it happens with crash sections," he added.

Good to know they regularly forgot partners in the goddamn hall.

He moved out of the way and held the door open, waving me on. "Uh, you can come in now."

The clinical scent of antiseptic bowled me over as I followed him into the sterile white operating room. A handful of doctors and nurses were grouped around Bailey, separated by a sheet hung at waist-height. To spare her from the carnage, I assumed, which I caught a glimpse of on the way in and wished I hadn't. Cuts and minor injuries didn't faze me, but organs on display were another story.

The minute her face came into view, everything inside me hurt.

She looked so vulnerable hooked up to a million machines with the anesthesiologist standing by her head.

Bailey locked eyes with me, and her chin wobbled. "I'm scared."

I was too.

"I'm here now." I stroked her forehead, hoping to have some calming effect in the midst of the chaotic operating room.

"She's doing great," Dr. Harris said from the other side of the curtain. "Baby's almost out."

"See?" I said. "Almost done."

Moments later, a cry pierced the air. The best sound I'd ever heard.

"It's a girl," someone called out.

With those three words, my entire life changed.

A daughter.

"Hi there, Baby Carter." I glanced down at the tiny fist wrapped around my index finger. Even her teensy fingernails were perfect. Long eyelashes rested against her chubby baby cheeks while she slept peacefully in the plastic bassinet.

It was like someone cut my heart out of my body and put it in this football-sized bundle of love. And I knew I would do anything for her, just like I would for my wife.

Bailey tilted her head, studying my face. "Are you surprised she's a girl?"

"A little," I admitted. "But she's perfect." Our little family was perfect.

Until now, I didn't know it was possible to feel whatever it was I was feeling. I couldn't even put it into words. I wanted to call my mother and apologize for every time I'd made her worry or didn't show up at home when I was supposed to.

Because now I knew what it was like to have a piece of my heart out there in the world, separate from me, and it was terrifying.

"She has your hair," Bailey murmured.

I laughed softly. She did. A full head of dark, downy hair sticking up all over the place just like mine in the morning. Hopefully, her personality was more like her mother's, or we were both in for some headaches down the road. Like, starting at age two and lasting until at least twenty.

"I think she has your nose," I said. "It's cute."

The covers rustled as Bailey shifted in the hospital bed and pulled herself upright, wincing. "We should probably settle on a name."

"Have you decided on one yet?" We had narrowed the list down to three top contenders, but Bailey was going to make the call. Only seemed fair, especially with the way the delivery had gone.

"No." Bailey frowned, glancing over at the portable bassinet. "I keep going back and forth."

Carefully, I eased onto the bed beside her and leaned my head against hers. "I'm sure she won't mind if we wait a day or two. How are you feeling?"

Bailey finally slept for a couple of hours around dinnertime, but she was almost as pale as the sheet beneath her. What we both needed was to go home and sleep in our own bed, but it would be a few more days before they discharged her.

"Other than the fact that I was cut open and stapled shut this morning? Fantastic."

I suppressed the reflexive urge to cringe. A C-section was no joke. Anyone who said that wasn't "real birth" deserved a swift punch to the throat. I was still blown away by how strong she had been through everything. How strong she was still being.

"I would have done it for you if I could." I meant it; if it meant she didn't have to go through that again, I'd do it ten times over myself.

Bailey looked up at me with a wry smile. "You could never handle the morning sickness."

"Probably not," I admitted. Throwing up was one of my most hated things in the world. I was borderline phobic of puking—and poor Bailey had done a lot of it over the past nine months.

"You do so much for me already," she said softly. "I know you're going to be the best dad there is."

"I'm sure as hell going to try."

I reached over and hit the dimmer on the light switch. Beside the bed, our daughter made a tiny mewling noise and stirred, then settled back to sleep.

Bailey slid her arm over my stomach and snuggled up against me. Her breathing slowed, deepening and turning more regular. For a minute, I thought she'd dozed off.

"Oh, no." She lifted her chin, eyes wide. "Are you going to be one of those dads that threatens to beat up her boyfriends if they mess with her?"

I gave her an innocent look. "No."

"You sure?"

"Of course, James. I'll teach her how to do that herself."

BONUS CHAPTER #4 – DILF

BAILEY

Three years later
Denver, Colorado – May

I shut the front door behind me and locked it, then placed my yoga mat in the entry closet. Peals of laughter echoed down the hallway behind me. Daddy-daughter days were hard to swing, scheduling-wise, but they were always a huge hit. I was happier with some time off to recharge too.

A sense of contentedness settled over me, blanketing me with warmth. I strolled down the hall and poked my head into the play-room to investigate. "What do we have here?"

Tatum was wearing a frilly yellow princess dress while she perched in a pink chair, swinging her legs and pretending to drink out of a blue plastic teacup. The other three chairs were occupied by a stuffed elephant, a baby doll, and a plastic dinosaur.

Chase was sitting on the floor in front of the tiny pink table, awkwardly attempting to fit his legs underneath. He had purple bows in his hair and hot pink nail polish on his fingers and I'd never been happier to call him mine.

Tatum beamed. "We're having a tea party."

"Looks like fun," I said.

Chase pushed to stand, patting Tatum on the head as he passed by her on his way to me. Leaning in, he gave me a quick peck on the lips. "Hi, baby."

"Eating in the playroom?" I quirked a brow, trying and failing to look stern. There were orange cracker crumbs all over the hardwood floor. We had a rule about eating at the table in our house. Or we *tried* to. But some of us were better at enforcing the rules than others.

"She said please…" He slid an arm around my waist, giving me a sheepish grin. No one could stay mad at that face. It was an impossibility. There was nothing better than seeing a gigantic hockey player wrapped around our daughter's little finger. "Did you have a good day with Shiv?"

My solo day off had been glorious. After yoga, lunch, and mani-pedis with another adult, I felt like a human being again. I loved being a mom, but with Chase's road trip schedule, sometimes I got worn out from parenting alone.

Chase kept saying we should hire a part-time nanny, but with Tatum starting preschool in the fall, I didn't see the point. I had things handled; it was just busy. I worked in the mornings, during naps, or after Tatum went to bed. It was a good way to fill my spare time alone while Chase was gone.

Though being pregnant again meant my "spare time" was about to disappear entirely.

"It was nice," I said. "How was mini-skate?" So far, Tatum loved skating lessons. But I wasn't sure who was more excited about them: father or daughter.

"It was fun!" Tatum called, pouring more tea for her stuffed elephant. The tulle of her frilly princess stress rustled while she bustled around the table like a busy hostess tending to her dinner party guests.

Chase nodded. "She skated circles around the other three-year-olds. Most of the four-year-olds too." Not all that surprising, given she was also taller than most of the four-year-olds. We really did make giant kids.

"So you're judging the toddler skate now."

"She comes by it naturally."

"Nice flex, Carter."

He folded his arms and leaned against the wall, jutting his chin at me. "Maybe I meant she got it from you."

"You didn't." I laughed. "I like your hair, by the way."

"What?" With a frown, he patted his head. His fingers landed on the rows of purple satin bows that matched the ones in Tatum's pigtails. "Oh yeah." He grinned, tugging them out and combing his hair with his fingers. "We were playing beauty salon before our tea party."

Playing pretend was one of Chase's parenting strengths. I tried to play along too, but Tatum had bluntly informed me that I wasn't nearly as good at it as he was. I was more suited to things like reading stories, making crafts, and taking her on outings like the zoo.

"I guess that explains the nails."

He surveyed his fingers, holding them up in display. "I dig it. I think I'll keep it on for the game tonight," he said. "You know, for good luck."

In the background, Tatum stood and rearranged the chairs. She scolded the elephant and dinosaur, who'd apparently been naughty. Between my love for following the rules and Chase's stubborn streak, I was pretty sure we were raising a future lawyer. Maybe even a judge.

Either way, the world was in for a reckoning when she got older.

"Oh, before I forget," I said. "Derek wants to know if we're coming to the cabin for Fourth of July weekend." Tatum would like nothing more than to run amok with her cousin, splashing in the lake and staying up too late to watch the fireworks.

"Sure, as long as your doctor is cool with you traveling."

Pregnancy was a pain that way. It was like being on house arrest toward the end, for fear I'd go into labor while out of town. Even more so knowing I'd have another C-section; I didn't want just any doctor slicing me open. I wanted my doctor.

"I won't be in my third trimester yet.... It'll be okay, but I'll check. He wants to book a tee time. Says Eagle Ridge books up fast."

"Guess he's got lots of spare time now that they've been eliminated for the season." Chase smirked.

"Be nice." I poked him in the side of his ribs, where I knew he was ticklish.

Chase flinched and stifled a laugh, grabbing my hand and kissing it before releasing it. "Come on, it's just a little friendly competition between teams." He rubbed his stubbled jawline and cocked his head thoughtfully. "Though this does mean he has more time to work on his golf game. He's going to kick my ass on the course again this year."

Behind him, Tatum accidentally knocked over the tea set, and it scattered all over the floor. She stared at it for a moment, tiny face threatening to crumple. Her bottom lip tugged into a pout as she kneeled down to pick up all the pieces. I checked my watch, confirming that it was nap time. Past it, actually—which showed.

I murmured, "Do you want to put her down while I take a shower?"

"Yup." Chase kneeled down to Tatum's height. "Come on, kiddo. Let's go read and have a little rest."

She nodded obediently, holding out her arms. If I had tried to put her down for a nap without a five-minute warning, she would have rioted.

He scooped her up with one arm and cradled her against his hip. When he brought her over to me, Tatum wrapped her arms around my neck and patted me on the back with her little hands. My heart nearly burst from the sweetness of the gesture. She smelled vaguely of fruit-flavored candy, which I suspected had also been part of this rule-breaking tea party. It was a really wild Saturday afternoon in the Carter household.

"Bye, Mommy."

"Bye, sweetheart." I kissed the top of her head before she turned away and clung to Chase. She leaned her head against his shoulder, eyelids already growing heavy. Her braided pigtails rested against his white tee, her hair the same shade of dark brown as his.

"Where's Moo?" she asked as they disappeared through the doorway. Moo was the ridiculous oversized pink cow that Derek had bought her for Christmas last year. It was cute, but it was almost as big as Tatum was. Naturally, it was her favorite.

Chase's voice carried down the hall. "Pretty sure he's in your bed. Let's go see…"

Half an hour later, I had just pulled a clean shirt over my head when Chase walked into our bedroom. "She just fell asleep," he said. "We read *The Paper Bag Princess* ten times, and she conked out clutching her hockey bear."

I didn't have the heart to tell him that starting a nap this late meant Tatum would be up late tonight too. He'd find that one out the hard way at bedtime when we played Jack-in-the-box with her popping out of bed every two minutes.

His brow creased. "Wait, did you finish your article?"

"Submitted it this morning." After writing, rewriting, revising, and re-revising it more times than I could count. I didn't get writer's block often, but when I did, it was a bear.

Plus, working on an article about playoff predictions was tough when the byline read Bailey Carter. Chase Carter was *in* the playoffs, so the optics were tricky; I didn't want to come across as lacking in objectivity. Even if I was. Obviously, I wanted his team to win.

"Who'd you pick to win the Cup?" Chase sat on the bed across from me, tilting his head.

I zipped up my light gray hoodie—which was straining over my belly already—and avoided his eyes. "Uh… Anaheim." I peeked up at him.

He raised his eyebrows, but he didn't say anything.

"You know that's what the numbers say," I added. "Statistically speaking."

Chase grinned. "Fuck the numbers."

"I still think you'll win, but when I'm writing for work, I can't let my personal opinions influence what I say too much. Gotta listen to the data too."

I eased onto the bed beside him and leaned against his broad shoulder. He laced his fingers in mine, squeezing gently, and let out a low *hmph*.

We both knew I thought Colorado would win, deep down, but I had to keep personal and professional separate as much as possible—especially as a woman in a male-dominated industry. Sadly, I was no stranger to online trolls haunting the comments section of my sports reporting articles, accusing me of being partial and unprofessional any time an article I'd written mentioned Chase or his team. What was I supposed to do, pretend my husband didn't exist?

"You're going above and beyond to avoid the illusion of bias. I'll give you that. But you know we're going to crush them in the next series." His fingers landed on my bare ring finger, tracing the skin, and his smile faded. "Where are your rings?"

He was probably worried I'd lost my new one. It was technically meant to be an anniversary band, but when we found out we were pregnant again, he got too excited and gave it to me early. At any rate, I knew exactly where that stunning diamond eternity band was—in my dresser, because it no longer fit on my sausage finger.

"My fingers are too swollen. I took them off to shower last night and couldn't get them back on. I didn't want to force it and risk them getting stuck."

He frowned, massaging my hand. "Really? That didn't happen till the end last time."

"I guess that's a perk of having twins: the accelerated extra-strength symptom package," I said. "When do you have to leave for the game?"

"Not for a couple of hours." Chase turned his body to face me. His mouth tugged, eyes blazing a path down my body and saying more with a single look than words ever could. "Why?"

"You know why."

"Mmm." He wrapped both hands around my waist, pulling me closer, and smiled against my lips. "I love pregnant horny James."

BONUS CHAPTER #5 - FOREVER

BAILEY

Denver, Colorado - One month later
Stanley Cup Finals - Game 7

Game seven.

I'd never wanted something for someone else so much in my life.

Siobhan and I sat on the edges of our seats in the owner's box, watching the clock count down to zero. The buzzer blared, marking the start of the second intermission. The players on the ice hopped onto the bench, then made their way down the hall to the locker rooms. Tonight's game had been impossibly tight so far, and the stakes were unimaginably high.

After a nail-biting second period, the score was tied one to one. Not ideal, but the last few minutes of the second period had been a little sloppy on the defensive side. For now, I was just relieved Colorado wasn't down. Hopefully, they'd come back in the third with a new fire lit beneath them.

In the seat beside me, Siobhan groaned and leaned back in the black leather club chair. "Oh my god. I'm going to have the worst heartburn from those spicy wings." She grimaced and rubbed her round belly beneath her white jersey. Although our due dates were close together, we looked nothing alike. She was roughly half my size because it was her first pregnancy—and because she was only having one baby.

"On the plus side," I said, "old wives' tales claim that having heartburn means your baby will be born with lots of hair. Maybe Luna will have a full head of hair like Tatum did when she was born."

Tatum still did, actually. She insisted on keeping her hair long "like a princess" and made me style it in all kinds of elaborate ways that required the assistance of YouTube videos, a million different combs and brushes, and infinite patience. I'd finally perfected the art of the french braid, at least, but my buns were not up to her satisfaction. I needed to work on that before ballet classes started up again.

Her own attempts were almost as good as mine—that is to say, also not great. If anything, Chase was the best hairstylist in the family. I guess that went along with the whole *good with his hands* thing.

"Did you have heartburn with Tatum?" She frowned as if trying to recall, then grabbed another hot wing despite her complaint moments earlier. Couldn't fault her for it; food tasted so much better when I was pregnant. I didn't know why; it just did. It was like how Chase felt about eating after games.

Which brought us to one massive perk to being a player's wife: box seats with in-suite food service. Especially when eating for two, like Siobhan, or for three, like I was. And especially when I needed to bury my feelings beneath a pile of junk food because the tension was too much to handle.

If we were this on-edge, I could only imagine how Dallas and Chase felt. Dallas had already made it to the playoffs twice—and won once—but it was a first for Chase. I wanted the win for him so badly I could feel it. Then again, he'd been confident going into tonight. He'd given me a kiss and strolled out the door like it was any other game. Maybe I was more nervous than he was.

Stress gripped me again, so I did the only reasonable thing. I grabbed a tortilla chip covered with melted cheese and dipped it in salsa and guacamole, then crammed it into my mouth. I swallowed and added, "Maybe I would have had more heartburn last time if I'd been able to keep food down."

"No kidding." Shiv shot me a sympathetic look. "I was nauseous for about a month, and it was torture. I didn't even actually throw up. But at least you're not sick this time, right?"

Miraculously, I wasn't. After having hyperemesis gravidarum the first time around—which was the technical term for throwing up constantly throughout my entire pregnancy—I was at a higher risk of having it again. A twin pregnancy was complicated enough, so I was thankful I could eat at all.

"Right," I said. "Now I'm just eating us out of house and home." I swore I was catching up to Chase in terms of food consumption. All I did lately was eat, nap, and play dolls with Tatum. Maybe I was the preschooler in this equation.

"Oh, stop." Shiv's cherry-red lips tugged into a smirk. "You look beautiful. You're tall, and you carry pregnancy well. I'm just going to look like I swallowed a watermelon in another month or so."

I laughed. "Not likely." Contrary to her protests, it was already clear Shiv would be one of those pregnant women who were all belly and barely needed maternity clothing until the end. A.k.a., not me.

After yet another bathroom break for the two of us, the game resumed with Dallas hopping onto the ice for the first shift. Despite what I'd hoped, Denver didn't crush Anaheim out of the gate. Anaheim didn't show up any better, either. Both teams were tired—and it showed.

For the first ten minutes of the third, the game remained tight, with lots of scoring opportunities on both sides, but without any luck getting the puck past either goalie.

We watched with bated breath while Dallas took possession again, skating up the side and pivoting into position to take a shot. Svenson, one of Anaheim's star defensemen, picked up speed and headed right for him. My grip on the armrest tightened as Svenson crouched and plowed right into Dallas—serving him with a knee to the stomach in the process. Dallas spun into the boards, catching the side to steady himself.

Shiv gasped, her hand flying to cover her mouth. "What the fuck was that?"

"Dirty hit," I said, shaking my head.

Dallas took a second to regain his bearings before gliding back into position, though his movements were slower than usual. He was probably winded, at a minimum, if not sporting several bruised ribs. It seemed like an obvious call, but play continued without a whistle.

From the player's bench, Chase mouthed a string of expletives and gestured to the officials, angrily pointing at Dallas. Chase was asking the same thing as Shiv, only using far more descriptive language. When he didn't get a response, he stood and leaned over the boards, continuing his verbal tirade.

When he didn't get the response he was looking for, he flopped back onto the bench and shook his head, leaning his elbows on his knees. Even at a distance, I could see the rage across his face.

"And no call? Nothing?" Siobhan turned to me, her mouth wide open.

"That should be a five-minute major," I said. "Intent to injure. Or a five-minute minor, at the very least."

She let out a growl, throwing her head back. "The officiating in this game has been a goddamn joke."

"Yep. They haven't called things evenly at all."

While fans often thought their teams were being unfairly singled out, this time, it really seemed to be the case. It wasn't just the lone, isolated hit. There had been a pattern—Anaheim getting away with questionable behavior while Colorado got called for anything that was even borderline.

The refs needed to pick a lane and decide whether they were putting their whistles away in a free-for-all or keeping the players accountable. On *both* sides.

I wanted Colorado to win that much more because of it.

Shifts changed, and Dallas climbed off the ice while Chase

hopped on and skated like a madman into Anaheim's zone. The fire I'd been hoping to see had been lit, at least for him.

If Svenson's intention had been to activate pissed-off Carter mode, he'd succeeded. And he'd probably find out the hard way shortly, because some things hadn't changed—Chase was still a force to be reckoned with on ice. No one wanted to find themselves on the receiving end of one of his hits.

Shiv and I grimaced as Chase slammed another player from Anaheim into the boards, sending a crunch across the arena so loud we could hear it from the second-level box seats. A cheer erupted from the crowd, peppered with angry boos from a handful of Anaheim fans. This time, at least, there wasn't a whistle for Colorado.

Siobhan drained her second Sprite and nervously combed through her glossy dark hair with her fingers. "This is so freaking stressful. It would be so much more tolerable if we could drink."

"No kidding," I said. Most of the time, I didn't mind not being able to drink while pregnant, but a drink or three to take the edge off would have come in handy tonight. Earlier in the game, Siobhan nearly threw her soda after a bad call that sent Dallas to the penalty box for a minor infraction. The other team had committed far worse sins without any recourse.

"I forgot to tell you," she added, "Dal bought non-alcoholic beer for me last week. He was trying to be nice, and I didn't have the heart to tell him it was awful, but now I'm scared he'll keep buying it. It tasted like a bale of hay." She made a face.

"Hay?" I teased. "How much hay have you eaten?"

"You know what I mean."

The clock continued to count down, each second crawling by like an eternity. Less than five minutes in the third period remained, and it was still tied. We sat on the edges of our seats, praying silently. All Colorado needed was one goal. One blessed goal, and the game would be theirs.

"I hope they don't go into overtime," I said. "For their sake and ours."

Unfortunately for everyone involved, it did. Sudden death overtime—twenty minutes of five-on-five. The first team to score would win.

My heart rate spiked to an all-time high watching the players cluster down near Colorado's net. Anaheim cycled the puck, gaining the upper hand in the play, and a sense of impending doom crept up on me. All night, I had been certain Colorado would win, but their defense was tired, lagging behind and struggling to keep up. If things continued like this, there was a good chance Anaheim would score and take the game.

Before I could doom spiral, a whistle blew. One of Anaheim's players had speared someone on our side, and the officials final called a long overdue penalty against them, granting Colorado a much-needed power play.

"'Bout freaking time," Shiv muttered, letting out a sigh of relief.

"They got this." I said it to reassure myself as much as her.

Chase and Dallas hopped onto the ice for the power play, both tearing up the ice with a renewed level of energy. Shiv and I fell silent, the two of us too tense to speak. This was it—the golden scoring opportunity. Eight minutes into overtime, five-on-four.

Colorado's right winger took possession of the puck, flying up the side to bring it into Anaheim's zone. Chase was perfectly in position to receive the pass, and he skated back a few strides, sending it to Dallas in front of the net. Before Anaheim's defense could cover the distance, Dallas shot the puck past the goalie, sinking it in the bottom right corner.

All the players on the ice froze, as if in disbelief.

The buzzer sounded, marking a career-defining moment for the entire Colorado team and kicking the players on the ice back into motion. Shiv and I let out whoops of joy, leaping out of our seats. Or more accurately, awkwardly sliding out of our seats due to our pregnant bellies.

"Oh my god!" Shiv squealed and wrapped me in as tight a hug as our bellies would allow. I squeezed her back, moisture welling behind my eyes.

We broke apart and returned our attention to the ice, where the Colorado players were huddled together, hugging and patting helmets. A surge of pride hit me as I watched Chase celebrate with his teammates.

I'd been there for his first NHL game, his first playoff game, and now, his first Stanley Cup win. After years of grinding—including several trades, plus a knee injury and surgery that sidelined him for months—he'd finally achieved the ultimate goal.

"They did it," Shiv murmured beside me.

I grinned while fighting back tears. "They sure did."

After fighting through the crowds to reach ice level, we squeezed past the people exiting the ice and stepped onto the playing surface to join Chase and Dallas, along with the other players and their families.

My heart swelled the moment I laid eyes on my husband, who was grinning and hugging one of his teammates. His eyes landed on me and widened, a look of excitement shifting into one of disbelief.

In a few quick strides, he was towering over me with a stern frown across his handsome face. With his skates on, he had closer to a foot on me in height.

"Get your adorable butt off the ice, Mrs. Carter."

I glanced down, realizing my error too late. "Uh… I can balance just fine."

In truth, I'd been so caught up in the excitement that I'd forgotten about the safety factor entirely. While Chase tended to be overprotective, in this case, he was right—being four months pregnant with twins meant I shouldn't have been shuffling around on a sheet of ice.

Especially someone as clumsy as me—though I'd never admit that to my husband.

"Maybe when there was one of you." He raised his eyebrows, fighting back a smile. "But you need to stay on solid ground until those babies come out."

He slid a hand around my torso, carefully steering me around his teammates and their families and back over to the benches. In my periphery, I spotted Dallas and Shiv, who appeared to be having a similar exchange while he escorted her off the playing surface too.

At least I wasn't the only one who'd had a momentary lapse in sanity.

I'd blame it on pregnancy brain—it's a real thing. Last week, my phone was in the fridge for over an hour before I realized where I'd left it. And maybe having twins meant my affliction was twice as bad. That was my story anyway, and I was sticking to it.

Once I was safely off the ice, Chase planted his elbows on the boards and leaned over. He tugged off his gloves and curled his fingers, beckoning me closer.

"Now that you're safe," he said, "come here so we can celebrate."

I looped my arms around his neck, and he dipped his head, bringing his mouth to mine. He was a sweaty mess, and while it probably should have grossed me out, somehow I loved him even more for it. It helped that I was used to sweaty, post-hockey Chase.

His hands lingered around my waist, and he studied me with a smile. "How was it up in the sky box?"

"A little stressful," I said. "But you played a good game."

"It was, wasn't it? That last assist I made to Ward"—he pushed his dark hair out of his face, letting out a low whistle—"it was a beaut."

"You know what I love about you?"

Chase gave me a crooked grin. "Everything?"

"Everything," I agreed. "Especially your modesty."

"Modesty is overrated." He tipped forward again, giving me another quick kiss on the lips.

Cheers and whistles echoed throughout the arena, the volume nearly deafening. All around us, fans continued to go wild. It was a big win—not only for the team, but for the franchise too.

"I'm so proud of you," I said. "You deserve this."

"Couldn't have done it without you."

CHASE

It was past after three a.m., and the house was silent.

My mom, who'd been babysitting for us, was sleeping in the spare room across from Tatum. Bailey was out cold in our bed, having fallen asleep almost immediately when we got home just after midnight. And I was sitting upright in Tatum's bed, where I'd just gotten her back to sleep after a nightmare.

Sometimes, I fell asleep in her bed during times like this, but not tonight. Turns out, winning the Stanley Cup could leave a person a little wired. An adrenaline buzz still coursed through my veins, rendering sleep an impossibility.

Tatum sprawled across my nap, her breaths slow and even now that her fears about spooky bats lurking in her room had been soothed. I gently lifted her head and shifted, placing a pillow beneath her for support as I slid out of her bed. Bending down, I planted a quick kiss on her forehead before padding out of the room.

How had I gotten so lucky? An incredible little family—soon to be not so little. Career I loved. Best life partner I could have ever asked for.

Things weren't perfect, but they were pretty damn close.

After washing up and brushing my teeth in the master bathroom, I crept back into our bedroom as quietly as I could to avoid waking Bailey. I almost succeeded, but the bathroom door squeaked behind me as I pulled it shut, and she groaned, stirring beneath the covers. Ever since having Tatum, Bailey was an incredibly light sleeper, even though our girl had been sleeping through the night for over two years.

"You okay?" Bailey rolled onto one elbow in the dark and peered up at me. "What are you doing up?"

"Tatum had a nightmare, so I laid with her until she fell back asleep." I pulled back the covers and slid into bed beside her, placing an arm along her lower back to tug her closer.

"Oof," she said, shifting. "Now that I'm awake, I've gotta pee. Be right back."

I felt bad for her. Peeing was practically a part-time job at this point.

A minute later, she returned and nestled in under the comforter, her belly brushing against my bare torso. I placed a hand on her stomach, still marveling at the fact that there were two babies in there.

We would be outnumbered once they arrived, three kids to two adults. It was going to be chaos in the best possible way. Couldn't wait.

"Baby A was being a real pain earlier," Bailey whispered in the dark. "Wouldn't stop kicking during the game."

I chuckled, kissing the top of her head and inhaling the familiar rosemary-mint scent of her shampoo. "How do you know it was Baby A?"

"Because he wouldn't stop moving in the ultrasound. Clearly trouble. Clearly takes after you. Carter genes through and through."

"Hmm, sounds a lot more like you."

Bailey laughed softly. "No way. Baby B is much calmer. She definitely takes after me."

As much as I tried to protest, we both knew she was 100 percent right. And now I felt even worse for waking her, because if she was this chatty, then she was just as awake as I was now.

"You could have woken me to get Tatum," she murmured, stroking my upper arm with the tips of her fingers. Some of the tension I had been holding eased in response to her touch. Sometimes Bailey was the only thing that could center me. "I wouldn't have minded."

Wake my pregnant wife? Not a chance. It was bad enough I traveled so much, putting her on full-time solo duty all too often. When I was around, I made a point to make up for that—for both of my girls.

"I was up anyway. Plus, you need the rest. You looked pretty wiped on the drive home." As in, she nearly fell asleep leaning against the window.

My best friend and I both had pregnant wives in tow, so the post-Cup celebration wasn't nearly as crazy as I'd always envisioned it to be. But it was perfect in its own way. Winning with Dallas was the icing on the cake.

She made a little grunt of dissent. "After a game like that, you're the one who needs rest."

"Too wired," I admitted. At the rate I was going, I might never sleep again.

"It is a pretty big deal." Bailey scooted up a few inches. She brought her face to mine in the dark and kissed my cheek, smiling against my skin. "Will probably take a few days to fully sink in."

"Probably."

If it ever did. I suspected it was one of those things that would always feel a little surreal.

Our lips came together in a soft, chaste kiss. Briefly, I considered pushing my luck for more, but she was probably too tired. It was the season of life we were in, and I was okay with that. We had the rest of our lives to do all those other things…often.

I nuzzled below her ear. "I love you."

"I love you." Bailey yawned and pressed her forehead to my shoulder, her long hair tickling my arm. "Call it pregnancy intuition, but I had a feeling you guys would win. Did you have a hunch too? You seemed pretty confident heading into the game."

"With the way the series had gone, I figured it was pretty fifty-fifty. But I knew I was coming out ahead no matter how the game ended."

She paused and peeked up at me. "What do you mean?"

While making it to the Stanley Cup finals was an impressive accomplishment in and of itself, it wasn't exactly a win-win scenario—especially for someone like me, who has a competitive streak the size of the Amazon River.

There were lots of ways to win, though, and some of them mattered more than others.

I slid a hand to her back and pulled her closer once more. She curled into me, fitting perfectly against my body like she always did.

"A cup is for one season. I have you forever."

ACKNOWLEDGMENTS

To my husband, who is my Chase. Thank you for your unconditional support and for showing me what love really is.

To my sons, I adore you both and hope you never read this or any of my other books.

To both of my editors, Mel and Beth, I could not have done this without you. You are both not only incredibly talented, I am lucky to call you my friends. Thank you for being so understanding with me while I worked on this book during a difficult time in my life.

And to all my readers, especially those of you who jumped on the Carter-James ship while Offside was in the process of being written: thank you for loving my sweet, filthy-mouthed antagonizer as much as I do.

ALSO BY AVERY KEELAN

Rules of the Game Series

Book 2: Shutout - Tyler & Sera

He's the tall, tattooed stranger I hooked up with on Halloween... and now he's my new roommate.

After a sudden cross-country move, I'm stuck crashing with my older brother and two of his hockey teammates for sophomore year. I'm not thrilled about shacking up with three athletes and their stinky gear, rotating door of hookups, and tendency to inhale every snack in the house. Just one reason of *many* that hockey players aren't my type.

When I walk in the front door with an armload of boxes, however, I'm faced with another problem.

My anonymous fling from two months ago is Tyler Donahue, the superstar goalie for my brother's team.

Lakeside University Series

The Enforcer (Nash & Vi)

The Sniper - Early 2024

The Power Forward (Connor & Reese) – TBD

The Captain (Drew & Savannah) –TBD

Standalone Novels

Otherwise Engaged

ABOUT THE AUTHOR

Avery Keelan is an award-winning author of sports romance and contemporary romance, a lifelong hockey fan, and a diehard coffee lover. She writes swoon-worthy happily ever afters with hot hockey heroes, snarky banter, and enough steam to fog up a mirror.

With undergraduate degrees in Commerce and Psychology, Avery specialized in government policy and legislation in a previous life. She lives in Canada with her husband and their two children, along with two spoiled rescue cats who like to sit on her keyboard at inopportune times.

facebook.com/authoraverykeelan
twitter.com/averykeelan
instagram.com/averykeelan
tiktok.com/@averykeelan
amazon.com/author/averykeelan
goodreads.com/averykeelan
pinterest.com/Averykeelan
bookbub.com/authors/avery-keelan

Printed in the USA
CPSIA information can be obtained
at www.ICGtesting.com
LVHW031916200224
772359LV00005B/288